Praise for Jasper Fforde

'Jasper Fforde is seriously funny . . . packed with magic and invention: a spiky heroine called Jennifer Strange, an unruly young princess and most importantly a flying car and plenty of dragon action. Watch out, Terry Pratchett!'
Sunday Express on *The Eye of Zoltar*

'True literary comic genius'
Sunday Express

'Reading a Fforde novel feels like taking off on a magic carpet, only to be picked up by another and another and taken on new flights of fantasy . . . just sit back and enjoy the ride'
Scotsman

'Terrifically inventive . . . full of fun'
Daily Telegraph on *The Last Dragonslayer*

'No summaries can do justice to the sheer inventiveness, wit, complexity, erudition, unexpectedness and originality of the works, nor to their vast repertoire of intricate wordplay and puns'
The Times

'I love to dive into Jasper Fforde's books. They're wildly imaginative but he makes you believe every word . . . Great stuff'
David Baldacci

'Highly recommended. Very funny'
Independent on *The Last Dragonslayer*

'Jasper Fforde has one of those effervescent imaginations that never throws in one joke when he can fit in two or three . . . he created his mad but logical parallel version of the Welsh marches with loving detail'
Independent on *The Last Dragonslayer*

'Hanging on to the Leviathan for dear life, the small Australopithecine was soon thousands of feet in the air . . .'

The Eye of Zoltar

Book Three of The Last Dragonslayer Series

JASPER FFORDE

HODDER

First published in Great Britain in 2014 by Hodder & Stoughton
An Hachette UK company

This paperback edition published 2015

1

A CIP catalogue record for this title is available from the British Library

B-format paperback ISBN 978 1 444 70730 4
A-format paperback ISBN 978 1 444 70731 1
Ebook ISBN 978 1 444 70729 8

Typeset in Bembo by Palimpsest Book Production Limited, Falkirk, Stirlingshire

Printed and bound by Clays Ltd, St Ives

Hodder & Stoughton policy is to use papers that are natural, renewable and recyclable products and made from wood grown in sustainable forests. The logging and manufacturing processes are expected to conform to the environmental regulations of the country of origin.

Hodder & Stoughton Ltd
338 Euston Road
London NW1 3BH

www.hodder.co.uk

For Ingrid, Ian, Freya and Lottie

Also by Jasper Fforde

The Last Dragonslayer Series
The Last Dragonslayer
The Song of the Quarkbeast

The Thursday Next Series
The Eyre Affair
Lost in a Good Book
The Well of Lost Plots
Something Rotten
First Among Sequels
One of Our Thursdays is Missing
The Woman Who Died a Lot

The Nursery Crime Series
The Big Over Easy
The Fourth Bear

Shades of Grey

The Eye of Zoltar

'I don't do refunds'

The Mighty Shandar

Where we are now

The first thing we had to do was catch the Tralfamosaur. The obvious question aside from 'What's a Tralfamosaur?' was: 'Why us?'. The answer to the first question was that this was a *Magical* Beast, created by some long-forgotten wizard when conjuring up weird and exotic creatures was briefly fashionable. The Tralfamosaur was about the size and weight of an elephant, had a brain no bigger than a ping-pong ball and a turn of speed that allowed it to outrun a human. More pertinent for anyone trying to catch one, Tralfamosaurs weren't particularly fussy over what they ate. And when they were hungry – which was much of the time – they were even *less* fussy. A sheep, cow, rubber tyre, garden shed, antelope, smallish automobile or human would go down equally well. In short, the Tralfamosaur was a lot like a Tyrannosaurus Rex, but without the sunny disposition and winning personality.

And we had to capture it. Oh, and the answer to the 'Why us?' question was that it was our fault the rotten thing escaped.

Perhaps I should explain a bit about who I am and

what I do, just in case you're new to my life. Firstly, I'm sixteen, a girl, and an orphan – hey, no biggie, lots of kids don't have parents here in the Kingdoms because of the huge number of people lost in the endless Troll Wars that have been going on these past sixty years. With lots of orphans around, there's plenty of cheap labour. I got lucky. Instead of being sold into the garment, fast-food or hotel industries, I got to spend my six years of indentured servitude with a company named Kazam, a registered House of Enchantment run by the Great Zambini. Kazam did what all Houses of Enchantment used to do: hire out wizards to perform magical feats. The problem was that in the past half-century magic had faded, so we were really down to finding lost shoes, rewiring houses, unblocking drains and getting cats out of trees. It was a bit demeaning for the once-mighty sorcerers who worked for us, but at least it was paid work.

At Kazam I found out that magic had not much to do with black cats, cauldrons, wands, pointy hats and broomsticks. No, those were only in the movies. Real life was somewhat different. Magic is weird and mysterious and a fusion between science and faith, and the practical way of looking at it is this: magic swirls about us like an invisible fog of emotional energy that can be tapped by those skilled in the Mystical Arts, and then channelled into a concentrated burst of energy from the tips of the index fingers.

The technical name for magic was 'the variable electro-gravitational mutable subatomic force', but the more more usual term was 'wizidrical energy', or, more simply, 'crackle'.

So there I was, assistant to the Great Zambini, learning well and working hard, when Zambini disappeared – quite literally – in a puff of smoke. He didn't return, or at least, not for anything but a few minutes at a time and often in random locations, so I took over the running of the company, aged fifteen. Okay, that *was* a biggie, but I coped and, long story short, I saved dragons from extinction, averted war between the nations of Snodd and Brecon and helped the power of magic begin to re-establish itself. And that's when the trouble *really* started. King Snodd thought using the power of magic for corporate profit would be a seriously good wheeze, something we at Kazam weren't that happy about. Even longer story short, we held a magic contest to decide who controls magic, and after a lot of cheating by the King to try to have us lose, he failed – and we are now a House of Enchantment free from royal meddling, and can concentrate on rebuilding magic into a noble craft one can be proud of.

I now look after forty-five barely sane sorcerers at Kazam, only six of whom have a legal permit to perform magic. If you think wizards are all wise, sage-like purveyors of the Mystical Arts with sparkling wizidrical energy streaming from their fingertips, think again. They are for the most part undisciplined, infantile, argumentative and infuriating, and their magic only works when they *really* concentrate, which isn't that often, and misspellings are common. But when it works, a well-spelled feat of magic is the most wondrous thing to behold, like your favourite book, painting, music and movie all at the same time, with chocolate and a meaningful hug from someone you love thrown in for good measure. So despite everything, it's a good business in which to work. Besides, there's rarely a dull moment.

So that's me, really. I have an orphaned assistant named Tiger Prawns to help me, I am Dragon Ambassador to the world – of which more later – and I also have a pet Quarkbeast, which is at least nine times as frightening as the most frightening thing you've ever seen.

My name is Jennifer Strange. Welcome to my world.

Now: let's find that Tralfamosaur.

Zambini Towers

Myself, Tiger and those forty-five sorcerers all lived in a large, eleven-storey, ornate former hotel named Zambini Towers. It was in a bad state of repair and even though we had some spare magic to restore it to glory, we decided we wouldn't. There was a certain *charm* about the faded wallpaper, warped wood, missing windowpanes and leaky roof. Some argued that this added a certain *something* to the surroundings that made it peculiarly suitable for the Mystical Arts. Others argued that it was a fetid dump suitable only for demolition, and I kind of sat somewhere between the two.

When the call came in I was standing in the shabby, wood-panelled lobby of Zambini Towers.

'There's a Tralfamosaur loose somewhere between here and Ross,' said Tiger, waving a report that had just been forwarded from the police. They'd taken the call but had passed it on to the zoo, who passed it on to Mountain Rescue, who passed it back to the police, who then passed it on to us when the zoo refused it a second time.

'Anyone eaten?' I asked.

'All of two railway workers and part of a fisherman,' said Tiger, who was only just twelve and, like me, a foundling. He was stuck here for four years and after that he could apply for citizenship, or earn it fighting in the next Troll War, which probably wouldn't be far off. Troll Wars were like Batman movies: both are repeated at regular intervals, feature expensive hardware, and are broadly predictable. The difference being that during the Troll Wars, humans always lost – and badly. In Troll War IV eight years ago, sixty thousand troops were lost before General Snood had even finished giving the order to advance.

'Three eaten already?' I repeated. 'We need to get Big T back to the zoo before he gets hungry again.'

'How long will that be?' asked Tiger, who was small in stature but big on questions.

I swiftly estimated how much calorific value there was in a railway worker, and matched that to what I knew of a Tralfamosaur's metabolism with a rough guess at how much of the fisherman had been consumed, and came up with an answer.

'Three hours,' I said, 'four, tops. Which sorcerers are on duty right now?'

Tiger consulted a clipboard.

'Lady Mawgon and the Wizard Moobin,' he replied.

'I'll help out,' said Perkins, who was standing next to me. 'I haven't been terrified for – ooh – at least a couple of days.'

Perkins was Kazam's youngest and newest graduate, having had a licence for less than a week. He was eighteen, so two years older than me, and while not that powerful magically, showed good promise – most sorcerers didn't start doing any really useful magic until their thirties. More interestingly, Perkins and I had been about to have our first date when the call came in, but that was going to have to wait.

'Okay,' I said to Tiger, 'fetch Mawgon and Moobin, and you should also call Once Magnificent Boo.'

'Got it,' said Tiger.

'Take a rain check on that date?' I said, turning to Perkins. 'In the Magic Industry, it's kind of "Spell First, Fun Second".'

'I kind of figured that,' he replied, 'so why don't we make *this* assignment the date? Intimate candlelit dinners for two are wildly overrated. I could even bring some sandwiches and a Thermos of hot chocolate.'

'Okay,' I said, touching his hand, 'you're on. A sort of romantic uncandlelit "recapturing a dangerously savage beast for two" sort of date – but no dressing up and we split the cost.'

'Game on. I'll go and make some sandwiches and that Thermos.'

And with another chuckle, he left.

While I waited for the other sorcerers to arrive, I read what I could about Tralfamosaurs in the *Codex*

Magicalis, which wasn't much. The creature was created magically in the 1780s on the order of the Cambrian Empire's 1st Emperor Tharv because he wanted 'a challenging beast to hunt for sport', a role it played with all due savagery. Even today, over two hundred years later, people still pay good money to try to hunt them, usually with fatal consequences for the hunter. Oddly, this made Tralfamosaur hunting *more* popular as it seemed citizens were becoming increasingly fond of danger in these modern, safety-conscious times. The Cambrian Empire was now making good money out of what it called 'jeopardy tourism' – holidays for those seeking life-threatening situations.

The first to arrive in the lobby was Wizard Moobin, who, unlike all the other sorcerers, was barely insane at all. Aside from his usual magical duties he also worked in magic research and development. Last month, Moobin's team had been working on a spell for turning oneself momentarily to rubber to survive a fall, the use of instantaneous 'turning to stone' enchantments as a way of transporting badly damaged accident victims to surgery, and a method of reliable communication using snails. Aside from this he was good company, aged a little over forty, and was at least polite and gave me due respect for my efforts. Tiger and I liked him a great deal.

'The Tralfamosaur escaped,' I told him when he walked into the lobby, 'when you and Patrick surged this afternoon during the bridge rebuilding. Two quarter-ton blocks of stone were catapulted into the sky.'

'I wondered what happened to them,' said Moobin thoughtfully.

'One fell to earth harmlessly in an orchard near Belmont, and the other landed on the Ross-to-Hereford branch line, derailing a train that was transporting the Tralfamosaur to Woburn Safari Park as part of some sort of dangerous animal exchange deal.'

'Ah,' said Moobin, 'so we're kind of responsible for this, aren't we?'

'I'm afraid so,' I replied, 'and it's already eaten three people.'

'Whoops,' said Moobin.

'Whoops nothing,' said Lady Mawgon, who had arrived with Tiger close behind, 'civilians have to take risks with the rest of us.'

Unlike Moobin, Lady Mawgon was *not* our favourite sorcerer, but was undeniably good at what she did. She was originally the official sorcerer to the Kingdom of Kent before the downturn of magical power, but her fall from that lofty status had made her frosty and ill tempered. She had recently entered her seventieth decade, scowled constantly, and had the unsettling habit of gliding everywhere rather than walking, as if beneath the folds of her large black dress she was wearing roller skates.

'Even so,' I said diplomatically, 'it's probably not a good idea to let the Tralfamosaur eat people.'

'I suppose not,' conceded Lady Mawgon. 'What about Once Magnificent Boo?'

'Already in hand,' I replied, indicating where Tiger was speaking on the phone.

Once Magnificent Boo had, as her name suggested, once been magnificent. She could have been as powerful as the Mighty Shandar himself, but was now long retired and saddled with a dark personality that made Lady Mawgon seem almost sunny by comparison. The reason for this was simple: she had been robbed of her dazzling career in sorcery by the removal of her index fingers, the conduit of a sorcerer's power. The fingers had remained hidden for over three decades until recently recovered by us, but even reunited with the dry bones, the only magic she could do was wayward and unfocused. These days she studied Quarkbeasts and was the world's leading authority on Tralfamosaurs, which was the reason we needed her.

'She'll meet you there,' said Tiger, replacing the receiver. 'I'll stay here and man the phones in case you need anything sent over.'

Once Perkins had returned with the sandwiches we trooped outside to my Volkswagen Beetle. There were arguably much better cars in the basement at Zambini Towers but the VW was of huge sentimental value: I was found wrapped in a blanket on the back seat outside the Ladies of the Lobster orphanage one windswept night many years before. There was a note stuffed under the windscreen wiper:

> Please look after this poor dear child as her parents died in the Troll Wars.
> PS: I think the engine may need some oil and the tyre pressures checked.
> PPS: We think her name should be Jennifer.
> PPPS: The child, not the car.
> PPPPS: For her surname, choose something strange.

The car was kept – all items left with a foundling were, by Royal Decree – and was presented to me when the Blessed Ladies of the Lobster sold me to Kazam aged fourteen. After I'd checked the tyre pressures and added some oil it started first time, and I drove to my first job in my own car. If you think fourteen is too young to be driving, think again. The Kingdom of Snodd grants driving licences on the basis of *responsibility*, not age, something that can frustrate forty-something blokes no end when they fail their responsibility test for the umpteenth time.

'Shotgun!' yelled Lady Mawgon, and quickly plonked herself in the passenger seat. Everyone groaned. Being in the back of the Volkswagen meant sitting next to the Quarkbeast, a creature that was often described as a cross between a labrador and an open knife drawer, with a bit of velociraptor and scaly pangolin chucked in for good measure. Despite its terrifying appearance and an odd habit of eating metal, the Quarkbeast was a loyal and intelligent companion.

'Right,' I said as we moved off, 'does anyone have a plan as to how we're going to recapture the Tralfamosaur?'

There was silence.

'How about this,' I said. 'We modify our plans with regard to ongoing facts as they become known to us, then remodify them as the situation unfolds.'

'You mean make it all up as we go along?' asked Perkins.

'Right.'

'It's worked before,' said Lady Mawgon.

'Many times,' replied Moobin.

'Quark,' said the Quarkbeast.

Tralfamosaur Hunt Part 1: Bait and Lure

The train that had transported the Tralfamosaur had been derailed about four miles out of Hereford. The locomotive had stayed upright but most of the goods wagons were now lying in an untidy zigzag along the track. There was a huge number of police cars, ambulances and fire engines in attendance, and the night scene was lit by large floodlights erected on towers. A willowy officer named Detective Corbett introduced himself and then escorted us up the track, past the shattered remnants of the goods train.

'The engine driver was the first eaten,' said Corbett as we stared at the wreckage. 'See these footprints?'

He snapped on a torch and pointed at the ground where a Tralfamosaur footprint was clearly visible.

'The creature headed north-east,' said Moobin after looking at several other footprints. 'Any reports from the public?'

'Nothing so far,' said Corbett.

'A Tralfamosaur can be surprisingly stealthy,' said Lady Mawgon. 'Discovering one near you and being eaten often happen at pretty much the same time.'

Corbett looked around nervously.

'The roads are locked down inside a fifty-mile perimeter,' he said in a hasty 'I'm leaving pretty soon' sort of voice, 'and everyone has been advised to stay indoors, or in a cellar if they have one. Artillery batteries have been set up if it tries to go in the direction of Hereford, and if you are unsuccessful by first light, King Snodd has agreed to send in the landships.'

'What about—' began Moobin, but Corbett had already gone. We stared at the remnants of the Tralfamosaur's railway carriage, then looked around. It was a dark night, and only a light breeze stirred the branches of the trees. Of the Tralfamosaur, there was no sign. Sending in the landships was a last resort: four-storey armoured tracked vehicles of immense power, they could overcome everything except Trolls, who impertinently called them 'Meals on Wheels'.

'I'm not sure a squadron of landships chasing after a single Tralfamosaur would do anything but cause a huge amount of unnecessary damage,' said Perkins. 'What's the next step?'

'No idea,' said Lady Mawgon. 'Moobin?'

'Not a clue. Let's face it, recapturing seventeen tons of pea-brained enraged carnivore isn't something we do every day. How was it captured last time?'

'Liquorice,' came a loud voice from behind us, and we jumped.

'I'm sorry?' said Lady Mawgon.

'Liquorice,' repeated Once Magnificent Boo, who had just arrived on her moped. We all felt silent. Boo never used more words than was absolutely necessary, rarely smiled and her eyes were so dark they seemed like black snooker balls floating in a bowl of cream.

'If you listen very carefully to my plan we will have the Tralfamosaur recaptured before the break of dawn,' said Boo. 'My plan is sound, and if followed to the letter, has a reasonable chance of succeeding without anyone being eaten.'

'Define "reasonable chance",' said Lady Mawgon, but Boo ignored her and carried on: 'We require only a grenade launcher, six pounds of industrial-strength liquorice, two spells of Class VIII complexity, a shipping container, a side of bacon, an automobile, several homing snails, a ladder, and two people to act as bait.'

Perkins leaned across to me and whispered:

'Boo was kind of looking at us when the "two people as bait" thing came up.'

'I know,' I whispered back, 'it's possible to refuse, but the thing is, who are you more frightened of: Once Magnificent Boo, or a Tralfamosaur?'

An hour later Perkins and I were in my Volkswagen, parked up near a crossroads on high ground a mile or two from the damaged railway carriage. We could see the stars through the open sunroof, and the pinkish glow of the Quarkbeast where it was sitting on a wall close by, sniffing the air cautiously.

'Enjoying the date so far?' I asked in a cheery tone.

'It could be improved,' he replied.

'In what way?'

'Not being used as Tralfamosaur bait, for one thing.'

'Oh, come on,' I said playfully. 'It's a lovely night to be eaten by a nine tons of hunger-crazed monster.'

Perkins looked up through the open sunroof at the broad swathe of stars above our heads. As if on cue, a shooting star flashed across the sky.

'You're half right,' he said with a smile, 'it's a lovely night. Crazy or nothing, right?'

I returned his smile.

'Right: crazy or nothing. Let's check everything again.'

I flicked the two glow-worms above the dash with my finger. A faint glimmer of light illuminated the two 'SpellGo' buttons that Moobin and Lady Mawgon had placed on the dashboard. Spells could be cast in advance and lie dormant until activated by something as easy to use as a large button. One was labelled 'Bogeys' and the second 'Float'.

'Got the rocket-propelled liquorice launcher handy?' I asked.

'Check,' said Perkins, patting the weapon, which, instead of having an explosive warhead, had a lump of industrial-grade liquorice about the size of a melon.

It smelled so strongly we had to poke it up out of the sunroof to stop our eyes watering. Tralfamosaurs love liquorice and could smell it from at least a mile away if the wind was strong enough.

We both jumped as a snail shot in through the open window and skidded to a halt on the inside of the windshield, leaving a slippery trail across the glass. Homing snails were one of Wizard Moobin's recent discoveries. He had found that all snails have the capacity to do over one hundred miles per hour and find their way to a given location with pinpoint accuracy, but didn't because they were horribly lazy and couldn't be bothered. By rewriting a motivating spell commonly used by TV fitness instructors, communication using homing snail was entirely possible – and more reliable than pigeons, which were easily distracted.

The snail was steaming with the exertion and smelled faintly of scorched rubber, but seemed pleased with itself. We gave it a lettuce leaf, popped it in its box and Perkins opened the note that had been stuck to its shell. It was from Lady Mawgon.

'Reports from worried citizens place the T three miles down the road at Woolhope.'

Woolhope was the Kingdom's sixth-largest town and home to twelve thousand people and a Marzoleum processing plant. I had a sudden thought.

'It's heading for the flare.'

Marzoleum refineries always had a gas flare alight from a tall tower and it was this, I guessed, that would attract the Tralfamosaur. Brain the size of a ping-pong ball it might have, but when it comes to looking for food at night it was no slouch. Fire and light, after all, generally denoted humans.

'There,' I said, stabbing my finger on the map near a place called Broadmoor Common, just downwind of Woolhope. 'He'll be able to smell us easily from there.'

I whistled to the Quarkbeast, who jumped into the back of the car, and we were soon hurtling along the narrow roads as fast as we could. It was about 3 a.m. by now, and I drove, I agree, recklessly. The police had locked down the area tight and everyone had been told to stay in their homes, but even so, I was half expecting to run into a tractor or something. I didn't. I ran into something much worse.

The Quarkbeast cried out first, a sort of *quarky-quark-quarky* noise that spelt danger, and almost immediately, my headlights illuminated something nasty and large and reptilian on the road ahead. The Tralfamosaur's small eyes glinted dangerously as it looked up. It was bigger than I remembered from my occasional visits to the zoo, and it looked significantly more dangerous out in the open.

There were about fifty yards between it and us and Perkins and I sat there for a moment, the engine of the Beetle idling. It stared at us blankly for some moments until I realised we were upwind, and it probably wasn't aware of the liquorice. I slowly backed away, but the Tralfamosaur didn't follow. Quite against my better judgement I stopped, and then inched slowly forward again. It still didn't seem that interested.

'Better show yourself,' I said to Perkins, 'and try to look appetising.'

'Yes,' he said sarcastically, 'I'm well known for my pie impersonations.'

Perkins took a deep breath, undid his seat belt, stood up through the sunroof and waved his hands. The effect was instantaneous. The Tralfamosaur gave out a deafening bellow, and charged.

I slammed the car into reverse and swiftly backed away. Luckily there was an open gateway nearby, and I reversed into this, pulled the wheel around, thumped the gear lever into first and drove off with the Tralfamosaur in close pursuit. Part one of the plan was now in operation.

Tralfamosaur Hunt Part 1: Chase and Capture

The Tralfamosaur could now smell the liquorice, and it took a wild bite at the car as we accelerated away. We felt the jerk as a single tooth caught in the bodywork, but a moment later the metal split, releasing us. I glanced into the rear-view mirror as we took off back the way we had come, and could see the Tralfamosaur glowing red in the tail-lights as it chased us with a heavy, lumbering gait. Thankfully, a Volkswagen is speedier than a Tralfamosaur, and we maintained a safe distance.

We took a left at Mordford, then a right over the River Wye, where the Tralfamosaur, now quite hungry, stopped to sniff at the ironically named Tasty Drinker Inn. The Tralfamosaur was so distracted by the smell of citizens hiding inside that we had to reverse almost to within reach of it before the creature changed its mind, and, overcome by the sheer succulence of the liquorice, once again moved after us, knocking over two cars in the car park and demolishing both bridge parapets as it lumbered across.

'Wow,' said Perkins, watching the spectacle while hanging out of the window, 'I think I've seen everything now.'

'I sincerely wish that were the case,' I said, 'but I doubt it. You're new to the magic industry. Pretty soon, stuff like this will be *routine*.'

After another ten minutes I took a tight left turn into a field. I had left the gate open ready and hung an oil lamp on the gatepost so I wouldn't miss it. I had to slow down to take the corner, however, and the Tralfamosaur, seizing the opportunity, closed his teeth around the rear bumper. The back of the car was lifted high in the air, held there, and then with a tearing noise the bumper ripped off. Almost immediately the car fell back on to the grassy slope with a thump and bounced back into the air. The Quarkbeast was catapulted off the rear seat to hit the roof, where he became stuck fast when his scales got embedded in the steel.

Undeterred, I put my foot down and aimed the car towards the second pair of oil lamps, positioned where we had removed a length of fencing between the field and the railway.

'Stand by for SpellGo one,' I yelled as we drove up the stone ballast and on to the railway track, the tyres bumping noisily across the sleepers. Perkins' hand hovered over the first of the two spell activation buttons.

'*Now!*' I shouted and Perkins thumped the one

marked 'Bogeys'. There was a bright flash and a buzzing sensation and the Volkswagen's wheels were transformed into railway bogeys, that is to say, train *wheels*. They immediately slotted on to the rails and the ride smoothed out. We were now, technically at least, a train. I didn't need to steer so let go of the wheel, pressed on the accelerator and looked out of the window.

The Tralfamosaur was close – and even more angry. It was snapping at us wildly, driven on by the over-powering smell of liquorice.

And that was pretty much when we entered the Kidley Hill railway tunnel. The Tralfamosaur followed us inside and the engine sound and angry bellows bounced off the tunnel sides to create a noise that I would be happy never to hear again.

'Right,' I yelled. 'Timing is everything for this one. I'm on the SpellGo button, you're on the grenade launcher.'

'Right-o,' replied Perkins, and shouldered the weapon as he stood up in the sunroof and faced, not the beast, but the other direction – the far tunnel opening we were fast approaching.

I accelerated to give us some distance between the creature and us, then came to a halt alongside a single green lamp I had left there earlier. I switched off the engine and flashed my headlights. In the distance a light flashed back at us, then stayed on. Perkins took aim at the light with the grenade launcher and flicked off the safety.

I placed my hand over the SpellGo button marked 'Float' and stared out of the broken rear windscreen. I could hear the footfalls of the Tralfamosaur and its panting, but could not see it, and after a few more moments everything went quiet.

'Now?' asked Perkins, finger hovering on the trigger.

'When I say.'

'How about now?'

'When I say.'

'Has it gone?'

'It's moved back to stealth mode,' I whispered. 'It's there all right, somewhere in the darkness.'

I peered into the inky blackness but could still see nothing, then had an idea and stamped on the brake pedal. The brake lights popped on, bringing much-needed extra luminance to the brick-lined railway tunnel. It was a good job they did. The creature was less then ten feet from the rear bumper and I could see its small black eyes staring at us hungrily in the warm red glow.

'*Now.*'

There was an explosive detonation as Perkins pulled the trigger, and the liquorice rocket flew down the railway tunnel, illuminating the tunnel sides as it went. There was a metallic *thang* noise as the rocket hit something. It didn't explode, of course – the warhead had been replaced with liquorice.

I thumped the SpellGo button marked 'Float'. There was another buzzing noise and the car lurched upwards. Not to the roof of the tunnel, of course, as that would not have allowed us to escape, but into one of the three ventilation shafts that connected the railway tunnel to the world outside. The shaft was quite large but even so the Volkswagen bumped against the sides as it rose, eventually pitching forward into a nose-down attitude that offered a good view looking straight down. The car's headlights now illuminated a confused-looking Tralfamosaur below us, standing on the shiny railway lines. It pondered us for a moment, then followed the trail of liquorice scent left by the grenade launcher. As soon as it vanished, we looked at one another and smiled. We were, for the moment at least, safe.

We bumped and scraped up the ventilation shaft to finally emerge into the early morning light. Moobin was waiting for us as planned, and a dozen men deputised from the nearest town placed hooks around the bumpers of the now lighter-than-air Volkswagen. The men heaved on the ropes as the car swung around in the breeze, and after a lot of grunting the floating car was tied to the front of two heavy tractors. I breathed a sigh of relief. It had been an exciting and dangerous night. As we sat there for a moment reflecting upon recent events, the Quarkbeast fell from the roof of the car back on to the rear seat with a thump.

'Are all our dates going to be like that?' said Perkins.

'I hope not,' I replied with a smile, 'but it was quite fun, wasn't it? I mean, it's not like we were killed or eaten or anything, right?'

'If your idea of a good date is not being killed and eaten, you'll never be disappointed.'

And he leaned towards me. I think I may even have leaned towards him, but then a voice rang out from below:

'Are you coming down from there?'

It was Moobin.

'Another time,' I whispered.

A ladder was placed against the car and we climbed down to join Moobin, who congratulated us both before we walked down the hill to the tunnel entrance. A shipping container had been reversed up to the portal, and the Tralfamosaur, urged on by the liquorice grenade fired into the back of its new prison by Perkins, had swiftly been contained. We could hear the sound of contented chewing through the thick steel of the container; we had left several slabs of bacon in there for it, as well as half a bison.

The third part of the plan was soon completed; the floating Beetle had been hauled down the hill and anchored to the shipping container with self-tying string. The Tralfamosaur was now fast asleep and snoring, pretty much worn out after the night's excitement, something that could be said for most of us.

'A fine job,' said Once Magnificent Boo in a rare moment of congratulation, although you wouldn't know it from looking at her – her mood seemed as dark as normal.

She then climbed the ladder to the Volkswagen, gauged the speed of the wind, slammed the door and ordered the ladder away.

'Ahoy, Moobin and Lady Mawgon,' she called out, 'I need Jenny's car to be another fifteen tons lighter.'

The two sorcerers complied, and with a straining of wires and creaking from my car, the Volkswagen lifted the container into the air. Within a few seconds the breeze had caught the strange flying machine and it was over the treetops and drifting away in an easterly direction. I joined Moobin and Lady Mawgon, who were also watching my VW rise rapidly into the dawn sky.

'She's a bit high for just going to the zoo,' I said.

Moobin and Lady Mawgon said nothing, and I figured out then what was happening.

'She's not going back to the zoo, is she?'

'No,' said Moobin quietly, 'she's carrying the Tralfamosaur across the border to the Cambrian Empire. They have wild Tralfamosaurs there and it can do . . . whatever it is Tralfamosaurs do.'

'I'm not sure the King will be pleased,' said Perkins. 'The Tralfamosaur was a valuable tourist attraction for the Kingdom and one of his personal favourites, even after the Queen insisted he stopped feeding his enemies to it.'

'The Queen was very wise to do that,' Moobin replied, 'but I don't believe Once Magnificent Boo gives two buttons for what the King thinks.'

And with the dawn sky lightening, we watched the Volkswagen with the shipping container slung below it drift high into the early morning. Pretty soon it was high enough to catch the sun, and it was suddenly a blaze of orange.

'I'm going to miss the Volkswagen,' I said.

'Don't be so sentimental,' said Lady Mawgon, 'it's only a car.'

But it wasn't just a car. It was my *parents*' car. The one I had been abandoned in. Wizard Moobin turned to Perkins and myself and smiled at us in turn.

'Good work, you two. Come on: breakfast is on me.'

Angel Traps

Prince Nasil was already up when I walked into the converted dining room we used as the 'nerve centre' of Kazam. It was here that the the day's work was arranged, and where all sorcery-related meetings took place. It had been two weeks since the Tralfamosaur escapade, and the company had returned to what we called normality.

'Hello, Jennifer,' said Prince Nasil cheerily. 'Any news of Boo?'

'Nothing yet,' I replied, 'but we know she got there as she released a homing snail once landed, which told us she and the Tralfamosaur were safe in the Cambrian Empire.'

'If my carpet hadn't been damaged so much on that trip up to the Troll wall,' said the Prince wistfully, 'I might have been able to help.'

He was referring to a recent high-speed flight to Trollvania. The trip had further damaged an already worn-out magic carpet, and the Prince needed it rebuilt if he were to resume any sort of aerial work.

'Look at that,' said the Prince, holding up a tatty

and threadbare excuse for a rug, 'already ten thousand hours and two centuries past rebuild.'

'What can we do?' I asked.

'We need more angel's feathers,' he announced, in much the same way as you might ask for an oil change on a car.

'O-kay,' I replied as angel's feathers were, by their very definition, somewhat tricky to obtain, 'and where would we find angels?'

'Oh, they're everywhere,' he said in a matter-of-fact tone, 'keeping an eye on stuff. But they're fleet of wing and catching them is the devil's own job. Here.'

He handed me a wire-mesh box that had a hinged flap on a tensioned spring.

'An angel trap,' he said without a shred of shame. 'Baited with marshmallows, it's possible we might be able to catch one.'

I looked at the trap dubiously as Tiger walked in. The Prince handed him an angel trap too, explained what it was and that the first person to trap an angel won a Mars bar.

'Should we be trapping angels?' asked Tiger, who, despite being not that old, knew right from wrong. 'I mean, is that ethical?'

'I very much doubt it,' replied the Prince cheerfully, 'but it's a lot better than running intensive angel farms like they used to in the old days – that was the real reason behind the dissolution of the monasteries.'

'I didn't know that.'

'Not many people do.'

'Where's the best place to leave an angel trap?' asked Tiger as soon as the Prince had gone.

'Angels are everywhere,' I said, 'but usually only intervene during times of adversity.'

'You should have had one of these when you were chased by the Tralfamosaur,' said Tiger, and I nodded in agreement.

'Have you seen this?' asked Wizard Moobin as he walked into the offices holding a newspaper. 'The unUnited Kingdoms are gearing up for Troll War V. The foundries have been working overtime – the orphan workforce are receiving extra gruel allowances.'

Moobin was referring to the Kingdom's main source of income, which was manufacturing landships, primarily to fight the Trolls.

'I can't think there's much appetite for another Troll War,' added Moobin. 'Most nations in the unUnited Kingdoms are still bankrupt from the last one. The only ones who really benefit are King Snodd and the weapons manufacturers.'

We all fell silent for a moment, contemplating a potential Troll War V. This, I knew with sadness, would produce only three things: profit for the King, more orphans – and Troll War VI.

'Speaking of kings,' I said, 'I have an audience with His Majesty at eleven.'

'Any idea what he wants to see you about?' asked Moobin. 'If he wanted to have us executed for losing the Tralfamosaur, he would already have done so.'

'I think he blames Boo for that. Besides, given our recent triumph, even he would think twice about any monkey business.'

The 'recent triumph' in question was the appointment to the Royal Advisory Position known as Court Mystician, a job the King wanted to award to a corrupt sorcerer named Blix, in order that the King could more easily exploit the power of magic. We had fought and won a magic competition over it, with Blix's House of Enchantment now absorbed into ours. Blix himself was currently transformed to granite, which was bad for him but good for Hereford museum, which had him as their chief exhibit.

'Even so,' said Moobin, 'be careful of the King. Ah! Customers!'

The bell had just sounded in our consulting room, and we got to work. The morning was spent discussing jobs from potential clients who had heard about our triumph in the magic competition, and were waking up to the idea that home improvements could be done by magic. We discussed realigning houses to face the sun better, and having entire trees moved. We agreed to find some lost keys, animals and grannies, and then, inevitably, had to turn down the usual half-dozen who wanted us to do what we couldn't do:

make people fall in love, bring someone back from the dead and, on one occasion, both.

The most interesting client was a man who proposed that we send him into orbit within a steel ball, from there 'to watch the sunset upon the earth, and muse upon immortality' until his air ran out. It was a ridiculous idea, of course, but luckily 'ridiculous' was never a word treated with much scorn at Kazam – most of magic was far, far beyond ridiculous. Magnetic worms, for instance, or removing the moles from Toledo, or giving memory to coiled cables on telephones, or echoes, or bicycles staying upright – or most strangely, the once serious proposition to magic a third ear on to the Earth's four billion rabbits to 'lessen pain when lifting'.

'Right,' I said, checking my watch as soon as we had told our low-earth orbit client to return with a doctor's note that declared him sane, 'time for a trip to the palace.'

I'd had to find another car the morning after my Volkswagen floated away. Luckily, there were many forgotten cars lying dormant under dust sheets in the basement of Zambini Towers. After looking at several I'd chosen a massive vintage car called a Bugatti Royale. Inside it was sumptuously comfortable, and outside, the bonnet was so long that in misty weather it was hard to make out the radiator ornament. I chose it partly because it started pretty much first time, partly because it looked nice, but mostly because it was the biggest.

The Royale, however, had one major drawback: the steering, which was *unbelievably* heavy. Lady Mawgon dealt with the problem by spelling me a simple Helping Hand™, which looks more or less like a severed hand but can do all manner of useful hand-related work such as kneading bread, copying letters or even taking the Quarkbeast for a walk. Although helpful, having a disembodied hand on the Bugatti's steering wheel was admittedly a bit creepy, especially as this one was hairy and had 'No More Pies' tattooed on the back.

I took Tiger and the Quarkbeast, and ten minutes later was weaving through Hereford's mid-morning traffic.

Audience with the King

The castle at Snodd Hill was outside the Kingdom's capital, not far from where the nation shared a long border with the Duchy of Brecon, and a short one with the Cambrian Empire. The sun had enveloped the castle with its warm embrace, which was fortunate, as it made the dark, stone-built structure less dreary than was usual. The 'Medieval Chic' fashion was still very much the rage, which is okay if you don't mind lots of weather-beaten stone, mud, funny smells, poor sanitation and lots of beggars dressed in blankets.

I left the car in the reserved Court Mystician parking place with Tiger and the Quarkbeast settling down to a game of chess, then trotted past an ornate front entrance guarded by two sentries who were holding halberds that were polished to a high sheen. I gave my name to a nearby footman, who looked at me disparagingly, consulted a large ledger, sniffed, and then led me down a corridor to a pair of large double doors. He rapped twice, the doors opened and he indicated I should enter.

The doors closed behind me and I looked around. Log fires crackled in hearths the size of beds at both ends of the room, and instead of courtiers, military men and advisers milling about, there were maids, servants and other domestic staff. This wasn't so much Business at Court, but home life. The King's spectacularly beautiful wife Mimosa was present, as were their Royal Spoiltnesses, Prince Steve and Princess Shazine. The Princess was engaged in studies but because she was so utterly spoilt, she had a university lecturer to do her schoolwork for her.

The whole scene looked suspiciously relaxed and informal. The King, I think, wanted me to see his softer side.

'Ah!' said the King as he spotted me. 'Approach, subject!'

King Snodd was neither tall nor good looking nor had any obvious attributes that might make him even the tiniest bit likable. Of the many awards he'd won at the annual unUnited Kingdom Despot Awards, the high points were: 'Most Hated Tyrant' (twice), 'Most Corrupt King of a medium-sized Kingdom' (once), 'Best original act of despotism adapted from an otherwise fair law' (three times), 'Worst Teeth' (once) and 'Despot most likely to be killed by an enraged mob with agricultural tools'. He was, in short, an ill-tempered, conniving little weasel with a mind obsessed only with military conquests and cash. But weasel notwithstanding, he *was* the King, and today seemed to be in a good mood.

I approached and bowed low, and he permitted me to kiss his large gold signet ring.

'Your Majesty,' I said with all due solemnity.

'Greetings, Miss Strange,' he said cheerfully, spreading an arm wide to indicate the hall. 'Welcome to our little oasis of domestic normality.'

Normality was not a word I'd choose. I didn't know anyone whose food taster had a food taster, nor anyone who had made mice illegal, taxed nose hairs or changed their curtains hourly 'so as not to afford good hiding places for assassins'.

'And an apology may be due for that regrettable incident two weeks ago,' he added, 'when it might have appeared that I used the power of the state to attempt to win the magic contest.'

'Water under the bridge,' I said diplomatically.

'Your forgiving air does you credit,' came a melodious voice close at hand. It was Queen Mimosa, who was as elegant a figure as I had seen anywhere. She held herself with poise and quiet dignity, and whenever she moved it was as though she were walking on silk.

'Your Majesty,' I said, bowing again.

The King and the Queen could not have been more different. The sole reason the Kingdom of Snodd enjoyed a better-than-normal reputation these days was Queen Mimosa's guiding hand. Popular rumour said she agreed to marry the King and bear his children in order to give a better life to his subjects, and if true, this would be a very noble sacrifice indeed. Before marriage she had been just plain Mimosa Jones, a medium-ranked sorceress in her own right, and it was rumoured that the Queen was a Troll War orphan herself, which might explain the large amount of charity work she did on their behalf.

'Now then,' said the King, eager to get down to business as he had, apparently, an execution to witness at midday, and didn't want them to start without him, 'since you and the rest of those irritatingly disobedient enchanters have the odd notion that magic should be for the good of many, I am having to come to terms with the fact that my relationship with sorcerers cannot be as one-sided as I might wish. Wife? Translate.'

'He means,' said Queen Mimosa, 'that he knows he can't boss you around.'

'Exactly,' said the King, 'but there is a matter of extreme delicacy that we need to speak about.'

He turned to where his daughter the Princess was waiting for her homework to be done for her.

'Peaches, would you come over here, please?'

'What, now?' she asked, rolling her eyes.

'If it's not too much trouble, sweetness.'

The Princess walked over in a sultry manner. I was the same age as her, but we could not have had more different upbringings. While I spent my first twelve years eating gruel and sharing a dormitory with sixty other girls, Princess Shazine had been indulged in every possible way. She wore clothes cut from the very finest cloth, bathed in rainwater imported at huge expense from Bali, and had her food prepared by Michelin-starred chefs. In short, her every whim satisfied in the most expensive way possible. But while extremely obnoxious she was undeniably very pretty with glossy raven-black hair, fine features and large, inquisitive eyes. Although I'd never met her, she was very familiar. She could barely catch a cold or be seen with an inappropriate prince without it becoming front-page news.

'Yes?' said the Princess in a pouty kind of voice, arms folded.

'This is Her Royal Highness the Crown Princess Shazine Blossom Hadridd Snodd,' announced the King, 'heiress to the Kingdom of Snodd.'

The Princess looked me up and down as though I were something considerably less important than garbage, but made quite certain she did not make eye contact.

'I hope this interruption to my valuable time has a purpose.'

'Pay attention, Princess,' said the Queen in the sort of voice that makes you take notice, 'This young lady is Jennifer Strange. The Last Dragonslayer.'

'Like totally big yawn,' replied the Princess, looking around her in a bored fashion. 'Magic is so last week.'

'She is also manager of Kazam Mystical Arts Management and a young lady of considerable daring, moral worth and resourcefulness. Everything, in fact, you are not.'

The Princess looked shocked, not believing what she had heard.

'*What?*'

'You heard me,' replied the Queen. 'Soft living has rendered you spoilt and obnoxious beyond measure – a state of affairs for which I admit I am partly responsible.'

'Nonsense, Mother!' said the Princess haughtily, 'everyone loves me because I am so beautiful and charming and witty. You there.'

She pointed to one of the King's servants whose job it was to clean up after the royal poodles, who were numerous, unruly and not at all house-trained.

'Yes, My Lady?' said the servant, who was a young girl no older than myself. She was pale, had plain mousy hair and was dressed in the neat, starched dress of the lowest-ranked house servant. She also looked tired, worn and old before her time. But she somehow held herself upright, with the last vestiges of human dignity.

'Do you love your Princess, girl?'

'Begging your pardon yes I do, My Lady,' she said with a small curtsy, 'and am surely grateful for the career opportunities your family's benevolence has brung to me.'

'Well said,' said the Princess happily. 'There will be an extra shiny penny in your retirement fund; it will await you on your seventy-fifth birthday.'

'Her Ladyship is most generous,' replied the girl and, knowing when an audience has ended, went back to cleaning up after the royal poodles.

'You see?' said the Princess.

'A character reference from a Royal Dog Mess Removal Operative Third Class is hardly compelling, Princess. Our minds are made up. If Miss Strange agrees, you shall take counsel from her, and try to improve yourself.'

The Princess's mouth dropped open and she gaped inelegantly like a fish for some moments.

'Take counsel from an *orphan*?' said the Princess in an incredulous tone.

I could have taken offence, I suppose, but I didn't. You kind of get used to it. In fact, truth to tell I was getting a bit bored, and was instead wondering whether Once Magnificent Boo was safe in the Cambrian Empire, and if my Volkswagen had ended up in a tree or something.

'You may shake hands with Miss Strange,' continued the Queen, 'and then we will discuss your education. Is this acceptable with you, Miss Strange?'

'Only too happy to help,' I said, not believing for one second that the Princess would agree to such a thing.

'Good,' said Queen Mimosa. 'Shake her hand and say "good afternoon", Princess.'

'I'd rather not,' retorted the Princess, looking me in the eye for the first time. 'I might catch something.'

'It won't be humility,' I replied, staring at her evenly, and figuring that this was probably what they thought the Princess needed. If my head was off my shoulders in under ten minutes, I was wrong. The Princess went almost purple with rage.

'I have been *impertinenced*,' she said finally. 'I insist that this orphan be executed!'

'I'm not sure "impertinenced" is a word,' I said.

'It *is* if I *say* it is,' said the Princess, 'and Daddy, you did say for my sixteenth birthday I could order someone executed. Well, I choose her.'

She pointed a finger at me. The King looked at Queen Mimosa.

'I *did* sort of promise her she could do that, my dear. What sort of lesson is it if I don't keep my word?'

'What sort of lesson is it to a child that she can have someone executed?' retorted the Queen, and glared at him. Not an ordinary glare, but one of those fiery, hard stares that leave your neck hot, cause you to fluff your words and make you prickly inside your clothes.

'You're right, my dear,' replied the King in a small voice.

Updating his style of medieval violent monarchy

to Queen Mimosa's benevolent dictatorship was a bitter pill to swallow, but the King, to his credit, was at least trying.

'I will not be talked to like this—' began the Princess, but the Queen cut her short.

'—You *will* shake Miss Strange's hand, my daughter,' she said, 'or you will regret it.'

'Come, come, my dear,' said the King, attempting to defuse the situation, 'she is only a child.'

'A child who is vain, spoilt and unworthy to rule,' said the Queen. 'We will not leave this kingdom in safe hands if the Princess is allowed to continue her ways. So,' concluded the Queen, 'are you prepared to greet Miss Strange, Princess?'

The Princess looked at her parents in turn.

'I would sooner eat dog's vomit than—'

'ENOUGH!' yelled the Queen in a voice so loud that everyone jumped.

'Leave us,' she said to the people in the room, and the royal retinue, well used to being able to make themselves scarce at a moment's notice, all made for the door.

'Not you,' she said to the royal poodle cleaner-upper who had been quizzed earlier.

'My dear . . .' began the King when the servants had left, but his entreaties fell upon deaf ears. The Queen's fury was up, and instead of holding his ground he cowered in front of her.

And that was when I felt a buzzing in the air. It was subtle, like a bee in fog at forty paces, but it meant only one thing – a spell was cooking. And if that was so, it could only be from the ex-sorcerer, Queen Mimosa.

The Princess crossed her arms and stared at her mother.

'You will do as you are told, young lady,' said the Queen in a measured tone, 'or you will not be in a position to do anything at all.'

'Do your very worst!' spat the Princess, her face curled up into an ugly sneer. 'I will not be ordered about like a handmaiden!'

The Queen, very slowly and deliberately, pointed her index fingers at the Princess. These were the conduits of a sorcerer's power, and when brought out or pointed anywhere near you, it was time to run, or beg, or duck for cover. The King must have seen this before, for he winced as a powerful surge of wizidrical energy coursed from Queen Mimosa's fingers. There was a thunderclap, several drapes fell from the walls, and all the window glass suddenly decreased in size by a tenth and fell out of the frames with an angry clatter.

This wasn't the spell, of course, just the secondary effect. When the peal of thunder had receded into the distance, I tried to figure out what spell had been cast, but nothing seemed to have changed.

The Princess changed

I looked at the King, who was as confused as me, then at the Queen, who was blowing on her fingers as sorcerers are wont to do after a particularly heavy spelling bout. She seemed quietly confident, and not unduly worried – something *had* happened, I just wasn't sure *what.*

That was when I noticed the Princess, who had such a look of confusion on her face it was hard to describe. She stared at her hands as though they were entirely alien to her. The King had noticed her odd behaviour, too.

'My little Pooplemouse?' he said. 'Are you quite well?'

The Princess opened her mouth to say something, but nothing came out. She tried again and looked as though she was going to cough up a toad or something, which is not as odd as it might sound, as that was often a punishment bestowed upon disobedient children by their mother-sorcerers.

The Princess opened her mouth again and this time found her voice.

'Begging your pardon, Your Majesties, but I don't half feel peculiar.'

'My dear,' said the King, addressing the Queen, 'you have given our daughter the voice and manners of a common person.'

'My nails!' came a voice behind us. 'And these clothes! I would not be seen dead in them!'

We turned around. The servant who had been ordered to remain had broken strict protocol and spoken without being spoken to first, one in a very long list of sackable offences. The Queen caught the servant's eye and pointed to her reflection in the mirror. The servant looked, then shrieked and brought her raw hands up to her face.

'Oh!' she said. 'I'm so plain and ugly and common! What have you done, Mother?'

'Yes,' said the King, 'what have you done?'

'A lesson to show our daughter the value of something when you have lost it.'

'That's our daughter?' asked the king, staring at the servant, then at the Princess, who had started to pirouette in a mildly clumsy fashion in the centre of the room, listening joyfully to the faint rustle of the pink crinoline dress she was wearing. The Princess might not be enjoying being a servant, but the servant didn't seem too bothered about being a princess.

'You haven't—?' said the King.

'I most certainly have,' replied Queen Mimosa. 'The

Princess has swapped bodies with the lowliest servant in the household.'

The Princess looked aghast.

'I've learned my lesson!' she shrieked. 'Turn me back, please! I will do anything – even shake hands with that hideous orphan person.'

She couldn't even remember my name. But impressed from a technical viewpoint, I turned to the Queen.

'Remarkable, ma'am. Where did you learn to do that?'

'I studied under Sister Organza of Rhodes when a student,' she said simply. 'The good sister was big on the transfer of minds between bodies.'

'Please turn me back!' yelled the Princess again, throwing herself to her mother's feet. 'I will *never* blame the footmen for my own stealing or demand people are put to death.'

'I may have to insist you change her back,' said the King with uncharacteristic firmness.

'I won't ever make fun of our poor royal cousins for only having two castles,' pleaded the Princess.

'I can't have a daughter with lank hair and a pallid complexion,' added the King. 'It might attract the wrong sort of prince.'

'Our daughter needs to be taught a lesson,' said the Queen, 'for the good of the Kingdom.'

'There are other ways to punish her,' said the King,

'and in this matter I will be firm. Return my daughter this instant!'

'Yes,' howled the Princess, 'and I promise *never* to pour weedkiller in the moat again – I'll even restock the ornamental fish with my own servant's pocket money!'

'That was you?' said the King, turning on her suddenly. 'My prized collection of rare and wonderful koi carp, all stone dead at a stroke? I had my fish-keeper stripped of all honours and sent to work in the refineries – *and you said nothing?*'

He turned to his wife and gave a short bow.

'I suppose it might be for the best,' he said wearily.

'*What?!?*' yelled the Princess.

'Right,' said the Queen, clapping her hands. 'Miss Strange, I am entrusting you with our daughter's further education. I hope she will learn something from the experience of having and being less than nothing.'

'I won't go,' said the Princess. 'I shan't be made to wear old clothes and eat nothing but potatoes and scratchings and have to share toilets with other people and have no servants. I shall savagely bite anyone who tries to take me away.'

'Then we shall have you muzzled and sent back to the orphanage,' said the Queen, 'and they will allocate you work in the refineries. It's either that or going quietly with Miss Strange.'

These words seemed to have an effect upon her, and the Princess calmed down.

'I shall hate you for ever, Mother,' she said quietly.

'You will thank me,' the Queen replied evenly, 'and the Kingdom shall thank both your father and me for delivering them a just and wise ruler when we die.'

The Princess said nothing. It was the servant-now-princess who spoke next.

'This is a very beautiful room, like,' she said. 'I'd not really noticed before what with not being allowed to raise my eyes from the floor and all. Is that a painting of a great battle?'

'That one?' said the King, always eager to show off his knowledge. 'It is of one of our ancestor's greatest triumph against the Snowdonian Welsh. The odds were astounding: five thousand against six. It was a hard, hand-to-hand battle over two days with every inch won in blood and sinew, but thank Snodd we were victorious. Despite everything, we were impressed by the fighting spirit of the Welsh – those six certainly put up a terrific fight.'

'Look after her, won't you?' said the Queen in a more concerned tone. 'I trust in your judgement to educate my daughter, and whatever happens, you will not find the Kingdom or myself ungrateful. Bring her back in a month or two and I will restore their minds to the correct bodies. Protect her, Miss Strange, but don't cosset her. The future of the Kingdom may very well be in your hands.'

The Princess quietened down after a while as she realised her mother meant it, and we were shown from the hall.

'No one is curtsying me,' she said in a kind of shocked wonderment as we walked unobserved down a bustling corridor in the palace. 'Is that what being common is like?'

'It's a small part of what being common is like,' I told her.

'Do you think that horrible servant will get my body pregnant?' she asked as we trotted down the steps. 'I've heard about you girl orphans having no morals and having babies for fun and selling them to buy bicycles and fashion accessories and onions and stuff.'

'We think of nothing else,' I said with a smile.

Tiger and the Quarkbeast were still playing chess when we got back to the car.

'Who's she?' said Tiger as we walked up.

'Guess.'

'From the look of her,' said Tiger, 'an orphan servant, probably bought for indentured servitude within the palace and used for menial scrubbing duties or worse. Here,' he added, fishing in his pocket, 'I've got some nougat somewhere I was keeping for emergencies – and you look as though you could do with a bit of energy.'

He handed her the nougat, which was mildly dusty

from where it had sat in Tiger's pocket. The Princess ignored it, and him.

'I smell of dog poo, carbolic soap and mildew,' she said, sniffing a sleeve of her maid's uniform in disgust, 'and I can feel a bogey in my left nostril. Remove it for me, boy.'

'Holy cow!' said Tiger. 'It's the Princess.'

'How did you know that?' asked the Princess.

'Wild stab in the dark.'

'Hold your tongue!' said the Princess.

'Hold it yourself,' said Tiger, sticking out his tongue.

'I dislike that ginger nitwit already,' said the Princess. 'I'm going to start a list of people who have annoyed me so they can be duly punished when I am back in my own body.' She rummaged in her pockets for a piece of paper and a stub of pencil. 'So, nitwit: name?'

'Tiger . . . Spartacus.'

'Spart-a-cus,' said the Princess, writing it down carefully.

'If anyone finds out you're the Princess,' I said after having a worrisome thought, 'I'd give it about an hour before we have to fight off bandits, cut-throats and agents of foreign powers. For now, you'll take the handmaiden's name. What is it, by the way?'

The Princess seemed to see the sense in this.

'She doesn't have a name. We called her "poo-girl" if we called her anything at all.'

I told her to take the orphan ID card out of her top pocket.

'Well, how about that,' said the Princess, reading the card. 'She *does* have a name after all, but it's awful: Laura Scrubb, Royal Dog Mess Removal Operative Third Class, aged seventeen. Laura *Scrubb*? I can't be called that!'

'You are and you will be,' I said, 'and that's the Quarkbeast.'

'It's hideous,' said the Princess. 'In fact, you all are. And why is there a disembodied hand attached to the steering wheel?'

'It's a Helping Hand™,' explained Tiger, 'like power steering, only run by magic.'

'Magic? How vulgar. I am so *very* glad I inherited no powers from my mother.'

I reversed the Royale out of the parking place and headed back towards town. The Princess, once past her fit of indignation at how hideously unsophisticated we all were, spent the time staring out of the window.

'I'm not allowed past the castle walls,' she said in a quiet voice. 'What's that?'

'It's a billboard advertising toothpaste.'

'Doesn't it come ready squeezed on to your toothbrush every morning and evening?'

'No, it doesn't.'

'Really? So how does it get from the tube to the toothbrush?'

I didn't have time to answer as a car had swerved in front of us. I stamped on the brakes and recognised it immediately: a six-wheeled Phantom Twelve Rolls-Royce, with paintwork so perfectly black you felt as though you could fall into it. There was only one person I knew who was driven around in the super-exclusive Phantom Twelve, and I was certain that this was not a chance encounter.

An impeccably dressed manservant in dark suit, white gloves and dark glasses climbed out of the Phantom Twelve, walked across and tapped on the window.

'Miss Strange?' he said. 'My employer would like to discuss a matter that concerns you both.'

We were stuck in the middle of a roundabout.

'What, here?'

'No, miss. At Madley International Airport. Follow us, please.'

The Rolls-Royce pulled away and we followed. The car would contain Miss D'argento, an agent, like me. But she wasn't any ordinary agent – she didn't look after film stars, singers, writers or even sorcerers. She didn't even look after careless kings who found themselves temporarily without a kingdom and needed a public relations boost. No, she was the agent for the most powerful wizard either living, dead or, in his case, otherwise: the Mighty Shandar.

The Mighty Shandar

The trip to the Kingdom's international airport did not take long, but instead of going to the main departures terminal we were led into a large maintenance hangar that contained a Skybus 646 cargo aircraft which was emblazoned with Shandar's logo – a footprint on fire. The rear of the cargo aircraft was open, and a large wooden crate was being unloaded by a forklift. I parked the Bugatti and watched as Miss D'argento alighted elegantly from the rear door, held open by the manservant.

The D'argentos were what was termed a 'Dynastic Agency' in that they had been looking after the business interests of the Mighty Shandar ever since his appearance as a featured 'Sorcerer to Watch' in the July 1572 edition of *Popular Wizarding*. As far as anyone can tell, there have been eleven D'argentos in the employ of the Mighty Shandar, and all but one female. Miss D'argento was perhaps a year or two older than me – about eighteen – and was dressed as perfectly elegantly as a socialite twice her age.

I climbed out of the car and waited for the forklift

truck to deliver the crate in front of us. While this happened, I noticed several other henchmen dotted around the hangar. They were all dressed in black suits, dark hats, white gloves and large sunglasses. I peered at the one closest to us. There was no flesh in the small gap between where his glove ended and his shirt cuff began. It was an empty suit, animated by magic. Usually you can tell a drone by their mildly jerky and decidedly unhumanlike movements, but these ones were top class – at a distance you'd never know at all.

'Notice anything odd about the henchmen?' whispered Tiger.

'Yes,' I said, 'drones.'

'Drones?' asked the Princess.

'Watch and listen,' said Tiger.

'Good afternoon, Miss Strange,' said Miss D'argento in a cultivated voice, her high heels click-clicking on the concrete floor as she approached us, 'congratulations on winning The Magic Contest. I reported it to the Mighty Shandar, who expressed admiration for your fortitude.'

I nodded towards the closest drone.

'They move well for the non-living.'

'Thank you,' said D'argento. 'Shandar does us all proud.'

'And from purely professional interest,' I added, 'are you running them on an Ankh-XVII RUNIX core?'

'You know your spells,' said Miss D'argento with a

smile. 'We run them with the Mandrake Sentience Emulation Protocols disabled to make them less independent. Make no mistake, they are twice as dangerous as real bodyguards for they fear no death.'

She wasn't kidding. Pharaoh Amenemhat V of the Middle Kingdom was said to have attempted to expand Egypt along the Mediterranean with an unstoppable drone army of sixty thousand. They got as far as what is now Benghazi before Amenemhat V was killed in battle.

I told Tiger and the Princess to wait in the car while the forklift placed the crate in front of us and then reversed away. Almost immediately, several of the lifeless drones unlatched the crate and wheeled the two sections apart to reveal the Mighty Shandar.

But it wasn't a flesh-and-blood Shandar, it was Shandar as he spent most of his time these days: stone. Every fold in the fabric of his clothes, every pore in his skin, every eyelash was perfectly preserved in glassy obsidian. This was how the Mighty Shandar could still be a power to be reckoned with four centuries after his birth, for in stone, you don't age.

But spending time *in petra* was not without dangers. The world is littered with sorcerers who have turned to stone for some reason, only to have an arm, leg or head fall, or be knocked or sawn off. Those that return to life generally bleed to death before they can be saved. But given the right storage facilities and barring erosion, accidental damage or mischief, a sorcerer could live hundreds of thousands of years without a second of their own life having passed.

'The Mighty Shandar celebrates his four hundred and forty-fourth birthday next year,' said Miss D'argento, 'yet in his own personal life he is only fifty-eight. He doesn't get out of stone for anything less than a million an hour, and at current life-usage rates will live to 9,356.'

She looked at Shandar's features, unclipped a feather duster from inside the crate, and flicked some dust from the statue.

'He spent the entire seventeen and eighteenth centuries turned to stone,' continued Miss D'argento proudly, 'but that was mainly for tax purposes. Four generations of my family never spoke to him at all.'

'You must be very dedicated.'

'Dedication does not even *begin* to describe our commitment to the Mighty Shandar,' said D'argento, 'but enough chit-chat. Read this.'

She passed me a sheet of paper. I scanned the contents, and my heart fell. It was a letter from Representatives of the unUnited Kingdoms to the Mighty Shandar, outlining a case of 'Breach of Contract' they had filed with the unUK's highest court.

'The thing is,' said D'argento in a half-apologetic tone as I read the lawsuit, 'that the Mighty Shandar doesn't do refunds.'

The problem was this: the Mighty Shandar had been contracted to rid the Kingdoms of Dragons four centuries before, and was paid a lot of money to do so. His plan required the last Dragon to die of old age, something that I personally intervened to ruin. There were now two Dragons left, and that was two more Dragons than the contract stipulated. Unless he rid the Kingdoms of all the Dragons he'd have to return the cash. And it was a *lot* of cash, paid to him four centuries ago – the interest alone would fund at least half a Troll War.

'We have the money,' said D'argento. 'The Mighty Shandar's share in Skybus would cover the debt pretty much on its own. No, it's the *principle* of the matter. A job was left unfinished, and we're not keen to make a habit of it. Clients might lose confidence, and in business, confidence counts.'

'I agree with that,' I replied, 'but Dragons aren't much into eating people any more – it's probably the last thing on Feldspar and Colin's mind.'

'They have names?'

'Certainly. In the first month of their new life they did a goodwill tour around the world to promote their "not eating people or burning stuff" agenda, and they are at present in Washington, DC, reading the entire contents of the Library of Congress in order to understand a little more about humans.'

'Admirable, I'm sure,' said Miss D'argento, 'but the

refund issue still stands. Don't take my word for it, for you are to be honoured: the Mighty Shandar wants to speak to you *personally*.'

Miss D'argento checked her watch and somewhere a clock struck two. Almost immediately the statue of Shandar turned from black to grey to a sort of off-white. There was a pause, then Shandar took a deep breath as life returned to his body, and the off-white coating seemed to burst off his skin and clothes like dry skin. He staggered for a moment, shook himself and looked around.

'Welcome back, O Mighty Shandar,' said Miss D'argento, beaming and clicking a stopwatch. 'It's two o'clock on the afternoon of 14 October 2007. You've been *in petra* for sixty-two days. We're currently at Madley International Airport in the Kingdom of Snodd.'

She handed him a damp towel so he could refresh himself, then a clipboard and pen.

'Ongoing progress reports, sir.'

His eyes scanned the text.

'I'll take two minutes,' he said, his voice a deep baritone that seemed to transmit confidence, awe and leadership in equal measure.

'This is Jennifer Strange,' said D'argento, gesturing in my direction, 'as you requested.'

He looked across at me. He was a handsome man, tanned, appeared healthy and was imposingly large. His eyes, which regarded everything with the minutest attention to detail, appeared not to blink, and were of the brightest green, like a cat's.

'Miss D'argento? Make that four minutes.'

He shook my hand.

'I'm *very* pleased to meet you at last. A worthy opponent is the only opponent worth opposing.'

His handshake was firm, yet cold, which is hardly surprising; a few seconds ago he had been stone.

'You assisted the Dragons in destroying my carefully laid plans,' he added in a quieter voice. 'Plans four centuries in the making. All that work for nothing, and now they're asking for a refund. Worse, you have damaged my hundred per cent wizidrical success rate and bruised my credibility as a sorcerer of considerable power.'

I didn't know what to say so I said nothing. He had a point to make, and he'd make it soon enough.

'For any one of those reasons I should banish you to the icy wastes of outer Finlandia.'

'If that was your plan you would already have done so.'

'Very true,' he said with a half smile, 'but I'm not into revenge. It has a nasty habit of biting you back when you least expect it. I have a feeling that punishing you would upset the delicate Good–Bad balance.'

Most sorcerers believed in what they called 'The Balance'. Simply put, all life requires *equilibrium* to survive. For every death there is birth, for every light there is dark, for every ugliness there is something that shines with the greatest lustre. And for every truly heinous act, there are always multiple good acts to compensate. It's why evil despots are always defeated, and why a truly awful reality TV show can never go on for ever.

Shandar looked at the clipboard for a moment, signed something, then continued to read while he spoke to me. Someone as powerful as Shandar would be able to read two books and converse with three people at the same time – even in different languages.

'You seem a resourceful young lady, Jennifer. I'm not often beaten, and the experience has renewed a sense of excitement that I have not felt for a long time. You appreciate that I have almost unlimited power at my disposal?'

'I know that, sir, yes.'

'Are we sure about this?' asked the Mighty Shandar, pointing to a clause in one of the notes he was looking at.

'Yes, sir,' replied D'argento. 'They want the state of Hawaii moved to the middle of the Pacific.'

'I thought it was fine between Wyoming and Arkansas.'

'The venerable Lord Jack of Hawaii said the move is on account of the climate – and they want to retrofit the collective memory so everyone thinks it's always been there.'

'Standard stuff,' said Shandar, signing the contract, 'and they didn't quibble over the price?'

'Not a murmur.'

He sighed and shook his head.

'Where *have* all the good negotiators gone?'

'Two minutes gone,' said Miss D'argento, consulting her stopwatch.

'So with my power almost unimaginable right now,' he continued, turning back to me, 'your friends the Dragons are easily exterminated. Take it from me that I could – and would – destroy them in a twinkling, thus completing the contract and avoiding a refund.'

'Then you will take on the might of Kazam as well, Mighty Shandar,' I said, 'for we will do *anything* to prevent you harming a single scale of a Dragon.'

It was a bold speech, and I felt myself shiver in fear of how he might react. He appeared not to hear me at first and spoke again to his agent.

'We're not doing this,' he announced quietly as he handed an unsigned contract back to Miss D'argento. 'There are quite enough boy bands on the planet as it is.'

He turned back to me.

'The combined power of your sorcerers would not equal a thousandth of my power,' he said.

'I know that,' I replied, 'and so do they. But it would not stop them. They would all die defending one of their own, and the Dragons, masters of the magical arts themselves, are one of us.'

The Mighty Shandar regarded me thoughtfully. I'd not consulted the sorcerers on any of this, but I knew them well enough, and so did he.

'Then I have a proposition for you, Miss Strange. Are you listening?'

'I'm listening.'

'As you can see, my time is strictly rationed. I have no spare time to search for rare and exotic trinkets to add to my collection of Wonderful Things. Miss D'argento is too busy with managing my affairs, and drones are all very well for heavy lifting and the odd senseless act of violence, but they have no finesse. So: find something for me and I'll leave the Dragons alone and take the indignity on the chin.'

'I'm still listening,' I said. 'What do you want me to find?'

'A magnificent pink ruby the size of a goose's egg. It belonged to a wizard I admire greatly. You can find me . . . the Eye of Zoltar.'

'That's a tall order,' I said, having absolutely no idea what he was talking about, but keeping that to myself. It didn't pay to look an idiot in Shandar's presence.

'One minute to go,' said Miss D'angelo, consulting her stopwatch.

'Do we have a deal?' asked Shandar.

I didn't need to think for long. If I didn't agree to

find this 'Eye of Zoltar' then Shandar would attempt to kill the Dragons, and we would be honour bound to try to stop him, and that would end in our collective annihilation.

'I'll find you the Eye of Zoltar,' I said, 'whatever it takes.'

'Good choice,' said Shandar with a grin. 'I knew you'd agree.'

'Any clue as to where it is?' I asked. 'The world is a big place.'

'If I knew where it was,' snapped Shandar, 'I'd get it myself.'

Since the meeting was clearly at an end, I returned to where the Princess and Tiger were waiting for me. From the Bugatti Royale we watched as Shandar talked quietly with D'argento, signed some more forms and eventually, when his four minutes were up, changed rapidly back into obsidian.

The drones quickly crated him up, and the forklift reappeared and placed the crate back into the rear of the cargo aircraft. Once that was done a clothes rail that had been standing unnoticed to one side was approached by the drones, and they deftly jumped back on to their coat hangers, the empty suits returning to what they had been – creatures given life only by the will of Shandar. The human manservant wheeled the clothes rail into the back of the aircraft, swiftly followed by Miss D'argento in the Phantom Twelve.

A minute later the rear cargo door was closed, and the engines started up. By this time tomorrow they could be anywhere on the planet.

I tapped the Helping Hand™ to bring it out of sleep mode and it dutifully pulled the wheel around and we drove out of the hangar. We paused on the perimeter track to watch Shandar's aircraft lumber almost impossibly into the sky with its tiny wings, then headed towards Zambini Towers.

'The Eye of Zoltar?' said Tiger when I'd finished relating what Shandar had said. 'What on earth's that?'

'I've no idea. The person to consult is someone with a clearer idea of what the future might bring.'

'I'm no clairvoyant,' said Tiger, 'but I think I know who you mean.'

The Remarkable Kevin Zipp

The Remarkable Kevin Zipp was one of Kazam's most accomplished clairvoyants. When we walked back into the offices at Kazam he was checking out baby futures. Not in a stocks and shares kind of way, obviously, but what a baby's life had in store for them. It was a good way to earn ready cash, as Kazam was constantly short of money. Two mothers had their tots with them, and Kevin was checking each by holding on to their left foot for a moment.

'If she wants to go out with someone named Geoff when she's sixteen,' he said as the first mother stared at him anxiously, 'try to get her to go out with Nigel instead.'

'There's a problem with Geoff?'

'No, there's a problem with Nigel. Ban Geoff from her life and he'll become unbelievably attractive and she'll forget all about Nigel, and believe me, she needs to. Nigel is big trouble.'

'How big?'

'*Really* big.'

'Okay. Anything else?'

'Not really – although you might consider joining the National Trust and holidaying in Wales. It's quite nice, I'm told, and not always raining.'

'Oh. Well, thank you very much,' said the mother. She handed Kevin a ten-moolah note and moved off. The second mother presented her baby to Kevin, who once again held the baby's foot. He closed his eyes and rocked slowly in his chair for a moment.

'This is preposterous,' said the Princess. 'I've never seen a more ridiculous load of mumbo-jumbo in my entire life!'

'You're young yet,' I said, 'lots of time to see some gold-standard mumbo-jumbo, and quite frankly, this is the place to see it.'

'Concert pianist,' Kevin murmured thoughtfully, still holding the baby's foot, 'and make sure he likes boiled cabbage, tasteless stew and runny porridge.'

'He'll be a pianist?' asked the mother excitedly.

'No, he's going to murder one – aged twenty-six – so better get him used to prison food from an early age . . . hence the boiled cabbage.'

The mother glared at him, slapped the money on the table, and left the room. Kevin looked confused.

'Did I say something wrong?'

'Perhaps you should temper the bad news with good,' I suggested.

'I couldn't tell them the *really* bad news,' he replied. 'The "concert pianist" thing was their *minority* timeline; their *senior* timeline – the most likely one – has them both not lasting the week. Oh, before I forget: this came in today.'

He handed me a letter. It was postmarked from Cambrianopolis, the capital city of the Cambrian Empire, and looked official.

'Oh dear,' I said as I read the letter. 'Once Magnificent Boo's been arrested for "illegal importation of a Tralfamosaur".'

'That's a trumped-up charge,' said Tiger. 'The Cambrian Empire has herds and herds of the things – people pay good money to hunt them, for goodness' sake.'

'There's a reason,' I added. 'She's been transferred to Emperor Tharv's State-Owned Ransom Clearance House, ready for negotiations.'

'The Cambrian Empire are *still* kidnapping people?' said Tiger. 'When are they going to enter the twenty-first century?'

'I think they have to consider entering the fifteenth century first,' said Kevin.

Traditionally, it was princes and kings and knights and stuff that were ransomed as you could get a lot for them, but pretty much anyone was fair game in the Cambrian Empire. If you weren't royal, the release fees could actually be fairly modest – some people cost less to release than a parking clamp, which is kind of depressing and very welcome, both at the same time. But the long and short of it was that if we wanted Boo back, we would have to pay. And that would mean going over there with a letter of credit and doing a deal of some sort.

'I spoke to Moobin and he's writing you out a note that will be good for twenty thousand. I think he wants you to nip over there and negotiate.'

Cambrianopolis was less than a couple of hours' driving from here, but I didn't relish the idea, even with a 'Safe Conduct' voucher attached to the letter.

'Why me?' I asked.

'Because you're about the most sensible person in the building. Who's that?'

He had noticed the Princess for the first time.

'This is Laura Scrubb. She'll be with us for a week or two.'

I nodded to the Princess, who reluctantly shook hands with Kevin, then made a point of smelling her hand with obvious distaste before wiping it on her uniform.

'She's the Princess, isn't she?' said Kevin with interest, peering more closely at what might appear, at first glance, to be an undernourished handmaiden.

'I'm afraid so,' I replied, 'but keep it under your hat. If she's kidnapped by agents of a foreign power we'll have to waste a lot of time and energy getting her back.'

'Probably do her the power of good,' said Kevin,

'and knock some sense into her thick overprivileged head.'

'You are *so* disrespectful,' announced the Princess haughtily, getting out her list and pencil again. 'Name?'

'Kevin Spartacus.'

'Related to this nitwit here?' she said, pointing at Tiger. 'That figures, and I don't know who to pity more.'

She scribbled the name he'd given her on the piece of paper while Kevin peered at her as one might gaze at a particularly intriguing variety of beetle. I was suddenly worried – I'd seen that look before. He was seeing something, or he had *seen* something. Something in the future, and something about the Princess.

'This is very interesting,' he said at length. 'Yes, very interesting indeed. *Definitely* keep her identity a secret.'

And so saying, he prodded the Princess with a bony finger and said: 'Fascinating.'

'I'm not here to be studied,' said the Princess. 'I am here to study *you*.'

'You will almost die several times in the next week,' said Kevin Zipp thoughtfully, 'but will be saved by people who do not like you, nor are like you, nor that you like.'

'That'll be you lot, then,' said the Princess, looking at Tiger and me.

'It might help if you were to invest in a bit of warmth,' said Kevin.

'If you have foreseen I am to be saved then it doesn't much matter what I do, now, does it?'

'I only foresee a version of the future,' said Kevin, 'how it unfolds is up to you. Despite what I can see, we are all of us, in some way or another, responsible for our own destinies.'

The Princess didn't make any retort to this, and instead asked where the lavatory was. I told her and she stomped off.

'Was that true?' asked Tiger. 'The near-death thing, I mean?'

'Oh yes,' said Kevin with a shrug, 'she'll come within a hair's breadth of death – may even meet it. It's all a bit fuzzy, to be honest. But I'll tell you this: the Princess will be involved in the next Troll War, which will be when least expected. It will be bloody, short – and the aggressors will be victorious.'

'We will?' I asked in surprise, for in the past the Troll Wars had been noted only for the swift manner in which humans had been utterly defeated.

'Yes. Strange, isn't it? Then again,' he added cheerfully, 'I've been wrong before. And don't forget that what I see is only a *possible* version of events – and sometimes a knotted jumble of potential futures all seen as one.'

This, unfortunately, was true. Fate is never precisely determined. The strange thing is that *all* of us are clairvoyant. Any future you can dream up, no matter how bizarre, still retains the faint possibility of coming true. Kevin's skill was of dreaming up future events that were not just *possible* but *likely*. As he once said: 'Being a clairvoyant is ten per cent guesswork and ninety per cent probability mathematics.'

'So,' said Kevin, 'aside from princesses looking like handmaidens, what news?'

'Lots. I'm looking for something called the Eye of Zoltar. Heard of it?'

'Sure. It's had Grade III legendary status for centuries.'

A Grade III legendary status meant that the Eye was 'really not very likely at all', which isn't helpful, but better than Grade II: 'No proof of existence', and especially Grade I: 'Proven non-existence'.

'Grade III, eh?' I said. 'That doesn't sound good.'

'So were unicorns at one time,' said Kevin, 'and the coelacanth. And we all know they exist.'

Kevin then frowned deeply, looked at me again, and a cloud of consternation crossed his face.

'Who *precisely* wants you to look for the Eye of Zoltar?'

I told him about the meeting with the Mighty Shandar and the options regarding the refund, and Kevin thought for a moment.

'I need to make some enquiries. Call a Sorcerers' Conclave for an hour's time.'

I told him I would, and he dashed off without another word.

'Kevin's seen something in the future,' said Tiger, 'and I don't think he likes it.'

'Yes,' I said, 'I noticed it too. And when clairvoyants get nervous, so do I.'

The Princess came back in, holding a roll of loo paper.

'Do I fold it or crumple it before I . . . you know?'

Tiger and I looked at one another.

'Don't give me your silent-pity claptrap,' said the Princess crossly, 'it is a *huge* sacrifice to live without servants, a burden that you pinheads know nothing about. What's more, this body is covered with unsightly red rashes and I think I may be dying. My stomach has a sort of *gnawing* feeling inside.'

'Have you had it long?'

'Since I've been in this hideous body.'

'You're hungry,' I said simply. 'Never felt that before?'

'Me, a princess? Don't be ridiculous.'

'You're going to have to trust that body when it starts telling you things. Let me have a look at the rash. Growing up in an orphanage tends to make you an expert on skin complaints.'

She made what I can only describe as a 'hurrumph' noise and I led her off grumbling in the direction of the Ladies.

Fortunately for the Princess and for Laura Scrubb, the rash was not bad and likely the result of sleeping on damp hay. After instructing her – and not *assisting* her – on the loo-paper problem, I took her down to the Kazam kitchens and introduced her to our cook, who was known by everyone as Unstable Mabel, but not to her face.

'Where did you find this poor wee bairn?' said Mabel, ladling out a large portion of leftover stew and handing it to the Princess. 'She looks as though she has been half starved and treated with uncommon brutality. From the palace, is she?'

'That's an outrageous slur against a fine employer,' said the Princess, shovelling down the stew. 'I'll have you know that the Royal Family are warm and generous people who treat their servants with the greatest of respect and only rarely leave them out in the rain for fun.'

Unstable Mabel, whose insanity did not stretch so far for her to be totally without lucid moments, looked at me and arched her eyebrow.

'She's the Princess, isn't she?'

'I'm afraid so.'

The Princess stopped mid-gulp, her manners apparently forgotten in her hunger.

'How does everyone know it's me?'

'Because,' said Mabel, who was always direct in speech and manner, 'you're well known in the Kingdom as a spoilt, conniving, cruel, bullying little brat.'

'Right,' said the Princess, getting out her piece of

paper, 'you're going on the list too. Everyone on it will be flogged due to the disrespectful manner in which I have been treated. Name?'

'Mabel . . . Spartacus.'

The Princess started to write, then stopped as she realised the ongoing Spartacus gag was doubtless a leg-pull.

'You're only making it worse for yourself,' she scolded. 'I hate every single one of you and can't wait for the moment when I leave.'

And she gave us both a pouty glare and folded her arms. Mabel turned to me.

'Can I make a suggestion?' she said.

'Yes, please.'

'Take her down to the orphan labour pool and have her allocated to sewer cleaning duties for twenty-four hours. She'll have to live outside for a couple of days afterwards due to the stench that no amount of scrubbing will remove, but it might teach her some humility.'

'I hate all of you,' said the Princess. 'I hate your lack of consideration, lack of compassion and the meagre respect you show your obvious betters. If you don't take me home *right now* I will hold my breath until I turn blue, and then you'll be sorry.'

I stared at her for a moment.

'No need for that,' I said with a sigh, taking my car keys from my pocket. 'I'll just apologise to the

King and the Queen and tell them their daughter is beyond my help, and probably anyone else's. You can live out your spoilt life without effort, secure in the depths of your own supreme ignorance, and die as you lived, without purpose, true fulfilment or any discernibly useful function.'

She opened her mouth but shut it again and said nothing. I carried on:

'You don't need me to drive you home, Princess. You know where the door is and you can walk out of it any time you want – but I'd like you to appreciate that Laura Scrubb, the orphan with whom you are not even worthy to share skin disorders, cannot walk out of a door to anywhere until she's eighteen, and even then it's to a life of grinding poverty, disappointment, back-breaking toil and an early death, if she's lucky.'

The Princess was silent for a moment, then pulled up a sleeve and looked at Laura's rash.

'Okay,' she said, 'I'm staying. But only because I choose to do so for educational reasons, and not because any of your words meant anything to me, which they didn't.'

'Good,' I said, 'and you'll *choose* to do what I tell you rather than endlessly complaining and putting people on your list?'

The Princess shrugged.

'I might *choose* to do that, yes.'

I stared at her and she lowered her eyes, took the list out of her pocket and tore it into tiny pieces.

'Pointless anyway,' she grumbled, 'what with everyone called Spartacus.'

And she chuckled at the joke. It showed she had a sense of humour. Perhaps she might become bearable, given time.

'Okay, then,' I said, 'let's get you into some clean clothes and out of that terrible maid's outfit.'

'Thank you,' she said, with a resigned sigh, 'I'd like that.'

I led her up to my bedroom, found some clothes about the right size and told her not to come down until she had showered and washed her hair.

She fumbled with the buttons on her blouse uselessly until I helped her.

'Hell's teeth, Princess, did you not do *anything* for yourself at the palace?'

'I did my own sleeping,' she said after a moment's thought, 'usually.'

I gathered up her tatty clothes as she took them off, then chucked them in the recycling. As I left to alert everyone to the Sorcerers' Conclave I heard her scream as she mishandled the mixer on the shower.

Sorcerers' Conclave

The sorcerers were all convened in the Kazam main offices an hour later. Wizard Moobin was there, as was Lady Mawgon, Full and Half Price, Perkins, Prince Nasil, Dame Corby 'She whom the ants obey' and Kevin Zipp, who was busy scribbling notes on the back of an envelope.

They all listened to what I had to say, from D'argento's appearance to Shandar's offer of a deal. Find the Eye of Zoltar, or he'd kill the Dragons, and us too if we tried to stop him. I didn't tell them about the Princess as they'd all guess soon enough.

'Zoltar?' said Perkins when I mentioned it. 'Anyone we know?'

'Zoltar was the sorcerer to His Tyrannical Majesty Amenemhat V,' said Moobin, 'and was ranked about third most powerful on the planet at the time. He turned to the dark Mystical Arts for cash, as we understand it, and was killed in an unspeakably unpleasant way not long after Amenemhat V himself.'

'And the Eye?' I asked. 'I'm thinking it wasn't a real one.'

'It was a jewel,' said Dame Corby, reading from the *Codex Magicalis*. 'It says that Zoltar liked to use a staff, the top of which was adorned "with a mighty ruby the size of a goose egg". Cut with over a thousand facets and said to dance with inner fire, the ruby was always warm to the touch, even on the coldest night. It is said that the Eye worked as a *lens* to magnify Zoltar's huge power. After Zoltar's death the Eye changed hands many time but not without mishap – lesser wizards "were changed into lead" when they attempted to harness its huge power.'

'Changed to *what*?' said Perkins.

'Lead,' said Dame Corby. 'You know, the heavy metal?'

'Oh,' said Perkins.

'Does it say what happened to the Eye?' I asked.

Dame Corby turned over the page.

'Changed hands many times – traditional reports of a curse, death to all who beheld it, ba-da-boom-ba-da-bing, usual stuff. It was definitely known to be in the possession of Suleiman the Magnificent in 1552, and was said to be instrumental in maintaining the might and power of the Ottoman Empire. It was thought to have been on one of the trains that T. E. Lawrence derailed on the Hejaz railway in 1916. It was suggested Lawrence may have owned the Eye until he died in a motorcycle accident in 1935 but nothing was found in his effects. No one's heard of the Eye after that.'

'I'm not so sure,' said Kevin Zipp, 'and I'll relate to you a conversation I had with an ex-sorcerer named Able Quizzler a few years back.'

Everyone leaned closer.

'Quizzler was part of the team that did the early spelling work for levitating railways,' said Kevin, 'but when I met him he was scratching a living doing voiceover work for I-speak-your-weight machines. He told me how he had spent the last forty years attempting to find the Eye of Zoltar, and with it restart his sorcery career. He had almost given up when he heard stories of a vast, multifaceted ruby that seemed to dance with inner fire, was warm to the touch and gave inexplicable powers to those skilled enough to tame it – and changed the unworthy to lead.'

'The metal lead?' said Perkins, who was having trouble grasping this.

'Yes, the metal lead.'

'And where was this?' asked Lady Mawgon, who suddenly seemed interested.

'The Eye of Zoltar was apparently seen around . . . the neck of Sky Pirate Wolff.'

Up until now everyone had been hanging on Kevin's every word, but as soon as he mentioned Wolff, everyone sighed and threw up their arms in exasperation.

'Oh, for goodness' sake,' said Moobin sceptically, 'if

there is a tall story kicking around, then fourteen pence to a pound Captain Wolff will be at the bottom of it.'

I knew of Captain Wolff, of course – everyone did. She was a mythical figure, also of Grade III 'really not very likely at all' status, who had more wild stories attached to her than almost anyone on the planet. She was blamed for many acts of aerial piracy but never caught, and sightings of her were sporadic, sketchy and prone to exaggeration. It was said that she had tamed a Cloud Leviathan personally, which is a bit like saying you rode a Zebricorn into battle after catching one. The Leviathan, an aircraft-sized flying creature of obscure origins, was seen only rarely, and photographed just once, about eight years before. The photograph was front-page news in the world's newspapers and downgraded the Leviathan's legendary status from Grade IV, 'not very likely, to be honest', to a Grade V: 'okay, some basis in fact, but still partly unexplained'.

It was also speculated that Sky Pirate Wolff's hideout was in the legendary Leviathans' Graveyard, the place where Cloud Leviathans go to die, reputedly located somewhere on the misty heights of the mountain known as Cadair Idris. The facts were all a bit hazy, but if Wolff were somehow real, this is how she'd want it – and Wolff's skill at taming a Leviathan would explain the ease with which she could apparently capture entire jetliners on the wing, the loss of the liner *Tyrannic* and even the capture and destruction of Cloud City Nimbus III, where every man and woman was made to walk the plank – it rained Cloud City citizens for weeks, some say.

'Sky Pirate Wolff doesn't exist,' said Moobin. 'It's more likely the *Tyrannic* was lost at sea, no one knows what happened to Nimbus III, and as for pirates boarding jetliners, it's more probable the scallywags stowed themselves aboard inside the wheel-wells.'

There then started an argument about whether the legendary pirate existed or not, whether it was safe or even possible to hide oneself in wheel-wells, and the wisdom of chasing after Grade IV legends and half-truths told by Able Quizzler, an old man driven insane by a quest that had dominated his life.

'Okay, okay,' I yelled above the arguing, 'let's all just calm down. Kevin, finish your story, please.'

'Last time we spoke, Able Quizzler told me that the Eye of Zoltar was within his grasp. I think it's a lead worth pursuing.'

'When and where was this?' asked Lady Mawgon.

'Six years ago, in a place called Llangurig. But I trust Able. We go back a while.'

Everyone went quiet.

'Llangurig is well inside the Cambrian Empire,' observed Moobin, 'in a region notorious for bandits, wild beasts, emulating slime mould and other perils. It's too dangerous.'

'So is fighting Shandar,' I said. 'Where's the harm in travelling to Llangurig to see if I can find Quizzler? After all, the refund isn't due for another month – and I could negotiate for Boo's release at the same time.'

This had an effect on the gathering, but before we could discuss it further there was a whooshing of wings and some brief bickering, and two dark shapes flew by the window.

'That's just what we need,' said Lady Mawgon, 'a couple of infants.'

And with a clattering at the window, two Dragons attempted to get in at the same time. They elbowed each other petulantly, breaking the window frame and panes of glass as they did so.

'Hey!' I said in my loudest voice, and they suddenly went silent. I was about the only one who could control them.

'Cut it out, you two – what happened to that bit where Dragons were creatures of great dignity, learning and wisdom?'

'Sorry, what did you say?' said Colin, removing one of his iPod earbuds. 'I was listening to the Doobie Brothers.'

The Dragons

The two Dragons I found myself vaguely responsible for were called Feldspar Axiom Firebreath IV, and Colin. They were each the size of a pony, and were decidedly reptilian in appearance, manner and gait. They had long jaws with serrated teeth, ornate head frills, a long barbed tail and explosively flammable breath. Their wings were a triumph of design in that when they were unfolded they took up the entire room and were as translucent as tissue paper, but when folded fitted neatly into dimples on their backs. They had muscular arms and legs, both of which carried sharp talons that needed to be clipped often as they would otherwise damage the hotel's parquet flooring.

But despite their appearance, which was both elegant and terrifying in equal measure, they acted like particularly dumb teenage brothers, only with an IQ immeasurably higher, and better taste in clothes and friends.

'Welcome home,' I said. 'Were you impressed by all that learning?'

'Good in parts,' said Colin thoughtfully, 'but generally inclined to repetition.'

'That's it?' said Wizard Moobin. 'Our entire intellectual output dismissed in a sentence?'

'We can discuss human literary output further if you'd like,' said Feldspar, 'but we'd only get as far as Aristotle before you'd do that thing where you stop working and fall apart. What's it called again?'

'Dying?'

'That's it. But your output isn't *all* boring. We thought that a few humans were actually *really* smart, but they were too rare to be of any real use, and rarely became leaders where they could actually change things.'

'And,' added Colin, 'I was a little disappointed over all that killing.'

Colin was a strict pacifist, and as much a vegan as any Dragon ever could be.

'There *is* quite a lot of it in our history,' I conceded.

'I knew how *much* before I went,' said Colin, 'I was just unprepared for the range of ridiculous excuses you lot use in its justification. It's somewhat bizarre to learn that many of you think that other humans are somehow different enough to be hated and killed, when in reality you're all tiresomely similar in outlook, needs and motivation, and differ only by peculiar habits, generally shaped by geographical circumstance.'

'We're not *all* bad,' I said, suddenly finding myself defending my own species.

'No,' agreed Colin, 'some of you are hardly rubbish at all, and a few – there are always a few – are quite exceptional. Mind you,' he added, 'you can always take solace in the fact that humans are generally better than Trolls.'

'Better than Trolls?' said Lady Mawgon scornfully. 'Praise indeed.'

'*Generally* better,' repeated Colin, in case she had misunderstood.

We all fell silent, and Feldspar looked around the room carefully.

'Is this a Sorcerers' Conclave?' he asked, and I nodded.

'It's about the Mighty Shandar,' said Moobin, and he outlined the refund issue, and how finding the Eye of Zoltar might help.

'I thought he might want to kill us,' said Colin in a matter-of-fact manner, 'most do. We'll defend ourselves as well as we can, but it won't be much of a fight – neither of us will be full-grown and at Peak Magic for at least another century, perhaps two.'

'. . . which is why we need to find the Eye,' I said, 'heard of it?'

'Nope,' said Colin, 'but then our Dragon trans-death memory is weak at present. If you want to give us thirty years or so for our forefathers' memories to settle and coalesce, we'd be happy to help then.'

'That might be too long,' said Moobin.

'Humans!' said Feldspar. 'Always in such a hurry. Well, must be off. I'm on a princess-guarding gig, and the venue needs my approval for suitability. Tall tower, abandoned castle, island, that sort of thing.'

'You never mentioned this,' said Colin, mildly annoyed.

'I don't have to tell you *everything*. Besides, it's only for thirty years or until successful abduction of said princess by said brave knight.'

'You wouldn't catch me doing any princess-guarding,' said Colin grumpily. 'It's so depressingly *medieval*, and besides, guarding princesses and vaporising knights with a white-hot ball of fire is not the publicity we Dragons need right now.'

'How about guarding but without doing the ball of fire thing?' asked Moobin.

'It's an idea,' replied Feldspar thoughtfully, 'although I'm not sure you *can* guard princesses without roasting a few knights. It'll be fine. I get to meet the princess and if we don't hit it off I can always turn them down.'

And so saying he flew out of the window.

'Okay,' I said, using my authoritative voice, the one I usually used when I had to make some sort of wise or portentous pronouncement, 'it looks like I'm going into the Cambrian Empire on a dual mission. Firstly, I'll head for Llangurig to find Able Quizzler and see if there is any truth in his claim that the Eye of Zoltar is in Pirate Wolff's possession.'

'And secondly?' asked Lady Mawgon.

'I'll drop in and see if I can negotiate for Once Magnificent Boo's release. I'll be gone for two days, three at most.'

There was a mild grumbling of discomfort. Whenever I went away or had a day off, things generally went a bit chaotic at Kazam, but they understood this was important.

'Okay, then,' I said, eager to move on, 'who's coming with me? Not you, Tiger, you're staying here to look after things in my absence.'

'I can be tactical air support,' said Colin. 'I might not be large enough to carry anyone, but I can manage reconnaissance duties.'

'Thank you,' I said. 'Anyone else?'

There was silence, and for a good reason.

'I'm not sure *any* of us can come with you,' said Moobin apologetically. 'The transportation of licensed sorcerers across borders has been strictly controlled for some time. We could get travel permits, but it would take six months or more.'

'If we sneaked across the border and were caught we'd end up no better off than Once Magnificent Boo,' added Lady Mawgon.

'My carpet and I aren't going anywhere until I get some more angel feathers,' said the Prince gloomily, 'but if you shout I'll come running and do what I can.'

'I'm too lazy,' admitted Kevin Zipp, 'and can foresee

more terrors than I think it will be helpful to tell you about.'

This was worrying. I didn't mind going on my own, but I'd prefer company.

'I'm in,' said Perkins. 'Officialdom moves slowly both in the Kingdom of Snodd and the Cambrian Empire. It's doubtful if my licensed-sorcerer status has even left the Ministry of Infernal Affairs out-tray. The worst they can do is refuse me entry.'

'Thank you, Perkins.'

'My pleasure. Never been on a quest before.'

'Hang on a second,' I said. 'Let's all get this perfectly clear – this is *not* a quest. All we're doing is travelling into the Cambrian Empire to find evidence that Able Quizzler chanced upon the Eye of Zoltar.'

'Besides,' said Moobin, 'all quests need to be approved by the Questing Foundation.'

'Exactly,' I said, 'and we don't want *them* involved.'

'So what if we do find evidence of the Eye of Zoltar?' asked Perkins.

'Then we carry on, I guess, and see what we can find.'

'It will be dangerous,' said Dame Corby, 'the Cambrian Empire always is. My Uncle Herbert went there to do some mild mega-pike fishing and was stuffed and mounted by the Hotax.'

'I'm thinking I shouldn't ask this, but what's a Hotax?' asked Perkins.

'A sort of cannibalistic savage with an unhealthy enthusiasm for taxidermy.'

'I *knew* I shouldn't have asked.'

'Don't forget to keep your angel traps on you at all times,' said Prince Nasil, '*especially* when imminent death is close by. Did I tell you they liked marshmallows?'

'Yes,' said Perkins and I, pretty much at the same time.

'Here,' said Moobin, handing me a piece of paper, 'you'll need this.'

It was a letter of credit to the Ransom Clearing House. Effectively worth twenty thousand.

'I'd like to go higher for Boo but that's all we can spare. Try and knock them down, won't you?'

I said I'd do my best, and put the note in my pocket.

'Right, then,' I said to the group as they got up. 'The duty roster is posted on the board and don't forget to fill out your paperwork. Tiger will help you.'

'Thanks for agreeing to come with me,' I said to Perkins as the meeting broke up.

'You can't go on your own,' he replied. 'Besides, Kevin once let slip that I would grow old in the Cambrian Empire. If I'm eventually to retire there, it makes sense to at least visit the place. What's the plan, by the way?'

'We drive to the border in the Bugatti posing as a couple going on holiday.'

'And then what?'

'And then we improvise.'

'Sounds like an *excellent* plan.'

'What about me?' asked the Princess, who I'd forgotten about, but who must have overheard everything. 'Shall I be a Tralfamosaur research student from a well-born family who has fallen on hard times but is otherwise treated as her high station befits?'

'You're not coming because it's too risky,' I said. 'Besides, we can't take a princess into the Cambrian Empire without an import licence.'

'But I'm not the Princess right now,' said the Princess. 'I'm an undernourished orphan named Laura Scrubb with unsightly red rashes on my arms and legs.'

'She's got a point,' said Perkins.

I thought for a moment. The King and Queen had told me she needed educating, and a fact-finding mission to the wildly unpredictable Cambrian Empire might be just the thing.

'Okay, Princess,' I said, 'you're in – but if you blow your cover and get kidnapped, your father will have to mortgage the Kingdom you might one day inherit to get you out.'

'I'll take that risk,' she said with a toss of her head. 'Now, shall I be a Tralfamosaur research student from a well-born family who is treated as an equal?'

'No, you're my handmaiden.'

She thought about this.

'Will I have to do any ironing?'

'*Can* you do ironing?'

'No.'

'Then probably not.'

'Okay,' she said with the first smile I'd seen, 'game on.'

To the border by Royale

As soon as our local filling station was open in the morning I checked the oil level and topped up the fuel on the Bugatti Royale. As an afterthought I added a couple of cans of spare petrol to the cavernous boot, then drove the car back to Zambini Towers, where I packed a spirit stove and a billycan for tea. I fetched several cases of 'one meal' expanding biscuits from Mabel and an enchanted tent that would swear angrily to itself when self-pitching, and thus save you the effort.

Perkins was the first to appear, dragging a leather suitcase behind him.

'A few things Moobin and Mawgon put together for me,' he explained. 'Potions, spells, temporary newting compound, anti-curse cream, that sort of stuff.'

'Keep it well hidden,' I said. 'I don't want to spend the next week in prison, trying to convince a judge we're not dangerous magical extremists or something.'

'Promise,' said Perkins, and by clever use of

perspective manipulation, tucked his heavy suitcase into the Royale's glovebox.

Tiger appeared.

'This is the best guide I could find,' he said, handing me a copy of *Enjoy the unspoilt charms of the Cambrian Empire without death or serious injury*.

'Not exactly a confidence-inspiring title, is it?'

'Not really. I got you this one, too.'

He handed me a book entitled *Death and injury avoidance techniques for the discerning traveller in the Western Kingdoms*. I put both guides in the door pocket of the Royale, and, since there was a bit of time, briefed Tiger as best as I could.

'Okay,' I said, 'Lady Mawgon and Moobin will be working on the spell for getting the mobile phone network running again. Keep Patrick of Ludlow confined to earth moving, tree transplanting and other lifting – let Dame Corby and the Prices do the subtle work. The Instant Camera Project will need testing once Mrs Pola Roidenstock has finished perfecting the "develop before your eyes" spelling. She'll need help thinking up a good name to sell it under, too. The rest of the work you'll find on the board, but, well, you know pretty much how it works by now.'

'I can contact you if I have any questions, yes?'

'Not by the usual channels – the Cambrian Empire has cut itself off from the outside world. Despite that, I'll call every day at seven in the evening to check in. If you don't hear from us for forty-eight hours, then alert the King. Do you have the conch?'

Tiger held up his conch shell, I showed him mine, and we touched them together to reinforce the twinning. They were a left and right pair, ideal for long-distance communication. We could have used winkles, which fit easily in the ear, but the reception was poor as limpets used the same bandwidth for their inane chit-chat.

'And Tiger,' I added, 'would you take care of the Quarkbeast? They hunt them for fun in the Cambrian Empire.'

'Sorry I'm late,' said a voice, and with a whooshing of wings and a flurry of dust Colin alighted on the pavement beside us, startling some pedestrians, who ran away screaming in terror. 'I've got to open a supermarket this morning so I'll meet you inside the Cambrian Empire later on.'

'Good luck with that. What news from Feldspar and the princess-guarding gig?'

'To be honest,' said Colin, 'I'm jealous I'm not doing it. Lots of grub, comfy digs and the castle is superb – just the right amount of ruined, off the coast of Cornwall and with angry seas all around.'

'Is there a volcano?' I asked, knowing how these things go in and out of fashion.

'No, but Feldspar gets Wednesdays off so we'll be seeing him from time to time, and the princess he's guarding has a relaxed attitude to being a prisoner, and often nips into Truro to meet friends.'

'Speaking of princesses,' said Perkins once Colin had left, 'I thought ours was coming with us?'

'I thought so too.'

We waited another five minutes and I rechecked everything was in the car.

'I left my angel trap behind,' said Perkins, 'it just didn't seem right.'

'Me too.'

The Princess kept us waiting for a half-hour for the simple reason that it was customary for princesses to never be on time for anything.

We headed west once she had turned up, towards the six miles of frontier the Kingdom of Snodd shared with the Cambrian Empire. The route took us past Clifford, where my old orphanage stood gaunt and dark against the sky, tiles missing from the roof and broken glass in the windows, the shutters askew. Part of the roof was missing, and one of the gable ends of the building had collapsed into a pile of rubble, exposing the interior to the rain. Not much different to when I lived there, in fact. I thought of dropping in to see Mother Zenobia, but we had work to do.

We negotiated the border post leading out of the Kingdom of Snodd without a problem, then drove slowly across the bridge that spanned the River Wye, at this point the border between the nations. On the

Cambrian bank there were tank traps, minefields and razor wire, and beyond this were batteries of anti-aircraft guns, and behind *them*, obsolete landships manned by a ragtag collection of Cambrian Army irregulars.

'Are the fortifications there to keep people in or out?' asked Perkins as we drove past several Cambrian border guards, who eyed us suspiciously.

'Probably a bit of both.'

We stopped behind a queue of vehicles once we were off the bridge, and waited to be called forward to the customs post. To our left was a large board reminding visitors of the many items that it was illegal to import. Some of them were quite straightforward, such as weapons, aircraft, record players and 'magical paraphernalia', but others were quite bizarre, such as spinning wheels, peanuts, flatworms, Bunsen burners and anything 'overtly red in colour'.

The Cambrian Empire was a large, ramshackle and lawless nation composed almost entirely of competing warlords, constantly warring tribes and small family fiefdoms, all of whom squabbled constantly. Despite the small fights that were constantly going on, the citizens of Cambria were fiercely loyal to Emperor Tharv, who lived in a magnificent palace within the fashionably war-torn and picturesquely ruined capital city Cambrianopolis.

For one of the largest kingdoms in the unUnited

Kingdoms – it was on the site of what was once mid-Wales – there were very few people living here, owing possibly to the aforementioned bickering. Most visitors entered the empire to explore or hunt in the Empty Quarter, a twelve-hundred-square-mile tract of former Dragonlands that had moved seamlessly into the hands of the Cambrian Wildlife Trust upon the death of a Dragon fifty years before. Many asked why Emperor Tharv would do something quite so sensible, but his madness, it seemed, was unpredictable. He once claimed to have trained up a thousand killer elephants with which to lay waste the unUnited Kingdoms, along with devising another plan whereby he vowed to destabilise the yogurt market by flooding the industry with cheap imports. But conversely, he had also instigated the best National Health System in the Kingdoms, along with a robust childcare regime that allows young women to go out marauding, thieving and kidnapping with their husbands.

'It says here that most foreign currency is earned through jeopardy tourism,' said Perkins, reading from *Enjoy the unspoilt charms of the Cambrian Empire without death or serious injury*. 'People after excitement and adventure, even if it means possible loss of life.'

'I guess that's where this bunch are going,' I said, indicating the steady stream of men and women eagerly queuing to cross into the nation.

'For some it will be for the last time,' said Perkins.

'It says here tourism mortality rates haven't dropped below eighteen per cent in the past nine decades.'

I looked again at the queue of tourists. If what Perkins said was correct, eighteen out of every hundred people wouldn't be coming back.

'My father sold Emperor Tharv an option on my daughter for his son,' said the Princess absently.

'You don't have any children,' said Perkins, 'and neither does Emperor Tharv. How could Tharv offer the hand of a son he doesn't yet have?'

'It's called "dabbling in the princess options market",' she replied, 'and it's not uncommon. In fact, a third of the Emperor's private income is earned on marriage trading options. Only last year he paid fifty thousand moolah for an option on the hand of my second daughter *if* I had one, for his son, *if* he has one. His son doesn't have to take up the option, but if he does it'll cost him a further million. Nice little earner for us and good for the palace coffers. For Emperor Tharv, he has now gambled on not only securing a good marriage for his grandson at a competitive price, but also gained a tradable asset – he can sell that option to anyone he pleases. If I actually *have* a second daughter the option jumps in value, and if she turns out to be beautiful, clever and witty, Tharv can make more money from selling the option. Conversely, if my second daughter turns out to be a vapid, airheaded little dingbat, his option value sinks to nothing.'

'So *that's* how the options market works,' said Perkins, 'and there was I, thinking it was complex.'

'Is that why queens have so many children?' I asked. 'For the option rights?'

'Exactly so,' said the Princess. 'The King of Shropshire managed to build most of his nation's motorway network by the trading options on his twenty-nine children.'

There was a pause.

'I don't suppose,' began Perkins, 'you know anything about Collateralised Debt Obligations, do you?'

'Of course,' said the Princess, who seemed to be oddly at ease with complex financial transactions. 'First you must understand that loss-making financial mechanisms can be sold to offset—'

Luckily we were saved that particular explanation as a Skybus Aeronautics delivery truck was allowed out, and they waved us into the border post of the Cambrian Empire.

The Cambrian Empire

I pulled forward and wound down the window as the border guard moved towards us. It was only then that I noticed that the Helping Hand™ was still firmly attached to the steering wheel. This was illegal magical contraband, and likely to be confiscated. Without time to remove it, I hid my own hand high in my cuff and pretended the Helping Hand™ was my own. The border guard stopped by the driver's-side window and looked at me suspiciously.

'Hello!' I said brightly.

'Good afternoon,' he said, looking at me again, then at the car. 'Is this . . . a Bugatti Royale?'

'Yes.'

'What's the chassis number?'

'41.151,' I replied, since it was what *everyone* asked me, along with the body type, offering a stiff admonishment for using it as a daily driver. Apparently the Bugatti Royale is quite rare but, well, we need a car, and it *is* a car first and foremost.

'I see,' said the guard, 'and why is one of your hands really hairy and like a man's?'

I lifted my arm and the Helping Hand™ – as its name would suggest – did as it was meant to do – *help*. The hand moved with my arm, and with the join hidden by my sleeve, the hand looked eerily as though it were attached to me.

'I lost my own in a car accident,' I said, thinking quickly. 'This one belonged to a landship engineer who was accidentally dragged into the number-three engine. All they could salvage of him was an ear, this hand and a left leg, which is currently doing useful service attached to a bus conductor somewhere in Sheffield. I've not heard where the ear is these days.'

'And the tattoo about pies?' he asked, referring to the 'No More Pies' tattoo on the back of the hand.

'You know, we never did find out.'

'Okay,' said the guard, who seemed to have fallen for my capacity for invention, 'papers?'

I handed him our IDs and personal injury waivers, something that is mandatory for all visitors to the risk-desirable nation. He stared at them for a moment.

'Purpose of visit?'

'Negotiation for the safe release of a friend,' I said, showing him the letter from the Cambrian Empire's Kidnap Clearance House, 'but before that, a day or two of holiday in the Empty Quarter – who knows, we might even indulge in some mid-level jeopardy.'

He looked at us all and then saluted smartly.

'Welcome to the Cambrian Empire. There's a Tourist

Information Office down the road where you can decide which particularly perilous pursuit you'd like to attempt first.'

I thanked him and drove the half-mile down the road to where the small border town of Whitney was doing a brisk trade preparing tourists for their excursions. The shops sold supplies, maps, guidebooks and 'Get Me Out of Here' emergency escape package deals at grossly inflated prices, and parked on the street were a parade of armoured four-wheel-drive trucks, ready to take visitors off into the interior. I parked the Bugatti and turned off the engine.

'Keep an eye on the car, one of you,' I said. 'I'm going to find a guide.'

I climbed out of the car and headed for the Tourist Information Office. I hadn't gone five paces when I was accosted by young backpacker carrying a guitar. He was wearing a baggy shirt open to the chest, flip-flops, fashionably ripped jeans, and beads woven into his blond hair.

'Hey, Dragonslayer babe.'

'I'm on holiday,' I said, well used to being recognised in public.

'The name's Curtis,' said Curtis. 'Want to hang out, play some guitar, talk about the latest fashions, the best places to be seen, and just generally chill?'

'You must be mistaking me for someone who is shallow and indifferent,' I said. 'Goodbye.'

'Wait, wait,' said Curtis, who clearly did not take no for an answer. 'The full name is Rupert Curtis Osbert Chippenworth III. From the Nation of Financia. *Chippenworth*, yes?'

He said it in a way that suggested I was expected to know who he was, and yes, I had heard of the Chippenworths – a family of huge wealth and privilege from the financial centre of the Kingdoms.

'Let me guess,' I said, 'you're here to have a few dangerous scrapes so once you have been shoehorned into your cushy and undemanding job you'll have something interesting in your past to brighten an otherwise unremarkable life?'

'Pretty much,' he said, completely unfazed by my assessment. 'So listen, I know you run Kazam, so got any "S"? Y'know, something to while away the dull evenings between bouts of excitement and terror?'

'S?'

'*Spells*,' he said in a low voice, 'the weirder the better, but none of that "changing into animals" stuff because it can totally do your head.'

He laughed in a clumsy attempt to charm me. The use of magic for recreational purposes was stupid, dangerous and irresponsible. Supplying mind-altering spells to idiots like Curtis would also have you drummed out of the magic industry quicker than you could say Zork.

'No,' I said, 'and here's why: you'll start with

something simple like a Pollyanna Stone that tells you what you want to hear. Pretty soon you'll be moving on to stronger and heavier spells that promote unrealistic levels of optimism and self-delusion. After that you'll be dependent on them, always looking for the next spell, and then, when the spells lose their power, you'll be lost, frightened and bewildered, and your life will tip into a downward spiral of recrimination and despair.'

'Okay, okay,' he said, backing away from my icy stare, 'I only asked. Boy, some people are so *square*.'

He returned to where his friends were waiting and they went into a huddle, throwing the occasional dirty look in my direction. I ignored them, and entered the Tourist Information Office.

The woman behind the desk was middle aged and dressed in the traditional badger skins. She had a tattoo on the left side of her face to denote her clan and status, and wore the 'ABTA Silver Star' medal on her left breast, denoting Tour Guide valour, probably something to do with her missing left arm.

'Welcome, noble traveller and adventurer,' said the woman in a long-rehearsed patter, 'to the land that Health and Safety forgot. In these risk-averse times, the Cambrian Empire is one of the few places where danger is actually dangerous. The possibility of actual death brings fear and excitement to even the most mundane of pastimes; the adrenalin surge in knowing you have cheated death by a whisker is a wild ride to which you will wish to return time and time again. Now, what do you fancy?'

She indicated a board behind her, with each activity outlined next to a price, and how dangerous it was by way of a Calculated Fatality Index. The most dangerous was a six-day 'wrestling with flesh-eating slugs' holiday at 58 per cent, which I took to mean that for every hundred tourists willing to risk the dangers, fifty-eight would end up as a sort of semi-digested gloop. Below that was Tralfamosaur hunting with a Fatality Index of 42 per cent, and the list went down in danger from there, past 'prodding a Hotax with a stick' to 'searching for the source of the River Wye' and then to 'watching Tralfamosaur from a distance' before the least dangerous activity of all, a shopping trip to Cambrianopolis. This, while relatively risk-free by Cambrian standards, could still lose one visitor out of a hundred.

'Mostly to crush injury, hold-ups and food poisoning,' explained the tourist officer when I asked, 'and the Fatality Index does rise to 2.2 per cent during the January sales. Now, what are you after?'

I had to think carefully. If I just said we were going to Llangurig, I wouldn't even need a guide. But if Quizzler was right and the Eye of Zoltar was with Sky Pirate Wolff, I'd need the best guide there was. I decided to opt for the most adventurous scenario.

'Party of three to discover the legendary Leviathans' Graveyard, please,' I replied, 'and when there to meet up with Sky Pirate Wolff – by way of Llangurig to visit a friend.'

The woman looked more amused than shocked.

'Yes, yes, very funny,' she said. 'Seriously, what would you like to do?'

'As I said.'

'Listen,' she said, lowering her voice and beckoning me closer, 'the reason we don't list excursions to search for the not-very-likely Leviathans' Graveyard is *because* of Sky Pirate Wolff. The last two expeditions both suffered an 86 per cent Fatality Index. *Risk* of death is our selling point; *almost certain* death is not. Dead tourists don't come back and spend more money.'

'I'll be okay,' I said, 'I'm big into peril.'

'Oh yeah?' she said, unconvinced. 'How big?'

'I . . . sleep in the same room as a Quarkbeast.'

The tourist woman blinked twice. The Quarkbeast's fearsome reputation was known all over the Kingdoms.

'Leviathans' Graveyard and Captain Wolff, eh?'

'If it's not too much trouble.'

'Okay, then,' said the tourist office woman, 'there *is* one guide I can think of who might be willing to help you search for the Leviathans' Graveyard, but they won't be cheap and this didn't come through me. Wait outside and I'll let them know.'

I thanked her and walked back out into the autumn

sunshine and noticed the Bugatti had gone. Our luggage was sitting in the dust by the roadside, and sitting on top of our luggage was Perkins.

'Where's the car?'

'Requisitioned by agents acting for Emperor Tharv,' said Perkins meekly. 'I tried to stop them but there were eight of them, and they all had very sharp swords.'

'Couldn't you have using a simple occluding spell or something?'

'Yes, well, I *could* have done but it all happened so fast. But they did say thank you very politely and issued a receipt.'

Crime in the Cambrian Empire was always business, never personal. You'd not be a victim of crime here without an apology, an explanation of why you were being robbed and then a receipt to facilitate an insurance claim. Perkins passed me the receipt, which conveyed, in very official-looking language, that the car had been claimed by the Emperor as anything in the nation could be, but the note said that I would be compensated – to the value of one Bugatti Royale.

'That's a blow,' I said, looking around, 'what about the Princess? Don't tell me they requisitioned her as well?'

'No, she went shopping.'

The Princess returned a few moments later.

'I had ID tags made for us so our bodies can be identified just in case,' she said cheerfully, handing us the discs. 'The man in the shop said they were Tralfamosaur gastric juice and flesh-eating slug ooze resilient. Where's the Bugatti?'

I showed her the receipt.

'Oh,' she said, studying the piece of paper, 'how interesting. Since it's issued on Emperor Tharv's order, technically it's a one Bugatti banknote.'

'And how would we redeem it?' asked Perkins. 'Go and ask Tharv for the equivalent in sports cars and take the change in motorcycles and hood ornaments?'

The Princess shrugged.

'I don't know. Shall I go and see if I can find a hire car?'

'Make sure it's good on all terrain,' I replied, 'and armoured.'

The Princess trotted off, enjoying her new-found freedom. It must have been quite a change for her, not being harassed by the press on her choice of boyfriends, her weight or who she would be voting for on *The Kingdom of Snodd's Got Talent*.

While we waited, Perkins and I checked our budget as I hadn't thought we'd be needing to hire a car, and a specialist guide was going to cost. We had enough, I figured, so long as we didn't eat out too often.

'Almost like a holiday, isn't it?' said Perkins, looking at the tourists moving here and there, organising their jeopardy gleefully.

'If you say so,' I replied absently, since I'd never

been on a holiday, and wouldn't know what to do if one chanced along.

'Sort of peaceful,' said Perkins, 'tranquil even.'

At that precise moment there was a tremendous concussion from somewhere close at hand. Before I could even begin to gauge from where the explosion had come, there was another crack, then another, and within a short time the air was filled with a sound like constant rolling thunder, so loud and heavy as to be almost directionless. I looked up and noticed that the anti-aircraft guns less than a hundred yards away were firing into the sky. I had once been on the receiving end of anti-aircraft fire while attempting to escape on a flying carpet, and I can tell you that it is *most* unpleasant. I looked up to see what they were shooting at, and my heart froze as a distinctive silhouette jinked and twisted as the anti-aircraft shells exploded all around it.

'Oh dear,' said Perkins, 'that's Colin.'

Colin's fall

And so it was. Colin, obviously finished with his supermarket opening, had dropped in to see how things were going and had been mistaken, we supposed, for a trespassing aircraft. We could do little but watch anxiously as Colin attempted to turn around and head back the way he had come. Unluckily, he was disoriented by the smoke, noise and hot shrapnel, and wandered farther into the Cambrian Empire's airspace. Eventually there was a black puff of smoke, and Colin rolled on to his back and began to fall towards the earth. We could see that one wing was tattered and frayed where the skin covering had been torn, and the other beat the air ferociously in a vain attempt to control his descent.

I looked at Perkins; his index fingers were already pointing at the Dragon. He thought quickly and mumbled a few words under his breath.

'Looking good,' I said. The Dragon had stopped struggling as Perkins transformed him into something else. I then noticed a green glint as the sun caught the figure, and I realised that the Dragon had not changed into anything usefully energy-absorbing, but *glass*. The impact upon hitting the ground would be catastrophic.

'Try again,' I said, as quietly and casually as I could, given the circumstances.

Perkins *did* try again, and the Dragon was immediately no longer glass, but an ornate decorative Dragon carved from marble. The resultant impact with the earth would have the same fatal effect, and possibly leave a large hole, too.

'Okay, okay, I've got it,' said Perkins, and let fly again.

Colin was now less than a thousand feet from the earth and still whirling about as the air rushed past his now rigid wings. Gravity, never a close friend to Dragons, would doubtless raise the historical score to Dragons: nil, Gravity: sixty-three.

Perkins tried again and Colin changed to bronze, then a shiny metallic lucky Chinese Dragon with a waving front leg, then to alabaster. All of these feats, while powerful and complex in themselves, really helped us not one jot, and as Colin passed the three-hundred-foot mark and was changed by Perkins into a delicate ice sculpture, I did the last thing available to me. I punched Perkins hard on the arm. It was a risky undertaking and could have gone either way – to him getting the spell correct, or failing utterly.

'What the—?'

'Get it together,' I snapped, 'or you and me are done.'

Actually, him and me were not yet an item so we couldn't be done, but I had to think that it might be something he valued, and give him an emotional boost to get the spell right. With only two hundred feet and a second or two to a nasty, shattered end, Perkins tried again and Colin changed abruptly to a dark matt-black substance.

I held my breath.

Colin hit the road with what I can only describe as probably the loudest, deepest and most dense-sounding *thud* I had ever heard. He narrowly missed two backpackers and a car as he momentarily spread out across the road to a flat disc about six inches thick. In an instant the rubber molecules that now made up his body sprang back into shape and Colin was catapulted high into the air. So high in fact, that the anti-aircraft guns opened up again, but this time with less accuracy, and none of the shell bursts came close. Pretty soon Colin was on his way back down but this time he landed five hundred yards or so farther away, and a second later was catapulted back into the air. We watched with growing despondency as Rubber Colin bounced off into the distance until he vanished below a low hill to the north.

'Blast,' said Perkins, lowering his now steaming finger in case anyone noticed he was responsible. They hadn't, and Perkins suddenly looked tired and sat on our luggage, head in hands.

'You okay?' I asked.

'I think so,' he said. 'I've not spelled that strongly before. Do I look okay?'

He looked tired and drained and somehow . . . different. More world-weary. I told him he probably needed an early night and he nodded in agreement.

'Was that Colin?' asked the Princess, walking back toward us.

I told her it was but to keep it under her hat. Magic was *strictly forbidden* in the Empire, and Perkins certainly didn't want to be outed as a sorcerer.

'How far do you think he went?' she asked, staring at the horizon.

Perkins looked at his watch.

'He'll be bouncing for the next ten minutes or so. Best guess – thirty or forty miles.'

'How much wizidrical energy to change him back?' I asked.

'Bucketloads if you want it done immediately,' replied Perkins thoughtfully, 'but the spell will wear off on its own within a few days. Either way, he's not flying out of here on his own – not with a wing like that.'

'But he's safe as a rubber dragon until he turns back?'

'Sure – so long as no one tries to make car tyres or doorstops or gumboots out of him. But it's not all bad,' he added. 'At least he'll be waterproof if it rains.'

I sighed. This was a bad start to our search. I pulled my compass out of my bag and took a bearing on the hill behind which Colin had bounced, then drew a line on my map. It was, luckily enough, pretty much in the same direction we were to travel. If our calculations were correct, Colin would be running out of bounce not far from Llangurig.

'They had run out of armoured cars,' said the Princess 'so I persuaded them to upgrade us to a military half-track at the same rate.'

She looked at Perkins, who was still sitting, head in hands.

'Do you think we should upgrade this to a quest?' she asked.

'It is *not* a quest,' I said emphatically. 'If it was we'd need to register with the International Questing Federation, adhere to their "Code of Conduct" and pay them two thousand moolah into the bargain.'

This was true. The Questing Federation were powerful, and would insist on a minimum staffing requirement: at least one strong-and-silent warrior, a sage-like old man, and either a giant or a dwarf – and all of them cost bundles, not just in salary but in hotel bills too. To go on a quest these days you needed serious financial backing.

'No,' I said more emphatically, 'this is a search, plain and simple.'

'Jenny?' said Perkins, still with his eyes closed.

'Yes?'

'Why *were* they shooting at Colin? At barely the size of a pony and with fiery breath no more powerful than a blowlamp, he's not exactly dangerous.'

A voice chirped up behind us.

'They shot him down because all aerial traffic in the Cambrian Empire is banned.'

I turned to see who was speaking, and that was when we first met Addie Powell.

Addie Powell

Her face was dirty, she had no shoes, and she was dressed in a loose, poncho-style jacket that was tied at the waist by a leather belt upon which hung a dagger. It was the costume favoured by the Silurians, a tribe who lived on the lower slopes of the Cambrian Mountains. She had three small stars tattooed on the left side of her face that told me she was a daughter of middle rank, a braid in the left side of her hair denoting no parents, and a ring on the third toe of her left foot – she held financial responsibility for someone, likely a younger sibling, or a grandmother. I guessed she was about twelve or thirteen, but it was hard to tell. Children grow up fast in the Empire. She may have been as young as ten.

'Hungry?' I asked, for Silurians value hospitality above everything, and the girl nodded. I dug some cheese out of my bag and offered it to her. The girl paused for a moment, approached warily with one hand on the hilt of her dagger, took the cheese and sniffed at it.

'Hereford Old Contemptible,' she said expertly,

'with chives and extra-mature. My favourite. Thank you.'

She sat down on a rock beside us, took a bite of the cheese, chewed for a moment, then said:

'New in the Empire?'

'Half an hour ago.'

'Was that rubber dragon anything to do with you?'

'Um – no.'

'Ah-ha. Did I just see your Bugatti being towed away?'

I nodded.

'Not unusual,' said the child. 'Our Glorious Emperor is a bit of a petrolhead. He sees a car he likes, he takes it. But at least he's willing to pay for it. He's odd like that. He cries bitterly when signing execution orders and always pardons his victims afterwards.'

'There's a lot to be said for not holding a grudge.'

'I suppose so. Why do you have "No more pies" tattooed on the back of your hand?'

'It's sort of like "nil by mouth" only with . . . pies,' I replied, having no real idea why. 'Actually,' I added, 'it's not mine at all.'

I took the Helping Hand™ out of my cuff, and tweaked the second knuckle for two seconds to put it in sleep mode. The Helping Hand™ made some rapid hand signals that were pre shut-down diagnostics, then went limp. The girl did not seem that taken aback, but then if you've been brought up in the strife-torn Cambrian Empire, seeing a hand without a body attached probably wasn't such a big deal.

'You're a sorcerer?' she asked.

'I *know* sorcerers,' I told her. 'The hand is enchanted, but not by me.'

'I see,' said the girl, 'and why do you want to find Sky Pirate Wolff?'

I raised an eyebrow.

'News travels fast,' I said.

'Gossip has been clocked at 47.26 mph out here,' explained the child, 'the fastest recorded anywhere in the Kingdoms. Gossip is so fast, in fact, that we have no need for newspapers or a postal service. The only place where news does not travel is across the border. I know nothing of your culture other than you seem mostly well meaning, are ridiculously wealthy by our standards, and regard anything dangerous as somehow fun.'

She was right. Little crossed our nations' borders in the way of information. A war might be raging in your own country, and the first thing you'd know about it was when you returned home to find your house a smoking ruin, with armed militia eating the contents of your freezer and 'Viva el Presidente' daubed on the walls.

'So, said Addie, 'what do you want with the captain?'

'We're curious,' I said, not wanting to give too much away, 'and we like an adventure. We hear Wolff rides the Cloud Leviathans, and we'd like to see one up close.'

She stared at us for a moment, head cocked on one side, sizing us up.

'The best place to start,' she said 'is the legendary Leviathans' Graveyard, where the huge beasts go to die. Many have sought the ivory in the dead animals' jaws, and many have been lost in the attempt. Actually,' she added, '*all* have been lost in the attempt, which is why it's kind of off the tourist trail. When can you leave?'

'As soon as our transport arrives, and our guide.'

'Your guide is here,' said the girl with a smile. 'My name is Addie Powell, and I agree to take you to Cadair Idris as long as you accept my terms.'

'Don't take this the wrong way,' I said, 'but you seem quite young for a guide.'

Addie narrowed her eyes.

'Don't take *this* the wrong way, but the last person who said that ignored my advice and is now carrion in the Empty Quarter. If they'd done what I'd said they'd be inheriting a kingdom about now. Besides, it's not the age, it's the mileage that counts.'

She definitely looked as though she had seen the mileage. Her eyes had a hard look in them, and I noticed a scar on one cheek, and one of her fingers was missing.

I apologised, told her I had complete confidence

in her abilities, and we all shook hands. I introduced everyone, even the Princess, who made an awkward half-curtsy.

'Will it be risky?' I asked as we sat down to negotiate her fee.

'Risky?' said Addie. 'Put it this way: statistically speaking, you're dead already, your bones gnawed by wild animals and now bleached in the sun, your life only fractured lost moments, memories in those who knew you best.'

'Very . . . jolly,' I said.

Addie shrugged.

'There are many dangers and I don't want you to start whining when someone gets eaten or drowned or something. But here's the deal: a Golden Moolarine each for wherever you want to go for the next week, and for that I can promise you a fifty per cent survival rate.'

'I thought the official Fatality Index was eighty-six per cent?'

Addie smiled.

'I can offer better odds than the official rate. It is a gift passed down from one tour operator to the next – a sixth sense that tells me how many we will lose. I am never wrong. But let's be clear on this: half of your party will die, or be lost or eaten. Are you sure you want to shoulder that responsibility?'

I looked at Perkins, who nodded.

'Yes,' I said.

'Then we have a deal,' said Addie, and we shook on it.

At that moment an ex-military half-track turned up in a cloud of yellow Marzoleum fumes. I'd not seen one of these up close before. The front two wheels were for steering, and at the rear there were caterpillar tracks, like on a landship. It was also protected by a quarter-inch of armour plate on the sides and bottom, but not the top, which was open, but could be covered by a canvas tarpaulin. Perkins and I looked at it doubtfully.

'Where we're going, there are no roads,' said Addie. 'This was a good call. We leave in half an hour. Wait here.'

'Fifty per cent casualties?' said Perkins as soon as Addie had gone and we had signed the half-track's rental agreement. 'That's . . .'

'. . . one and a half of us, plus two and a half fingers if you count the Helping Hand™,' said the Princess. 'Bags I not be the one half-dead, especially in Laura's body.'

'You should be more serious, Princess,' said Perkins.

'And you should hold your tongue when talking impertinently to royalty, Mr Porkins.'

'It's *Perkins*.'

'Perkins, Porkins, Twitkins – like I give a monkey's.'

'No one is dying or losing fingers,' I said, 'and we've

got a few magical moves that should help us get home safely. And Princess, hold your tongue. You're Laura Scrubb right now, and will be until we get you back to the palace.'

We chucked our baggage inside the half-track and I climbed into the driver's seat to figure out how to drive the vehicle. It didn't seem much different to the Bugatti, in fact, and I was just reading the bit in the instruction manual about track maintenance procedures when a voice made me look up.

'Hey!'

It was Curtis and two others. All young, all dressed kind of hip, all looking a bit smug, confident and stupid.

'Hey, Dragonslayer dude,' said Curtis, grinning at me, 'heard you were heading off through the Empty Quarter towards Cadair Idris to do some Cloud Leviathan spotting. Sounds dangerous, and well, we're like totally up for it.'

'This is a private expedition,' I said sharply, 'you're not coming.'

'Too late,' he said, 'we've already okayed it with your tour guide, and she's taken our money.'

'Is that right?' I asked Addie, who was walking up with a bedroll on her shoulder.

'Yes indeed,' she said, 'a larger party fares better for all manner of reasons, and if it comes to a scrap, seven people are better than four.'

'I really don't think—'

'I'd like you to trust my judgement on this one, Miss Strange.'

We stared at one another for a moment. There was something she wasn't telling me, but I had to trust her – only a fool ignores a local guide.

'Okay,' I said, 'welcome aboard.'

'Awesome,' said Curtis, readying himself for introductions. 'These are my buddies. Meet Ignatius Catflap.'

He indicated the shorter of the two. Ignatius had a shock of black hair and seemed to be trying a little too hard to grow a beard. He was chewing gum and his red-rimmed hungover eyes blinked stupidly as he was introduced.

'Hi,' he said. 'This is just like going on a trip to some weird and awesome dangerous place.'

'It's not *like* it, you dope,' said the Princess, 'it is.'

Ignatius stared at her in surprise.

'A *little* bit forward for a handmaiden, aren't you?'

'She's kind of a bodyguard as well,' I said. 'Try and be nice to the morons, Laura.'

'Yes, ma'am.'

'Ignatius' family own the Catflap Corporation,' piped up Curtis, as though it were exciting and relevant. 'They make novelty placemats.'

'They do *what*?' I asked.

'Placemats,' said Ignatius, 'mats to put your plates on at mealtimes. I'm here doing research into our planned "Extreme Jeopardy Range". Each mat will depict a frightful end suffered by someone here in the Cambrian Empire. What do you think?'

'I'll tell you what I think: that "tasteless" was a word invented just for you.'

'. . . and over here is Ralph,' said Curtis, eager to move on and indicating the second of his friends, 'another of my old school chums.'

The third traveller was tall and slender, and rubbed his hands together nervously when he spoke. He seemed the least idiotic of the trio and looked to be here as a hanger-on, probably against his better judgement.

'Hello,' he said quietly, 'Ralph D. Nalor. Pleased to meet you. I'm – um – twenty in June.'

'Anything else?' I asked.

He thought for a moment.

'Nothing springs to mind.'

After shaking hands – it was best to at least *attempt* to get along, I felt – and after they'd stored our baggage in the back of the half-track, Addie told us she wanted our attention.

'Right,' she said, climbing on to the half-track's bonnet to address us, 'the first thing to remember is there is only one rule: do as I tell you, no matter how insane. If we are held up by armed bandits, I do the talking. If we are all kidnapped, I do the talking. If *you* are kidnapped, then make polite conversation with your captors until I come to bargain for your release. That might take up to a year *but I will come*. Trying to escape is considered unspeakably rude, as is wailing, crying and pleading for your life, and is the quickest and easiest way to get yourself killed. The tribes who populate the Cambrian Empire are a murderous bunch of cut-throats, bandits and ne'er-do-wells, but they are polite, hospitable and won't tolerate bad manners. Does everyone understand?'

'Yeah, little girl, anything you say,' said Curtis with a smirk.

Addie looked at him for moment, made a quick movement and in a moment her dagger had punctured Curtis' collar and pinned him to the tree upon which he leaned.

'Sorry,' said Addie, 'did you say something?'

'I said,' replied Curtis, firmly rattled, 'that you're totally the boss-dude.'

'Okay. Now, altogether: what's the one rule?'

'Do as you say,' we all said in unison.

'Stand on one leg,' said Addie, and we duly complied.

'Good,' she said, and five minutes later we pulled the half-track onto the road and headed off into the interior of the Cambrian Empire.

Addie explains

We headed north along the main Cambrianopolis road. I was driving with the Helping Hand™ making easy work of the half-track's ridiculously heavy steering. Perkins was in the passenger seat with Addie sitting between us, with the Princess just behind. The fields we drove past contained cultivated almond tree groves, from which refined Marzoleum was derived, a syrupy oil that could be used for fondant icing, sunblock, window putty, aviation spirit – and pretty much anything else in between. Curtis and his friends had been standing up in the back because they thought it looked cool and manly until the dust, flies and road debris got in their eyes and mouths, so with eyes streaming and throats sore, they bravely sat in the rear instead.

I looked back to make sure they weren't within earshot, then said to Addie:

'Why were you so keen for Curtis and his dopey friends to come along?'

'Simple. We need those three to make up the fifty per cent fatalities.'

This made me uneasy.

'That's not a great thing to hear.'

'Perhaps not, but this is: you'll go home safely and Curtis and his losers get to be the honoured dead. What's not great about that?'

'A lot,' I replied. 'Everyone matters, even those three.'

'I don't think that they do,' said the Princess, who had been listening in to the conversation. 'If they never came back it wouldn't change much. Their families would be a bit glum but I dare say they'd get over it. Besides, you don't come to Cambria without accepting at least the *possibility* of tragedy.'

'I know you're not actually a handmaiden,' said Addie astutely, 'what with your unservantlike manner and all, but you speak my language.'

'Well, I *don't*,' I replied. 'I'm not having those three used as cannon fodder.'

'They knew the risks,' said Addie, 'and so did you when you agreed to the trip. I offered you a fifty per cent Fatality Index, and you accepted it. No point getting all precious about it now.'

'We were taking the responsibility for *ourselves*,' I said, 'not other people.'

'And you still are,' said Addie with a shrug. 'I can only guarantee the fifty per cent. I can't say for certain who will live and who will die.'

Addie's logic was somewhat strange, but did ring true – sort of. We a fell silent for a few moments.

'Have you lost many tourists?' asked Perkins.

'Hundreds,' said Addie in a nonchalant manner. 'I used to keep count but after a while, there were just too many. You always remember the first and the youngest and the one you liked the most, but after that they're simply a blur.'

'Wait a moment,' said the Princess. 'Jennifer, myself, Porkins, you, Ignatius, Ralph and Curtis only make up seven. If you expect a fifty per cent casualty rate, how's that meant to work?'

'We'll pick up someone on the trip,' said Addie, 'we always do. It'll pan out correctly, you'll see. I have a gift.'

'I'll believe that when I see it,' said the Princess. 'What's that up ahead?'

I looked out. On the road ahead someone had painted 'SORRY' in large letters.

'Hunker down,' shouted Addie and we all did as she said. The half-track had a large armoured flap that could be swung down in front of the windscreen in case of attack. Addie reached up and released the catch; the flap swung down with a bang, leaving me a small slot to see through. A second or two later the first bullet hit the armoured half-track, followed by a second, then a third.

'Don't stop,' said Addie.

I did as she asked, and the air was suddenly heavy with the crack of rifle fire and the metallic *spang* of bullets as they bounced off.

'Okay,' said Addie as if we were doing nothing more unusual than driving through heavy hail, 'here's the plan: we'll enter the Empty Quarter presently and stay at the Claerwin reservoir tonight; they have some Pod-poles. Tomorrow afternoon we'll reach Llangurig and visit your friend. We'll stay the night there and then head off into mountain Silurian territory to get to the foot of Cadair Idris. We'll search for the Leviathans' Graveyard on its rocky slopes until you give up – which you will, because the graveyard doesn't exist – and then return.'

'Good plan,' I said, 'although our movements really depend on what my friend in Llangurig says – I'm not mad keen on going any farther if I don't have to.'

I wasn't wildly keen on climbing the mountain. Cadair Idris was known not just for its stark beauty – a soaring pinnacle of sheer rock almost six thousand feet in height, the highest in the Cambrian range – but for the number of people who had vanished on its rocky slopes. Despite numerous expeditions, no one had reached the summit in modern times, or if they had, no one had returned. I'd risk our lives if there was a chance of finding the Eye of Zoltar, but not if there wasn't.

'Don't worry,' said Addie, mistaking my silence for nerves, 'Cadair Idris will be fun.'

'Ever been there?'

'No. That's why it will be fun.'

As we drove on, the rifle fire slowly diminished, and after a minute it stopped completely, and Addie gave us the all-clear so we could raise our heads above the armoured body of the half-track.

'What was that?' asked Perkins.

'What was what?'

'The rifle fire?'

'Oh, *that*. I don't know. A local warlord who is annoyed they built a bypass around his village. It's cut travel times by a third and reduced congestion, but it also means he can't extract money from travellers – so he fires on any car that passes. It's nothing really serious.'

'Unless you're not in an armoured car,' said Perkins.

'But everyone is,' said Addie simply. 'Take the next left and continue on for about twenty miles.'

The half-track was neither fast nor quiet, so to conserve fuel and our eardrums I drove as slowly as practical, and we spent the time taking in the spectacular local countryside. The nation was utterly unspoilt. There were almost no modern buildings, shopping malls or fast-food joints, and no advertising hoardings, electricity pylons or other modern contrivances. Once away from the almond groves, broadleaf forests covered much of the lowlands, and the small houses dotted haphazardly about were constructed of stone with riveted steel roofs, and all were in some manner fortified.

'What's a Somnubuvorus?' asked the Princess, who

had been reading *Enjoy the unspoilt charms of the Cambrian Empire without death or serious injury*.

'It looks like a cross between a baobab and a turnip,' explained Addie, 'and about the size of a telephone box. It's actually not a plant at all, but a fungus that releases puffs of hallucinogenic spores into the breeze. Anyone who inhales them suddenly becomes convinced that being near the Somnubuvorus will enlighten and enrich them with hard-hitting and devastatingly relevant social and political commentary. Then, of course, you are soon overcome with a sense of listlessness and torpidity, and fall fast asleep.'

'It sounds like what would happen if you weaponised French cinema,' I observed.

'Yes, pretty much, only French cinema doesn't secrete enzymes from its roots and dissolve you while you sleep.'

'Yag,' said the Princess, and returned to the book.

I had a thought.

'Why did the gunners shoot down Col— I mean, that Dragon just before we left?'

'That's easily explained,' said Addie. 'Emperor Tharv deplores mankind's need to defy gravity so he's banned all aerial traffic above his Empire. But because he wants to be equitable and just in all matters, he thinks that it would be unfair if birds, bats, insects and so forth were allowed to fly – so he banned them, too.'

'And that included Dragons?'

'Right. But here's the real issue: Emperor Tharv comes from a long line of dangerously insane rulers, and the greatest difficulty in taking over from the *previous* dangerously insane ruler is to demonstrate that you are as crazy, or even *crazier*. When Emperor Tharv took over from his father, he declared that he would train an entire legion of killer elephants to invade the rest of Wales.'

'I heard something about the killer elephant story.'

'It was just sabre-rattling. Firstly, elephants don't make good deranged killers, being generally good natured, and secondly, the idea fell foul of the "Killer Elephant Non-Proliferation Treaty", so Tharv simply banned all flying instead. The high jump and pole-vault are illegal, pogo sticks and skipping are banned, and even jumping off chairs and tables is frowned upon.'

'But that's absurd,' said Perkins. 'Are you saying that geese and pigeons and bees and and bats and Dragons and stuff can't fly in the Empire?'

'That's *exactly* what I'm saying.'

'And how does he expect to enforce that?'

Addie shrugged.

'He *can't* obviously, except—'

'Except what?'

'Except . . . have you seen anything that flies since you arrived?'

I thought about this, and looked around. Now she mentioned it, I didn't think I had.

'Right,' said Addie, 'weird, isn't it? We've got a lot of jeopardy here in the Empire, but not many things that flap.'

We all fell silent as we considered this.

'If there are no aeroplanes in Cambria,' said Perkins, pointing towards two lorries that had stopped in the road for their drivers to chat, 'what about them?'

The lorries were painted with the pale blue logo of Skybus Aeronautics, and as we watched the one heading into the Empire lumbered forward with a grinding of gears while the one heading out accelerated rapidly away.

'Aircraft components,' said Addie. 'Emperor Tharv may not support flying, but he does apparently have an aircraft component factory somewhere in the Empire.'

'It doesn't sound a very consistent policy, does it?'

Addie shrugged.

'Perhaps not. But as insane as he is, he does okay for us. Do you get free healthcare and child support in your country?'

'No.'

'We do. And even though the Cambrian Empire boasts the lowest life expectancy in the Kingdoms what with all the civil war and jeopardy tourism and stuff, at least we get to live our short lives in a varied fashion: full of interest, fun and adventure. Which would you prefer? A short life as a tiger or a long one as a rabbit? I'm with the tiger.'

'We're in broad agreement,' I replied after giving the matter some thought. 'The only place where we part company is that I think everyone should have the *choice* to be a tiger or a rabbit – or anything in between.'

Flesh-eating slugs

We stopped for lunch at one of the many tea rooms that dotted the roadside, each one of them designated, by mutual consent, a neutral area where even rival warlords could stop and have a cup of tea and a currant bun without risking a dagger between the shoulder blades. The lunch was excellent – simple, yet tasty – but the meal was marred by Curtis and Ignatius' brash behaviour – they thought it amusing to talk loudly, flick food at one another and generally act like the complete idiots they were. We apologised as we left, and were told cheerily that 'youthful high spirits' were generally tolerated, but if we set foot inside the café again, Curtis and Ignatius would both be 'tied inside a sack and beaten with sticks'.

We were back on the road within ten minutes.

'Hello,' said Ignatius, who had clambered to the front of the half-track to talk to us.

'I'm not listening to anything but an apology,' I said.

'It was only a *little* food fight,' he said with a grin, 'barely worthy of the name.'

'What do you want?' I asked.

'There's a slug farm coming up,' he said, pointing to his copy of *Ten animals to avoid in the Cambrian Empire*, 'and I thought we should stop and have a look.'

I looked at Addie, and she nodded.

'They're quite amusing in a gooey kind of way,' she said, 'and who knows? With a bit of luck he'll be eaten by one.'

'Oh, come on!' said Ignatius with a smile. 'I'm not *that* bad.'

Addie stared at him in a 'Yes you are' kind of way and he smiled sheepishly and rejoined his friends in the back. We took the next turning on the right, and parked in a dusty car park alongside a half-dozen armoured tour buses. Addie told us to go on ahead without her as she'd seen flesh-eating slugs many times. Ralph said he'd not come either, as he had a peculiar allergy to 'anything without legs, such as cats.'

'Cats have legs,' said the Princess.

'They do, don't they?' agreed Ralph in a confused manner, but declined to join us anyway. So myself, Perkins, the Princess, Curtis and Ignatius trooped into the farm.

After paying the entry fee we walked down between circular concrete pits, each containing about a dozen slugs the size of marrows. They were the colour of double cream, had grooves along their bodies, and were covered by a slimy gel that smelt of rotting flesh. The slugs had no eyes, a single mouth with razor-sharp fangs, and atop their small heads were an array of antennae of varying size and function that waved excitedly as we walked past. They were, in a word, repulsive, and if any creature had 'avoid' stamped all over it, the flesh-eating slug was it.

'Woh,' said the Princess, 'that is *so* gross.'

'It's about the only placemat design that we are already agreed upon,' said Ignatius excitedly, producing a camera from his bag. 'You may be interested to know that we only ever do six designs in a set of placemats.'

'Is that a fact?' I said.

'Yes. Although the average seated meal is only 3.76 persons, you might be forgiven for thinking that four designs might suffice, but no. A dinner of six is not unusual, and by employing numerous focus groups and conducting market research, we have discovered that while repetition of placemat design is acceptable in a group larger than six, in any group *smaller* than six it is not. Thus, six designs. Clever, eh?'

'Where's the nearest Somnubuvorus?' said the Princess. 'I want to throw myself into it.'

'The nearest *what*?'

'Never mind,' I said. 'Laura, stop antagonising the nitwits.'

'Yes, ma'am,' said the Princess, doing her best curtsy

yet. The matter was soon forgotten and we joined the crowd milling around one of the feeding troughs. The slug farmer was giving a talk.

'. . . the slug's mucus – or slime – can be used in all manner of products from meat tenderisers to skin exfoliant to paint stripper to battery acid, and an adult slug can ooze almost a gallon a day, if kept moist. Any questions before feeding time?'

One of the other tourists put up their hand.

'Is it true that enriched slug slime is part of Emperor Tharv's secret chemical weapons stockpile?'

'That was always conjecture and never proved,' said the farmer, 'but knowing Tharv, almost certainly.'

'Can we wrestle them?' asked a stupid-looking young man who turned out to be Curtis.

'This is a *farm*,' said the slug farmer testily, 'not a circus. If you want to fight one, then go to an official slug-wrestling salon, or ever easier, find a slug. They sleep until midday, usually in the damp shade of limestone outcrops. Any more questions? No? Okay, then let's feed them.'

The farmer went on to explain that keeping intelligent slugs in captivity denied them the stimulation of hunting prey for themselves, so they made them do tricks for their supper. For the next five minutes we watched the slugs balance balls on their antennae, play a passable rendition of the *Beer Barrel Polka* on descant recorders and then do synchronised backflips, to sporadic applause. The show finished with an entire pig carcass being chucked into a trough containing a dozen slugs. The pig was devoured in a little under thirty seconds and with such uncontrolled ferocity that when the pig was nothing but bones, there were only ten slugs left.

'That often happens,' said the farmer sadly.

We walked back outside once the show was over. I bought Mother Zenobia some skin exfoliant for her feet, while the Princess wrote a postcard to her parents.

'I was disappointed not to see someone being devoured,' said Ignatius as we returned to the car park, 'or lose a foot at the very least.'

'If you cover yourself in lard first you can wrestle them quite easily,' remarked Curtis, reading from a leaflet, 'and make a fortune in prize money.'

'Anyone eaten?' asked Addie as we climbed back into the half-track.

'No one even got nibbled, worse luck,' grumbled Ignatius. 'Are you okay, Ralph? You look a little . . . strange.'

'It's nothing, dude,' said Ralph, who *did* look unusual – drunk, almost, 'probably the altitude. I'll be fine.'

'Did you do anything to him?' I asked Addie once I'd climbed into the driver's seat.

'Not me,' she said. 'I went to the loo and when I got back he was sweating and muttering about anchovies.'

'Mule fever?' I asked.

'No, probably just Empty Quarter nerves.'

I looked at Ralph again; he seemed to have relaxed somewhat, although I could see his pupils contract and dilate quite rapidly several times a second.

We drove for another half-hour and presently came across the dormant marker stones that marked the extent of what had once been Dragonlands. There was a large and very chewed sign that read:

DANGER
Empty Quarter
Remain Vigilant or Remain Here

The Empty Quarter

The Empty Quarter was exceptionally well named. It took up almost exactly a quarter of the Cambrian Empire and was, well, empty: an unspoilt tract of rolling upland roughly squarish in shape, and forty miles across. No one was mad enough to live here and for the most part the Quarter was simply thousands of acres of scrubby grass, hog-marsh, stunted oak and the occasional bubbling tar pit.

We moved off full of expectation, but after half an hour of driving had seen nothing more exciting than a distant herd of Buzonji and the fleeting glimpse of a Snork Badger's corkscrew tail. We passed several armoured cars returning from a failed Tralfamosaur shoot, and were then overtaken by two off-road motorcycles which we re-encountered three miles up the road, the bikes twisted and mangled and with no sign of the riders.

'We'll probably never know,' said Addie when Curtis asked her what happened. 'Only half the missing are ever accounted for. Death certificates here in the Empire have a box marked "Non-Specific Peril-Related Fatality" – and it gets ticked a lot.'

'It would be a good place to kill someone you don't like and get away with it,' said Curtis thoughtfully.

'We think that happens too,' said Addie, 'but natural justice has a way of making good.'

We drove on, and on two occasions met armed road bandits about whom Addie seemed curiously unconcerned. She took one look at their clothes and general demeanour and told me to drive on and ignore them, which I did without incident. The third roadblock was somehow different, and Addie instructed me to slow down and stop.

'These kidnappers are Oldivicians,' explained Addie, '*much* more dangerous. Our tribe and theirs had a brief misunderstanding recently and things are still a little tender.'

'How recently?' asked Perkins.

'Three centuries. Let me do the talking.'

We pulled to the side of the road and three armed men walked up with an arrogant swagger. They were dressed in the traditional woollen tweed suits of the Oldivicians, with leather boots and a flat cap. Like Addie, they also displayed a complex series of tattoos on the side of their faces to denote kinship, position and allegiance. They were armed with ancient-looking weapons, and wore twin bandoliers of cartridges criss-crossed across their torsos. It looked too as though they had already done some business that day – they had a downcast-looking prisoner already with them, sitting on a rock close to where their Buzonjis tramped the soil impatiently.

'Hello, Addie,' said the first bandit in a cheerful manner, 'tour work good these days?'

'Haven't lost anyone for almost a month now, Gareth,' she replied, 'so not bad. How's the kidnapping business?'

'It's rubbish to be honest with you, Addie,' he said. 'It's got about and no real celebrities attempt to cross the Empty Quarter unless with bodyguards and loaded with heavy weaponry.'

'We live in sorry, untrusting times. You going to let me pass?'

'Perhaps. Have a look, Rhys.'

One of the other bandits stared at us while consulting a well-thumbed copy of *Müller's Guide to Kidnappable Personages*, which I noticed was over three years old. I'd probably make next year's edition. Luckily, he wouldn't recognise the one person who was definitely in *Müller's* – the Princess. Rhys stared at us all in turn, looked back at Gareth and then shook his head. But Gareth, it seemed, wasn't convinced.

'Anyone in there we should know about?' he asked.

Addie shifted her stance to rest her hand on her dagger. Gareth noted this and changed his stance, too. His compatriots, through long practice, picked up on this. I even heard a safety catch release. The tension in the air seemed to have risen tenfold. Addie spoke next, and it was menacing in its softness.

'The thing is, Gareth, that if you ask me if there's anyone kidnappable with me, then I'm honour bound to answer, and then you'll ask me to turn them over, and I'll tell you that you'll have to kill me before I'd do that, and my tribe and your tribe are in a blood feud but it's our turn to kill one of yours, and if you kill me then an Oldivician will have killed two Silurians in a row, and that's all-out war between our tribes and it's last man standing. You want that?'

As they stared at one another in a dangerous manner, something odd happened. Ralph started glowing with a pale yellow light, and then floated a couple of feet out of the half-track. Everyone's eyes were suddenly on him.

'Well, what do you know?' said Gareth with a smile. 'You've got a *sorcerer*. They're worth bundles. Grab him, lads.'

Perkins and I looked at one another as the bandits moved forward.

'Ralph can't be a sorcerer,' I whispered, 'we know all of them.'

They pulled the glowing Ralph out of the back of the half-track, holding him down by his shoelaces as if he were a helium balloon in a breeze. He was giggling stupidly and mumbling something about camels, and as we watched bright sparks started to fizz out of his ears. He then turned blue, then red, then green, then burped out a large iridescent bubble that burst to produce a flock of brightly coloured butterflies.

I glanced at Ignatius and Curtis, who were themselves now giggling stupidly at Ralph's predicament, and I suddenly had a terrible thought.

'Perkins,' I said, 'did you leave your bag in the half-track when we went to look at the slugs?'

Perkins hurriedly opened the leather suitcase that would have contained all his potions, balms and one-shot spells written on rice paper. It was, predictably enough, empty. Ralph, like Curtis, must have had a fondness for abusing magic and, finding some spells unattended, had consumed the lot.

Ralph was now beginning to stretch and flex in a peculiar manner, as though a pony were inside him trying to get out. I'd not seen anyone have a magic overdose, but I'd heard about it. The lucky ones turn themselves inside out, and die a horribly painful death. The unlucky ones get to turn themselves inside out *for ever.*

'Fun's over,' said Gareth to Ralph, who was still floating in the air and now doing some rapid transformations between a piano, a walrus and a wardrobe and then back again, 'give it a rest and come down here *immediately*.'

Ralph, predictably enough, ignored him.

'Blast,' said Perkins, thumping the side of the half-track with his fist, 'I'm responsible for this.'

'No, it's hard cheese for the idiot whatsisname,' said

the Princess. 'If he's stupid enough to consume a bagful of unknown spells, then he can deal with the consequences.'

I looked at Perkins, and he looked back at me, and he sighed. With the skill of Mystical Arts comes a certain . . . *responsibility*.

He stood up.

'It's me you want,' he said to Gareth the Bandit. 'That bloody fool is suffering the symptoms of acute magic poisoning. Do what you want with me, but I need to help him before he bursts.'

Ralph responded by freeing himself from his captors and doing three somersaults in mid-air, braying like a donkey and then momentarily turning into a tiger and back again, all the time giggling uncontrollably. Ignatius and Curtis were laughing too, and cheering him on, and even some of the bandits were beginning to find it amusing. But just then Ralph's foot expanded explosively to four times its normal size, shredding his boot and covering us with scraps of tongue, laces, leather lowers and man-made uppers. No one was laughing any more.

'Go on, then,' said Gareth.

Perkins stretched out an index finger and began to concentrate. Doing a standard Magnaflux Spell Reversal was tricky, but I knew he wasn't planning on that – it would be too complex given that there were now thirty or forty spells coursing through Ralph's body. No, he'd be trying the grandmaster of all the reversals: the rarely tried, personally draining and supremely risky Genetic Master Reset.

Ralph stopped giggling as his head swelled to twice its size and then back again, followed by a curious rippling of his skin that morphed his front into his back and then into his front again, which is a lot more unpleasant to behold than it is to describe. Even Ignatius and Curtis grimaced.

Ralph started to scream in pain. Not that 'stubbed your toe' sort of pain, but more a kind of 'detached kneecap' kind of pain, only with seven simultaneous childbirths, neuralgia and a tooth abscess all mixed in as well, for good luck. The sort you hope you never get to experience.

While Ralph screamed, his ear migrated across his face with a sound like tearing cloth and the tips of his fingers shot off and ricocheted dangerously about the small group, smashing a wing mirror and causing two of the bandits to duck for cover.

And that was when Perkins let fly.

There was a burst of energy from his fingertips and a cold fireball burst out from Ralph which then expanded to a sphere about thirty feet wide, paused for a moment in a wonderful display of crackling light, then collapsed rapidly to a ball of light that enveloped the still-screaming Ralph before vanishing in a twinkling of bright lights. There was a distant rumble and all was quiet. Ralph, such as we knew him, had gone.

It's an Australopithecine

'Where's Ralph gone?' said Ignatius. 'And who's that?'

He was pointing at a small, hairy and very primitive-looking man about four foot high with a flattish face and a protruding upper and lower jaw. He had a mild stoop, long arms and legs and was completely naked. He stared at us all with a furtive manner as Perkins sat back heavily in his seat, exhausted.

'That's Ralph as an Australopithecine,' I said. 'What Perkins did was a Genetic Master Reset – the only thing that could release him from the spells was a complete scouring out of anything that made him Ralph. And since Ralph *was* human, a Master Reset brought him back to the first thing that would eventually turn out to be Ralph that wasn't *quite* human.'

'You turned Ralph into a caveman?' said Curtis, staring accusingly at Perkins.

'It was either that,' murmured Perkins, still with his eyes closed after the effort, 'or resetting him to Standard Rabbit. Believe me, Australopithecine is better. At least this way he can evolve back into a human. A rabbit, well, that just stays a rabbit.'

'Evolve back? That's a relief,' said Ignatius. 'I promised his mother I'd have him back in a week.'

Perkins and I exchanged looks.

'It'll take a little longer than a week,' I said.

'I suppose we could keep him in a spare room or something,' said Ignatius. 'How much longer?'

'About 1.6 million years. I'm sorry to say that Ralph will spend the rest of his days as a primitive version of a human. He'll still be Ralph, only with one third brain capacity, some peculiar habits and a mostly obsolete skill-set. Despite this, he'll pick up a few words and may even learn how to use a spoon.'

'Ook,' said Ralph, staring at us all with his small dark eyes. He still looked a lot like Ralph, just shorter and hairier and more extinct.

'Turn him back, you sorcery piece of scum,' said Curtis, taking a menacing step forward. 'I don't believe this. *You turned my best friend into a caveman?*'

It was Perkins' turn to get angry now, but he wasn't going to. Firstly, he was exhausted, and secondly, it wasn't in his nature. But it was in mine.

'Listen here, numbskull,' I said, pressing a finger against Curtis' chest. 'Ralph as you know him isn't coming back. And just so you know, Perkins didn't *have* to help him. But when he did, he gave up some of his own life to do so. That's right, *idiot*. Notice anything different about Perkins? He's aged a decade. He gave those years to save your dumb friend's life, so the next time you open your stupid gob it will be to say: "Thank you, Mr Perkins, we are not worthy of your generosity". Understand?'

Curtis and Ignatius frowned and looked at Perkins curiously. Now they looked, they could see he *was* older. A few minutes ago Perkins had been a spotty-faced eighteen-year-old, but now he was a handsomish man in his late twenties. A Genetic Master Reset takes a lot of wizidrical energy, and if there's not enough in the air about you, there is only one place you can go: your own life spirit. Magic is a form of emotional energy bound up inside everything that lives, and since all life is one, we are all part of that same magical energy. *Life is magic, and magic is life*. But the broader point was this: Perkins had given ten years of his life to help Ralph, whom he neither knew nor liked.

Ignatius and Curtis went silent, and stared at one another with, I hope, a sense of shame. Gareth and his bandits, who had been watching the spectacle with a kind of appalled curiosity, decided they had seen enough.

'We're done,' said Gareth. 'Lower the finger, wizard, and do *exactly* what we say.'

Perkins was too tired to do anything other than what he was told. Within a few seconds he had been hauled out of the half-track and made to sit on the ground. Gareth went through Perkins' papers and they soon ascertained who he was and that he was totally kidnappable. While this was going on, Addie had moved across to where I was sitting in the driver's seat.

'You might have told me you had a wizard with you,' she said.

'There's lots of things I haven't told you.'

'Like what?'

'Like we're actually looking for the Eye of Zoltar. The guy in Llangurig we need to visit is called Able Quizzler, and he connected the Eye to Sky Pirate Wolff.'

She sighed.

'I can't speak for Able Quizzler, but Sky Pirate Wolff hasn't been seen in years, if she was ever seen at all, and the legendary Leviathans' Graveyard is exactly that – legendary.'

'Even so,' I said, 'I'd still like to look.'

Addie looked at me and realised just how serious I was.

'If you're chasing dreams and legends across Cambria, Jenny, you must want the Eye of Zoltar pretty badly.'

'If we don't find it then our two Dragons are to be killed by the most powerful wizard in the land, and we will be honour bound to die attempting to save them.'

'And would one of those Dragons be rubber right now, the same one you denied knowing anything about?'

'Something like that.'

'Terrific. Anything else? Surprises, I mean?'

I thought about the Princess.

'There *might* be more . . . It's an instalment kind of thing. Will you still be our tour guide?'

'Of course,' said Addie. 'Deluded tourists chasing after barely credible legends is not just our bread and butter, but also very entertaining. I think you're mistaken, but I'll still help you.'

I thanked her, and my attention was taken by a comment from the bandit named Rhys.

'How much can we ransom him for?'

'We're not going to ransom him,' announced Gareth, 'we're going to give him away.'

The two other bandits stopped and stared at Gareth suspiciously.

'To the *Emperor*,' continued Gareth. 'His Tyrannic Majesty will look favourably upon such a valuable gift.'

The two bandits nodded enthusiastically, and my heart fell. Emperor Tharv would indeed welcome the gift. He needed sorcerers, and for one reason only: to help him develop a powerful Thermowizidrical Device with which to threaten his neighbouring kingdoms. Needless to say, this would not be a good thing.

'It's time we left,' said Addie in a low voice, 'before Gareth starts wanting the half-track as well.'

'No way,' I said. 'I can't leave without Perkins.'

'You don't have a choice – unless you think you can kill those three and get out of the country before the rest of their tribe catches up with you?'

'I have . . . a Dragon,' I said. 'Admittedly he's rubber right now, but he'll be turning back pretty soon.'

'And *if* he does, and *if* he can get here, will he be willing to kill them to get Perkins back?'

I thought about Colin's strictly pacifist nature.

'Actually, probably not. But he can be seriously scary – talons, teeth, barbed tail, fiery breath, that sort of thing.'

'I'm sure that's very scary where you come from, but considering the loathsome creatures that squirm, squelch, drift or creep around this country, a Dragon has a terror rating of two. And to put that into context, a Tralfamosaur is a five, and my gran is an eight.'

'Your gran must be very scary,' I said.

'She ate a live whippet once,' said Addie, 'which *is* pretty scary, especially during a wedding.'

'What did the bride and groom say?'

'She *was* the bride. I think she wanted to make a statement to her in-laws.'

'That would be quite a statement,' said the Princess, pulling a face.

'There must be something we can do about Perkins,' I implored. 'He's a good friend, and I *really* like him.'

Addie shrugged.

'It's not like he's dead,' she said. 'You'll meet him again some time, I'm sure.'

'True,' I replied, 'but I also think Emperor Tharv might reopen research into Thermowizidrical Weapons if he had access to a sorcerer.'

Addie thought for a moment.

'You're right,' she said, 'and *that* would be a screaming disaster. Wait here.'

She patted me on the arm, and approached the three bandits, who were all congratulating themselves on their good fortune.

'How much for him?' she asked, pointing not at Perkins but at the man who was the bandit's *previous* kidnap victim.

'Getting into the kidnap business, Addie?'

'Tour guide pay is not what it used to be.'

Gareth thought for a moment, then nodded. They went into a huddle for some bargaining, and two minutes later Addie returned with their previous victim. He was in his mid-sixties and dressed in a tweed jacket and plus-fours. He had a genial demeanour, an impressive moustache, but didn't look as though he'd slept in a proper bed for a week.

'This is Mr Wilson,' said Addie, 'and we're leaving.'

The others needed no second bidding and hurriedly clambered aboard the half-track.

'Why did you buy him?' I said to Addie in a low voice.

'I have a plan to get your Perkins back,' she said, 'and there can't be any witnesses.'

I stared at her to see whether she was pulling my leg, but she wasn't. She nodded in the direction of the bandits, who were readying to leave.

'Better say your goodbyes.'

I walked across to Perkins.

'Hey,' I said, 'how are you feeling?'

'Not great,' he said. 'They want to present me to Emperor Tharv as a gift. I've never been a gift before.'

I leaned forward to kiss him on the cheek, and took the opportunity to whisper: 'Trust us. You'll be fine.'

The bandits then mounted Perkins on a spare Buzonji and were soon lost to view in a swirl of dust. I watched them go and then returned to the half-track. I was, as you might imagine, of a somewhat heavy heart. Perkins was the closest thing to a boyfriend I had, and despite our recently increased difference in ages, I didn't want to lose him. I looked at my watch. At seven I would contact Tiger using the conch and report what had happened. Moobin or Lady Mawgon would doubtless know what to do.

At the Claerwin

'Hello, everyone,' said our new travelling companion as soon as we were on the move, 'you don't have to call me Mr Wilson – Wilson is just dandy. I'm an ornithologist.'

'A what?' asked Curtis.

'It's someone who studies birds,' said the Princess.

'Hadn't you heard?' said Curtis with an impertinent laugh. 'Birds have all but vanished in the Empire.'

'Which makes the sport of birdwatching *quintriply* fascinating,' said Wilson. 'Think of the thrill of finding a bird where there aren't any. Marvellous.'

'You're mad,' said Curtis.

'Bit rude,' said Wilson cheerfully. 'Who's the hairy chap and does he know that his thing is showing?'

'That's Ralph,' I said, 'and I don't think he cares if it's showing or not.'

'Ook,' said Ralph, sort of in agreement.

'An ornithologist?' I said, still considering Wilson's earlier statement.

'It's how I managed to negotiate his release so easily,' said Addie. 'Gareth mistook *ornithologist* for *anthologist*.

Practitioners skilled in the art of collecting works of poetry are sound, tradable commodities out here, while birdwatchers just eat your food and say: "Ooh, stop the car a minute, I think I can see Painted Dillbury".'

'Where?' asked Wilson excitedly, before realising it was simply an example. 'The funny thing,' he added, 'is that I *am* also an anthologist. I didn't tell them because they never asked. I'm very grateful, by the way. As a special treat I'll tell you all about the Cloud Pippit. The sparrow-sized bird has a density only slightly greater than helium and nests upon rising columns of air—'

'Bored now,' said Curtis.

'Still rude,' said Wilson.

'Where are you heading?' I asked.

'This way, now,' he said, pointing in the direction we were going. 'I have no plans. You?'

'Llangurig,' I answered, 'and then perhaps to Cadair Idris.'

'To watch Leviathans?' he asked, suddenly excited.

'It's possible.'

'Not *exactly* birds, but they do fly and have as yet unobserved mating rituals – I'm in.'

'It's on a fifty per cent risk factor,' I said, 'and we've not lost anyone yet so mathematically speaking you could still be fair game.'

'I'm still in,' said Wilson with a grin. 'I've heard Leviathans are a total blast.'

There were no other incidents of note in the next hour, and after driving through a narrow gorge where we had to pay two sub-quality bandits an insultingly low fee for the privilege to pass, we came upon the Claerwin lake, a large body of water nestling quietly about twenty miles inside the Quarter. We drove along the banks of the lake for a mile or so and arrived at one of the many campsites dotted about the countryside, expressly for the use of travellers eager to spend a safe and unmolested night.

'Okay,' said Addie as we pulled into the deserted campsite and parked next to the shattered remains of long-abandoned armoured vehicles, 'I know it's not late, but we'll camp here for the night. It'll be a long day tomorrow if we're to make Llangurig before nightfall.'

We climbed out of the half-track and stared at the lake, which was about a mile across.

'It looks almost perfectly . . . circular,' said Curtis.

'I read in *Conspiracy Theorist* magazine that the lakes around here are craters from top-secret Thermowizidrical Device weapons tests back in the eighties,' said Ignatius.

'Thermowizidrical . . . *what*?' asked Curtis.

'Using magic to cause explosions,' I said, 'usually two contradicting spells that draw increasing amounts of power as they attempt to cancel each other out. If left unchecked the spell will break down and then either fizzle out or go supercritical and violently explode. Crucially, the two spells could be potentially just written down – the power to take out a city block or two from a few scribbles on the back of an envelope.'

'There was magical fallout for years following the testing,' said Addie, 'resulting in all sorts of odd occurrences: balls of light, strange apparitions, levitations. We think it's how Buzonjis were created. That a pony and an okapi were too close to one another drinking at the lake and, bingo – fused by a wayward spell.'

'Wow,' said Ignatius, 'it's like we're standing near the location of a massive weapons test area or something.'

'It's not *like* we are,' said Curtis, 'we *are* standing on the site of a weapons test area.'

'Is it still dangerous?' asked Wilson.

'Not if we don't stay too long,' said Addie, 'forty-eight hours, max. If anyone notices any weirdness, raise the alarm.'

'What sort of weirdness?' asked Curtis.

'Metal corroding too quickly, sand changing into glass, growing extra toes – you'll *definitely* know it when you see it.'

'Like that?' he said, pointing to where a jetty had been built out into the lake, and to which several rowing boats had been tied. All three were floating in the air like balloons, held down only by the ropes that attached them to the jetty. Two of the rowing boats bumped gently in the breeze like inverted windchimes.

'Yes,' said Addie, 'kind of like that.'

We had a look around. There were several camping tables, barbecues and what looked like old leather sofas. I was about to sit on one when Addie stopped me. She kicked the sofa a couple of times and it eventually got up in a very fed-up manner and waddled off into the brush.

'*Physarum emeffeye metamorphica*,' said Addie, 'a sort of furniture-emulating slime mould. Annoying more than dangerous. Ten hours' sleep in one of those and it would digest all the stitching out of your clothes. I've seen them transform into Regency card tables, futons and barstools. One example that had disguised itself as an Eames Lounge Chair even got to the first round of bidding at an auction of contemporary furniture.'

'More magical fallout?' asked the Princess.

'In one,' said Addie, 'it's why we can't stop here for more than forty-eight hours. These will be your home tonight.'

She was indicating one of the more obvious features of the campsite: the pod poles.

To guard against night predation by Tralfamosaur, Hotax, Snork Badger or the Variant-N flesh-eating slug, it was wise to sleep inside a small pod that was situated atop a thirty-foot shiny steel pole that was anchored firmly to the ground. There was a ladder for access, of course, with the first section able to be hauled up out of reach.

While Curtis and Ignatius went off to find some fireberries for heat and light and Wilson went on a hunt for abandoned stores, Addie and I went to check the perimeter fence.

'Do you think Curtis and Ignatius are safe digging up fireberries?' I asked, knowing how easily the large, volatile, radish-like vegetable can ignite when handled roughly.

'Who cares?' said Addie. 'Hang the wire back on the post, will you?'

I did as Addie asked, and before long we had the perimeter fence, which was basically lots of tin cans hanging on a wire, back up.

'So what do we do if we hear the cans clinking?' I asked.

'It's not a question of *if*, but *when*,' said Addie, 'and hopefully when we're safe up our poles. I can only hope the Tralfamosaurs don't come. They can't reach us but the hungry smacky noises can keep you awake for hours.'

There was a mild *whompa* noise as the first fireberry ignited, and this was followed by several more dull concussions as other fireberries were lit and placed in baskets hung on high poles, for light. When we got back to the camp we found Ignatius had set up an awning attached to the vehicle and held up with two tent poles, and several bits of non-slime mould furniture had been gathered together for us to sit on.

Once the supper was on, Addie beckoned me aside and lowered her voice.

'I have an . . . errand to run. Don't wait up for me, and make sure everyone is up their poles by sundown or the moment the fence jangles.'

I told her I'd be a lot happier if she didn't take the half-track, but she just smiled, put two fingers into her mouth and gave out a silent whistle that made Ralph wince. There was a patter of hooves from nearby and an Appaloosa Buzonji approached rapidly from the south-west. I presumed it had been tailing us all day, keeping just out of sight. It trotted up, and tossed its head happily as Addie gave it a carrot. She released the stirrups from the finely tooled saddle, and expertly mounted up.

'If I don't come back, I'm dead and you're on your own.'

'I wish you wouldn't say things like that. What are you going to do?'

'You don't want to know. See you in the morning.'

And she galloped off like a bullet into the evening light, back the way we had come.

'She's very tough, isn't she?' said the Princess. 'Do you think she'd want to be my bodyguard when I'm a princess again?'

'Please don't tell her you're a princess,' I replied. 'What with rubber Dragons, Class III legend status amulets, pirates, Leviathans and a missing boyfriend whose age difference is now a teensy-weensy bit inappropriate, I've got about all the dramas I need.'

We sat down to wait while Wilson made supper over an extra-large fireberry that, unlike the smaller, brighter ones, burned slow with a dull red glow. Ralph, newly Australopithecine, was fascinated.

'Ook?' he said, as I held one of the light-giving variety in my cupped hands, the beams of light spilling out past my fingers.

'Ook?' he said again, as I placed the fireberry in his small, nut-brown hands.

Curtis and Ignatius stared at their former friend with a mixture of dread and disgust.

'We can't take him back to his family like that,' said Curtis, 'primitive, barely house-trained and with his thing showing.'

'I agree,' said Ignatius, 'it would be kinder to just turn him loose and let nature take its course. We can tell Ralph's family he fell into a swamp or got eaten by slugs or something.'

'Or we could just put it to S.L.E.E.P,' suggested Curtis.

'That would be the humane thing, I suppose.'

'Ook?' said Ralph, who had been listening with a confused expression.

'Wow,' said Curtis, 'it's like it almost understands us.'

'Can you sit farther away?' I said to Curtis and Ignatius.

'Any particular reason?'

'How about "your lack of compassion disgusts me"?'

'Whatever you say, boss-girl,' said Curtis sarcastically.

'And,' I added, 'if you so much as touch a hair on the head of the Australopithecine, you'll have me to reckon with.'

'We were just *joking*,' said Curtis in the sort of way that suggested they weren't. But they moved away. Ralph watched them leave but elected to stay with us.

'I don't like that Curtis fellow one bit,' said the Princess. 'He keeps on staring at my whatnots. I mean, I know they're not the royal whatnots which are protected from prolonged staring by the death sentence, but even so, Laura's whatnots are whatnots none the less, and he shouldn't stare at them.'

I told her I was in firm agreement, having experienced something similar from Curtis myself.

'Shall I kill him?' said the Princess after a pause. 'My father insisted I was trained in the art of silent assassination, "just in case".'

'Just in case of *what*?'

'Lots of things,' said the Princess. 'Doing away with a dopey royal husband to take over a kingdom, for one. It happens more than you think, believe me.'

'Wouldn't going to marriage counselling be safer?'

'What, and have to discuss our marriage problems with a stranger? Don't be ridiculous. So, shall I kill him?'

'Absolutely not. You can't kill someone for staring at whatnots, royal or otherwise – not even if you are a princess.'

I looked at my watch.

'Hold the fort – I'm going to call home.'

Speaking on the conch

Communication conches work best on a relatively clear line of sight, so I climbed a low hill to the west to where the bleached bones of a long-dead Tralfamosaur were lying in the grass. I sat on the skull, waited until the time was precisely seven o'clock and then spoke quietly into the conch.

'Kazam Base from Jennifer Mobile, come in, please.'

There was a whistling from the large shell, several clicks and a buzzing sound, but nothing intelligible.

'Kazam Base from Jennifer Mobile, come in, please.'

There was only static, so I said:

'Tiger, can you hear me?'

There was more buzzing and a gentle warbling sound, then the conch sprang abruptly into life.

'. . . testing, testing, one two three – is this thing working?'

It was Moobin. I responded, gave him a position report and asked how things were.

'Hello?' said Moobin again. 'Jennifer, can you hear me?'

'I can hear you.'

'Jennifer, are you there?'

'I'm here.'

It was soon clear that Moobin *couldn't* hear me, probably because the communication spell was being disrupted by the thermowizidrical fallout. Moobin realised this too.

'Hello, Jennifer, it's possible that you can hear me and I can't hear you. I'll be brief because there have been a few developments and we're kind of busy. Nothing too serious so no need to come home – keep looking for the Eye of Zoltar and take especial care of the Princess. If you're getting this message, send us your first homing snail to confirm. But remember: defend the Princess and find out what you can about the Eye of Zoltar.'

He repeated the message, but didn't elaborate on what 'developments' had occurred, and after a while stopped transmitting and the conch went silent. It seemed odd that he was urging me to find the Eye when he had been the one against it, but wizards were unpredictable at the best of times. I took out my pocketbook and wrote:

> *Received your message but due to interference can't transmit. Claerwin tonight, Llangurig tomorrow, Perkins kidnapped, Colin changed to rubber, Bugatti confiscated, have employed excellent guide. Request more information on 'developments'. Handmaiden well. Weather good, Jennifer.*

I checked the spelling, folded the note up small and then stuck it to the side of the homing snail. I removed the snail's head-cosy, tapped the shell twice and it was gone in a puff of dust. We were about fifty miles from home, so at homing snail cruise speed it would be there in about an hour, always supposing it could negotiate the heavily fortified border. I'd never heard of a snail being put off by a tank trap, a river and a minefield, but you never know.

'All well?' I said as I walked back into camp.

'We thought we heard a Snork Badger sniffing outside the perimeter,' said the Princess, 'and Ignatius spotted a Hotax encampment two miles away.'

'Where?'

'Over there.'

She pointed to the lake, where I could see a floating island of logs and hog-brush and a small wisp of pink smoke rising from a fireberry. Hotax often used floating homesteads as it kept them clear from danger, although quite what *they* might regard as dangerous, given they were very dangerous themselves, was never clear.

'What exactly *is* a Hotax?' asked the Princess as Wilson doled out Omni-rice, which is a sort of camping rice dish with everything in it.

'They're a primitive and barbaric tribe of humans,' I said, 'who have only a rudimentary language, little understanding of the modern world and are cannibalistic, with a curious habit of preserving their victims after death.'

'To assist them on their long journey through the afterlife?' asked the Princess.

'That would be vaguely honourable,' I replied, 'but no, it's thought they do it for fun. They'd have all been exterminated long ago, but Emperor Tharv thinks they're good for jeopardy tourism and reputedly has a pet Hotax called Nigel.'

'I wish I'd not asked,' said the Princess, looking about nervously.

The Omni-rice was actually quite good. The inclusion of custard and pilchards helped enormously, and we ate in silence for a while, then had marshmallows for pudding. The conversation was quite animated, but only between Wilson, myself and the Princess. Curtis and Ignatius kept to themselves, but their conversation was not hard to follow.

'I'm thinking we just tell his parents it was mule fever,' we overheard Ignatius say, obviously still referring to Ralph.

'Agreed,' replied Curtis, 'but we'll need to find somewhere for him to stay in case he does go home. I wonder if we can sell him to a circus freak-show or something? At least that way we can recoup some cash.'

'Good idea,' said Ignatius.

'Ook,' said Ralph.

Worry of the dangers that lurked beyond the perimeter increased as the light faded, and by the time it was dark, we were all talking not so much for fun, but to stave off the nervousness.

Ignatius brought out two packs of cards and suggested canasta, but we couldn't agree on the rules, so someone else said that Addie had a Scrabble set, but none of us thought it would be good manners to rifle through her bag without her around, so we didn't do that, either.

We eventually agreed that someone would tell a story but no one volunteered, so we all sat in a circle and I spun a bottle. The bottle pointed at Wilson.

The naval officer's tale

'Ooh,' said Wilson, 'let's see now. I could tell you more about the Yellow Helium Pippit, but I can see some of you find ornithological matters of less than passing interest.'

He looked at Curtis and Ignatius as he said this.

'So I will tell you of a time forty-one years ago when I was barely twenty-two and a communications officer in the port rudder control tower of the S.P.I. Isle of Wight, during Troll War I.'

I could sense the small party settle quietly to listen. Of all the nations in the unUnited Kingdom, the steam-powered Isle of Wight was the only one that was movable, unless you count some of the marshier sections of the Duchy of Norfolk. While usually moored off the Solent in the south of England, the floating Isle of Wight was fully seaworthy, and in times of peace used to cruise off the Azores to avoid the long damp winters of the British archipelago.

'I went through naval college, and at the time that Troll War I began I was communications officer in the port rudder control room. This was when the island's engines and rudders were controlled not directly by the command centre at the front of the island, but by a series of secondary control centres which took orders from the admiral via a telephone system. My job as communications officer was to answer the command telephone when it rang and relay the orders to Rudder Captain Roberts, who was one of those implacable naval officers who had made the Isle of Wight such an efficient movable island in peacetime and war.'

Wilson gathered his thoughts, then continued.

'It was the morning of the first push of Troll War I, and we'd steamed up the coast to Borderlandia the week before on the pretext of full power tests in the Irish Sea. The plan was that as soon as the Troll War began, we were to cruise up and down the coast firing broadsides to divert the Trolls from the main landship advance.

'So there we were, making good headway up the west coast of Trollvania at eighteen knots, shelling the Trolls from about two miles offshore, and from our control tower we could see distant explosions in the wooded landscape of Trollvania. There was a bit of retaliation from the Trolls, but nothing spectacular. A few of their siege engines fired boulders at us, but all fell woefully short – we were well out of range.'

'Do you get any sense of speed while at sea?' asked Ignatius.

'Not really,' replied Wilson. 'When you're under way the only real sensation you get is the distant *thrum* of the engines, the plumes of black smoke coming out of the funnels, and the sometimes disconcerting changes in direction of the sun as you go about.'

Wilson paused for a moment, and then continued.

'As we were turning about for the third run up the coast, the order was given to move to within 750 yards of the coast to more accurately rake the Troll's positions with high-explosive shells.'

'Wouldn't you run aground?' asked Ignatius.

'The waters were well charted,' said Wilson, 'and although large, the island has a shallow draught, enabling us to move in close to shore.'

He gathered his thoughts and then continued.

'We had some initial success shelling their positions, with the main observation tower reporting direct hits upon the Trolls manning their siege engines. Our rejoicing was short lived, of course, for the Trolls had tricked us: they had been firing their boulders purposely short to make us *think* we were out of range, so now that we had been enticed closer the Trolls opened up with everything they had. Large rocks the size of cars and buses rained down upon the land, taking out shore batteries, centres of communication and eventually the main observation tower.'

Everyone was silent, so Wilson took a sip of water and continued.

'Naturally, as soon as the bombardment started we felt the engines increase in power and the order "full hard starboard rudders both" came down the telephone. We immediately complied, but as the combination of full hard rudder and full power kicked in, the island began to tip. Anything loose in the control room slid across the floor. Charts fell from the plotting table, and the tea trolley rolled across the floor and was upended near the stairwell.

'The tilt increased as the rudders bit, *decreasing* the depth beneath the port side of the island – and the port propeller hit a submerged reef. The one-hundred-foot-wide propeller stopped dead, but with the engine still at full power the prop shaft was twisted like a tube of damp cardboard, effectively putting one engine out of action.'

'Did you know this at the time?' asked the Princess.

'We pretty much guessed,' said Wilson. 'A fearful shudder ran through the entire island. The island rapidly fell back on to an even keel and slowed, while all about the *thump thump thump* of incoming boulders punctuated the deathly silence in the rudder control room. We all stared at one another, horrified at what was happening.'

'I remember reading something about this,' said Ignatius. 'It sounds jolly exciting.'

'*Terrifying* would be a better word, for things were just about to get that much worse. A well-aimed boulder had destroyed the starboard rudder control tower, communications were down, and the starboard rudder was still stuck hard over to port. We now had one engine out, only one rudder, and the Trolls' strategy was apparent – the course upon which we were heading would run us aground off the coast of Trollvania, and once there, we could be boarded and overrun by Trolls, who have never been anything but savage in their treatment of humans. Putting the engine full astern wouldn't help us as the island would ultimately run aground backwards, destroying the second engine, and *also* placing us at the mercy of the Trolls. The only course of action would be to get both rudders to starboard, but the point was that *both* had to be moved – one to port and one to starboard would do nothing at all.

'After ordering our rudder to starboard in case we too should be hit, Rudder Captain Roberts told us all to 'stand fast at our posts' despite the boulders falling closer and closer to the control room, then called his second-in-command to his side, a career petty officer named Trubshaw.

'"Listen here, Trubshaw," said Captain Roberts, "you've got to get over to the other rudder control room and bring the starboard rudder hard over, no matter what. Drive like the wind, old girl."

'It was a good plan, it was the *only* plan, and if it wasn't executed in about half an hour the island would run aground and the Trolls would board us. After that, it would be all over. Trubshaw just had time to salute before a massive boulder ripped through our control room and I was knocked off my feet. When I stood up, there was nothing left of Trubshaw, the other ratings or even the control room, which was a ragged mass of tangled steel and broken glass. I called in to report the damage, but all communications were down. I crossed to the rudder captain, who was barely alive; his body was half crushed beneath a steel stanchion.

'"It's up to you now," he told me, "and this one's from the admiral: hard a starboard both, *all other considerations secondary*."'

'What does that mean exactly,' asked the Princess in the pause that followed, '"all other considerations secondary"?'

'Exactly what it says,' replied Wilson, 'that I was to fulfil my orders with no consideration to anything else. This was the most important order I was to carry out – that *anyone* on the Isle of Wight was ever to carry out – and nothing could stand in my way. Everything and everybody was expendable in the execution of this one order. If the Trolls boarded the island, all would be lost, the hundred thousand inhabitants eaten or enslaved.'

'Wow,' said Ignatius, 'it's like you could do anything.'

'It's not *like* I could do anything, my muddle-headed friend, I *could* do anything. I took my car and drove like the wind to the starboard rudder control centre on the other side of the island. Twice the road was blocked by rubble, and twice I had to abandon my vehicle, climb across the rubble and requisition another car to carry on. When I got to the starboard rudder control room I found Rudder Captain Gregg on duty with a junior officer in attendance. I told him my orders were from the admiral himself and he told me to calm down, to leave, and only return "when I was acceptable to be presented to a superior officer".'

'What did that mean?' I asked.

'I had lost my cap,' said Wilson, 'so was not *technically* in uniform. I didn't know it at the time, but my ear was half hanging off, and my face was covered with blood. I must have looked quite a sight.

'I told Rudder Captain Gregg that if he did not get the rudder hard over to starboard all would be lost, but the rudder captain insisted that he would only accept orders direct from the admiral or the admiral's staff – and that if I didn't leave he would have me arrested.'

'What an idiot!' said Curtis. 'What did you do?'

'I took out my service revolver and shot him dead, right there and then. His second-in-command made a move to stop me, so I shot him, too.'

He stopped again, and I saw his eyes glisten at the memory.

'To be fair to Rudder Captain Gregg,' continued

Wilson, 'I think he was probably in shock, and his number two was just being loyal. In any event, I was now the ranking officer so called "Rudder hard a starboard expedite!" and with a groaning and shouting from below, the order was executed. The island swung about, and within an hour we were heading back to the open sea, and safety. Communications with both rudder command posts was restored, and we limped back to port for extensive repairs.

'The Isle of Wight, once the finest seaborne island in the world, was a shadow of its former self. We lost seventeen hundred men and women and three-fifths of all buildings were destroyed in the bombardment. We didn't set sail again for another nineteen years, and haven't participated in a Troll War since.'

'What happened to you?' asked Curtis after a pause. 'I mean, you shot two officers.'

Wilson's expression changed. He sighed, and I saw his shoulders sag.

'I'll let you in on a secret,' he said quietly. 'Although I was there on that fateful day, I'm *not* the officer who saved the island. I told it first person to make it more exciting. No, the young man who saved the day was Brent, an officer of considerable resource, resolve and steely-eyed adherence to duty. He's now Admiral Lord Brent of Cowes, the most decorated officer we have ever honoured.'

There was a pause.

'So what were you doing on that day?' I asked.

'I was the second officer in the *starboard* rudder control room, the one who was shot by Communications Officer Brent. I should have assumed command from Rudder Captain Gregg and got that rudder hard over on my own initiative, but I didn't. I was tested, and found wanting. I failed not just myself and the service, but everyone on that island. Consumed by shame, I left the Isle of Wight soon after, never to return.'

Wilson fell silent after he had concluded the story, deep in thought, and after we all agreed that it had been a good story even if it wasn't his, we spun the bottle again.

A deal with Curtis

This time, the bottle pointed towards the Princess.

'Goody,' she exclaimed, clapping her hands. 'I'll use this opportunity to explain *precisely* how the financial futures market works.'

'This should be a bundle of laughs,' grumbled Curtis, but the Princess ignored him.

'The first thing to remember about futures is that they are a contract for the supply of *specific* goods at a *specific* price at a *specific* time in the future—'

'What was that?' said Ignatius, staring into the darkness.

'Oh no you don't,' said the Princess crossly, 'I'm not going to have my fascinating account of financial derivatives sidelined by the old "what was that?" trick.'

'I thought I heard something too,' I said, 'a clinking of tin cans.'

All of a sudden we were on our feet, staring into the darkness. Something was either trying to get through, or had got through and was now inside, staring at us from the darkness.

'What do we do?' whispered Curtis.

'We get ready to scoot up your pod poles,' said Wilson. 'Better to be safe than eaten, as the saying goes.'

We started to back off towards our pre-allocated pod poles. And while pre-allocation might seem a bit sad and nerdy and controlling, it can actually save lives if you can imagine sixteen panicked tourists all trying to climb up the same pole. As soon as we were fifteen feet up a lever could be tripped and the first section of ladder would be drawn upwards by an internally falling weight. As you can see, the terrors of the Cambrian Empire have been well catered for over the years.

We were all creeping slowly towards our poles when there was a faint crack and a rustle in a nearby hedge. With images of Snork Badger, Hotax and flesh-eating slugs in our minds, everyone ran for it. There was then a scream from the Princess, and I looked back to see her rolling on the ground.

'My face!' she yelled. 'Get it off me!'

I jumped down and ran towards her. She was clutching her face and there seemed to be a trail of glistening slime up her arm, but if it *was* a flesh-eating slug, it was a tiddler.

'Hold still, for admiral's sake,' said Wilson, who had reached her first, 'and we'll get it off—'

'Wait!' I yelled, and they both stopped struggling. I pulled the Princess's hands away and then plucked . . . the homing snail from her face.

'There's no panic,' I said, 'I think this was meant for me. But you know, I think it's really time to turn in before something genuinely nasty finds us.'

There were mutterings of agreement at this and those already halfway up their pod poles continued on, leaving Wilson, the Princess and me on the ground.

'If you're okay,' said Wilson, 'I'll be off to bed.'

'Thank you,' said the Princess, and clasped his hand for a moment.

'It was only a snail,' replied Wilson, 'barely dangerous at all.'

'But you didn't know that when you came to my aid,' replied the Princess.

He looked at us both without saying anything, and I detected a sad, resigned look in his eyes.

'I am bound to help wherever possible,' he said sadly. 'I was found wanting once. It won't happen again.'

'Is that why you're out here?' I asked, realising that Wilson probably wasn't here for the birdwatching after all.

'Back home, my name is forever linked with cowards and ditherers. I am here looking for a second chance – a time of extreme jeopardy where my intervention can make a difference.'

That can't be too difficult out here, surely?' I asked.

'You'd be surprised,' said Wilson, 'simply saving a life is not enough. My act of contrition has to have far-reaching consequences, so that years from now, someone will say: "Without Wilson, all would have been lost".'

He sighed, then bid us goodnight.

We wished him the same and he scooted nimbly up his pod pole.

'I feel a fool to have been frightened,' said the Princess sadly, wiping the snail-slime off her face with a handkerchief, 'most unregal. A princess should be resolute in the face of danger, and unflinching. I'd be a rotten queen.'

'Queenliness is a skill that must be learned,' I told her, 'and this is the place to do it.'

'I hope so,' she said with a sigh, then added, after a pause: 'I was so obnoxious to you back at the palace. You must think I'm a complete arse.'

'Don't even think about it,' I replied. 'You and I are both victims of a random chance of birth: you a princess, me an orphan. But we're both working against it to improve ourselves.'

'I suppose *technically* speaking I'm an orphan too,' said the Princess, 'or at least, I will be until I get my body back.'

'It's the mind that defines the person,' I said, 'not the body.'

'Oh,' she said, 'looks like I am a princess after all. What does the note say?'

I had been unfolding the message stuck to the shell

of the homing snail, and let the Princess read it over my shoulder by the light of the nearest fireberry.

> *Received your msg, contents noted. Use* *EVERY EFFORT* *to secure return of Perkins, then find Rubber Colin. Will be waiting at the conch seven tomorrow if possible, much happening and not any of it good, take no risks with yourself or the handmaiden and carry on search for EofZ with all determination. Raining here in Hereford, Tiger says hi – Moobin.*

I read the note twice, trying to figure out what he meant, if anything. There seemed to be something going on that didn't sound brilliant, and a sense of urgency over our task.

'He underlined "Every Effort" and capitalised it,' said the Princess. 'Do you think that's an "all other considerations secondary" kind of deal?'

'I think so,' I replied, 'and if I know Addie, that's the approach she'll take to get Perkins back. What's worse, I think I asked her to do it, which makes me responsible.'

'How does that feel?'

'Not good. Good night, ma'am.'

'Laura,' said the Princess, 'just call me Laura.'

We climbed our pod poles, but I got quite a shock when I clambered into mine, for I wasn't alone. Curtis was there, and he smiled in that 'I'm so cute' manner that I found so utterly odious. Worse, he was lying on my bed, all sort of stretched out and pretend-relaxed.

'You'd better have a good reason for being up my pod pole,' I said.

'Oh,' he said with a chuckle, 'is it yours?'

'You know it is. Out.'

The smile dropped from his face.

'I thought we could be friendly over this, but never mind: although today I'm a tourist, I'm also a businessman, and a businessman is always on the lookout for new business opportunities.'

'You said "business" three times in that sentence.'

'So?'

'It's bad syntax.'

'No it isn't.'

'Yes it is. It's like me saying: "You're the dumbest dumb person I've ever had the dumb luck to meet".'

'You're very sarcastic for someone so young.'

'You noticed?'

Curtis scowled.

'Fun's over,' he said. 'This is why I'm here: I thought at first that you were out here for a holiday too, but then I got to thinking. You're Jennifer Strange, the Last Dragonslayer. You run Kazam, who have recently established themselves as the only licensed House of Enchantment in the world. You are personal Court Mystician to King Snodd and Dragon Ambassador.

You are probably the most powerful and influential person working in magic today.'

This was worrying. Idiots like Curtis I can handle so long as they stay being idiots – I have a terrible temper and can fight dirty, if pushed – but when idiots stop being idiots and start sounding smart, that's another matter entirely.

'So what are you saying? You want to write my CV?'

'I'm saying that it's a little suspicious: you're heading off towards Cadair Idris mountain with a half-track loaded with fuel and the most experienced guide in the Empire, purportedly to look for Leviathans.'

'So?' I said. 'Everyone needs a holiday.'

'With a handmaiden who I suspect isn't a handmaiden, an illegally imported sorcerer and a rubber Dragon? This is a quest, isn't it?'

'It's a *search*.'

'No way. This smacks to me of an arduous journey towards greater spiritual understanding of oneself and a greater truth.'

Blast. He'd rumbled us.

'. . . and if the International Questing Federation find out you're questing without a licence you'll be in serious trouble, and not just with them – the Cambrian authorities don't like anyone questing out here without a permit. A call from me and you'd be in custody quicker than you can say "blackmail" and you can kiss goodbye to whatever it is you're looking for.'

We stared at one another for a moment.

'I want to know what you're looking for,' he said. 'It's something of *extraordinary* value, isn't it?'

I had to think quickly.

'I'm not telling you anything,' I told him. 'Go on, call the Questing Federation. I'd die before I'd tell you anything.'

Curtis drew a knife from his pocket. It was a flick-knife and although I could have disarmed him relatively easily and punched him painfully in the eye, I didn't. A second or two later and he had me in an armlock and the knife at my throat.

'Let's try again,' he said. 'What are you looking for?'

'Go to hell.'

I stamped hard on his foot and struggled. There was an opportunity to break the grip he had on the knife and punch him in the eye, but I did neither and pretty soon he had me in an armlock once more and I cried out, even though the pain wasn't that bad. He held the knife so close I could feel the coldness of the blade, his hands gripped me tightly, and I could feel his breath against my ear. This was good news as I now had Curtis *precisely* where I wanted him: convinced he was stronger, and smarter. And now he was an idiot again, I could act.

'Okay, okay,' I said in a strained 'please don't hurt me' kind of voice. 'It's no big deal. We need . . . Leviathans' teeth. They're useful in spells. In particular, we're trying to reanimate the mobile phone network, which will require a couple of dozen.'

'Leviathans' teeth?'

'Yes; we usually extract them from the Leviathan bites we find on jetliners' tails, but the attacks have dropped off these past six years.'

The Leviathans' tooth story was nonsense, of course. No one had used them in potions for years on account of the whole 'growing antlers side effect' controversy of the 1720s, and we certainly didn't need them to spell mobiles into existence. Only one thing was true: Leviathans *did* chase jetliners – like dogs chase cars, some say.

'So without Leviathans' teeth the mobile phone network won't work?'

'And a lot of other spells too,' I said, 'and here's the deal: keep quiet about the quest and help us to find the Leviathans' Graveyard. It's where the creatures go to die and if we can find it, there'll be hundreds of tons of dry bones for us to search through. Your silence and assistance will be rewarded: five Leviathan teeth for you to trade with as you see fit. Deal?'

'I'll stay quiet and help you,' said Curtis, 'but for twenty.'

'I can go as high as ten.'

'Fifteen.'

'Okay,' I said, 'you've got a deal.'

He relaxed his grip and took the knife from my throat.

'Well now, *partner*,' he said with a greedy smile, 'this sounds so much better. And this Leviathans' Graveyard is somewhere near the top of Cadair Idris, yes?'

'So legend has it. And now you know where we're heading, you can get your objectionable carcass out of my pod.'

'Only too happy to oblige, Jennifer. See you tomorrow.'

He smiled again, convinced that he had somehow managed to secure a valuable commodity with minimum effort when in fact he'd negotiated away his own strong position for something of zero value.

After he had gone, I closed the door and bolted it, then took a deep breath. Curtis was out of my hair for a while, but now I knew he would use violence to get what he wanted, I'd have to keep a careful eye on him. But if Addie was right and he was along for the trip only to make up the fifty per cent casualty rate, I half hoped he would hurry up and become a statistic. I then felt guilty for half hoping he would die, then felt stupid for feeling guilty about half hoping he would die. This might have gone on for a while, so I pinched myself out of the emotional-guilt feedback loop and set out my bedroll on the bed.

I lay on my back and stared out at the night sky through the skylight, and listened to the jangling of the perimeter fence as the night creatures stalked over our camp. Something bad was going on back at home. Moobin was suggesting I use 'Every Effort' to regain Perkins and despite the fact that Moobin had been against looking for the Eye of Zoltar, he was now asking me to carry on with all due determination. Something wasn't right. I was still trying to figure it out when I fell fast asleep.

Slow boat to the Land of Snodd

When I awoke the sun was up, but not by much. I had been disturbed twice in the night. Once as a Tralfamosaur herd moved through in a noisy manner, and then again when Ignatius found a gherkin-sized flesh-eating slug sucking on his toe as he lay asleep in bed. He screamed and dislodged it, which was a relief as we then didn't have to help him.

I unbolted the door of my pod and cautiously looked out. A ground fog had crept in, which offered good cover for a Hotax attack, so it would be wise to remain vigilant until the fog cleared. I folded up my bedroll, tidied the pod, collected my belongings and then signed my name in the visitors' book before descending the pole to get the breakfast going, all the while keeping a wary eye out.

The half-track had been shoved a few feet sideways by a clumsy Tralfamosaur, but aside from a small piece of bent armour plate, no damage had been done. There were Snork Badger footprints aplenty, and here and there were the shiny trails of flesh-eating slugs. If we wanted to earn a few moolah we could have scraped up the trails and sold them to any glue supplier, as slug slime is that gooey substance you find in glue-guns.

'Ook?' said Ralph, appearing from the brush, seemingly unharmed by his night out in the open. He would have been more used to sleeping with dangerous creatures all about him, even though most of the nasty creatures he might have known would have died out by the end of the Pleistocene.

'Sleep well?' I asked, and he stared at me in an uncomprehending sort of way.

'G-ook,' he said, making an effort to emphasise the 'G'. I think he was learning to speak. Or relearning, at any rate.

'L-ook,' he said, and showed me the flint knife he had been making.

'May I hold it?' I asked, putting out a hand, and after looking at me suspiciously for a moment, he gave me the knife. It was well balanced, with a carved bone grip in the shape of the half-track. The blade was finely curved, dangerously serrated and was so thin as to be almost translucent. I smiled appreciatively, and handed it back. He gave an odd half-smile and placed it in a large ladies' handbag he had found somewhere, then hung the bag over the crook of his arm.

'Jennifer,' I said, pointing at myself.

'J-ookff,' he said, then pointed at himself and said: 'R-ooff.'

'You're getting it,' I said with a smile, then nodded as he pointed at various things around the campsite, the small part of what was once Ralph's brain attempting to speak through an Australopithecine voice box.

'Hfff t-Ook,' he said, pointing at the half-track. After a while he settled down by himself, practising pronunciations, and eating some beetles he'd collected.

I had noticed with dismay that Perkins' and Addie's ladders were still down, indicating that they'd not returned. I also noticed Ignatius' ladder was down, so checked his pod – it was empty. I found a few slime trails and oddly shaped footprints at the base of his pod pole, but no evidence of Ignatius himself. It was only on a search for a fireberry with which to cook breakfast that I found Ignatius. He was huddled – wedged might be a better word – in one of the wooden rowing boats, which, as previously noted, were lighter than air because of the Thermowizidrical fallout, and were dangling straight up, tethered to earth only by a frayed rope tied to the jetty. Ignatius was alive, awake, and was staring at me with a shocked expression on his face.

'Are you okay?' I asked.

'No, I am *not* okay,' he said. 'Several large creatures, two small ones and a slimy thing tried to eat me in the night.'

'That's an uneventful night here in the Empty Quarter,' I said. 'Didn't anyone explain the dangers before you came out here?'

'No, they did not,' said Ignatius in an aggrieved tone. 'They said this experience would be like the most amazing and enjoyable dangerfest known to man.'

'And . . . ?'

'They said it would be *like* it – not *actually* it. You all must be stark staring bonkers wanting to be out here. I'm going home.'

'Fair enough,' I said, glad to be rid of him. 'You can pick up a G'mooh in Llangurig.'

'I'm not going a step farther. You can call me a G'mooh as soon as you find a payphone. It can come and get me. I'm not shifting.'

G'mooh was an acronym for 'Get Me Out of Here', the slang and universally accepted name for a Fast Exit Taxi, which will guarantee those who have lost their nerve a speedy way out of the Empire. The G'mooh drivers are usually battle-damaged former tour guides who will stop at nothing to return their passengers to safety. It's expensive, but few haggle.

'Okay,' I said, 'if you want to stay out here on your own, but I'd not . . .'

I stopped talking because Ralph was lolloping up the jetty towards Ignatius, and when he reached him, stared up at where Ignatius sat huddled in the vertically moored boat.

'Go away, monkey-boy,' said Ignatius. 'Go on, shoo.'

But Ralph did *not* shoo, and instead flicked the taut rope that anchored the rowing boat with an inquisitive forefinger. He then looked up at Ignatius.

'No mmnk . . . *boy*.'

'What did he say?' asked Ignatius.

'I think he said he wasn't a monkey-boy.'

Ignatius laughed.

'Well, he *is*, that much is obvious – and a nasty piece of genetic throwback, to boot.'

Ralph frowned for a moment, rummaged in his handbag and brought out the razor-sharp flint knife. Without pausing he sliced cleanly through the rope that tethered Ignatius to the ground. The rowing boat, with Ignatius inside it, began to rise gently in the morning air.

'Ralph!' yelled Ignatius, suddenly panicking. 'What in—!'

'Wait there,' I said, 'I'll throw you a line!'

I ran to the half-track and rummaged in the tool locker for a length of cord. By the time I had found one, Ignatius was about twenty feet above me, drifting east. I tied a spanner to the end of the line and readied myself to throw it to him.

'It's okay,' he yelled excitedly. 'The wind is taking me towards the border. Cancel the taxi, I'll be home and safe in an hour or two!'

'Hang on, Ignatius,' I said, having seen civilians

try to use magic for their own ends and it all going horribly wrong, 'I don't think this is a good idea.'

'Nonsense,' said Ignatius happily, 'by the time the magic wears off I'll be home and dry.'

'Wait . . . !'

But I was too late. The rowing boat was now drifting faster as the breeze caught it, even bumping against Curtis' pod pole as it went past. Curtis popped his head out to see what was going on, and was surprised to see Ignatius drifting past.

'I'm off home,' said Ignatius. 'Join me?'

Curtis said he wouldn't but wished him well and they agreed to meet up at a bar in London some time when all of this was over. Their voices roused everyone else, who also wished Ignatius well but probably, like me, were actually fed up with him. The rowing boat rose until it reached its maximum height of about six hundred feet or so, and continued to drift in the direction of the unUnited Kingdoms.

Now awake, the group came down from their pod poles. The fog had now dispersed and the risk of Hotax attack lessened, so they washed in the lake while they swapped notes about the night's noises, terrors and close calls, then we all sat down to a breakfast of coffee and bacon and eggs. By the time we had finished, Ignatius and his rowing boat were simply a distant dot in the morning sky.

'I've just had a thought,' said the Princess. 'I mean, aren't there anti-aircraft batteries along the border?'

'That's just for aircraft coming in,' said Wilson. 'They'd have to be either mad or vindictive to shoot at anyone leaving – wouldn't they?'

And as if to prove that Emperor Tharv's orders to his military were precisely those things – mad *and* vindictive – we saw small puffs of anti-aircraft fire explode around the small dot. It was a slow-moving target, and Ignatius didn't stand a chance. There was a large explosion and we saw a few bits fall to earth trailing smoke.

'That was hard cheese,' remarked Curtis without a shred of compassion. 'Should have stuck with us – or taken a parachute.'

'I trained in the navy,' said Wilson, 'and the first thing you learn is that parachutes are not generally required while boating.'

'Ook-ook-ook,' said Ralph, with a slight curling of the lip that I took to be an early hominid smile.

'Do you think he planned that?' asked the Princess.

'I'm not sure Australopithecines *can* plan,' I said, 'but you never know.'

'Okay,' I said, as soon as we had given Ignatius a minute's silence as a vague sort of respect, 'this is where we are: Addie went to rescue Perkins last night and told me that if she didn't return she was dead.

It's now nine o'clock. I say we leave it until midday before assuming the worst. After that, we head off towards Llangurig. Any objections?'

There weren't any, of course, and we settled down to wait.

Leviathans explained and some tourists

It rained in the morning for about half an hour, but we sheltered under the awning attached to the half-track. At eleven o'clock two Tralfamosaurs moved through the camp, so we climbed the poles until they were safely past. The morale of the small group was not high. Despite the fact that none of us had liked Ignatius and his demise had tipped Addie's guaranteed 50 per cent survival rate in our favour, a member of our group had still died, and somewhere he would be mourned. Curtis was being unbearably smug as he thought he had one over on me, so was best avoided. I'd told the Princess about his visit the previous evening. She again suggested she kill him, which I again refused. So with neither of us talking to Curtis and Ralph not talking very well, Wilson was about the only person we could all turn to for a chat. He was in a good mood, and spent the time writing up his birdwatching notes in a blue exercise book.

I looked over his shoulder and noticed that aside from the odd pigeon and a wren or two, the 'birds I've seen this week' page was almost completely blank.

'Not much luck seeing birds, then?' I asked. 'Tharv's ban must be working.'

'The absence of birds has nothing to do with him,' said Wilson. 'Birds have a hard time living out here. The successful ones either learn how to burrow like sand martins, puffins or blind mole-sparrows, or have a huge turn of speed like the swift or Falcon X-1. Anything else that flaps is otherwise . . . devoured.'

'By what?'

'The Cloud Leviathans,' said Wilson as though it were obvious. 'The beasts swoop low across the land ingesting huge volumes of air along with everything that's in it. The air is then compressed in the Leviathan's muscular chambers, and when the run is over, the beast swallows the flying creatures and vents the compressed air through pressure ducts on its undersides, assisting with extra lift at the end of a feeding run.'

'Sort of like whales in the ocean?' asked Curtis.

'Absolutely,' said Wilson. 'Leviathans have been known to swallow flocks of starlings more than ten thousand strong, and are suggested as the reason behind the passenger pigeon extinction in North America. It's the reason birds migrate, too – to avoid being eaten. I'm not surprised at the lack of birds. Since Cloud Leviathans are about the size of a smallish passenger jet, they can get pretty hungry.'

'How does it fly with such ridiculously small wings?' asked the Princess, holding up a blurry photograph she'd found in a copy of *Ten Animals to Avoid in the Cambrian Empire.* The creature was sort of like a stubby plesiosaur, with four seemingly inadequate-sized paddle-shaped wings, and a large mouth on the underneath of a broad, flat head.

'No one's ever studied them at length,' said Wilson, 'firstly because they are rare – fewer than five, it's suggested – and secondly because they have a chameleonic skin that allows them a limited invisibility. No one has ever seen a body, far less a skeleton, hence the theory of a legendary graveyard – somewhere they all go to die.'

'Do you think it's likely Sky Pirate Wolff trained one?' I asked.

Wilson thought for a moment.

'It's always *possible*, of course, and I've heard the stories about aerial piracy, the destruction of Cloud City Nimbus III and the RMS *Tyrannic*, but I'm fairly sceptical. As the Princess noted, it doesn't look like a good flyer, so how could it support the weight of a team of pirates?'

We all fell silent after that, and I considered Sky Pirate Wolff, and whether she existed or not – if not, then the Eye of Zoltar might not exist either, but I was not necessarily here to *find* the Eye, but to ask Able Quizzler what he knew – something I could still do, even with our current difficulties.

★

On the dot of twelve and with Addie and Perkins not returned, I decided we should leave. I wrote what we were doing on a sheet of paper and left it taped to the bottom of Addie's pod pole. Wilson suggested he take the wheel and after some grinding of gears we departed along the the compacted dirt road marked 'Llangurig and the North', to which the Cambrian Tourist Board had helpfully added: '32% chance of being devoured, but good scenery with ample picnic spots'.

We hadn't gone more than two miles when we came across a dusty Range Rover parked on a grassy lay-by at the side of the road. We slowed down as we passed, and looked in at the driver and passenger, who were staring at the view. They didn't look up and, sensing something might be wrong, I instructed Wilson to stop the half-track a little way down the road.

'Wait for us here,' I said to the Princess and Curtis, then walked cautiously back to the Range Rover accompanied by Wilson and Ralph, who didn't seem to want to stray too far from my side.

'Everything okay?' I asked the driver of the Range Rover, but he didn't reply. He was a well-dressed middle-aged man who was holding a camera in one hand while the other rested lightly on the steering wheel. His brow was wrinkled, as though he had just seen something, but he made no movement. Something definitely wasn't right.

'Hello?' I said, and waved a hand in front of the driver's face. He didn't even blink.

'Mine's unresponsive,' I said, 'what about yours?'

'Same,' said Wilson, staring uneasily at the passenger. She was seemingly frozen in mid-stretch, her mouth partially open as though just finishing a yawn.

'Mule Fever?' I suggested.

'If it was, they'd have ears long before the paralysis set in,' replied Wilson.

'I can't feel a pulse,' I remarked, holding the driver's wrist, 'and the skin feels hard and waxy.'

'Hotax did this,' said Wilson.

I looked at the motionless people.

'What are you saying?'

'I'm saying,' said Wilson, 'that the Hotax are not just murderously cannibalistic but big on conservation. They retain the discarded skin, hair and bones then preserve them perfectly. Look.'

He reached inside the car and lifted the hair from the back of the driver's neck to reveal a row of fine cross-stitching in the skin, then tapped the man's nearest eyeball, which was not human at all, but skilfully made of *glass*.

I peered closer. It was quite the most remarkable piece of work. As realistic as anything I had ever seen, and ten times better than the rubbish you get at the waxworks.

'Amazingly lifelike, aren't they?' said Wilson. 'The

families of Hotax victims often elect not to bury their relatives but instead use them as hatstands in the hall. Mind you, the good thing about a Hotax attack is that you don't know anything about it – just a slight prick in the back of the neck as the poisoned dart hits home. Then you're like this, preserved at the moment of death, for ever.'

'I . . . suppose I could think of worse ways to go,' I said.

'I could *definitely* think of worse ways to go,' agreed Wilson thoughtfully. 'Knowing Hotax they would have stripped the car for any tradable spares, too. Look.'

He lifted the bonnet to reveal an empty engine bay.

We stood for a moment, musing upon the Hotax's odd mix of utter savagery, skilled artistry and business sense in the car spares industry, when the roar of an engine punctuated the silence.

It was the half-track. We both turned, and whoever was driving clunked the vehicle swiftly into gear and it lurched off.

'Hey!' I yelled, and ran after it. As it drove away, the driver turned to see how close I was, and I recognised him immediately – Curtis. The half-track was not fast, but Curtis had a head start; I couldn't catch him.

'Tell me you didn't leave the keys in the ignition,' I said to Wilson as he joined me.

'Whoops,' he said, 'sorry.'

'Ook,' said Ralph.

'This is bad,' I said, looking around at the empty moorland and wondering what horrors lay hidden just out of sight, '*really* bad.'

'He's probably doing it as a stupid joke,' said Wilson without much conviction. 'He'll be back soon.'

'He's gone for good,' I said, realising what was happening, 'on a journey to the Leviathans' Graveyard.'

'Why?'

'Because he thinks Leviathans' teeth are key to the magic industry and wants them all for himself, I imagine.'

'Are they?'

'Not at all. But,' I added, 'it doesn't explain why he didn't dump my handmaiden by the side of the road.'

'I have a theory about that,' said Wilson. 'The Cambrian Empire has suffered a servant shortage for the past three decades, and it's not just handmaidens. Footmen, cooks, pastry chefs and even bootboys are in short supply. He probably wants to sell her in Llangurig and I dare say he'd get a good price.'

'He'd best be careful,' I said. 'Laura was trained in the art of silent assassination.'

'That might be a relief,' said Wilson, 'but if she kills him, can she drive a half-track?'

'Almost certainly not,' I said, reasoning that Curtis – who was strong – would not need much effort to overpower the Princess while she was in Laura's smaller and weaker body.

I sat down on a boulder by the side of the road and rubbed my face with my hands.

'This trip is getting worse and worse.'

'We might be able to buy her back,' added Wilson thoughtfully, 'unless she's good at ironing – a well-ironed shirt out here is as valuable as gold.'

'I've got a feeling the Prin— I mean, Laura's not that good at ironing,' I said, guessing that she'd not be able to identify an iron in a line-up of fruit. 'How far is it to Llangurig?'

'By road, about thirty miles,' replied Wilson, 'half that if we cut across country. But one thing's for certain—'

'We don't want to spend a night in the open.'

'Right.'

I walked to the other side of the road, picked up a stone and chucked it as far into the Empty Quarter as I could in a pointless display of anger and frustration.

I had entrusted the care of the expedition to a twelve-year-old who had lost Perkins to a group of bandits and then failed to rescue him, leaving Perkins at the mercy of Emperor Tharv and a possible – no, *probable* relaunch of his Thermowizidrical Device project. I had lost the Princess entrusted to my care and then woefully underestimated Curtis' greed, and given him a reason to abandon us to our deaths in the middle of the Empty Quarter, the most dangerous place in the Cambrian Empire, which is, in turn, the most dangerous place in the unUnited Kingdoms.

Terrific.

I think Ralph and Wilson sensed my anger and frustration, for they held back on the other side of the road for five minutes, then walked over to join me.

'Well now,' said Wilson, who seemed to have an overwhelming capacity for optimism in the face of unrelenting failure, 'I expect a lift may be along soon.'

'Between when we stopped last night and right now,' I asked, 'how many vehicles have passed us?'

'Well, none,' said Wilson, 'but that's not to say they won't. And although the Empty Quarter is the most dangerous place to be, we're not actually in the most dangerous place in it. Or at least, not *quite*. And we should count our blessings that we're still alive.'

'Whoop-de-doo,' I replied sarcastically, staring at the ground, 'happy days.'

'*Dan-jer!*' said Ralph in a sharp, urgent tone. I looked around but could not see where the danger lay. But Wilson could.

'Don't move,' he whispered.

'Hotax?'

'Sadly, no. Something much worse. Remember a second ago when I said we should count our blessings that we're still alive?'

'I remember that, yes.'

'I . . . I might have spoken too soon.'

A brush with death

I stared in the direction in which Ralph and Wilson were staring, but could see nothing. The Empty Quarter was living up to the 'empty' part of its name surprisingly well.

'I can't see anything,' I whispered.

'*Moribundus carnivorum*,' said Wilson in a low voice, 'moving in from the north-west.'

'*Mori* . . . what?' I whispered back.

'*Moribundus carnivorum*. A Lifesucker. It is nourished not by the energy and proteins, fats and starches *within* life forms, but the very *essence* of life itself.'

I looked again. There was nothing visible in the direction Wilson was pointing except a rabbit, nibbling the grass about thirty feet away, and steadfastly ignoring us.

'You mean the rabbit?'

'The rabbit? No, of course not the rabbit. I mean *behind* the rabbit.'

'I can't see anything behind the rabbit. Except . . .'

My voice trailed off as I saw the Lifesucker. Or at least, I didn't actually see it, but the *effect* it had on the grass as it slowly crept up on the rabbit. Where all around us the grass was bright and green and lush, there was a trail of brown and withered grass advancing slowly towards the rabbit like a gravy stain on a tablecloth. The brown stain of death was no more than six inches wide, and as the rabbit stopped nibbling and looked around cautiously, the encroaching area of dead grass stopped and waited.

'I see it now,' I whispered, 'it's stalking the rabbit.'

'It usually takes bigger prey than that,' Wilson whispered back. 'Must be hungry – it will take one of us if it picks up on our scent.'

'We can outrun it, surely?'

'Outrun death?' said Wilson, eyebrows raised. 'I think not.'

I turned my attention back to the approaching patch of dead grass behind the rabbit. When the Lifesucker was about a foot away from the unwitting creature, it pounced. The rabbit didn't know what was happening at first. It seemed shocked and made to run, but then faltered, convulsed for a moment, tipped on its side and twitched a few times before lying still.

'Sh-*ook*,' said Ralph, who, like us, was staring intently at the now-dead rabbit. The Lifesucker didn't only steal life, though, it seemed to strip away many of life's associated functions: warmth, moisture and beauty. In less than a minute the rabbit had aged and withered until it was nothing more than patchy fur stretched tautly across a dry skeleton.

'I've not seen anything like—'

'Shh!' said Wilson. 'It's strongest when freshly nourished. It will be hunting for more prey – I've seen one take an entire herd of sheep before finally collapsing into a gorged stupor. If you can push anything charismatic and life-confirming to the back of your mind and fill your head with thoughts of utter banality, now's the time to it.'

'How do I do that?'

'I usually start with daytime TV, and then work my way down through celebrity biographies to international road aggregate trade agreements.'

Despite Wilson's advice, it's hard to think of boring thoughts when requested, *especially* when there is death lurking nearby, so I instead attempted to relax, and I could see Wilson and Ralph do the same. The area of dead grass moved at a slow walking pace in our direction, then stopped a few feet from Ralph. The Australopithecine sensed the danger, remained utterly still and stared absently into the middle distance, his mind apparently blank. The dead patch of grass remained in one place for what seemed like an age, then moved on and past Wilson towards me in a slow, purposeful manner. I'd faced down death a couple of times, but never like this.

I stayed as still as I dared until the Lifesucker was

barely a yard from me, and that's when Wilson stamped his feet.

'Heigh-ho!' he yelled in a forced tone tinged with fear. 'Boy, am I feeling terrific today. So full of *life*. So much to do, so much to see! Everything in the world is there to witness, and I am the one to breathe in its many varied splendours!'

For a moment, it seemed to work. The dead patch of grass stopped, paused for a moment, but then carried on in my direction.

'Ook, ook!' said Ralph as he joined Wilson and danced an odd dance while making a strange trilling noise that, while not *exactly* musical, might become so given a few hundred millennia.

I hurried to get away, stumbled on a rock and fell heavily to the ground.

'Ha, hoo!' yelled Wilson as he moved closer to try to draw the Lifesucker away from me. Ralph joined him, but it wasn't working. Death was after me, probably because I was the youngest and had more of life left in me. A small frog died instantaneously as the patch of dead grass moved over it, and I found myself attempting to flee in an undignified rearward floundering movement while still lying on my back. I panicked, and just as Wilson was about to jump forward and put himself between the Lifesucker and me, a bellow rent the air.

'HOLD!'

I stopped. Wilson and Ralph stopped. Death, ever the opportunist, stopped as well – perhaps in case a tastier snack might suddenly have come within easier reach.

The newcomer was standing less than a dozen paces away. He wore walking breeches, stout boots, a checked shirt rolled up to the elbows, and carried a large rucksack. He had an agreeably boyish face, even though I guessed he was in his thirties, and his thick brown hair was tied up inside a red bandana, and he regarded me through the most piercing blue eyes I think I had ever seen. They didn't so much look *at* you as look *into* you.

He was weighing a stone up and down in his hand, presumably to ensure accuracy when it was thrown. I wondered whether you could kill death with a stone, until I realised it wasn't for death. It was for me. He swung his arm around, there was a sudden blaze of light and everything went black.

The name's Gabby

'Her life-force positively *glows*,' came an unfamiliar voice out of a darkness that was punctuated only by flashing stars. 'I can see why the Lifesucker homed in on her. Have you known her long?'

'Since yesterday,' said a familiar voice. 'Her party rescued me from some kidnappers. I think she's somebody big in the magic industry.'

'No kidding?' said the unfamiliar voice, which sounded impressed. There was a pause, then: 'Where did you find the Australopithecine?'

'His name's Ralph. He had a Genetic Master Reset.'

'I'm not sure what that means,' came the unfamiliar voice again.

'To be honest,' said Wilson – for that's who it was, I realised – 'I'm not really sure myself. I think it's a kind of magic.'

'There's not much round here that isn't. Does it trouble you that his thing is showing?'

'No, we're kind of used to it by now.'

'Ook.'

I opened my eyes to find Wilson, Ralph and the

stranger staring at me. Wilson was holding a damp handkerchief to my head.

'Am I dead?' I asked.

'If you were,' said the stranger, 'would you choose this place as heaven?'

I looked around. I was still in the Empty Quarter, leaning up against the Range Rover's wheel. If this had all been a bad dream, I was still in it.

'Sorry I had to knock you out,' said the stranger with a boyish smile, 'but your heart was belting out a funeral march so loud every Lifesucker on the planet could hear you.'

I looked at the handkerchief in Wilson's hand. There was only a smallish amount of blood.

'Thank you . . . ?'

'The name's Gabby,' said the stranger amiably, 'a traveller like yourselves.'

'Jennifer,' I said, shaking his outstretched hand, 'and this is Wilson.'

'I've heard of you,' said Gabby to Wilson. 'Been here a while. A lot of close scrapes, but you always got away.'

'I *will* die out here,' said Wilson. 'I'm choosing my moment – and I've been lucky.'

'I'm not so sure luck has much to do with it out here.'

'What, then?' I asked.

'Fate,' he said, 'and chosen moments winning out

over lost moments. But we don't choose those moments – those moments choose us.'

'I'm not sure I understood that,' said Wilson slowly. 'Jennifer?'

'Not really, no.'

Gabby shrugged.

'Actually, me neither. I heard it from a smarter guy. Was this your transport?'

He nodded towards the Range Rover, and I explained that up until an hour ago we had had a half-track but it had been stolen, along with all our luggage and a handmaiden.

'Llangurig, eh?' said Gabby after Wilson had explained where we were heading but not why we were heading there. 'Me too. We'd better get going if we're to have even a hope of finding a safe place to spend the night.'

'The Lifesucker,' I said with a start, suddenly remembering. 'Is it still around?'

'It'll always be around,' he said, 'and eventually return for you, as it will for us all. Death cannot be avoided for ever, but it can be postponed – in that respect it's very like the washing-up. Now, we must leave before the batteries run down.'

'Batteries?'

The reason for death's sudden lack of interest in me was that Gabby had coaxed it away by means of a small tape recorder that had the sound effects of a party in full swing. The joyous laughter and unrelentingly upbeat chatter of happy humans were considerably more attractive than unconscious me, and the patch of dying soil was currently circling beneath a tree into whose branches the tape recorder had been placed, in the same way that a dog might pace angrily about a tree when seeking a squirrel. The tree was now quite dead, of course, as was the ground beneath it where death paced angrily, but better it than me, I figured.

With nothing else for it, we began to walk along the empty road to Llangurig, keeping a watchful eye out for peril, with Ralph moving about like a spaniel on a walk, sniffing a plant here, scrabbling under a stone for a beetle or two there.

'What are you doing out here?' I asked Gabby. 'You don't look as though you're on holiday.'

'I collect information on death likelihood for a major player in the risk management industry.'

'Can you explain that in simple terms?'

'Everything we do has an element of risk to it,' he said, 'and by identifying the potential risk factor of everything humans do, we can decide where best to deploy our assets to avert that risk.'

'You work for an insurance company?'

'Our data is *used* in the insurance industry,' he said, 'but we also freelance. As you can imagine, a place as dangerous as the Cambrian Empire offers a unique opportunity for studying risk. For example, if two people are confronted by a Tralfamosaur, which of them is more likely to be eaten first? The one who panics, the one who runs, the one who looks most dangerous or the one who looks the juiciest? There are many factors.'

'I'm guessing "juiciest".'

'Yes, me too – it's not a good example.'

'You must know the Empty Quarter very well.'

'I can't stay away from this place,' he confessed with a smile, 'and studying people as they weigh up the risks involved in their various decisions is fascinating. Did you know that you are statistically *more* likely to die driving to the airport than you are on the flight you are going there to catch?'

'You've never flown by JunkAir, clearly.'

'There are always exceptions to the rule,' conceded Gabby.

No traffic came our way in the next hour, except two Skybus lorries, presumably taking aircraft parts out of the Empire. The lorries swept past, ignoring our attempts to get a lift even if it was in the wrong direction, and were soon lost to sight. The day grew warmer, and we spoke less as we walked. Wilson, usually fairly voluble and optimistic, fell silent, and even Ralph, who had earlier dashed around like a mad thing, seemed to be keeping a keener lookout. With Llangurig now twenty-five miles or so away by road it was not possible to get there before darkness, and a night in the open seemed inevitable. Although Gabby was confident he could deal with most dangers during the day, he could not guarantee our safety at night. Calculating risk required one to be able to first accurately sense it, and there were, by current estimates, over sixteen life forms out here that could kill before you were even aware of them.

'I think we should turn back,' said Wilson when we stopped for a rest. 'At least that way we'll have somewhere to stay for the night, and it's always possible a tourist party may chance along.'

He took off a boot and stared sadly at a blister, one of several.

'That might not be for a week or more,' I said, 'and I've got Perkins, a half-track and a handmaiden to retrieve.'

There was a rubber Dragon and the Eye of Zoltar to consider, too.

'We could cut *across* the Empty Quarter,' said Gabby thoughtfully. 'I know a Hotax trail that would take us direct to Llangurig past the Lair of Antagonista, the Dragon who once ruled these Dragonlands.'

'Cut across the Empty Quarter on *foot*?' asked Wilson in an incredulous tone.

'Sure,' replied Gabby. 'The Dragon lived here so long that local animal memory evolved to include it – the Dragon's been dead almost half a century, and still nothing goes near. I calculate the risk factor on sleeping near the old Dragon's lair as no more than four per cent.'

'Sounds good to me,' I said, since Dragons held no real fear for me. 'Ralph? What do you say?'

'*Yoof*,' said Ralph, staring at me curiously. His response might have meant 'yes' or 'no' or almost anything in between – but I felt I should ask him anyway.

'What the hell,' said Wilson with a shrug. 'Lead on and let's get it over with.'

And so it was agreed. About half a mile farther on we left the road to take a narrow path close to a roadside memorial to 'An Unnamed Tourist' who was 'Dissolved but not forgotten', but from the state of the half-buried headstone, probably was.

And after taking a deep breath and exchanging nervous glances, we struck off across the open country of the Empty Quarter.

The old Dragonlands

The Hotax path was easy to follow among the tussocky grass, but the going was slow. We encountered a jumble of boulders carved by the wind into curious and frightening shapes that had to be carefully negotiated, then gaping sinkholes, marshes and the occasional flaming tar pit littered with the charred bones of large herbivores.

We passed a herd of Elephino who were staring thoughtfully at their feet, as was their habit, then a Giggle Beetle migration, where a constant line of yellow-spotted carapaces stretched into the distance in both directions, chuckling constantly. We stepped across this, walked through a long-deserted village, then found an abandoned road, which was paved with large flat stones carved with curious markings.

'This would have been the Dragon's route to his lair,' said Gabby as we picked up the pace on the grass-fringed flagstones. 'In the pre-Dragonpact days when Dragons roamed freely and had the same prestige as kings and emperors.'

We followed the ancient roadway in a stop-start

fashion all afternoon. On one occasion we had to wait for a half-hour while a herd of Tralfamosaur moved through, and another time we paused owing to a strange noise, only to discover it was a small herd of Honking Gazelle, so named because their call is indistinguishable from a car horn. Indeed, a herd all honking in unison sounds *exactly* like a traffic jam in Turin.

We stopped for a break near a spring of fresh water that bubbled out of the ground and tasted of liquorice – there was probably a seam of the stuff lying somewhere underfoot.

'Anyone got anything to eat?' I asked, since I had left everything – food, drink, conch, Helping Hand™, cash, Boo's twenty-grand letter of credit – in the half-track.

No one had anything, although I noted that Gabby was carrying a full backpack, something he didn't remove as he sat on a grassy bank.

Ralph, sensing we were hungry, disappeared and returned five minutes later with a dead slug the size of a rat and about as appetising. I knew slugs *could* be eaten if you were desperate, but 'desperate' in this context meant 'perilously close to death', and we weren't quite there yet. Interestingly, since the flesh-dissolving enzyme was on the outside, it had to be turned inside out like a rubber sock and then eaten like a corncob. After our polite refusal, Ralph ate it himself.

We followed the road up a hill, crested the ridge and looked down upon a huge, dish-like depression in the ground about a mile in diameter. At the very centre of the depression was a large grass-covered dome, surrounded by a high wall that had partly collapsed. Nothing seemed to be growing near the abandoned lair and even from this far out there seemed to be a dark, almost oppressive feeling about the place. The breeze seemed to grow chillier, and high above, despite the grey overcast, a circle of clear blue sky could be seen directly above the grass-covered dome.

'Okay,' I said, 'we should be cautious. Long-unused spells may have recombined in unusual ways.'

As we walked, the strangeness of the redundant strands of magic did indeed manifest themselves in odd ways – the grass in the cracks between the paving stones seemed to shift underfoot as we walked, and once, when I looked back, the grass we had trodden upon had become nourished and healthier by virtue of our life-force. Stranger still, to either side of us and partially hidden by the scrubby grassland were what appeared to be statues carved from a reddish sandstone. One was human and three were Hotax – like a human only stockier, and with a broader, flatter head, I noted – but most were of animals. Several Buzonji, a Snork Badger, a pair of ground sloth and even Elephino, Honking Gazelle and a juvenile Tralfamosaur. They weren't statues, of course, but real creatures *enchanted* to stone, and it wasn't difficult to see the one factor that linked them all: each was caught in the middle of an expansive yawn.

'Don't yawn, anyone,' I said, pointing to the victims. 'A "Turning to Stone" defensive enchantment has recombined with a spell intended to be activated by yawning – creating something that is potentially fatal if you become tired or bored.'

They all nodded sagely and we quickened our pace to move more rapidly out of the danger zone.

We reached the outer wall of the lair, which would once have been ten or fifteen foot high and made of large, interlocking blocks like a three-dimensional puzzle. The Dragon's lair had once been a neat truncated dome, much like a cake, with the vertical edge supported by a twenty-foot-high wall of river stones interspersed with jewels. The lair's poor state of repair was due not so much to age, but to greed – as soon as the Dragon died people had come in and grabbed what they could. As we walked across the yard, we noticed that covers of rotting leather books lay scattered about, presumably from the Dragon's personal library. The brightly decorated pages from the ancient manuscripts would have been removed and sold as pictures to decorate anonymous suburban walls. Even those pages without pictures had been taken, the vellum to be scraped and sold and reused.

We walked a little way around the paved circular

courtyard, and that's when we came across the Dragon, or at least, the remains of it. His massive bones were lying in a heap where he had fallen. The jewel was missing from the forehead of his great skull, and we could see the evidence of axe-marks around his jaws where the teeth had been removed long ago – a Dragon's tooth has a sharp edge that never blunts, and is much prized in the manufacturing industries, and with a price to match. The ground, too, had been churned up over the years by treasure hunters eager to find some of the gold, silver and jewels with which Dragons are wont to line their lairs – the fine tiles that once decorated the floor were broken, spoilt and scattered about.

'What a mess,' said Wilson.

'It's like vandals stripped anything of value right out,' said Gabby.

'Marv-ook,' said Ralph in a soft voice.

'I know,' I said, 'this place must have been spectacular once.'

As the whole sorry scene unfolded before us I thought of the Mighty Shandar's role in the Dragon's destruction, and how the lair of the beast, one of the most powerful and mysterious places on earth, had been stripped like so many others like it for nothing more then souvenirs and cash, the multi-millennia of learning now lost. If Shandar's threat to make good on his promise to destroy all Dragons had been wrong before, it was trebly wrong now. Colin and Feldspar *must* survive, *must* thrive, and *must* one day inhabit a lair such as this, thinking deep thoughts and living a life in the pursuit of greater knowledge.

'This place has an inherent sadness stitched into its very fabric,' said Wilson. 'Can you feel it?'

'I can,' said Gabby, 'like a heavy damp chill. I think we should pick up the pace.'

'I agree,' I said, and with Ralph leading the way, we skirted past the massive bones and towards the back of the lair, and the route beyond.

As we stepped out from behind some fallen masonry Ralph stopped dead. We stopped too. There, bathed in the warm orange light of the setting sun and looking every bit as dangerous as its eight-ton bulk would suggest, was a Tralfamosaur. It was barely fifteen feet away, and was crouched, ready to spring. It cocked its head on one side, regarding us in a dinnery sort of way.

I'd been this close to a Tralfamosaur before. I'd seen the saliva glistening on the razor-sharp teeth and the tiny red eyes, but the previous time there had been the Volkswagen's windscreen between us, and there had been a plan. Here there was no plan, nothing between us, and the only possible thing acting in my favour was that Ralph was closer, and probably tastier.

Ralph realised it too and, unwilling to become an appetiser without a fight, quietly drew out his flint knife. The Tralfamosaur blinked at us all for a moment and flexed its front claws menacingly. I moved slightly as a precursor to darting *right*, hoping that if I did Ralph and the others might dart *left* and at least one or two of us might have a chance.

But as I moved, the Tralfamosaur moved with me. He had zeroed in on me, and it's not a pleasant feeling. As I was about to make my move to a boulder a dozen paces away a hand rested lightly on my shoulder. The Tralfamosaur cocked its head again, perhaps wondering whether he could take two of us at the same time.

I glanced sideways and realised it was Gabby. He had opened his mouth wide, displaying two perfect rows of fine white teeth. I didn't realise at first what he was trying to do but soon cottoned on. He was pretending to yawn and I did likewise: large yawns, expansive and pantomime-like. Ralph and Wilson, who had noticed us, also joined in.

Yawns are, oddly enough, quite infectious. Once one person in a room yawns, then others are likely to follow. And since we were only *pretending* to yawn and not actually yawning, I figured the spell would not affect us. The question was: would the Tralfamosaur join in the yawn we had started?

The answer was 'not really', and as we opened our mouths and pretended to yawn in a manner that would win no amateur dramatic prizes anywhere but would win gold in the 'Desperate Measures Challenge Cup', the Tralfamosaur peered at us hungrily and rose on his toes ready to lunge. It was a long shot, obviously, and we were beginning to think of instigating Plan B, which was pretty much along the lines of 'run like stink and hope for the best'. It was always prudent – and I give you this information for free as it might come in useful one day – when being attacked by a hunger-crazed carnivore the size of a bus to remind yourself that it has immeasurably higher mass, and that it cannot speed up, slow down or change direction as quickly as something considerably smaller – such as us. It was said that lively jumping, dodging and jinking could postpone the inevitable for at least a minute before brute force and speed across rough terrain finally ended the sorry spectacle. Even for the unskilled, the first bite could usually be avoided if you kept your eye on the beast.

So I fixed my eyes on the Tralfamosaur's, and as I watched, the jaws opened as a precursor to a lunge. I paused, wavered, then shifted my weight as I waited for it to make the first move.

But the move never came. The mouth opening had actually been a vast yawn, complete with the foul stench of rotting carcasses, and the Tralfamosaur had changed instantaneously into a dark granite statue that shimmered subtly as it was caught by the last dying rays of the sun.

'Ook,' said Ralph in a relieved tone.

We all looked at one another and burst out laughing – out of relief, I think, and not because it was funny, which it wasn't. We moved past the now-silent beast without talking and made camp in an abandoned armoured scout car. We found some fireberries and ignited them by twisting the stalks to the left sharply, and settled down for the night. It wasn't easy. There were snufflings, scratches, clicks and whistles as the nightlife of the Empty Quarter went about its nocturnal business. Thankfully, some distance away.

'Anything to eat?' I asked as hunger was beginning to gnaw.

'Ralph had a hunting look in his eyes as he left the camp,' said Gabby, 'but if he comes back empty handed or fails to come back at all, I have a Snickers somewhere.'

Thankfully, Ralph *did* return, and with a skinned swamp-rat. By using some scrap steel as a frying pan we soon had it cooked, and the rat was about as welcome as any food could be. Wilson and I settled down for the night, huddled in the wreckage of the armoured car with a large blanket of dried grass and heather pulled over us. Gabby sat separate from the pair of us, filling in a report in a leather-bound ledger.

'Paperwork,' he explained when I asked. 'The top floor wants to know everything we get up to down here.'

'I know the feeling,' I said, as the magic industry was a stickler for paperwork. As I stared up at the stars, which were bright and clear in the night sky, there was a screeching noise and a homing snail arrived hot and sweaty on my chest. It was muddy and bruised, one of its antennae was missing, and several scratches on its shell spoke of a narrow escape from a predator. It was past seven and since my communication with the conch hadn't happened – the conch was still in the half-track – Moobin and the others had sent a snail instead. I plucked off the message and read it by the light of the fireberry. The previous evening's message had been written in a neat hand, but this one seemed more hurried.

Jennifer,
Couldn't raise you on the conch so hoping all well. Eye of Zoltar more important than ever, and keep a close eye on the Princess. Tell Perkins from me that all other considerations are now secondary, and Kevin says that if you ever find yourself on the shoulders of giants and need to take a leap of faith, go for it.
Moobin

There was nothing I could do to respond, so I folded the message up and placed it in my top pocket. I wasn't happy. Did Moobin mean 'all other considerations secondary' in the same way that Wilson had described it in his story? 'To use whatever means available to carry out his task'? And a 'leap of faith from the shoulders of giants'? What was that all about? Giants died out years ago and had long ago been consigned to Grade VI legend status, the same as dodos: 'Once existed, but now proved to be extinct'.

I lay quite still for a while, the events of the past day going through my head while by the light of the fireberries I could see Ralph sitting sentry on a rock, flint knife at the ready. I tied my handkerchief around my head to guard against yawning, then tried to get comfortable against the remains of the seats in the abandoned scout car. It was chilly and after the day's events I thought sleep would be impossible. In less then five minutes I was proved wrong.

The morning feeding

I awoke with a chill in my joints. The air was cold, and a thick layer of fog had draped the land in a soft milky blanket. I coughed and looked up. It was early, and I could see Wilson fast asleep close by. Ralph was still perched on the rock where I had seen him the previous night, but he was now hunched over, fast asleep. Gabby was nowhere to be seen, and as I looked around and stretched I was suddenly aware of a distant whistling noise, like the wind that sings through the tassels of a fast-moving flying carpet.

The noise appeared to be coming from the north, and what's more, seemed to be getting louder. In another second Gabby came running into the campsite while wrestling to put on his backpack, and with a worried look on his face.

'*Hang on to something!*' he yelled. '*Leviathan on a feeding run!*'

Wilson was still asleep so I flung myself on top of him and wedged myself – and him – with both feet in a corner of the vehicle and my arms wrapped around the bent steering wheel. Gabby did the same, but around a door pillar.

The whistling increased and a breeze seemed to blow up – the fabled 'squall line' that preceded a low-level feeding run, intended to stir anything capable of flight into the air. A moment later and the air was flooded with birds of almost every description, eager to outrun the predator. I saw gulls tear past us, sparrows, a hawk, three herons, a pelican and two dozen starlings, all grouped together for protection. Many of them alighted in the wreckage of the vehicle and, momentarily unafraid of us, tucked themselves into any crevice they could find. Three puffins snuggled inside my coat and assorted sparrows, choughs, curlews and a woodpecker desperately attempted to wedge themselves beneath the armoured car's hull.

The whistling increased in strength and the wind in the squall line increased. My ears popped, and all of a sudden a cloud of insects moved past, tumbling and fluttering in the wind. Butterflies and bees, wasps, ladybirds and myriad others gathered together in a confused and erratic swarm, all in a vain attempt to escape. Dust and dirt and small stones and clumps of grass were lifted and whipped and whirled into the air by the wind. I looked up to see whether I could see the Cloud Leviathan – you'd have done the same, I assure you – and that's when I noticed Ralph. He was standing on his rock, flint blade in hand, peering at the colossus that was fast approaching. I could see the Leviathan now, or rather, I could see *parts* of it, the most obvious being the mouth – an oval gaping maw twenty foot wide and ringed by pearly-white teeth the size of artillery shells. The rest of the Leviathan seemed indistinct; more like a wobbly pattern in the air. In another few seconds the Leviathan was upon us, and as it went thundering overhead with the sound of a gigantic hoover, I caught a glimpse of Ralph jumping into the attack. Perhaps he thought a lone Australopithecine could bring down a Leviathan. Perhaps he wanted to be the first one to try. Perhaps deep down, the risk-averse loner that had once been Ralph D. Nalor wanted to end it all on the most daring endeavour of all. I don't know, but Ralph managed to sink his dagger into the leathery hide of the beast as it moved past, and was then carried away as the Leviathan continued on its feeding run, seemingly untroubled by its passenger.

The armoured car in which we'd sought refuge lurched as the Leviathan went over, and then all was still. The wind subsided, and the birds all hopped from their hiding places, rubbed their beaks and then flew off, apparently unperturbed. Gabby and I watched as the Cloud Leviathan, or at least the shimmering shape where we thought the Leviathan might be, reared vertically upwards, venting air from the twin rows of vectored nostrils on its underbelly.

'Isn't that Ralph?' I asked.

It was. Ralph was clinging to the belly of the beast as it rose several thousand feet into the air, streaming dust, feathers, dirt and grass as it went. Ralph was tenacious, that much was clear – he even had his large ladies' handbag still in the crook of his arm.

'Did I miss something?' asked Wilson, blinking and getting up.

'Kind of,' I said, pointing in the direction of the tiny dot that was Ralph, clearly visible on the shimmering outline of the barely visible Leviathan. It looked almost as if he were rising alone, unsupported by anything at all. In a moment or two the Leviathan rolled on to its side to head north, and Ralph was lost to view.

'Do you think he's okay?' I asked.

'He'll be fine for about as long as he can hang on,' replied Gabby.

We stared into the now-empty sky for a few moments in silence.

'He was a loyal companion to us both,' I said sadly.

'And will be missed,' added Wilson.

'Friends are always lost here in the Empire,' said Gabby philosophically, 'and we'll lose more before the trip is over, I wager.'

'Mathematically speaking you may be right,' I said,

thinking of Addie's predicted fifty per cent Fatality Index, 'but I hope not.'

'That Leviathan was low,' mused Gabby as he unhooked something from the jagged edge of the armoured car's shattered body. He laid the scrap of leathery material across his arm, where it changed colour to match his skin. He laid it across my skin and it darkened almost instantaneously to match mine.

'Scraps of Leviathan skin fetch a good price on the Cambrianopolis black market, I've heard,' said Wilson.

'If the Emperor's men find you with this your head will be off,' said Gabby. 'It's better to let it go.'

And so saying, he released the section of skin, which floated off into the air like a helium balloon.

'Leviathans are lighter than air?' I said, amazed at what I was seeing.

'How else do you think something so large could fly?' asked Gabby, then added: 'We'd better get going. With a bit of luck we can get to the edge of the Empty Quarter before something considers that we'd make a fine breakfast. And Jennifer?'

'Yes?'

'I think you've still got some puffins inside your jacket.'

It was true. They seemed to have taken a liking to the pockets, and had to be carefully removed.

We walked in silence for the next three hours or so, now and then pausing to hide from danger, drink from a mountain stream or nibble on some wild radishes. Eventually we came across the now-dormant marker stones that denoted the edge of the Dragonlands and the northern edge of the Empty Quarter. The stones were covered with a thick crust of lichen, and appeared forlorn and forgotten. Llangurig would be only a few miles away.

Gabby called a halt.

'Any particular reason?' I asked.

'Breakfast.'

'You have some?'

'No,' said Gabby with a smile, 'but they will.'

He pointed towards a stunted oak. The roots had grasped one of the marker stones tightly, and the overhanging branches partially hid a small group of people. A quick leg count told me this was a group of five people and I was suddenly suspicious until I realised that six of the legs belonged to one creature – a Buzonji – and that the other legs belonged to Perkins, and Addie. I blinked away some tears. I had convinced myself I would not see them again.

Friends reunited

'Heigh-ho!' said Addie cheerfully as she walked into the clearing. 'How are my tourists?'

I must say that I have rarely been so glad to see someone safe and well. Perkins, that was, and Addie a close second.

'Hey, Jenny,' said Perkins, and he gave me a long hug, taking the opportunity to whisper in my ear how much he'd missed me. I returned the compliment gladly and unconditionally, but I must confess that his increased age – he'd put on ten years with Ralph's Genetic Master Reset, remember – was not something I was going to get used to quickly.

'Are you okay?' I asked. 'Not harmed in any way, I mean?'

'I'm fine,' he said, 'but I can't say the same for the kidnappers.'

'Dead?'

He didn't say anything, but just looked at me and raised his eyebrows.

'Hail, fellow,' said Addie to Gabby, grasping his hand and shaking it warmly, 'good to see you again.'

'You know each other?' I asked, surprised, but unsure why I should be.

'He's my secret weapon,' said Addie. 'Everyone should have a Gabby to look after them.'

'You sent Gabby to keep an eye on us?' I asked.

'Only to remain on standby in case anything happened.'

I looked at Gabby, who shrugged.

'I should have said something, I suppose,' he said, 'but I didn't know until two minutes ago that Addie was okay, and, well, I'm just in it for the rescuing.'

I thanked him, and Addie quizzed Gabby further. Safe jeopardy tourism – any tourism, actually – I had decided, was all about information. The more of it you have, the better the decisions you can make.

'I found them two clicks north-west of the pod poles,' said Gabby when Addie questioned him. 'They'd lost their transport and were about to be emptied by a Lifesucker. I brought them here by way of the Dragon's lair.'

'Was that wise?' asked Addie.

'Perhaps, perhaps not,' said Gabby, 'but we made it without loss.'

'Except Ralph,' I said, 'who tried to attack a Cloud Leviathan while it was on a low-level feeding run. I think he had an exciting ride while it lasted.'

'And the others?'

I explained that Curtis had stolen the half-track

with my 'handmaiden' on board and Addie agreed Curtis would be heading towards Llangurig, almost certainly to sell Laura, as Wilson suggested.

She didn't yet know, of course, that Laura was anything but a handmaiden – but for now, while an odd one, she was a handmaiden nonetheless. I also told her Ignatius was dead.

'Flesh-eating slugs?' she asked. 'He never was a fast mover.'

'He tried to escape to the border in a rowing boat and was shot down by anti-aircraft fire.'

'Wow,' said Addie, 'I would never have seen *that* coming.'

'Neither did he.'

'If you don't need me for anything more,' said Gabby, 'I'll be off. I've got some raw recruits to train in the risk management business. Staff turnover is savagely high these days.'

We all shook hands. I thanked him again and after politely refusing an offer of breakfast, he was off at a brisk walk and was soon lost to view over a rise.

We sat on the warm grass, and a picnic breakfast never tasted so good. There was tea in a billycan, too, boiled up over the residual Thermowizidrical energy emanating from the runic markings on the fallen marker stones.

'So what's the deal with Gabby?' I asked.

'He's exactly what you see. Someone who assesses

risk of death, and steps in to intervene if the right conditions prevail.'

'Why didn't he save Ralph if he works for the insurance companies? Someone like that wouldn't come out here without adequate life cover.'

'Ralph wasn't human,' said Addie, 'and Gabby's instructions are clear. If he was rescuing non-humans, where would he draw the line? Tralfamosaurs? Rabbits? Ladybirds?'

'He was *definitely* a rum cove,' added Wilson thoughtfully. 'He never ate or drank, and I didn't see him sleep last night. He was still awake as I nodded off, and awake before me.'

'And me,' I said. 'And he never took off his back-pack. I only saw him struggling with it once, when he returned to camp this morning.'

'Listen,' said Addie, 'Gabby is what Gabby does and it's best not to ask too many questions. There are some things out here that defy ordinary explanation, and Gabby, well, he's one of them.'

'So . . . what about the kidnappers?' I asked, helping myself to another bread roll, but this time with peanut butter. I saw Perkins and Addie exchange looks.

'If you'd rather not—' began Wilson.

'No, we should tell you,' said Addie. 'I tracked them to a camp about five miles from Cambrianopolis,' she continued, taking a sip of tea, 'and then waited until dawn before walking into their camp. I told them my word of death was in the steel I carried, and that they could stay there alive if they relinquished Perkins, or stay there dead if they did not. I knew they wouldn't give him up, but it's traditional to offer some sort of deal.'

'Three against one?' I said. 'No offence or anything, Addie, but you're not even half their size. Did you think you had a chance?'

'What I lack in weight I make up for in savagery,' she said, 'and no offence taken. I weighed my chances in at about seventy/thirty in my favour. It would have been a hard hand-to-hand struggle, but I would have won out eventually. I would have left them to the flesh-eating slugs, set free their Buzonjis, and returned with Perkins. They knew I would have to do this when they took him. They would have *expected* me to come for them.'

'Did it pan out that way?' I asked.

'It would have,' said Addie, 'but for your friend here.'

I turned to Perkins.

'What did you do?' I asked him.

'She turned up and, yes, did the whole dopey tribal honour speech,' replied Perkins, 'which was quite stirring in a simplistic, barbaric and pointless-death kind of way, and I said that if she killed them I wouldn't come with her.'

'I told him he didn't have a choice,' said Addie, staring into her teacup, 'that I would bind him like a hog and return him whether he liked it or not.'

Wilson and I looked at Perkins expectantly.

'So,' said Perkins, 'I told her I would pop myself if she laid so much as a finger on any of them.'

I raised my eyebrows. 'Popping' was the last resort for a wizard, a simple spell that caused a haemorrhage in the brain. Unconsciousness would be instantaneous, and death would soon follow.

'That put me in a quandary,' said Addie, 'for it would be a treble failure. I would still have to kill the bandits as threatened, the Silurians and the Oldivicians would go to war, and the trophy in the argument – Perkins – would be lost too. There were no winners. So I did something I've never done before. I told them that I would not be killing them as there was no good reason for it, and that I would lose my honour in order to keep the peace between our two tribes.'

'I'm getting really confused over this whole honour thing,' I said. 'Isn't a willingness to die and to kill for an abstract concept of dubious relevance a bit daft?'

'I'd be the first to admit that it is,' said Addie. 'Honour is kind of what you get when you weaponise manners, but if you're brought up in a system where honour is valued more than life itself it makes a lot more sense. Some. A bit. Anyway: they attacked me as they were honour bound to do, and I defended myself as I was bound to do, but killed them in *self-defence*. I think it was what Gareth had planned. He had dishonoured himself by kidnapping Perkins in the first place and causing our tribes to fall out, then been the cause of me dishonouring myself, which then brought dishonour upon *himself*. By attacking me, he allowed me to restore my lost honour by killing him, and, odd as it might seem, his honour as well. He died with honour, and I thank and respect him for it. We didn't leave them to the slugs at all, and instead buried them with tribal honours, which is why we were kind of delayed. The ground was hard and we had to ride for miles to find a shovel.'

'I'm totally lost,' I said.

'Me too,' said Wilson.

'And me,' said Perkins, 'and I was actually there witnessing it.'

'Okay,' I said, 'what happened then?'

'We got to the pod poles long after you had left, found your note and followed your trail as far as the Hotax-attacked Range Rover. By that time is was late afternoon, so, we decided to find a hotel in Llanidloes.'

'So the plan is now . . . ?' I asked.

'Same as before, pretty much,' said Addie. 'We'll head into Llangurig and see if we can retrieve your handmaiden, the half-track and get some payback on that idiot Curtis.'

'And then?'

'See what Able Quizzler has to say for himself, I guess – and take it from there.'

This seemed the best plan, and after Addie had

instructed her Buzonji to head on home, she led us towards a path that led downhill.

'Any news from home?' asked Perkins. I showed him the latest note from the homing snail, and watched his reaction to the part that read 'all other considerations secondary'. I saw a look of consternation cross his face, but it was soon gone.

'They're keen to keep the Princess safe,' he said, 'and the Eye is still our number-one priority.'

'Maybe so,' I said, 'but if Able Quizzler hasn't any information about the Eye of Zoltar, I'm pulling the plug. We've lost two people already, and hunting Leviathans and a legendary pirate across Cadair Idris sounds like a fool's errand.'

'Fair enough,' said Perkins.

He pointed at Moobin's note again.

'What's all this about a "leap of faith"?'

'No idea,' I said, 'and why did Moobin want to tell you "all other considerations secondary"? Are we in some kind of trouble?'

'I'm not sure,' said Perkins. 'Perhaps he wanted to impress upon me just how important this mission was.'

Just then we came to a thin line of beech trees on the ridge, and Addie pointed towards a town on the valley floor.

'Behold,' she said in a dramatic tone of voice, 'Llangurig.'

Llangurig

Llangurig was situated on a bend in the river and was roughly circular. It was defended by a high wall that was curved inwards with an overhang at the top in order to better withstand attack by Tralfamosaur and other terrors. There was open countryside outside the walls but it was churned and shattered by recent conflict. And by recent, I mean *really* recent – several armoured vehicles were smouldering from a battle earlier that day.

'What are they?' I asked, pointing to what looked like two encampments, one a half-mile to the east of Llangurig, and one the same distance to the west. Each encampment seemed to have its own system of trenches and earthworks, within which I could see troops at readiness.

'Two conflicting sides,' said Addie, 'who have fought violently over Llangurig's territory for the past one hundred and forty years. A period of endless strife, aggression and political manoeuvring. The leaders of these two factions will stop at nothing to defeat the other, while in between them, the target of their endless battle awaits the outcome with long-bated breath.'

'Warlords?' I asked.

'If only,' replied Addie. 'At least power-hungry Lunatics *eventually* know when to call a truce. No, these two factions are fuelled by greed and are utterly ruthless in their pursuit of power, influence and territory.'

'You mean—?' said Perkins.

'Right,' said Addie, 'railway companies.'

I looked again. Now she mentioned it, the two encampments to the east and west did appear to have cranes and piles of building materials, coal, even a locomotive or two, and behind each fortified area was a railway, snaking out behind and soon lost to view in the endless green folds of the countryside. The area of churned soil and shattered earth was confined, I noticed, solely to the area around Llangurig.

As we watched, a salvo of artillery was fired from the railway company to the east, and a few moments later several shellbursts appeared close by their enemies in the west, who returned fire and felled an ancient oak that looked as though it had survived several near-misses in the past. While the artillery barrage continued, I noticed that engineers and armoured fighting vehicles on the western side were attempting to lay some railway track in the direction of Llangurig. This was soon noticed by those in the east, who sent forward some skirmishers to stop the engineers, which they managed to do – only three sleepers were laid, for a body count, as far as I could see, of five.

While this was going on the engineers in the east used a steam crane to deliver a completed section of track about thirty feet in length, which was met with a fusillade of small-arms fire from the west. As we watched, welders in heavy body armour ran out to fix the new section of track, and even though they welded with incredible bravery, the section of track was condemned by the Inspector of Works, who was dressed in a stripy umpire's outfit.

'Not enough ballast under the track,' said Wilson expertly. 'It would never have taken the weight of a locomotive, let alone fully loaded coal wagons.'

It all seemed very strange indeed, even by Cambrian Empire standards, which were admittedly quite broad. The two factions seemed to be fighting over the mile of empty ground between the two railheads.

'Okay,' I said slowly, 'and they are fighting because . . . ?'

'I'll tell you as we walk down,' said Addie, glancing at the sun to gauge the time. 'We want to get to town in time for the 12.07 ceasefire.'

'That seems very precise.'

'Railway militia are notorious sticklers for punctuality. They are sometimes late, but always apologise and let you know why, and if the ceasefire is *really* late, you can apply for a refund.'

'A refund of what?'

She shrugged.

'No one really knows.'

As we climbed down, the story unfolded itself courtesy of Addie's spirited storytelling. The conflict began with Tharv's grandfather, who was keen that the Cambrian Empire make full use of the then new railway technology to bring modernity and riches to the Empire. A flurry of railway companies sprang up to bid on the lucrative railway contracts but, owing to a misunderstanding, *two* railway companies were mistakenly awarded the potentially lucrative line from Cambrianopolis to the deep-water anchorages at Aberystwyth.

'After some wrangling,' concluded Addie, 'the Emperor decreed that whoever got to Llangurig first would control the line, so a flurry of building ensued. The Cambrian Railway Company built from the east, and the Trans-Wales Rails Corporation from the west. The companies met either side of Llangurig, and one thing led to another – angry words, a bloody nose, someone shot someone, and before you know it there was a war, which has lasted over a century. There are goods stacked high at the docks and in Cambrianopolis waiting to be transported by rail. If your great-grandfather ordered a Cambrian piano, it'll be in a warehouse somewhere, still waiting to be shipped.'

We stopped within sight of the town walls as the warring companies exchanged another artillery salvo and several brave railway militiamen were cut down by a scythe of machine-gun fire.

'How many people have died over this mile of railway track during that century and a half?' asked Perkins.

'Eight thousand,' said Addie, 'give or take.'

'Working for the railways is quite dangerous out here,' said Wilson.

'True,' said Addie, 'and each of those soldiers is fighting not for glory, but a share of the profits. If the company you fight for builds the track to Llangurig and you survive, you'll be rich beyond your wildest dreams.'

'What if you're killed?'

'You get a cardboard box to be buried in, and a fifty-pound Argos gift token goes to the widow.'

'Do they have any trouble recruiting?' asked Wilson.

'They're queuing up.'

'Someone should put a stop to this,' growled Perkins.

'The battle has been going on for so long and the profits to be made from the line are so huge that whoever wins bankrupts the other,' said Addie, 'so it really is a matter of corporate life and death. It's not profit running this war any more, but the dire financial consequences to the loser.'

'What if it's a tie?' I asked out of interest, 'Couldn't they share the line?'

'They would have to drive in the final two spikes at precisely the same time,' she said, 'and that's not likely to happen.'

We waited until the 12.07 ceasefire, and the guns fell silent. Almost immediately the two railway companies came out to remove their wounded and dead, and the gates of the city opened. A torrent of traders, walkers, vehicles, railway enthusiasts, TV crews, goatherds and other assorted townsfolk spewed forth, eager to get out and back again before the battle recommenced at 14.38.

We walked up to the gates and entered the town. It was not large, but it was busy. *Very* busy. Llangurig wasn't just a railway trophy town, but a frontier town. All the land north of here was unexplored and uncharted. Llangurig was a good starting point for tours into the rarely travelled and mostly inhospitable Plynlimon and Berwyn mountains.

'But the tours tend not to go to Cadair Idris,' said Addie. 'Even jeopardy tourism has its limits.'

'Any particular reason?' asked Perkins.

'The impossibly high level of fatalities, mostly. Dead tourists aren't good for repeat business.'

As we headed towards the nearest hostelry for something to eat, I noted there were numerous street traders buying and selling railway shares. These traders, who had names like 'Honest Bob' and 'Rock Solid Eddie' and so forth, had set up blackboards on the streets with up-to-date reports of the current worth of the companies. Given the fresh battle this morning, the shares of the Cambrian Railway Company were at present slightly higher in value than the shares of the Trans-Wales Rails Corporation, but from the look of the number of hastily scrubbed and rewritten figures on the board, this was a state of affairs that was constantly changing.

'The value of shares can go up as well as down!' came a cheery voice behind me. I turned to find the Princess beaming at me. She was, strangely enough, actually dressed as a handmaiden, but aside from that, looked remarkably well.

'Oh boy,' I said, 'am I glad to see you.'

'Likewise,' said the Princess, giving me a very unprincessly hug. 'Hullo, Wilson, hullo, Addie and Mr Perkins. Hang on, my goat shares have taken a dive.'

She was pointing at another trader, who was dealing in *commodities* – things that you could consume like orange juice, beef and goats. It seemed the price of goats had suddenly dropped.

'I was dabbling in the Llangurig Commodities Market,' explained the Princess, looking suddenly crestfallen, 'and I can't understand how goats could be so cheap. It just doesn't make any sense. Someone must be dumping cheap goats on the already saturated goat market. I thought the price couldn't go any lower, but what a fool I was.'

'Is that what you've been doing here for the past twenty-four hours?' I asked. 'Dabbling in goat shares at the Llangurig Commodities Market?'

'I've not had so much fun in years,' she said happily. 'The smallest thing can set prices tumbling. Shall I demonstrate?'

'No, please don't. What happened to Curtis and the half-track?'

'Gone, and not before time. Why not come over to the Bluebell Railway Inn? I can explain it over lunch.'

This seemed a good idea, and we trooped across to the inn opposite and ordered some food.

The handmaiden's tale

'So,' I said, once large tankards of tea had been placed in front of us by a burly barmaid who had a pair of Star Class locomotives tattooed on her forearms, 'what's been going on?'

The Princess moved her chair so she could see the stock traders through the window in case any prices changed, then began.

'I was watching you examine the Range Rover on the road yesterday morning – what was it, by the way?'

'Hotax attack. Two tourists stuffed.'

'Ah. Well, all of a sudden there is this colossal bang and when I wake up I'm rattling around on the floor of the half-track, bound and gagged and with a shocking headache. I figure Curtis must have whacked me on the head with a tyre iron or something. We get to Llangurig during the afternoon battle, then enter the town at teatime. Curtis immediately sells me to a local kingpin named Gripper O'Rourke, then stays the night over at the Llangurig Ritz to head out first thing this morning in the half-track. I don't know where.'

'Did he take any goats with him?' asked Addie.

'Four.'

'He'll be heading north to Cadair Idris,' said Addie. 'The goats are payment to cross the Mountain Silurians' territory.'

'Why Cadair Idris?' asked the Princess.

'To find the Leviathans' Graveyard. I told him the teeth were highly valuable to sorcerers.'

'Are they?'

'No, although they might have some novelty value. Where's this Gripper fellow? I've got to buy you back.'

The Princess chuckled.

'You won't have to. Let me explain: since handmaidens are quite valuable out here Gripper didn't have the cash to pay Curtis outright, and Curtis didn't trust that Gripper would send him the money he owed, so I suggested I float myself on the Llangurig Stock Exchange.'

'You did *what*?' asked Perkins.

'Floated myself. It's very simple. If you consider that I have a value doing handmaideny things, then I could incorporate myself as a company named "Laura Scrubb (Handmaiden) Ltd". I could then sell – or *float* – myself to buyers with the value split into one hundred shares. If you bought ten shares in Laura Scrubb (Handmaiden) Ltd, I would give ten per cent of my sixty-hour working week to you, or six hours.'

'Wouldn't just selling your time on an hourly basis work better?' I asked.

'This is much better,' said the Princess with a grin, 'because those Laura Scrubb (Handmaiden) Ltd shares are *tradable*. Gripper had a sixty per cent share but Curtis retained thirty per cent, which he immediately sold for seventy plotniks a share. Not a great price, but for an unknown commodity – me – it was the best price he could get.'

'So then what happened?'

'Okay, so to raise the value of Laura Scrubb (Handmaiden) stock I spent two hours being useful – making beds, walking dogs, washing up, polishing shoes, that sort of thing – and pretty soon everyone wanted a piece of Laura Scrubb to do their menial tasks for them and I was trading at two hundred plotniks a share. So the value of Laura Scrub (Handmaiden) Ltd went from seventy plotniks at flotation to two hundred a share in just two hours. Are you following me so far?'

'Kind of. So . . . Gripper's shareholding is now worth almost three times what he paid for it?'

'That's pretty much it. Okay, now this is where it gets good. See that woman behind the bar?'

We turned to see a kindly-looking woman with long black hair and a red face. She was chatting with another customer.

'Yes?'

'That's Madge Ryerson. She's a lovely lady but the worst gossip imaginable. Whisper something to her and it's all around town in a matter of minutes. I *suggested* to her that I do ironing as part of my handmaiden duties.'

'No one likes ironing,' said Wilson. 'Out here, a well-ironed shirt is hugely prestigious.'

'*Exactly*,' said the Princess. 'Within twenty minutes Laura Scrubb (Handmaiden) Ltd was trading at almost a thousand plotniks a share. In fact, shares in the Cambrian Railway Company *fell* as people sold those shares to buy into Laura Scrubb. And those that couldn't buy shares bought options to buy shares if they became available. I had Madge put it about that I can make a cracking apple and blackberry crumble and an hour later, shares in Laura Scrubb had peaked at three and a half thousand plotniks a share – the highest climb ever recorded on the Llangurig Stock Exchange.'

'But listen,' I said as the sandwiches arrived, 'you don't know the first thing about ironing. Hardly anyone does. The Guild of Master Ironers keep that secret arcane knowledge well guarded.'

'I know, so this is the clever bit, and you have to pay attention. I kept ten per cent of myself as payment for setting up Laura Scrubb (Handmaiden) Ltd, and at that peak value, my ten shares were worth *thirty-five thousand plotniks*, and I then sold them.'

'Wouldn't people get worried you were selling all your own shares?' asked Wilson. 'I mean, it's a bit suspicious, don't you think?'

'Good point,' said the Princess, 'so I set up a series of bogus companies so no one would know. I had the butcher's boy and the blacksmith's apprentice sell my shares for me a few minutes before trading ended. Then, the next morning – this morning, in fact – I denied I knew anything about ironing or apple and blackberry crumble, then put it about that I was going down with the mumps and would be unable to work for a month.'

'In order to lower the value of your shares?' I asked.

'Bingo. By ten o'clock, the share price at Laura Scrubb (Handmaiden) Ltd had bottomed out at one plotnik a share, and I then used the profit I gained last night to buy back all the shares. Once everyone had been paid off – Madge, the butcher's boy, a few dodgy accountants and several ratings agencies I omitted to tell you about for simplicity – I was twenty thousand better off and Laura Scrubb is a free woman. Admittedly,' she concluded, 'I lost half the profit on my ill-conceived goat commodities speculation. But I'm still flush – the sandwiches are on me!'

We all fell silent for a moment, musing on how basic the stock market seemed, and how easily it could be manipulated for gain.

'You like economics, don't you?' I asked.

'Everyone should know the basics,' said the Princess. 'Lasting peace will only be brought about through economic means – we should be trading with the Trolls rather than fighting them.'

'Good luck with that one,' I said, knowing how humans and Trolls like to fight to the death at every opportunity. 'But listen, Laura, wasn't any of that trading a teensy-weensy bit illegal? I mean, Gripper O'Rourke lost almost everything he put in, and all those people who bought shares in you are now out of pocket.'

'That's the stock market, buster,' she replied cheerfully, 'win some, lose some. Yes, maybe it was technically a *bit* illegal, but who's going to find out? By the time they realise they've been ripped off I'll be long gone. The Llanguriganeans are all a bunch of unsophisticated dullards who wouldn't know an illegal stock market manipulation if it fell on them.'

'Laura Scrubb?' said a man in a tweed suit who had just approached our table.

'Yes?'

'My name is Brian Lloyd. I work for the Llangurig Financial Services Commission. I have to inform you that all trading in Laura Scrubb (Handmaiden) Ltd has been suspended, and we are arresting you for eighteen counts of illegal manipulation of the stock market, nine counts of fraudulent accounting and six of misrepresentation and corporate fraud.'

'That's an *outrageous* suggestion,' said the Princess haughtily, 'but since I have neither the time nor the inclination to defend your clearly bogus charges, I'll be more than happy to deal with this here and now – shall we say two thousand, cash?'

'And one count of attempting to bribe a public official.'

'Whoops,' said the Princess as a constable snapped some handcuffs on her.

'Dear oh dear,' said Mr Lloyd, shaking his head sadly, 'you must think we're all a bunch of unsophisticated dullards who wouldn't know an illegal stock market manipulation if it fell on them.'

The Princess put on a good show of looking shocked and surprised.

'The thought . . . never crossed my mind.'

'Sure it didn't,' said Mr Lloyd. 'You rogue traders are all the same. You think it's just business and not stealing. It is. Constables? Take her away.'

'Here, Jennifer,' said the Princess, handing me the remains of her ill-gotten gains and an envelope stuffed with share certificates, 'better try and get me a good lawyer, a bent lawyer, or failing that, any lawyer. Oh, and buy Trans-Wales stock when it drops below one-twenty plotniks a share; if goats go above half a plotnik a head, sell the lot.'

The two constables took the Princess by the elbows and marched her swiftly to the door. I jumped to my feet and followed them outside.

'What's going to happen to her?' I asked as we crossed the street to the law courts, which also doubled up as the bakery, named, appropriately enough, All Rise.

'This is a railway town, so she'll be tried using the

fast-track method,' replied Mr Lloyd. 'The trial will begin after the 18.24 ceasefire but before the railway militia night raiding parties begin at 20.15. She'll be found guilty, of course, and will receive the penalty demanded by the law.'

'Which is?'

Mr Lloyd turned and stared at me.

'For a first offence, execution.'

'Execution?' I echoed. 'Isn't that a *little* severe?'

'If we didn't execute bankers and rogue traders found guilty of financial mischief, it might give them a clear signal that it's actually okay, and then where would we be?'

'The judge may show mercy,' I said.

'I doubt it,' said Mr Lloyd with something of a cruel smile. 'Judge "Gripper" O'Rourke has taken a *special* interest in this case.'

'Oh dear,' I said, then added: 'Sir, I wonder if you could direct me to the best lawyer in the town?'

'We only have one lawyer in the town, miss, and it's me. I will also be prosecuting this case. You may engage me if you wish to conduct the defence as well – I will make every endeavour to be just and fair.'

'I'm not sure that's allowed,' I replied.

'Me neither,' said Mr Lloyd, 'but it saves a lot of time. Oh, and in case you're thinking of bringing in a lawyer from elsewhere, only Llangurig lawyers can speak at Llangurig trials. Good day, miss.'

And with a tip of his hat, he was gone. I returned to where the others were sitting.

'She's going to be executed,' I said gloomily, 'tonight, and there's not a lawyer to be found in town. We must rescue her.'

'She did break the law,' said Addie. 'What do you think they should have done? Given her a bonus for her daring and ingenuity?'

I took a deep breath. It was time to tell them who she was.

'No, it's just that, to be honest, she's not Laura Scrubb at all. She's actually Princess Shazine, the heir apparent to the Kingdom of Snodd, and I swore to her mother the Queen I'd look after her.'

There was a shocked silence from Addie and Wilson. Wilson said that he doubted this very much as Laura's teeth, nails and skin complaints were hardly princessy, so I told him all about the King and the Queen wanting me to educate the Princess, and how Queen Mimosa used the Sister Organza mind switcheroo to do it.

'Any more surprises?' asked Addie sullenly. 'Another two dozen rubber Dragons or a few wizards or spells or you're actually Princess Tharvina in disguise or something?'

'No,' I said after thinking hard, 'you've got the lot.'

'We'll just tell the judge she's a princess,' said Wilson.

'They're not going to execute royalty. Not even Tharv does that, and he's as mad as a barrel of skunks.'

'Who will believe us?' said Perkins. 'She's in Laura Scrubb's body right now so we can't prove it's *not* Laura – and she did *say* she was Laura.'

'We could contact King Snodd,' suggested Wilson.

'With what?' I said. 'There are no public cross-border phone lines and my conch and last homing snail are in the half-track.'

We lapsed into silence, our appetites lost owing to recent events.

'Okay,' I said, taking out the cash that the Princess had handed me, 'I don't know how we're going to rescue her, but rescue her we will. I need ideas. Here.'

I divided the money equally between Wilson, charged to see whether there was anyone to bribe to postpone the trial, and Addie, charged with finding some transport.

'Transport to where?' she asked, since there was still some doubt as to whether our search was continuing, or whether we were going to head into Cambrianopolis to bargain for Boo's return.

'I'm not sure,' I said, realising that I first needed to find Able Quizzler. 'Just get me some wheels and I'll let you know.'

Wilson and Addie left the pub, leaving Perkins and myself at the table. I beckoned the barmaid over and asked whether she knew where I could find Able Quizzler.

'Able?' she said. 'Are you friends of his?'

'Yes.'

'Then you can pay his unpaid bar bill.'

'More colleagues actually,' I added quickly. 'Do you know where he is?'

'That I do,' she said. 'In fact, I can tell you *precisely* where he is right now.'

'A man of habit?' asked Perkins.

'*Very* fixed in his ways,' said the barmaid. 'You'll find him in the cemetery.'

'A gravedigger, is he?'

'No, he's dead – and has been these past six years.'

Trouble with gravediggers

Llangurig's cemetery was on the north side of the town. It was a dismal place, the grass patchy and the stones streak-stained by the rain. Even the fresh flowers on the graves looked tired, the clouds dark, the wind chill. Row upon row of headstones charted the history of Llangurig's railway conflict from the very first death in 1862 to the most recent, only forty-seven minutes previously. That latest addition was already buried owing to a hyper-efficient funeral service that could have someone in the ground before they were even cold. Ten graves had been dug in readiness for the inevitable casualties that evening, and with eight thousand inhabitants, the occupants of the cemetery outnumbered the Llangurig living five to one, and it was twice the size of the town itself.

'This is grim,' said Perkins as we walked past the headstones, each commemorating a young man or woman's life not lived.

'The loss seems more when you see them laid out like this,' I said.

'It doesn't make much sense,' added Perkins as we

walked along. 'If Quizzler had died, wouldn't Kevin have foreseen it?'

'Kevin doesn't see *everything*,' I replied, 'but I agree it's annoying. We'll find out what we can, grab the Princess and get out of town. Without any evidence about the Eye of Zoltar, we're not going any farther.'

Perkins hailed a passing gravedigger. His clothes were worn but respectable, his hands looked as though they were made of leather, and his shovel had been worn shiny by constant use. The gravedigger introduced himself as something that sounded like 'Dirk', and Perkins explained who we were looking for.

'Kin?' asked Dirk, staring at the pair of us suspiciously.

'A distant cousin,' I said, 'on my mother's side.'

'Ar,' said the gravedigger, 'follow I.'

The gravedigger led us past hundreds of headstones carved with a name, the date and a short epitaph in a typically railwayese style. They ranged from the direct 'Ran out of steam' or 'Hit the buffers' to the more poetic 'Shunted to a quiet corner of the yard' and 'Withdrawn from service'.

We turned left at a crossroads and followed another avenue of headstones.

'You must be kept busy,' I said to the gravedigger.

'Busier than a turkey neck-breaker at Christmas.'

'Nice simile,' said Perkins, 'full of charm.'

'Jus' thar,' said the gravedigger as he pointed at a simple cross marked 'Quizzler' and a six-year-old date.

'Ever meet him?' I asked.

'Only once,' chuckled the gravedigger, 'but he was in no mood for talkin'.'

'You know how he died?'

'Some say it were the grass what killed him.'

I sighed. Gravediggers always spoke in dark riddles. As a student at gravedigger college you'd have to master the art of random quirky banter before they'd even let you touch a spade.

'The grass?' I asked.

'Aye. Was all grass around here when he arrived, and he wasn't brought here by the undertaker, and we didn't dig his grave, neither.'

'Then who did?'

'He done dig it hisself. He done *everythin'* hisself 'cept read the sermon. Delivered hisself he did, then dug his own grave.'

Perkins and I looked at one another.

'So what you're saying,' I said slowly, 'is that he walked in alive, dug his own grave and was then laid into it?'

'Sort of,' said the gravedigger, 'only he didn't walk in here, and wasn't put into the grave. Came in fast he did and buried isself quicker than a sneeze. Heard him the other side of the yard.'

Perkins was becoming exasperated too.

'If I give you some money,' he said, speaking very slowly and firmly, 'would you tell us what the blue blazes you're talking about?'

The gravedigger wagged his finger and laughed again.

'Okay,' I said, 'I've almost got this. He arrived in a hurry but not from the entrances, and buried himself in almost no time at all while making a loud noise?'

'Aye,' said the gravedigger, disappointed at our failure to understand him, 'and you'll get nothing further from me, not till you've learned some smarts.'

The gravedigger turned to walk away, but Perkins called after him.

'Did you just . . . backfill over him after he landed?'

The gravedigger stopped, then turned slowly to face us. His eyes twinkled and he very purposefully looked upwards. I didn't need to follow his gaze; I knew what he meant. Able Quizzler had arrived in the graveyard not by walking, but by *falling*, and if he hit the grass hard enough to bury himself, it was from a great height.

'From a Leviathan, do you suppose?' I asked.

'No other explanation,' said Perkins, 'and Leviathans lead us on to Sky Pirate Wolff, and from there we get to the Eye of Zoltar – or do we?'

'Sadly, no,' I said after a moment's thought. 'We just get to Able Quizzler hitching a ride on a Leviathan. Ralph would have suffered the same fate – only I don't think he had the good luck to fall into a graveyard.'

I stood there for a moment, unsure of what to do. I would risk all our lives if there was evidence of the Eye of Zoltar, but not for evidence of a Leviathan. This was a magic expedition, not one in pursuit of an endangered species, fascinating though that might be.

'Right,' I said, finally coming to a decision, 'once we've got the Princess back we're moving on to Cambrianopolis to negotiate for Boo's release. My brief was to find evidence of the Eye. We don't have any so I'm pulling the plug.'

'Shame,' said Perkins. 'I was looking forward to climbing Cadair Idris and facing off all those terrors. jeopardy tourism has kind of grown on me.'

'Well, it's not growing on me,' I said. 'Come on.'

We walked back towards the entrance to the graveyard after giving the gravedigger a tip. We had almost reached the entrance when Perkins stopped.

'Jennifer?' he said.

'Yes?'

'I was just thinking. I mean, is it even *possible* for someone to bury themselves falling from a great height?'

'What's your point?' I asked.

'I'm thinking perhaps you'd only leave a dent in the ground, if that. Unless . . .'

'Unless what?'

'Unless you were made of something much, much heavier.'

'Like . . . lead?'

Able Quizzler must indeed have come into contact with the Eye of Zoltar. But far from it giving him the power he craved, he had instead been changed to lead, the fate of anyone unskilled who tried to tap its massive powers. He would have been on a Leviathan when it happened, too, and once lead he would simply have toppled off. Being changed to lead wasn't a great way to go, but probably quick.

'Well,' I said, 'Kevin was right about the Eye. Looks like we're heading north after all.'

The fast-track trial

We all reconvened at Mrs Timpson's Battlement Viewing Tea Rooms situated atop the town walls, which, as its name suggested, afforded the many railway and military enthusiasts drawn to Llangurig a clear view of the battles below. We were there for a more culinary reason: Mrs Timpson's was reputedly the best tea rooms in Llangurig, and I wanted at least to savour one last excellent scone, jam and clotted cream before we headed north.

'. . . even if this only shows the Eye of Zoltar was here six years ago, I'm for going on,' I concluded, 'but if anyone wants out, I understand.'

'I've got something to add before you all get too excited,' said Addie. 'I made a few enquiries and everyone who has ventured towards Cadair Idris to look for Sky Pirate Wolff or the Leviathans' Graveyard has vanished without trace.'

'How many?'

'Fifteen expeditions, two hundred and sixty people,' said Addie. 'A hundred per cent fatality rate, and that's weird. Even the most hideously dangerous undertaking leaves *someone*.'

'The Mountain Silurians?' I asked. 'They're pretty unpleasant.'

'Unpleasant but not gratuitously murderous,' replied Addie. 'They let people travel across their territory so long as they get paid in goats. No, I think there's something else. Something we don't know about – a hidden menace waiting for us out there at the mountain. Still want to go there?'

We all exchanged glances.

'You can only be talking to me,' said Wilson with a smile, 'because Addie we know would sooner accept death than dishonour her profession by baling out, and Perkins is as loyal and as unswerving as any man I have ever known.'

Addie and Perkins nodded their agreement at the assessment.

'As for me,' said Wilson, 'that brush with the Cloud Leviathan has really got my ornithological blood racing. Okay, it's not a bird, but the notion of lighter-than-air flight in the animal kingdom is the scientific discovery of the century. I'll be on the cover of *National Geographic*, so long as that woman with the gorillas hasn't done anything exciting that month. Listen, wild Buzonjis wouldn't keep me from this part of the expedition.'

I thanked them all, and asked how everyone had done since we last met. The short answer was 'not very well'. Addie had found us transport in the guise of a battered jeep that was now waiting for us fuelled and oiled at the North Gate.

'The jeep is a bit clapped out,' said Addie, 'but it should get us to Cadair Idris. I've also got eight goats in a trailer to barter safe passage with the Mountain Silurians.'

'Good. Mr Wilson?'

Wilson explained that he had tried a small test bribe on the clerk of the court but was simply met with stony defiance.

'I then went and told Judge Gripper O'Rourke that Laura was a princess.'

'How did that work out?'

'The judge laughed and told me that "everyone tried that" and "to come up with something a little more imaginative".'

'I could *try* magic to spring her,' said Perkins, 'but this is a tricky one. I've never used it *against* the accepted rule of law and . . . and that might cause some morality blowback.'

'Some *what*?' asked Wilson.

'Morality blowback. Using magic to accomplish something against the natural order of justice can do serious damage. To use magic for wrong you have to *believe* the wrong is correct, and I'm kind of thinking that because the Princess was trading fraudulently, somewhere in all of this is a form of justice – even if execution itself is unjustified.'

'Morality and magic is a minefield,' I said. 'It's why wizards never spell death – just newting or stone transformations and stuff. It's why Evil Sorcerer Geniuses always employ minions to do their dirty work. Even someone like Shandar would risk everything if he tried to actually kill someone or something *directly* using magic. Perkins is right. It's too risky.'

We all fell silent for a while. We heard the gates of the town swing shut, and a second or two later the warring railway companies commenced their 18.02 teatime 'Express Battle' special.

We had a good view as the two railway armies locked in combat once more, this time with tanks and flame-throwers. Within a very short time two Trans-Wales Rails armoured bulldozers advanced to lay ballast for the tracks. They might have succeeded, had the earth not collapsed beneath them, the result of some secret tunnelling by Cambrian sappers. As the battle increased in intensity, the Cambrian railwaymen brought out a completed sixty-yard section of track while under cover of a diversionary 'pincer movement' to the south.

As we watched the proceedings, the assistants of Honest Pete and Rock-Steady Eddie communicated by a series of bizarre hand signals to their masters in the street below as to how the battle was faring, and with every sleeper or length of rail that was added or removed, the company's share value rose or fell accordingly. By the time a short volley of mortars heralded the destruction of any small gains twenty-two minutes later, the shares had settled at about the same level as when the battle started. The railway tracks, it should be noted, had not progressed so much as an inch.

The railway enthusiasts who were with us made notes in their books as the dead and wounded were carried off, the town gates opened again and everything returned to Llangurig's version of normal.

'Senseless waste of time, effort and life,' said Perkins.

'So,' I said, checking my watch, 'any ideas on how to spring the Princess?'

There weren't, which was discouraging.

'Okay, then,' I said, 'we'll just have to improvise.'

We paid for the tea and scones and made our way towards the combined bakery and courthouse to take our seats for the trial. It was hot in the courthouse – it would be, since the bread ovens had only just completed the afternoon bake – and the public were busy fanning themselves.

'Where's Perkins?' I said to Wilson, as I'd lost sight of him coming in. He told me he didn't know, and offered to find him, but I said not to worry. I wanted the Princess to see at least two of us there.

She was duly escorted in by the two officers who had arrested her earlier. Mr Lloyd, prosecuting, was sitting at his bench surrounded by a mountain of paperwork. In the Cambrian Empire lawyers were paid not by time worked, but by using a complex algorithm that took into account the weight of the paperwork, the age and height differential between counsel and defendant, recent rainfall and the brevity of the proceedings. It was said the best way to make a profit as a Cambrian lawyer was if you were a tall octogenarian who could generate three tons of paperwork, conduct cases in the rain for no more than three minutes and only prosecute the under-twelves.

'All rise!' said the clerk, and we all rose dutifully as the judge walked in and took his seat. He rummaged for his glasses, and had the court sit before he read the charges. While he did so, the public – there were at least thirty of them, I think – tutted and went 'ooh' and 'aah'. The Princess looked on impassively, but did not glance in our direction. She may have been in the body of Laura, but she wanted to show us she could face the music like a princess if need be.

'How do you plead?' asked the judge.

'Not guilty,' said the Princess, and there were more muted whisperings in the courthouse.

'Nonsense,' said the judge, 'I've seen the evidence and it's highly compelling. Guilty as charged, for which the sentence is death. Anything to say before the punishment is carried out?'

'Yes,' said the Princess, 'actually I do—'

'Fascinating,' said the judge. 'Thank you, Mr Lloyd,

for such a well-tried case. The legal profession may be justly proud of you. What was that? Nineteen seconds?'

'Eighteen and a quarter, M'lud,' said Mr Lloyd, bowing deferentially after consulting a stopwatch. 'A new regional judicial speed record.'

'Good show,' said the judge, signing a docket the clerk had handed him. The scrap of paper was then passed to a bony old man who was sitting on a chair half asleep, and who awoke with a start when prodded.

'Executioner?' said the judge. 'Do your work, but make sure it's a clean cut – not like the messy job you did last time.'

'Yes, My Lord,' said the executioner.

I jumped up.

'Objection!' I shouted, and several people in the courtroom gasped at my audacity. 'This trial makes a mockery of the high levels of judicial excellence that we have come to expect from the great nation that is the Cambrian Empire. I counter that everyone has the right to be represented by counsel, to be judged by their peers, and all evidence subjected to scrutiny before any decision is reached. I move that this farce be declared a mistrial and the prisoner released forthwith!'

There was silence in the court. It wasn't a great speech. To be honest, it wasn't even a *good* speech, but several of the public were moved to tears and shook me by the hand, and I even heard a sob from someone in the front row.

'Your impassioned appeal has moved me, miss,' said the judge, dabbing his eyes with a handkerchief, 'and I accede to your wishes. The trial will be declared void, the prisoner will be pardoned and released, and her criminal record expunged, with our apologies.'

He indicated to the clerk, who swiftly drafted a pardon for the Princess.

'Th-thank you, M'lud,' I said, surprised by the results.

The judge signed the pardon with a flourish.

'There,' he said, handing the Princess the pardon.

'Thank you, M'lud,' said the Princess, then added, as soon as she had read it: 'Wait a moment, this is post-dated. I'm not pardoned for another hour – until *after* the execution.'

'How . . . ironically tragic,' said the judge. 'Executioner? Get on with it.'

'That's not fair!' I shouted.

'You shouldn't confuse justice with the law, my dear,' said the judge. 'I have done everything that the law and you have asked: I have been both resolute and merciful. Now stay your hand, or you shall be arrested for contempt.'

I felt myself grow hot. The veins in my temples began to thump and a prickly heat ran down my back as my anger rose. It would end badly if I went into a rage, and I battled to keep it down. I squeezed the chair in front of me and the wooden back-brace exploded into fragments in my hands. I felt a howling in my ears, which then became a whistling; a high-pitched squeal that . . . *sounded like a train whistle.* Everyone in the courtyard had heard it too, and it had come from outside. My temper subsided as the judge, the executioner, Mr Lloyd and the public all hurried out to see what was going on. I took a deep breath and beckoned to the Princess, who hopped over the barrier between the combined witness box and flour bin.

'All we have to do is keep you hidden for an hour,' I said, taking her hand and heading for the door. 'Quick, to the North Gate.'

We made our way to the town square and noticed that everyone was streaming out of the main gates with whoops of joy and resounding cheers. Hats were being thrown in the air, old women were crying in doorways and a brass band had struck up a triumphant tune. Just beyond the town gates I could see a shiny locomotive, big and bold and hissing with steam, where less than an hour ago there had been only battlefield.

'Go with Wilson,' I said to the Princess. 'I'll be with you as soon as I can. Something's . . . not right. Wilson, use force to protect her if necessary.'

'All other considerations secondary?'

'Exactly.'

I left them and ran out of the gates to find that ahead of me a mile of shiny new track connected the depots of Trans-Wales Rails and Cambrian Railway. The rails were dead straight, the sleepers perfectly aligned and the ballast looked as though laid carefully by hand. The jubilant townsfolk and equally jubilant and now very wealthy railway troops were dancing in the dust outside the short connecting piece of rail while the railway militia generals were shaking each other's hands in an annoyed but relieved fashion. The line was to be shared; profits would be equal; and better still, there would be no more senseless loss of life over an insignificant mile of railway line somewhere in the forgotten wilds of the Cambrian Empire.

'In less than ten minutes!' said one man, dancing past me.

'It is a miracle!' shouted another.

'It's nothing of the sort,' I muttered through gritted teeth, 'it's *Perkins* frittering his life away.'

I looked around, knowing he would still be about. Such a feat would have exhausted him, and he'd need help getting to the North Gate. I eventually found him sitting on a bench a little way away.

'That was quite something,' I said, my voice trembling. His face was obscured by his hands, and I dared not see what price his magic had exacted this time around.

'It was a win-win,' he said in a tired voice. 'My timing was good and the Princess lives, yes?'

'Yes.'

'And the Llangurig Railway War is over?'

'It is.'

He looked up at me and smiled. A mile of track in under ten minutes is a fearfully large spell. By my best estimation he was now in his early fifties. His hair was streaked with grey and there were wrinkle lines about his mouth and eyes. A small mole on his cheek was now more prominent, and he was wearing reading glasses.

'I thought it would only take six years from me,' he said with a smile, 'but it took over twenty. But then, I'm not so young as I was.'

'It's not funny,' I said. 'Here, take my arm.'

I pulled him to his feet and we stumbled back through the main gates and the deserted town. 'For Sale' signs had already sprung up, and townsfolk were loading handcarts with their possessions and beginning to move out, the town's purpose now vanished with the arrival of the railway. We were passing a parade of shops when I stopped outside a second-hand furniture store and stared in the window. I moved closer. This was *not* what I had expected.

'Will you look at that,' said Perkins with a smile as he followed my gaze, 'he'll never live this down.'

Sitting in the antique shop's window and surrounded by several pieces of furniture, a moose's head and various items of bric-a-brac was a large rubber Dragon, its scales perfect, its mouth open and a large array of black teeth on display in its rubbery mouth.

'I can turn him back instantly if you want,' said Perkins. 'It'll only take ten years off me.'

'*Absolutely not.* Your spelling days are over until we get you back to Kazam. I'll go and make enquiries while you sit down and rest.'

A bell rang above my head as I opened the door, and a few seconds later a middle-aged woman appeared from the back room. She stared at me over her half-moon glasses, and didn't look the type to take any nonsense, nor give any.

'I'm interested in the rubber Dragon,' I said, touching Colin's rubber scales with an index finger. In life they would have been hard and unyielding, but here they felt soft and pliable, like a marshmallow. 'Is it for sale?'

'Everything's for sale,' she said, 'make me an offer.'

I emptied the contents of my pockets on to the counter. There was a shade over eight hundred plotniks. The woman looked at the money, then chuckled derisively.

'The rubber scrap value alone is fifteen hundred. Give me two thousand and it's yours.'

'I don't have two thousand,' I told her. 'Eight hundred and an IOU for the rest.'

'I don't take IOUs.'

'It's all I have.'

'Then you aren't going to own a rubber Dragon today, and given that Llangurig is being abandoned, he'll be sold to the recyclers tomorrow, and made into bicycle inner tubes and pencil erasers.'

It wouldn't be a dignified end for such a magnificent beast, but I had an idea. It wasn't a good one. In fact, I think it might have been one of my worst, but I needed to buy Rubber Colin before anyone figured out who or what he really was.

'Then I'll trade,' I said. 'You give me the rubber Dragon, and I'll give you . . . me.'

I took my indentured servitude papers out of my pocket. I had two years to run at Kazam and after that I was free – or free to sell myself for another year or two, or whatever I wanted.

'I'll give you a year of me,' I said. 'I work hard and learn quick. That's got to be worth two thousand any day of the week.'

The shopkeeper looked at my orphan papers and stared at me suspiciously.

'There's something I'm missing here,' she said. 'No one in their right mind would swap a year of themselves for a rubber Dragon – unless . . .'

Her voice trailed off as a look of sudden realisation crossed her face. All of a sudden, she *knew*. A Dragon – *any* Dragon, in any condition, transformed or otherwise – would be worth a thousand orphan years. The cat was now out of the bag, and I wasn't sure what to do. I could have tried to steal Rubber Colin but wasn't sure how far I'd get with something I could barely lift, and besides, this was Llangurig, and it was perfectly legal to have a weapon hidden beneath the counter, and doubly legal – encouraged, actually – to use it on shoplifters. We stared at one another for a moment in silence.

I took back my indentured papers and pushed the eight hundred plotniks and an IOU for a further twelve hundred across the counter. We weren't bargaining any longer. I was going to tell her how it was.

'This for the rubber Dragon. Take it or we take him and you get nothing.'

'And how do you propose to take him?' she asked, her hand reaching under the counter.

'I have a sorcerer outside who can transform him back to a living, breathing and very angry Dragon in a twinkling,' I said. 'I know Colin personally, and believe me, he won't be happy to have been turned into rubber. Take the money. It's the best you're going to get.'

'You can't threaten me,' she replied defiantly. 'The law is on my side.'

I leaned forward and lowered my voice.

'And magic is on mine. Which do you think the more powerful?'

We stared at one another for a moment until, finally, she saw sense.

'Looks like you're the owner of a rubber Dragon,' she said, taking the money and the IOU.

'A wise choice,' I said in a quiet voice, 'but there's one other thing: I need a hand trolley.'

A few minutes later I had loaded Rubber Colin on to the trolley and was wheeling him along the street, Perkins at my side, steadying the rubber creature, which wobbled about all over the place in a very undignified manner. It was about the size of a pony, but weighed, thankfully, only about a tenth as much.

We stumbled to the North Gate, where Addie, Wilson and the Princess were waiting next to a battered jeep that was attached to a trailer that contained eight 'barter quality' goats.

'I'm not going to ask where you found that,' said Addie, pointing at Rubber Colin, 'but it's going to be a tight fit.'

It *was* a tight fit. Ridiculously so. But with Rubber Colin in the back of the open jeep, Wilson and Perkins on either side of him and with me and the Princess sharing the passenger seat, we could just about fit in. Addie coaxed the jeep into life.

'Is Perkins okay?' asked Addie. 'He looks kind of . . . old.'

'He's fine,' I said, even though he wasn't, not really. 'Let's just drive.'

So we did. We took the rough unmade road towards Cadair Idris and after an hour had passed we knew that the Princess's pardon was now official, and she was free.

We drove in almost unparalleled discomfort for another two hours until we reached a waterfall, where Addie knew there was a dry cave hidden behind some rhododendron bushes. We stopped and then sat in silence for some time, not moving, the eight goats bleating plaintively as they weren't used to being in a trailer and could smell the water. It had been a worrying afternoon, and the positive outcome of the trial notwithstanding, we could all feel the stress within the small group. We ignored one another for the forty minutes it took to settle in the cave, all of us working at our chores without talking. I chased out a boogaloo that had taken refuge while Addie and the Princess went to tether the goats near the river, and Perkins and Wilson wandered off to look for fireberries. Colin stayed in the back of the jeep, his lifeless rubber eyes staring unseeing into the gathering gloom.

We reconvened when the fireberries were ignited, the daylight had gone and the supper was about ready. It was Spam, but everyone was too tired to complain.

It was the Princess who finally broke the silence.

'Thank you,' she said, 'all of you. I knew you wouldn't let me down.'

'You should thank Perkins,' said Addie, pointing to where he was sitting on a stone farther back in the cave. He looked preoccupied and in that sort of dark place where you shun companionship, but are secretly glad when someone forces it upon you.

'Did he give more of himself?' asked the Princess anxiously. 'In years, I mean?'

I nodded.

'Over twenty.'

'Oh,' she said in a quiet voice. 'I must speak with him.'

She went over and spoke to him in a quiet voice. She took his hand in hers, and I saw him shrug, then smile, then nod some thanks of his own.

We opened some tins of rice pudding, which, along with the Spam and some pickled eggs, was all Addie could find for provisions at short notice, and washed it all down with a cup of tea.

Conversation after dinner was muted. We had come a long way and each of us had dodged death at least twice. The Princess kindly offered to tell us how hedge funds operated, but I could tell her heart wasn't in it and there were no takers. There would be no spin-the-bottle, no stories. The search had suddenly become more dangerous, more *real*.

Seven o'clock passed and no homing snail had arrived. I felt very much on my own, with only my wits to guide us.

The Princess placed her bedroll next to mine.

'I'm not doing very well, am I?' she said once we'd settled down and were staring at the roof of the cave, ready for sleep. 'I mean, this adventure is meant to make me less bratty and more wise and thoughtful and stuff but all that's happened is that you've all put your lives on the line to save me, but I've done little except need to be rescued. I feel like the worst princess cliché.'

'It could be worse,' I said, 'you could be screaming and swooning or demanding a bath in rabbit's milk or something.'

She agreed with this, and there was a pause. I hadn't much cared for her at the beginning, but I'd be sorry to lose her now. And not just because there was the hint of a fine queen about her, but because I actually quite liked her. I recalled Kevin's words: *You will be saved by people who do not like you, nor are like you, nor that you like.* It had been true then, but it wasn't so true now. None of us had saved the Princess from the executioner because she was just the Princess. We had saved her because she was part of whatever made us *us*.

'We'd have done the same if you were Laura Scrubb,' I said. 'We don't abandon our friends.'

'I'm glad,' said the Princess. 'Your friendship and trust mean more to me than everything I have, or everything I will ever be.'

There was no answer to this, so I nodded to say that I understood.

'What did you say to Perkins?'

'I conferred upon him the Dukedom of Bredwardine

– in recognition of his sacrifices in the service of the Crown. I know the honour system is the worst kind of bullshit, but the Snodd dukedom also allows the holder a twenty-five per cent discount at the Co-op, free bus and rail travel and two free seats at the Wimbledon finals every year.'

'He deserved it,' I said, then added in a louder voice so everyone else could hear: 'Don't tell the Federation, but I'm upgrading this search to quest status.'

The flickering light of the fireberry played upon the roof.

'About time too,' came Addie's voice in the darkness.

To the foot of the mountain

That night, I dreamt of my parents again. They were scolding me for leaving my conch on the half-track and telling me that I couldn't marry Perkins because he was 'old enough to be my father'. Then I was dreaming of Kevin Zipp, who said he had come to say goodbye and to not 'lose sight of all that is good'. After that I was chasing after Curtis and the half-track, and when I stopped and turned around, five Hotax were staring at me with their small pig-like eyes, and one of them was holding a surgeon's saw and another a bag of kapok stuffing and a sewing needle. I'd turned to run but found I couldn't for some reason, and that's when I was shaken awake. It was Addie.

She put her fingers to her lips and beckoned me to the rhododendrons that were hiding the entrance to the cave. She gently pushed the branches apart to reveal two pale blue Skybus trucks parked on the road next to the waterfall, almost identical to the ones we had seen before. The drivers seemed to be comparing notes about the journey, and from the manner in which their large, four-wheel-drive trucks were parked, one seemed to be heading off in the direction of the Cadair range, and the other, mud-spattered and dusty, seemed to be returning.

As we watched they shook hands, climbed into the cabs of their trucks and drove off in the directions I had guessed.

I looked at Addie and raised an eyebrow. She shrugged. She had no idea what they were doing here either.

'There are no manufacturing facilities in this direction,' she said, 'or at least, nothing that I know about.'

'Smuggling?' I said.

'It's possible,' said Addie, striding across to look at the tyre tracks. 'The Mountain Silurians used to illegally export spice, but if they are still doing it, why use Skybus vehicles?'

'I've counted at least six while I've been here,' I said, 'all heading to and from the border. Aviation parts, you say?'

'So I'm told,' said Addie, squatting down to study the tyre tracks, 'but I've never looked inside the lorries, so I don't know for sure. Notice anything odd?'

We were at a muddy section of the road, and Addie was pointing at the tracks. One was deep and well defined while the other vehicle had hardly made any imprint at all.

'One's laden and the other not,' I said. 'So what?'

'Because,' said Addie, 'the one that's heavy is the

one going *towards* the mountains – the lighter of the two is coming *out*.'

'They're delivering components *to* the mountains?' I said. 'That makes no sense at all.'

It wasn't the first time I'd noticed this. The first two Skybus lorries I'd seen had been halted while their drivers chatted. The one heading out accelerated away more easily than the one heading in.

'These vehicles are delivering something to the Idris mountains,' I said slowly, 'but what?'

'I don't know,' said Addie, 'but I'd like to find out.'

'What about Curtis and the half-track?' I asked.

'Just there,' said Addie, pointing at a ghost of an imprint on the dusty roadway, 'and by the look of it, he passed through here yesterday afternoon about midday. If he stopped for the night, he may be only six or seven hours' drive ahead.'

'It's not so much his capture or punishment I'm interested in,' I said, 'even though such a thing would be welcome. I'm really after the half-track, or to be more exact, my bag and what's in it.'

It was the conch, of course, the Helping Hand™ – I'd get hell from Lady Mawgon for losing it – and the letter of credit to negotiate for Boo's release.

'We better get a move on, then,' said Addie.

Perkins rubbed his head when I woke him. His new age had established itself more firmly overnight. His voice was deeper, his face more lined, his hair greyer. He moved with the more measured certainty of someone entering their fifth decade, and seemed more thoughtful in his responses – and was painfully stiff after the cold night in the cave.

'Ooh, bloody hell,' he said, rubbing his legs.

'Welcome to the club,' said Wilson, who'd had longer to acclimatise to the myriad changes that advanced age wrought upon the human body, 'and don't worry if you start forgetting the names of things or being less sharp than you once were. You may even have trouble . . . have trouble, um . . .'

'Finishing your sentences?' put in Perkins.

'Exactly so. All entirely normal. But with age comes wisdom.'

'I think wisdom comes with years, not age,' replied Perkins sadly. 'I've managed to separate the two. I think I'm going to be old *without* wisdom.'

'If that *is* the case,' said Wilson, 'you won't be alone.'

Addie suggested we let the Skybus trucks have half an hour's start so we would not be observed, but it took that long to get the goats herded into the trailer as they had a certain *bounciness* about them that didn't permit easy herding.

'They're called ISGs,' explained Addie once we had rounded up the goats and coaxed the ancient jeep's engine into life, 'for International Standard Goat.

They're a sort of one-size-fits-all-goat that does everything pretty well: climb, give lots of milk, soft fur, excellent meat. It was the legacy of Emperor Tharv's father, who became convinced that what the world really needed was animal standardisation. He managed to standardise the goat, honey bee, badger and hamster, and was working on the bird kingdom when he died.'

'It's why so many birds are small and brown,' explained Wilson, 'so he had moderate success.'

We drove for two hours, stopping to fill up the jeep's leaky radiator three times. We climbed steadily up the rough, winding track and once on the high Plynlimon pass we stopped for a moment to stretch our legs, change drivers and make a short devotion at the shrine dedicated to the once popular but now little known St Aosbczkcs, the patron saint of fading relevance. This done, we surveyed the scene that was laid before us.

Below us were bumpy foothills through which we could see the road slowly winding down towards the fertile valley floor, a random patchwork of natural woodland and open grassland. But beyond this valley and dominating our view was the place in which the Leviathans' Graveyard and Sky Pirate Wolff's hideout were most likely to be hidden: Cadair Idris. Although I'd seen pictures, the mountain was even more spectacular in real life. Sheer walls towered vertically from the valley floor, presenting a dizzying pinnacle of grey rock that was awe-inspiring and terrifying in equal measure. High waterfalls cascaded into space from high on the sheer rock walls where the water dispersed into clouds of water droplets that formed clouds that clung to the lower reaches of the mountain. Although it was reputedly the second-highest mountain in the unUnited Kingdoms after the peak named T4 in the Trollvanian range, the exact height of Cadair Idris had never been fully determined. The summit had never been out of cloud in living memory, making a triangulation survey impossible. 'Between six and seven thousand feet' was a pretty good guess. When the sun rose in the morning, the shadow of the rock would extend across three kingdoms.

'From here on in we're in Mountain Silurian territory,' said Addie.

'Can you see the others?' asked Wilson as we gazed out across the landscape.

Perkins spelled himself a hand telescope by creating two 'O' shapes with his index fingers and thumbs and conjuring up a glass lens in each. Early versions of the spell required an operator to focus the telescope manually, but later releases had autofocus as standard, with a zoom feature and auto-stabilisation useful add-ons.

'I can see the half-track. Looks like it's a couple of miles from the base of the mountain. Think he's still got your conch?'

'He didn't try and sell the Helping Hand™ in

Llangurig,' I said, for if he had he'd make several times the price of a handmaiden, 'so I'm hoping.'

Perkins scanned the parts of the road that were visible among the low hills and wooded areas. 'The Skybus truck is not far behind him.'

Because they were still moving, it seemed logical to presume that neither of them had encountered the Mountain Silurians, or if they had, goats had been successfully bartered.

We moved off soon after and as we descended into the dense woodlands of the Mountain Silurians' land, we noted how the increased rainfall had made everything lush and moist. Bottle-green moss grew in abundance on the rocks and trees, lichen clung doggedly to anything it could find, and we were constantly fording small streams and rivers.

All this time, the overwhelming size of the bleak pinnacle of rock that was Cadair Idris loomed over us menacingly. A better place for a pirate hideout would be impossible to imagine.

'Where are the Mountain Silurians?' asked the Princess. 'I thought you said they were fearless tribespeople who would kill us all for amusement unless we gave them goats?'

'I was wondering that myself,' said Addie. 'To get this far into their territory without being threatened with dismemberment and asked to pay tribute is unusual – I hope nothing's happened to them.'

'I'm really hoping something *has* happened to them,' said the Princess. 'Any jeopardy we can avoid is one more step toward survival.'

'I'll just be glad to quietly sit down somewhere with my pipe and a pair of slippers,' said Perkins, coming over a bit fiftyish, 'and read the paper.'

'You don't have a pipe,' I pointed out, 'or slippers.'

'Or a paper, yes, agreed – but there's a first time for everything.'

'Slow down,' I said, pointing to where a light blue vehicle had stopped ahead of us in a clearing. Addie pulled the jeep off the road and parked behind an oak tree. It was the Skybus truck. The driver had climbed out and was stretching his legs, then he reached into his cab, took out a roll of loo paper and walked off into the forest.

'Stay here,' said Addie.

She jumped out of the jeep and darted forward noiselessly, stopped for a moment, looked around and then moved forward again. Within a minute she was at the back of the truck, had opened the rear doors and looked inside. Just as quickly she shut the doors again, and slipped into the undergrowth. The driver duly returned, the truck restarted and then drove off towards the mountain. Half a minute later Addie rejoined us. She didn't look too happy.

'Everything okay?' I asked.

'I'm not sure,' she said, pointing behind us, 'and we've got company.'

I turned around to find that a dozen or so warriors riding Buzonjis had crept up on us completely silently, and were now less than twenty paces away. Each warrior was large, tanned and amply but not skilfully covered in blue warpaint. Every one of them was armed with a short sword and a lance, upon the point of which was a human skull, the steel tip of the lance piecing the top of the skullcap. These heads were traditionally harvested by lance in battle while in the charge, and remained there as a trophy. The warriors were all scowling at us in probably the most unpleasant and unwelcoming way I had ever witnessed. I heard Wilson swallow nervously. We didn't need to guess who they might be. They were the feared Mountain Silurians.

The Mountain Silurians

'All hail Glorious Geraint the Great,' said Addie, bowing low, 'the gutsy, gallant and gracious gatekeeper of the great green grassy northern grounds.'

It seemed, from Addie's flowery and clearly overblown greetings, that the Silurian chief himself had graced us with his presence.

We all bowed as Geraint the Great looked on imperiously, while the Buzonjis stamped their feet impatiently. After a pause that felt like ten minutes but was probably less then twenty seconds, Geraint the Great looked at one of his advisers, a giant of a woman dressed in the skin of a Welsh leopard, who nodded.

'Your alliteration is acceptable albeit mildly simplistic,' said Geraint. 'What do you seek, Addie the Tour Guide, champion of the blade, younger daughter of Owen the Dead, holder of the Tourist Good Conduct medal?'

'Our lives are in your hands,' continued Addie, bowing again and continuing the long-winded formal greeting. 'We wish only peace and goodwill, and are merely travellers seeking to pass through your sacred grounds.'

'To where?' asked Geraint.

'To seek the legendary Leviathans' Graveyard on Cadair Idris, Your Greatness, to venture there and return, safely and without hindrance.'

'The Rock Goddess shall not be defiled,' he intoned angrily, while the rest of the warriors muttered darkly to themselves. 'You shall be sacrificed to the mountain, your blood splashed about the rocks and your rotting carcasses picked apart by the condor. The mountain shall be appeased. You will die. I, Geraint the Great, have spoken.'

'We have brought gifts,' said Addie.

There was a pause.

'The mountain may be appeased . . . in other ways,' said Geraint the Great. 'We accept your gifts . . . so long as they're not more of those bloody goats. All we ever get given is goats, and let me tell you, we're sick of them. Sick of the sight of them, sick of the smell of them, and sick of the taste of them. Isn't that right, lads?'

The warriors gave out a hearty 'Uuh!' sort of noise and waved their spears in the air.

'We have so many goats,' continued Geraint the Great in an exasperated tone, 'that we even have to sell them at below market value to those milksops in Llangurig. If anyone were ever to try and offload those same goats back to us, our anger would be great, our violence most savage.'

'O-kay,' said Addie. 'Please wait, Your Greatness, while I consult with my fellow travellers.'

She turned to us.

'Looks like I was misinformed over the whole goat thing,' she said in a whisper.

'It explains why cheap goats are flooding the Llangurig Commodities Market,' said the Princess thoughtfully. 'How fascinating.'

'Not *really* important right now, ma'am,' said Addie. 'Has anyone got anything else we can barter?'

'I have two thousand plotniks,' said Wilson, opening his wallet. 'It's all I have in the world but you are welcome to it.'

'Any good?' I said to Addie.

'They're not fond of cash,' she replied, 'but I'll try.'

'Gorgeous Geraint the Great,' said Addie, turning back to the warriors, 'as weary travellers of limited means, we can offer only two thousand plotniks.'

The warriors all laughed uproariously.

'We despise your abstract monetary concepts. Value should lie in the commodity, and not be assigned arbitrarily to a device of no intrinsic value in itself.'

'I like this bunch,' whispered the Princess, 'they *totally* talk my language.'

'So we only barter,' continued Geraint the Great, 'but no more goats. We want washing machines, food mixers, toasters and other consumer durables. That nice man in the half-track gave us his iPod.'

That explained how Curtis got past, at least. We told him we had none of these things, nor any reasonable chance of finding any at short notice.

'Very well,' replied Geraint, 'you will return the way you came and we will take the novelty rubber Dragon in exchange for your lives.'

As he said it he pointed at Rubber Colin, who was still sitting, very much made of rubber, in the back of the jeep.

'The . . . novelty rubber Dragon is not for trade,' I said.

The chief rolled off his horse in a less-than-expert fashion and drew his sword.

'Then you will die,' said the warrior chief, 'and painfully – except for Addie, who will do our washing and cleaning for the rest of her natural life.'

Addie drew out her dagger and glared at the warriors.

'I will die protecting my friends.'

They were fine words and I knew she was good in a fight, but a dozen Mountain Silurians armed to the teeth against a twelve-year-old wasn't a fight I'd be betting on any time soon.

'Wait!' said the Princess. 'I can help you.'

'You can iron?' said the chief. 'That would indeed be a game-changer.'

'No,' said the Princess. 'I'll help you change your financially crippling goat surplus into a valuable trading commodity.'

Geraint looked at the Princess and narrowed his eyes.

'It's an attractive idea,' he said. 'We have thousands of the blasted things. How?'

'Well,' said the Princess, taking a deep breath, 'we would first form a Goat Trading Corporation and use this to bring together all the other goat-producing tribes in order to control the number of goats moving on to the market. Instead of buyers dictating goat prices based on free supply, the goat-producing tribes can limit production and peg their value to an agreed minimum goat price so that all producers get a fair deal. We can couple this with an advertising strategy to increase goat use awareness among the public, and even develop a breeding programme to generate expensive limited-edition goats for collectors. I think we can increase the value of goats tenfold in as little as six months, so long as all the other goat-producing tribes agree to join us.'

'What's she talking about?' whispered Addie.

'I have absolutely no idea,' I whispered back.

Geraint the Great stared at the Princess for a long time, then replaced his sword in its scabbard.

'It shall be so,' he said. 'You will consult with our accountant, Pugh the Numbers.'

One of the neater warriors climbed off his Buzonji as Geraint remounted his, and after Geraint had told us we were 'the guests of the Siluri', they were all gone, leaving the Princess to explain her complex marketing plans in detail to Pugh the Numbers.

It was almost an hour before we were back on the road again.

Cavi homini

'That's kind of weird,' said the Princess once we had driven a mile or two down the road in silence. We had dumped the trailer and freed the goats, so although still cramped in the jeep, we were at least a little faster.

'What's weird?' I asked. 'There's a wide choice out here.'

'The *quantity* of goats involved. Pugh the accountant said that Skybus Aeronautics gave them two thousand goats a month as payment for mining rights at Cadair Idris.'

'What were they mining?'

The Princess shrugged.

'He didn't say. But because the contract was well drafted, they couldn't convert the goats into something more usable. At least, not until now. I think the Goat Marketing Board will be a serious earner for the Mountain Silurians. It might even civilise them.'

'You did say that peace would be brought about only through economic means,' I observed.

'I did, didn't I?'

We reached the farthest extent of the wooded area

a half-hour later, and Addie pulled into the shade of a large lime tree. We climbed out to consider our next move.

'There's at least a mile of open country to the base of the mountain,' said Addie, peering at the landscape through binoculars, 'and we must be cautious – a lot of people have vanished travelling this way.'

I looked up at the sheer grey mass of Cadair Idris, the top swathed in clouds, and saw, for the first time, that one side of the rocky pinnacle seemed to have the remnants of a stairway cut into the stone. The road upon which we were parked led to the mountain, then branched to where we could see that some buildings had been constructed beneath the almost vertical southern face. They seemed quite new, too. I nudged Perkins and pointed. He spelled himself a hand telescope again and stared for a moment at the distant buildings.

'Several large buildings,' he said, 'and a barbed-wire perimeter with lots of people milling about. Looks like a manufacturing facility of some sort. The Skybus truck has just arrived and the gates are being opened to allow it to enter.'

'Manufacturing?' I said. 'Out here?'

'Looks like it. With a sizeable workforce, too, but they're too far away to see details.'

'Someone not subject to the hundred per cent fatality index, at any rate,' I said.

'Pugh the Numbers called them *Cavi homini,*' said the Princess.

Addie laughed and I asked her what was so funny.

'It's like Cloud Leviathan graveyards and Sky Pirate Wolff and the Eye of Zoltar – myths. The *Cavi homini* are spooks, bogles, mysterious men without morals, or form. They take what they want, and nothing can kill them. It is said they are only empty walking clothes, with nothing inside. The translation from Latin is—'

'Hollow Men,' I said with a shiver.

'Yes,' said Addie with a frown. 'You have these fairy stories in the Kingdom of Snodd as well?'

'No,' I said, 'we've got them for real, as have you. We call them drones. They are used by . . .'

I stopped talking as several pieces of a large and very unseen jigsaw puzzle that was hovering above me locked into place. The Mighty Shandar used drones, owned a large share of Skybus Aeronautics, and here in the empty land near Cadair Idris, Hollow Men were manufacturing something for Skybus and then shipping it out in the trucks we had just seen.

'Addie,' I said, 'just what did you see in the back of the Skybus truck?'

'Nothing,' she said, 'it was completely empty.'

'It couldn't have been,' I said. 'They come in heavy and go out light – you said so yourself.'

'I did say that, yes. The empty lorry I saw was one of the heavy ones being driven in.'

'Then there's *less than nothing* in the light ones going out?'

Addie shrugged.

'I don't get it,' said the Princess.

'Sometimes when magic and the Mighty Shandar are involved,' I said, 'it's better not to know the truth.'

'Jenny, I've found the half-track,' said Perkins, who had focused his fingerscope on the side of the mountain where I had seen the stone steps.

'And?'

'The vehicle's empty, but halfway to the top I can see a small figure – Curtis. I'd recognise that bandana anywhere. What do we do?'

'Do what we planned and climb Cadair Idris,' I said, 'by way of the steps, preferably.'

'And the Skybus facility and the Hollow Men?' asked Addie.

I shrugged.

'They're what – two miles away? I say we worry about them if they start heading our way.'

So that's what we decided to do. We got back in the jeep and headed off over the open land towards the mountain. I say 'open land' but that was true only in that there were no trees. The road rose and fell with the contours, and then tipped into a shallow ravine where the river crossed our path.

Addie slowed to a stop when we reached the river,

and we looked around at the morbid sight that met our eyes. We didn't speak for some moments.

'Holy cow,' said Perkins finally.

Addie switched off the engine and we climbed out. It was a medium-sized river, stony and fast moving and no more than a couple of feet deep. But it wasn't the river that we had stopped to see, it was the *bones*. There were, quite literally, thousands of them. All human, and in places piled so thick that they had clogged the river and raised the water level. There were vehicles, too. Some overturned by winter floods, others corroded to nothing and a few that looked as though they had been there less than a year.

'I'm thinking we've just discovered what happened to everyone who headed this way,' said Addie, 'ambushed and massacred.'

'Do you think the Mountain Silurians aim to kill us anyway?' asked Wilson. 'That they aim to kill us anyway?'

'After all my financial advice,' said the Princess, 'that would be a pretty dismal thing to do.'

Addie had approached the river and knelt down to inspect the bones.

'It won't be the Siluri,' said Addie, 'they're honourable people, if a little violent and not very sophisticated.'

She held up a cleanly sliced ulna, then a lower jaw cleaved neatly sideways.

'No, these are random wounds by a swiftly wielded

long sword. These people were overcome not by skill, but by numbers.'

'Drones,' I said. 'Hollow Men.'

We looked around nervously, but there was nothing – just the babbling of the brook, the gurgle of water through rocks.

'Over here,' said Wilson, who was standing next to a Land Rover half submerged in the river. The canvas top and seats had rotted, and the keys were still in the ignition. In the back were rain-stained sketchbooks full of illustrations of the Cloud Leviathan, and notebooks packed with notes, observations, discoveries.

'A scientific expedition,' said Wilson. 'All that learning. For nothing.'

Addie drew her dagger and looked around. We were in a dip in the ground. It was a bad place to stop and a good place to attack, depending on your perspective.

'These were all attacked *returning*,' I said quietly. 'Look at the direction in which the vehicles are pointing.'

Everyone looked. All the vehicles were headed towards the road we had just come in on. All these travellers had discovered secrets out here – Leviathans, Hollow Men, even something about Sky Pirate Wolff and possibly the Eye of Zoltar – but the secrets had stayed secrets; dead men and women tell no tales.

'You were right, Addie,' said Perkins, 'there *is* a hidden menace waiting for us out here. But even

Hollow Men have to come from somewhere – and the closest place is that facility. Even if they started to march right now, we'd still have half an hour or more to get away.'

'I think not,' said the Princess, who had moved away from the group and was staring at the ground near a small grassy hollow. 'We're surrounded.'

We joined her, and she pointed to four swords that were buried up to their hilts in the ground.

But it wasn't the swords alone that worried us. Positioned around them were four neat stacks of clothes tied up with string. There were trousers, shirts, pairs of shoes, gloves and jackets, ties and hats. All identical, all carefully folded and waiting to be conjured into life to do their master's bidding. Drones.

'All these people were killed by a small drone army, eager and willing to do one thing and one thing only,' I said. 'To stop anyone returning from Cadair Idris.'

'It would explain why Geraint the Great wanted my entire plan for the Goat Marketing Board up front,' said the Princess. 'He knew that people never return.'

'But why?' asked Perkins. 'What's the secret?'

'I'm only guessing here,' I said, 'but perhaps the facility we saw is a manufacturing facility for hollow suits for the drones to wear. Perhaps the magic is in the weave.'

'If that was so,' said Addie, 'the lorries would come

out heavier than they go in, but they don't, they're *lighter* on the way out.'

'And yet the lorry you saw coming in, the heavy one, was empty?' said Perkins.

'I know,' said Addie, 'it doesn't make any sense.'

'I've got a feeling it won't just be about Cloud Leviathans and Sky Pirate Wolff,' I said, 'it will be about drones, the Mighty Shandar and Skybus Aeronautics.'

Perkins looked around at the scene of the massacre.

'And I've a nasty feeling that our enlightenment may be short lived.'

'You say the jolliest things,' said Wilson, 'but we're not dead yet. Let's get going.'

Cadair Idris

I instructed the others to pick up half a dozen discarded swords just in case and we climbed back aboard the jeep in a subdued mood. We drove up and out of the shallow ravine, then across the empty grassland. As we drove, the mountain seemed to loom over us even more oppressively. All we could see now was a thin trail of cloud blowing from the summit high above. Now alert to drone clothes-packs, we noted several more on the way, all identical – a package of clothes with shoes and hat, tied up with string with a sword close by.

We parked next to the empty half-track and I rummaged through our baggage. Mercifully for us, Curtis was as lazy as he was unpleasant, and aside from taking all the cash, everything else was left untouched. My Helping Hand™ was still there, as was the letter of credit with which to negotiate for Boo's release. More importantly, there was also my last homing snail and the conch. I tried to raise Tiger straight away, but there was nothing but static and sounds of the sea from the conch. I'd not heard from them for over twenty-four hours – not even a homing snail – and I was beginning to get nervous.

'What are you doing?' I called to Perkins, who was twenty yards away, treading stealthily in the direction from which we had just come.

'See that bundle of drone clothes over there?' he called.

'Yes?'

'Watch.'

He took another six steps and the bundle of clothes sprang into life like a jack-in-the-box. Since the clothes were stacked in the vertical order in which they hung on the body, there seemed to be a slick liquidity about the movement. Stack of lifeless clothes one moment, lethal killing machine the next. The drone drew a sword that had been buried up to its hilt in the ground and brandished it menacingly.

Perkins stopped and backed away, and almost as quickly the drone dropped back into a pile of clothes again, the string retying itself neatly, the sword dropping to the ground harmlessly.

We had all been watching, and although expected, the display was still chilling. There were dozens of drone clothes-packs dotted around, blocking our passage back to Llangurig, and safety.

'Any ideas?' asked Wilson as soon as Perkins had rejoined us.

'Not a single one,' said Perkins, 'but we're alive so long as we don't try to leave the mountain.'

'I'm not staying here my entire life,' said the Princess. 'I've a kingdom to inherit.'

'And I've booked a group to go Elephino-watching next month,' said Addie.

'Drat,' said Wilson, 'and I was *so* hoping for a significant end to my life.'

'I've an idea,' I said, and brought out the homing snail. It seemed strange to think that our lives might rely on a snail fetching help, but it was pretty much our best and only hope. Sure, we could wait for Colin to derubberise, but then we'd need a further six months for his wing to heal from the anti-aircraft shell. Six months was a long time to scratch a living stuck at the base of Cadair Idris. The rations in the half-track would last us a week, tops, and quite where we'd find enough food to feed Colin during the winter I had no idea – I didn't even know whether he *could* fly again. Rescue seemed the best hope, always assuming Moobin and the rest could reach us and then get us out.

I opened a can of Spam and fed it to the homing snail, who guzzled it down greedily. He'd need every bit of energy if he were to break out of this. I wrote out a note.

Dear Moobin

Surrounded by Hollow Men, little chance of escape. Have Rubber Colin, aim to climb Cadair Idris, Shandar up to

no good, need help soonest, listening out on the conch at all times.
URGENT
Jennifer

I double-taped the message to the shell, then put the snail on the ground and removed its hood. It looked around for a moment, tasted the air, and was off like a bullet back across the open ground.

A drone sprang to life and made a wild running dive for the snail. It missed, but there was another drone and it too made a wild grab. But the snail, no slouch itself, jinked and the drone missed it. Within a second two dozen other drones popped up, each of them making a grab for the escapee. The snail dodged another three, but that was it. There was a squeal as it was caught, and then a sickening crunch. Their job done, the drones collapsed into piles of clothing again and all was quiet.

I felt Perkins put his hand on my shoulder.

'Come on,' he said, 'we've still got the conch. We'll monitor it constantly. Moobin and Tiger and the others must be as keen to contact us as we are them.'

I agreed, and after we had loaded as much food as we could from the half-track into our knapsacks, I taped a note explaining what had happened to Colin's hand. If we didn't return he should know what happened, and be warned about the drones. With nothing else to delay us, we began the long climb up the mountain.

The steps were finely hewn, but were annoyingly large. About the same as those in a house but multiplied by a factor of two – which made the going hard, but made me think they had been cut for *giants*, which would at least confirm the legend that the mountain was not a mountain at all, but a viewing platform for the giant Idris, who would have climbed these stairs in ancient times to study the heavens and philosophise about life and existence.

I wasn't the only person who found it hard going.

'It would make Idris about twelve feet tall,' panted Wilson, 'a good size.'

'But still one third the size of a Troll,' said Perkins.

'Is an ogre bigger or smaller than a giant?' asked the Princess.

'Human, ogre, giant, Troll,' I said, reciting the order of magnitude of the bipedal species, 'but there's sometimes a bit of overlap.'

'Ah,' said the Princess, 'good. That always puzzled me.'

The climb was hard work and in several places the stairway had broken away so we had to scramble across an empty patch where a precipitous drop led to the ground far below. The path took us up in a zigzag fashion so our view of the drones' manufacturing facility hove in and out of viewpoint as we climbed to the summit. From our lofty viewpoint the facility's use was no easier to divine, and after a while we had climbed so high that it looked like a few boxes, and we paid it no more heed. There was plenty of fresh water streaming out of the rock, which we all agreed was about the best that any of us had tasted, and even though the edges to the side of the path were vertiginous in the extreme, none of us felt at all nervous and instead experienced a certain sense of mountain elation, a sort of magic that glowed from the rock, a lingering after-effect of the giant Idris.

There were two rockfalls as we climbed up. One was a small torrent of rocks dislodged by a stream as it cascaded down, with gravel, small stones and weed, but the second was larger and potentially fatal. A large section of rock dislodged from above and came bouncing down the mountain, so we pressed ourselves flat against the rock face and watched as the boulders hit the face above us and actually bounced farther out, leaving us unscathed. The path did not come off so well, and another large chunk was torn out of the stairway. I looked up when the rocks stopped, and for a fleeting moment saw a figure that looked like Curtis peering down, and none of us were in any doubt it was he who had deliberately caused the rockfall. We spent the rest of the journey with at least one person keeping an eye out for any other skulduggery, but there were no more attempts on our lives.

We stopped for a bite at two, and then struck off with renewed vigour for the summit, eventually finding ourselves moving into the cloud at about four in the afternoon. The air felt damp and clammy, and fine droplets of water began to form on our clothes. There was not a shred of vegetation to be seen anywhere, and pretty soon the rocks themselves seemed to ooze water like leaky sponges. A few minutes later a pair of large stone gateposts loomed out of the cloud, with a pair of once ornate and now very rusty gates collapsed between them. We climbed over, the small group now subdued and quiet. Although we were still in cloud and visibility was poor, we knew we had reached the summit. We walked along a rock-cut walkway, under an archway and entered a paved semicircular area about a hundred yards in diameter. Around this semicircle were delicately carved reliefs of strange creatures battling with men in ancient armour, and in the centre, right next to the cliff edge where a slip would have one tumbling into space, was a chair carved from solid rock. The seat was at least five feet from the ground – it was a chair for a giant.

'The Chair of Idris,' said Addie, 'where he would have sat and considered questions of existence, and stared into the heavens.'

'This would once have been a full circle,' said Wilson, looking around. 'Half of this area has already fallen away.'

'In a few years the chair will go too,' came a familiar

voice, 'so count your blessings you have witnessed even this.'

Curtis walked out of the grey fog towards us, grinning. He had shown little remorse when Ignatius died, treated Ralph like an animal once he had devolved and left us to die in the Empty Quarter. He had also kidnapped the Princess, sold her in Llangurig and then tried to kill us with a rockfall. I should have hated him, but somehow, given the circumstances, I hardly felt anything at all. He would not escape back to civilisation either; the drones would cut him down before he'd gone twenty paces. It struck me as ironic that he knew nothing of his fate, but was the only one of us who vaguely deserved it.

'I've been up here two hours,' he said. 'The top of the mountain is not large and extends about as far as you can see in every direction. I've checked the lot. I'm sorry to say there is nothing up here but damp rock, ancient history and disappointment. There are a few human bones but nothing from a Leviathan, not even a tooth. It was a wild goose chase, Jenny. Addie was right after all – it's all legends, hearsay, old wives' tales. I should despise you for wasting my time, but hey, at least I got to climb Cadair Idris and see the giant's chair.'

'Yes,' I agreed, 'there is that.'

'Hello, Laura,' said Curtis as the Princess stepped out from behind the chair, 'no hard feelings, eh?'

'None,' said the Princess. 'I've never been kidnapped, knocked unconscious or sold before. It was very . . . educational.'

'Well,' said Curtis, checking his watch, 'you're all being very sporting over this. I confess I thought you'd be annoyed. But hey, I guess that's the rough and tumble of the Cambrian Empire. The big adventure, y'know? Perhaps we should meet up for a drink or something when this is all over. Perhaps we'll even get to laugh about it.'

'Perhaps we will,' I said, 'but not together. Not you and us. Goodbye, Curtis.'

He suddenly looked uneasy. Wary, perhaps, of our apparent relaxed attitude to him and how he'd left us to almost certain death in the Empty Quarter.

'Okay, then,' he said, his voice cracking with the briefest tremor, 'I'll get going. I should make Llangurig by nightfall. So long.'

'One more thing,' I said, 'I've taken the keys to the half-track, so you're in the jeep.'

'And if you touch our belongings,' added Addie, 'or try to sabotage the half-track or anything I will make it my sworn life's duty to hunt you down.'

He looked at us all in turn. I think he got the message.

'Jeep it is then,' he said.

He turned hesitantly, thought of something, glanced at us again and then walked away and was lost to view in the swirling fog. We listened to his footsteps retreat after we lost sight of him, and heard a rusty clang as he climbed back over the fallen gates. We heard a few steps as he began the long descent, then no more.

'So,' said the Princess, 'any ideas about this Eye of Zoltar thingy? I can't see a Leviathans' Graveyard anywhere.'

'Nor a pirate hideout,' added Wilson.

'Me neither,' I said, 'but the answer is up here somewhere, I can feel it.'

I asked everyone to search the mountain top to see whether Curtis had missed anything. They all fanned out and I was left by myself next to Idris' chair to think, for something didn't add up. If the Mighty Shandar had gone to the trouble of protecting the area with hundreds of drones, then there had to be a secret up here that needed protecting. And with this amount of effort, a seriously good secret. All we had to do was find it.

Perkins' secret

Perkins was the first to return. He had found nothing except a rock-cut shelter, presumably to offer meagre comfort to any travellers caught up here in bad weather, and it seemed that weather here could be very bad indeed.

'Bones and gristle and a few IDs,' he said when I asked him whether there was anything inside, 'and tattered remnants of luggage, a corroded radio and some water bottles. I also noticed that every surface slopes gently towards the edge of the cliff. A few good rainstorms and this place would be hosed down – almost like it's self-cleaning.'

'And the magic?' I asked. 'Can you feel it?'

He could, but it wasn't the buzz of modern wizidrical energy, which is more like the humming of power lines, but the low, almost inaudible rumble of old magic.

'I can feel it,' he said, 'but I can't pinpoint it. Almost like it's all around us.'

Addie returned next, then Wilson, followed ten minutes later by the Princess. They too had found nothing but damp rock and a few buttons, coins and shards of bone.

'Are we done?' asked the Princess. 'This place gives me the willies.'

I looked at their faces in turn. Their fate was my responsibility. It was my expedition, my wish to come up here, my need to see what lay hidden at Cadair Idris.

'Look,' I said, 'I'm really sorry. There's something up here, I know it. Something that explains all this – the Mighty Shandar, the facility down below, the drones, everything. Even the reason Kevin sent us all the way out here. Problem is, I just can't see it. Quizzler must have found the Eye of Zoltar elsewhere, which isn't so unbelievable; it was a legend that linked the Eye with Pirate Wolff, and only a half-legend that linked Woolf with the Leviathans' Graveyard. And with all clues amounting to nothing, we're done. We'll head back as soon as we've had a break. You go below the cloud and dry out. I'm staying up here a few more minutes.'

'I'm going to make some tea,' said Wilson, practical as ever.

'I'll help you,' said Addie. 'I don't like it up here. It all feels wrong. Princess? Come and help. I think Jenny and Perkins need to talk out our options.'

They left, and Perkins and I sat on a lump of carved stone. We said nothing for several minutes.

'Addie was right,' he said finally, 'we need to talk. I'm your best and only chance of getting out of this mess. I can't unspell the entire drone army, but I can probably disrupt them long enough to cover your retreat across the mile or so of open grassland.'

'Absolutely not,' I said. 'We leave as one, or leave as none. No more spelling your life away, Perkins. Ordinary sorcery only. Promise me?'

'If you had my powers you wouldn't hesitate to use them,' he said. 'You'd give your life without batting an eyelid.'

'This isn't negotiable, Perkins. This is about *us*. Promise me?'

He bit his lip and sighed, then rested his hand on mine. I could feel him trembling.

'I'm not what you think I am, Jenny, and there was never going to be an us. Not for long, anyway.'

I didn't say anything. I wanted us to be together but I knew also, deep down, that he was right. He was the only chance we had.

'I didn't tell you earlier,' he said, 'but Ralph's Genetic Master Reset wasn't the only spell I've done that I had to burn some of my own life spirit to undertake – the rubberising spell took two years out of me. In fact,' he said, dropping his gaze, '*all* spelling takes time off me. Every scrap of magic I've ever done has exacted a cost measured in weeks, months and years. Truthfully, how old do I look?'

'I don't want to hear this,' I said.

'You've got to, Jenny. How old?'

I stared at him for a moment.

'Fifty?'

'I'm sixty-one. Wizidrically induced ageing is kinder to the skin than sun and wind and years. I'm a fraud, Jenny. I can't do magic – at least, not without shortening my life. You know how old I really am? How long I've been on the planet, I mean?'

'I don't know,' I said as a nasty thought struck me.

'I'm fourteen, Jenny. I'm not a wizard, I'm a *Burner*. A one-shot throwaway, and like all Burners, I'm here for one reason only – to shine brightly for a fleeting moment to help others in their time of need.'

I'd never met a Burner, but he was right: they typically lasted only two or three big spells before they had mined their own life spirit to nothing. Some of the finest magicians on the planet had been Burners, who did one fantastic feat of magic, then were gone.

'No,' I said, tears springing to my eyes, 'no more magic. We can put you on other duties when we get back to Kazam.'

He shook his head sadly.

'It's all I've ever wanted,' he said, 'to be magically useful. Jenny, we have been charged to find the Eye of Zoltar, and protect the Princess at all costs. Moobin told me to undertake my duties with "all other considerations secondary". Moobin wouldn't have told me that if this quest wasn't of vital importance.'

He was right. Moobin wouldn't have taken the decision on his own, either.

'The greatest sorcerers give everything to their craft, and at least this way I get to spend the rest of my life with you. My mind is made up, Jenny. It's time you started treating me as what I really am – a useful resource to be expended wisely.'

I looked up at him and gave him a wan smile. I think I loved him more than ever at that particular moment. I'd be married in the fullness of time, and have children, and be widowed and marry again – but my heart, my true heart, the one that loves first and most strongly, would always belong to Perkins.

'They always said you can't make relationships within the magic industry,' I said, wiping my eyes, 'and some say that magic actively works to prevent it.'

'Yeah,' said Perkins, 'that's how I see it too.'

There was a pause.

'"A resource to be expended wisely"?' I repeated. 'That's really how you see yourself?'

He smiled.

'A bit harsh, yes, but I was trying to make a point. Remember Kevin foresaw I would grow old in the Cambrian Empire? He was right – it's just happening a bit more quickly than I thought.'

I sighed, pulled out my hair tie and rubbed my

fingers through my hair. It was knotted and matted from the three days I'd gone without a bath. I'd been an idiot to think this was anything but a quest. Searches were nice and soft and cuddly and no one need be killed. A quest *always* demanded the death of a trusted colleague and one or more difficult ethical dilemmas. I'd been in denial. I'd been a fool.

'I'm so sorry,' I said, 'for dragging you into this.'

'Nonsense,' he replied, 'I came of my own free will. Okay, it's a serious downer that the Eye of Zoltar isn't here, but at least we know that for sure. Ten minutes ago we didn't even know that.'

'Perhaps – but useless if we can't get to tell anyone.'

'Defeatist talk,' said Perkins, jumping to his feet. 'We can figure out the Shandar problem when we get home. Let's kick those drones where it hurts and get you headed for home.'

'I'm not sure that metaphor works with drones, who have no parts to hurt, but yes, let's go – what plans do you have to disrupt the Hollow Men?'

'I'm working on something,' he said with a smile.

We started to walk towards the archway that led to the gates and the stairway back down, and I turned to take one last look at the large semicircular area, from where the giant Idris would once have considered the cosmos.

'He wouldn't have seen much in this low cloud,' said Perkins, thinking pretty much the same as I.

And that was when we heard a rattle as several things struck the ground behind us. We turned instinctively to investigate, and saw a few human finger bones rolling on the ground. They hadn't been there before. Perkins and I frowned at one another as an ulna dropped out of the foggy murk above us with a wristwatch still attached by some dried gristle. I picked it up. It wasn't a watch, it was a wrist *altimeter*, such as a parachutist or aerialist might wear. There was something engraved on the back.

'*To Shipmate Fly-low Milo, the finest aerialist that ever there was*,' I read.

'Sounds like pirate grammar to me,' said Perkins. 'They missed out everything but the "Arr".'

'No, that's engraved on the strap, look here.'

'Oh. Right. But what does it mean?'

We both looked up at the tendrils of fog drifting past.

'The old magic we can sense is the *cloud*,' I said. 'There's a reason the top of Cadair Idris is constantly swathed in cloud . . . it's hiding something.'

I picked up a stone, and threw it upwards as high as I could. There was a noise as the stone hit something, and a second later we jumped aside as a small section of rotted aircraft wing complete with tattered canvas came wheeling out of the fog and crashed to the ground. There was something hidden above us. We couldn't find Pirate Wolff's hideout for the very simple reason that it wasn't meant to be found. That's the thing about pirates. It's not wise to underestimate their cunning.

'If there's something up there there must be a way of accessing it,' I said, looking around. 'We need to find the highest point.'

After a brief scout around in the damp fog, we found it – the high seat back of Idris' chair, one side of which was twenty feet above the hard stone ground, and the other a precipitous seven-thousand-foot drop through the fog to the valley floor below.

'Give me a hand,' I said, and Perkins helped me to climb on to the large stone seat. I looked around to see how to climb farther and found a useful handhold, then a foothold, and then another. The holds were impossible to see from below against the wet stone, but had been definitely cut for a purpose. I had soon climbed upon the seat back, a narrow rock ledge less than six inches wide. I made a mental note that if I *were* to fall, I would try to land on the safe side of the chair – and when I say 'safe' I'm speaking in purely relative terms: a painful drop twenty feet on to wet rock rather than a seven-thousand-foot fall to certain death below. I cautiously stayed low, and reached above my head into the cloud, which here seemed to be thicker and distinctly uncloud-like – more like smoke. My fingers touched nothing, so, with fortune favouring the bold, I stood upright on the narrow ledge, all vision vanishing as my upper body was enveloped by the fog. I was mildly disoriented and my foot slipped on the wet rock, but I regained my footing, my heart beating faster. I stood up straight and reached above my head, straining to touch something. I even stood on tiptoe, but nothing. I was about to give up and return to firm ground when Kevin's last message rang out in my head:

> *You may have to take a leap of faith if you find yourself on the shoulders of a giant.*

I was standing on Idris' chairback, about as close to his long-dead shoulders as I was likely to be, and if this wasn't a leap of faith, I wasn't sure what was.

I made a small jump and reached above my head, but felt nothing, and when I landed my feet slipped. For a moment I thought I would fall, but then I regained my balance.

'Come on, Jenny,' I said to myself, 'that was nothing like a leap.'

'Perkins?' I called out.

'Yes?' came a disembodied voice from below.

'I'm going to leap.'

'And trust in providence?'

'No,' I said, 'something better – I'm going to trust in . . . Kevin.'

And I jumped. Lept, actually. Even today I can't

remember whether I jumped on the cliff side or the summit side, but reasoning it out later it must have been the cliff side. Without the certainty of death, the leap wouldn't have worked.

Because it *did* work. I leapt as high and as far as I could and put out my hands, hoping to grab hold of something, and I did. But it wasn't the rung of a ladder, or a rope. It was a human hand, and it grabbed me tightly around the wrist, held me for a moment and then hauled me up until I was safe. I looked around and blinked, open-mouthed. I had not expected to see what I could see, nor the identity of the person who had just saved me.

The sky pirate's tale

'Surprised?'

'Just a little,' I said, looking around. I was still in cloud but sitting on a small, gently undulating platform that I soon figured was the distinctively broad flat skull of a Leviathan, and what's more, that it was floating in mid-air and supporting my weight. I knew the Leviathan was lighter than air, but I had not taken the next logical step to suppose the bones would remain so after death. To one side of me was a spiral staircase, made of Leviathan bones, which vanished upwards into the gloom, and on the other side of me was the man who had hauled me to this strange new world within the clouds. It was Gabby, the very same as I had seen him last. Youthful, sleeves rolled, still wearing his backpack.

'What are you doing here?' I asked.

'Hiding. I'm not always wanting to be found. But when you took that leap, well, I wasn't going to let you die.'

'For the second time.'

'Fourth, actually, but who's counting?'

'You are.'

'Agreed. But you didn't see me the other times. In my line of work, being seen can raise difficulties.'

'I don't understand.'

'No, few do – let me show you around.'

And so saying, he led the way up the creaking spiral bone staircase. We didn't have to go very far before we broke cloud, and emerged into the sunlight. I looked around. My mouth, I think, may even have dropped open.

We were standing on what I can only describe as a floating platform of massive Leviathan bones, all lashed together, and constructed on several different levels. There were walkways, stairways and even rooms, passageways and a main hall, the framework of each built solely of lighter-than-air Leviathan bones.

'The legendary Leviathans' Graveyard,' I breathed, for here indeed were the remains of perhaps hundreds of Leviathans, their bones used to make a hideout of crude beauty. Despite the lashed-bone construction there was elegance in the haphazard structure, and a certain recycled charm, for among the framework of bones was the booty of the aerial pirate – parts of aircraft stolen on the wing and adapted to make the hideout more like home. Wings became roofs, aluminium fuselage panels became footways, aero-engines as generator sets and winches. We were standing at what appeared to be a dock, ready to accept a Cloud Leviathan, with a large leather harness all set to strap a wicker balloonist's gondola on the creature's back, with harpoon guns on swivelling mounts, grappling hooks and cutlasses at the ready.

But for all this apparent readiness, the hideout was long abandoned. Everything was old, worn and weathered. Any exposed metal was corroded and the leather strips that held the Cloud Leviathans' bones together had begun to rot. There were bodies, too, or rather, *partial* bodies. The closest pirate to us had died while fighting as his arm was still holding a cutlass embedded in the handrail, but although most of him was now little more than skeleton half held together with dried gristle, his arm, half of his chest and head had been preserved at the moment of death – but as a dull grey metal.

I tapped the grey metal, and stared uneasily at the look of grim determination stuck permanently to the dead pirate's features, then tested the metal for softness with my fingernail. There was no mistake – he had been changed partially to lead.

'The Eye of Zoltar,' I breathed, 'it's here – or *was* here.'

I looked around to see whether there were other bodies, and there were, all of them either partially or completely changed to lead. It looked as though there had been a fight – and the pirates had lost.

'However did this place come about?' I asked as

we followed the trail of dead pirates towards the main hall, the walkway flexing beneath our feet as we moved.

'The Cambrian species of Leviathan has always lived on Cadair Idris,' explained Gabby. 'It is hatched here, breeds here, roosts here overnight and will eventually return here to die. Once dead, it floats in the air until it rots away, and its bones rise to form a mass about twenty thousand feet above the summit – and usefully become the nest where it lays its eggs. It's thought the first sky pirate tamed a Leviathan and then established a base in what was once the Leviathan's nest.'

'We're not at twenty thousand feet,' I said, noting as we walked past how another pirate was lead from the waist down.

'Agreed,' said Gabby, 'and it would be too cold to live up there. We think that much of this aircraft scrap – the engines and undercarriage and whatnot – is really just for ballast, to keep it hovering just above the mountain's summit. One of their first acts of piracy was to kidnap a sorcerer to ensure that the nest – now built into pretty much what you see now – was permanently obscured by cloud.'

'Which explains why the summit can never be seen.'

'Precisely. As the years went by the pirating business moved from captain to captain but was always fairly low key – until Sky Pirate Bunty Wolff took over. She had no qualms about plundering the biggest airliners quite literally on the wing – she would attack anything if there was rich booty to be had.'

'So was the attack on Cloud City Nimbus III and the loss of the *Tyrannic* her after all?'

'Absolutely. She always made sure there were no witnesses.'

'She sounds like a monster.'

We had arrived at the main hall. We stepped across another half-lead pirate holding a musket, and opened two doors that looked as if they too had been salvaged from an aircraft. The hall had been made up of an entire Cloud Leviathan ribcage covered with a patchwork of aircraft fabric, still with registration numbers and the names of almost every airline I could think of. It would have been used as a meeting place, for meals and grog and shanties – or whatever it is pirates sing.

'Three out of four missing aircraft can be attributed to Sky Pirate Wolff,' said Gabby as we walked across the creaking floorboards, some of which were missing, revealing the swirling clouds below, 'and she did very well out it. Murderous thug, of course; nothing glamorous in pirates – they're criminals, pure and simple.'

'Have you heard of something called the Eye of Zoltar?' I asked, as Gabby seemed to know a lot about a lot.

'No, but I presume it's related to Zoltar the sorcerer?'

'A pink ruby about the size of a goose egg,' I said,

'which seems to dance with an inner fire. It can be used as a conduit – a *concentrator* of wizidrical energy. But it's dangerous, too. In the wrong hands, it will—'

'Turn a person partially to lead?' asked Gabby as we passed yet another pirate who had suffered a similar fate to the rest.

'Wholly, sometimes,' I said, recalling Able Quizzler, who must have been entirely lead to have the energy to bury himself when he hit the ground.

'Nasty way to go,' said Gabby, 'but in pirating, an unpleasant death is very much an occupational hazard. You seek this jewel?'

'That we do,' I said, 'and all the clues point towards Sky Pirate Wolff.'

'Then you'd better meet her,' said Gabby, 'she's in here.'

Sky Pirate Bunty Wolff

Gabby opened an inner door from the main hall and we entered Sky Pirate Wolff's private cabin. The room was panelled with an interior stolen from the first-class lounge of a flying boat somewhere and once must have looked supremely elegant – before the rain had managed to gain access, turning parts of the panelling black with mould.

Sky Pirate Bunty Wolff had been completely turned to lead. It was a similar effect to being transformed to stone. Every pore of her skin, every muscle sinew, scar, blemish and hair, was perfectly preserved. She was dressed in traditional pirate uniform, although with a battered flying helmet in place of the tricorne hat. Her clothes had rotted badly, and a pair of pistols were still stuck in her waistband. One of her lead hands was resting on the tabletop, and the other was empty and held aloft, the fingers open as though showing us an apple or something. Upon her features was a look of shocked surprise. Her enleadening moment had not been expected.

'Is your Eye of Zoltar anywhere here?' asked Gabby.

'Certain to say it once *was*,' I replied with a sigh, checking an open safe behind Sky Pirate Wolff that was stashed with jewels, sadly none the size of a goose's egg, and nothing that was 'dancing with inner fire'. The Eye, I knew, would be unmistakable.

'Do you know when all this happened?' I asked.

'Six years ago,' said Gabby, 'give or take. We rarely intervene when it comes to pirates.'

I returned to Sky Pirate Wolff and looked at her hand, the one that was being held aloft. Looking closer, I noticed that her soft lead fingers had been bent apart. When she had been turned to base metal, she had been holding something – and it wasn't an apple.

'This is where the Eye of Zoltar was,' I said, pointing at her hand. 'Sky Pirate Wolff was holding it. She was talking to someone who was seated right here.'

I dropped into the seat opposite the lead statue, and immediately the pirate's dead eyes stared into mine.

'They were talking. The person sitting here uses the Eye to change Pirate Wolff to lead, then makes a run for it. The "people into lead" spell must be the Eye's default spell, or a gatekeeper or something.'

'It would explain the trail of partially leaded pirates all the way out,' observed Gabby. 'Whoever took the jewel used the lead transformation spell to cover their retreat.'

He was right, and I swore softly to myself. The trail, sadly, had long ago turned cold. If this all happened six years ago, the Eye could be anywhere on the planet. I searched Sky Pirate Wolff's room, then the main hall, but could find nothing that might have told us who took the Eye, let alone where it was now. Kevin Zipp had been right about the Eye's whereabouts – it was just his timescale that had been at fault.

We walked back the way we had come.

'Do you know who took it?' I asked.

'Sadly, I do not,' said Gabby, 'but it would have to be a sorcerer of some sort.'

'The Mighty Shandar is skilled enough to tap the Eye's power,' I murmured, 'but sending me to find something he already has doesn't make much sense.'

'And there's a good reason why Shandar wouldn't want you poking around out here,' said Gabby, 'and it has nothing to do with the Eye of Zoltar.'

I frowned and thought for a moment.

'The Skybus facility below?' I suggested.

Gabby nodded.

'What are they making?' I asked. 'And why do the empty lorries coming *in* weigh more than the ones coming *out*?'

'Because . . . they'd have to be.'

I stared at Gabby for a moment, trying to figure it out. We had by now arrived at the top of the bone spiral staircase. A few steps down and we'd be in the all-obscuring cloud again. I reached out to one of the

Leviathan bones and scratched off a small amount, which, once released, drifted upwards.

'Shandar's harvesting Cloud Leviathans?' I said, and Gabby smiled.

'Ever wondered how those huge jetliners seem to hang in the air on those tiny wings?' he asked. 'How Skybus lead the world in efficient aircraft that can fly twice as far on half the fuel? Ever wondered why Shandar has made so much money through Skybus, and how Tharv can afford for all his citizens to have free universal healthcare?'

'Tharv and Shandar are partners?'

'Very much so. The whole jeopardy tourism thing might sound like a long and very complex joke, but without it, Tharv and Shandar would not be as stupendously rich as they are. All those tourists in the Cambrian Empire snatched from the jaws of certain death, hundreds of times a day, month in, month out.'

And that was when it hit me. The answer had been staring me in the face the whole time. The Cloud Leviathans' lighter-than-air capability was not due to magic, nor some natural process. Prince Nasil had even mentioned it before he left: the same thing that keeps a flying carpet in the air also keeps up a Leviathan.

'Angel's feathers,' I said in a soft whisper. 'We were nearly hoovered up by the Leviathan the night before last. They do that feeding run every morning, sucking up not just the birds and bugs, but also many of the

Variant-G angels who are constantly employed in the Cambrian Empire. They are then digested to make the Leviathan lighter than air. jeopardy tourism is there for a purpose. High risk of death, high concentration of guardian angels.'

I paused, and looked at Gabby, who nodded.

'But,' I added, 'that's not the end of it, is it?'

'No indeed,' said Gabby. 'The higher-than-normal concentration of ingested angel's feathers leads to an excess, which is then expelled as all animal waste is expelled. The drones working in the facility below gather up the Leviathans' droppings with nothing more complicated than shovels, then extract the angel's feathers using Shandar-supplied magic. They then ship it out in the Skybus lorries. The refined material is known in the aeronautical industry as Guanolite, and is stuffed inside aircraft wings to assist with lift. That's what's going out in the Skybus trucks.'

'Which must explain,' I said slowly, 'why the trucks are lighter on the way out.'

'Of course. Fill a two-ton truck with concentrated Guanolite and the upward force will ensure it weighs effectively no more than a golf buggy.'

Gabby beckoned me to follow him as I fell silent for a moment, digesting this new information as we began the climb down the staircase. As I entered the cloud I felt the damp and clamminess touch my face and hands, and pretty soon we were standing on the

Leviathan skull, the spot where I had first entered this strange place.

'*Who are you?*' I asked. 'You know about this place, but you're not dead – you come and go as you choose.'

'You might say I have a version of "access all areas",' he said with a chuckle. 'As I think I explained, I collect information on death likelihood for a major player in the risk management industry.'

'I remember,' I said, 'and by identifying the potential risk factor of everything anyone does, you decide where best to deploy your assets to avert those risks.'

'That's pretty much it,' said Gabby. 'We save lives . . . when lives need to be saved.'

'It's not an insurance company, is it?'

'Not really, no. It's sort of . . . fate management. It's of vital importance that you – or anyone, in fact – do not die until you have fulfilled your function in the G-SOT.'

'G-SOT?'

'The Grand Scheme of Things. Bigger than me, bigger than you, and all are to play a part. It might be something simple like opening a door, encouraging somebody to do something, or even, as in Curtis' case, simply giving people a focus of someone to dislike. But sometimes it's for good – like bringing a tyrant to their knees and leading an enslaved nation to freedom.'

'Then my function in the Grand Scheme is still ahead of me?' I asked.

'It is. And Perkins, too.'

'He's going to burn himself out battling the drones on our return, isn't he?'

'To have a function is the right of all sentient beings,' said Gabby, touching my shoulder, 'to have a *vitally important* function is an honour not often bestowed.'

He smiled, then added:

'For operational purposes we like to maintain our Grade II legendary status: "No proof of existence". I can rely on your discretion, yes?'

'Yes.'

'Good. Time to go, but I calculate the jump from here back to the top of the stone chair has a 79.23 per cent Fatality Index – here.'

Gabby tossed a rope over the side and I heard the end fall on to the damp stone below. I thanked Gabby for his time and help, then slid down the rope. After a few more seconds my feet had touched the damp stone of the semicircle around Idris' chair, and I found a very astonished-looking Perkins.

'Okay,' he said, 'that was kind of strange, and I'm a sorcerer, so should be used to it. You jump into the cloud, vanish for half an hour and then return down a rope. What did you find?'

'Answers,' I said, 'but not the ones we're looking for. Let's find the others.'

He started to move, but I caught his arm, moved him around and kissed him. It was my first, and I think his too. I'd been meaning to do it for a while, but only with Gabby's words did the whole thing seem that much more urgent. He returned the passion, and it felt good – far better than I'd thought – and made me feel tingly in all sorts of places.

'What was that for?' he whispered as I rested my head on his shoulder and held him tight.

'Because.'

'Because what?'

'Just because.'

We both knew he'd be burnt out soon, and we attempted to get as much of a lifetime's worth of hugs as possible in the time available.

'Okay, then,' I said, and we avoided each other's gaze as we separated, 'let's find the others.'

We walked down from the summit and out of the cloud, where we found Addie, the Princess and Wilson, who had made some tea.

We rested for an hour while I told everyone what I had found, but without mentioning Gabby. I told them about Sky Pirate Wolff's hideout and her fate, that someone else had beaten us to the Eye of Zoltar years ago, and it could now be pretty much anywhere. I told them how the facility far below us was simply positioned where the sole remaining Cloud Leviathan roosted at night, and they scraped up the droppings each morning to process them into Guanolite.

'I can see why they have drones do the job,' said Wilson, 'it must be rotten work.'

'I'd say it was more to do with secrecy,' I replied, 'which also might explain the Cambrian Empire's no-fly zone. The last Leviathan is worth so much money it would be foolish to have it damaged in a collision with anything – or even discovered at all.'

'So all our careers in jeopardy tourism were simply there to facilitate the manufacture of angel-feather-fortified Leviathan droppings?' asked Addie. 'Hell's teeth, you just couldn't make this stuff up, could you?'

'Magic's like that,' I said.

There was a pause.

'So what now?' asked Perkins.

'We came out here to find the Eye, and we failed. So we're going home.'

'Past the Hollow Men?' asked Wilson.

'Yes,' I said, swallowing down my emotion and avoiding Perkins' gaze. 'We'll think of something, I'm sure.'

So after packing up and trying the conch for the umpteenth time without success, we turned to leave. It was with a heavy heart that I descended the steep steps, but I was consoled by the fact that I had it on good authority that Perkins' life would not be in vain – and I now had a pretty good idea what Gabby kept in his rucksack.

The plan

The first thing we noticed when we returned to the base of the mountain was Curtis. He had somehow decided not to leg it back to Llangurig straight away, and was instead standing at the edge of the empty scrub that separated us from the safety of the forest, a mile away. He had a deep frown etched upon his features.

'Did you see them?' I asked.

Curtis said nothing, and continued to stare off towards the woods, and safety.

'They're called Hollow Men or drones,' I explained, '*Cavi homini*. Nothing more than the personified evil will of the Mighty Shandar: empty vessels bidden to kill us, without thought, malice or guilt. It's why no one ever comes back from Cadair Idris.'

Curtis still said nothing, so I continued:

'I'm telling you this because we need to be a team to survive. Are you any good with a sword?'

'You're wasting your time.'

That sounded like something Curtis would say, but he hadn't spoken. It was Addie.

'Asking Curtis to help?' I said.

'Asking Curtis for *anything*.'

I looked quizzically at her, and she nodded towards Curtis, who, now I looked closer, wasn't just standing there looking thoughtfully out at the scenery, but simply standing there. I could even see the fine stitching down his neck.

'Hotax?' I said, waving a hand in front of Curtis' blank and unmoving features. He had been paralysed, captured, boned, eaten and then stuffed. It wasn't a pleasant way to go, but would at least have been painless, and ornamentally at least he was now quite impressive.

'The Hollow Men don't see the Hotax as a threat,' said Addie, 'the same as Tralfamosaur and Snork Badger and all the rest. Leave him. He had it coming.'

'No one deserves this,' I said.

'Perhaps not,' said Addie, 'but he was only ever along to make up the fifty per cent casualty rate I'd promised – and you agreed to him coming along.'

'That's true,' I conceded, then added: 'How are we doing on that?'

Addie counted the casualty rate on her fingers.

'Out of the eight in the team we've now lost three: Ignatius, Ralph and Curtis – which is pretty much what I'd planned. If I'm right we only need lose one more.'

'It's a nice mathematical theory,' I said, 'but I'm not sure the fifty per cent thing is working any more. We're fighting for our lives.'

'You're right,' she said sadly, 'but it helps to have something hopeful to cling on to, no matter how slender. Some people have a lucky gonk or a deity – I have statistics.'

She gave me a smile.

'Listen,' she said, offering her hand for me to shake, 'it's been a lot of fun. Most tourists just moan about the food and the weather and the transport and the hotels and stuff and then think of devious ways they can fleece me for a refund. You were different, and I'd like you to know that whatever happens, I'd tour-guide for you anywhere, any time – and with a generous discount.'

'Thank you,' I said, knowing that such a compliment was not often given, and a discount even less so, 'and on my part, you've been exemplary. If we survive this final push, I'll be giving you the best feedback I can.'

We shook hands again and parted. I walked across to where the Princess was helping Wilson and Perkins secure Rubber Colin in the back of the half-track. Because of the lateness of the hour and with rain due tomorrow we had decided to cross as soon as possible. Magic doesn't work so well in the rain, and although this meant the drones' powers would be diminished, it followed that Perkins' power would too. As soon as Rubber Colin was lashed down I asked Perkins about his plan.

'I'm not sure.'

'That's not helpful,' I said, 'we're kind of counting on you.'

'No, I mean, I'm not sure *yet*. I won't be able to come up with a countermeasure until I get an idea of the spell the Hollow Men are running. I can't defeat a hundred drones, obviously, but there may be some way I can disable them long enough for you to get away.'

I looked around. With me driving the half-track, the Princess no good with a sword and Perkins concentrating on a realistic countermeasure, that left only Addie and Wilson wielding swords to keep the Hollow Men at bay. And while they were easily dispatched by a sharp sword – they were hollow after all, and needed their clothes to move and fight – the sheer weight of numbers might prove too much. Not knowing how many there were didn't help, either.

'Is it worth derubberising Colin?' I asked. 'I know his fiery breath is not fully developed, but at close quarters it might do some damage.'

'I thought of that too,' said Perkins, 'but I read the washing label on those Hollow Men clothes we found earlier, and they were made of fire-retardant synthetic material. I'm going to keep the power I have for the countermeasure.'

'Whatever that might be.'

'Yes,' said Perkins, 'whatever that might be.'

'These swords were a bit rusty,' said Addie, showing me one of the weapons we had retrieved from the river earlier, 'but I've managed to get an edge back on them.'

'What do I do?' asked the Princess.

'You'll keep your head down.'

She looked at me petulantly.

'Like hell I will. If we're going to die, I'm going to go down fighting, even if I'm totally rubbish with a weapon.'

'Fair enough,' I said, and handed her a cutlass. She swished it in the air a couple of times.

'Pointy end towards the bad guy, right?'

'Right.'

I gathered everyone around.

'Okay,' I said, 'this is the plan. The Hollow Men are tireless, violent fighters, but we have one advantage: they can't run faster than a half-track. We're going to charge across as quick as we can. Addie, Princess and Wilson, you're on defence. Perkins here will let fly with whatever he can as soon as he figures out a weakness.'

'How long will that be?' asked Addie.

'I don't know,' said Perkins, 'but the closer they get the better I can sense the weave of their spell.'

'Terrific,' replied Wilson, 'so *let* them get close?'

'If you can.'

'Any more questions?' I asked. There weren't. 'Okay,' I said, 'good luck, everyone.'

We shook hands in silence, and as I looked from face to face I could see that none of us rated our chances that high. Even so, there was no hesitation from any of them. Truly, I was in the very finest of company.

Addie positioned herself on the bonnet of the half-track and Wilson in the rear left with the Princess in the rear right. Rubber Colin had been laid flat and covered with blankets, the note I'd taped to his hand amended to what we were attempting right now. If the worst came to the worst he would revert naturally and find himself in a deserted half-track in the middle of nowhere – and it was important he told Moobin and the others what had happened to us.

Once we were all positioned, I started the engine. Perkins sat down next to me and concentrated hard. I depressed the clutch, selected first gear in low range and gunned the engine. I figured there was about a mile before we were safe. At thirty miles an hour it would take us two minutes – always supposing we could get to that speed. I put out my hand and Perkins squeezed it.

'Crazy or nothing,' he said, and smiled.

'Crazy or nothing,' I replied.

I placed both hands on the wheel, gunned the throttle again and released the clutch. The tracks bit into the soft earth and we were away. Almost instantly a stack of clothes popped up into the air ahead of us and took the shape of a human. In a few seconds six more had joined it. I yelled 'Hold on!' and floored the accelerator.

Battle of the Hollow Men

Since we had a decent run-up, the first three drones were easily dispatched under the front wheels, and Addie expertly sliced another in half and Wilson two more. They were surprisingly easy to bring down as they were only as strong as their clothes. They remained animated when cut in two but the top half was dangerous only if you were near, and the bottom half not dangerous at all unless they gave you a kick. All this didn't really register, as my forward view was filled by several more Hollow Men popping into life. I was relieved to find that there didn't seem to be so many of them and I steered into them, the lifeless husks disappearing under the heavy treads, ploughed into the mud.

'Anything yet?' I shouted to Perkins.

'Not yet,' he said, concentrating hard, fingers on temples. 'I think they've been spelled in a non-standard reverse weave.'

I turned the wheel and accelerated towards a group of three and they too vanished under the front wheels.

'They're getting up again!' shouted Wilson as he fought off two more drones that had popped back into life as soon as the tracks had passed over them. One even managed to climb aboard, but was soon dispatched by the Princess, who had discovered that if a drone's right sword arm was sliced through, they had to stop and find the sword with their left before continuing.

Several more popped up and I steered towards them to help Addie slice through two in one go, then positioned the half-track to run over two more. All seemed to be going quite well, until I noticed three of them run *towards* the half-track and dive under the front wheels, something that suddenly made me wary.

'This is too easy,' shouted Addie.

'I'm not complaining,' yelled back Wilson, hacking a drone diagonally in half from the shoulder to the waist. I changed gear to speed up and the half-track suddenly lurched aggressively to the left. Addie was caught off balance and fell off the bonnet. I accelerated but this only made the swing to the left worse, and in a few more seconds we had spun around and were pointing not at the forest and safety, but back towards the mountain. I let in the clutch and came to a halt as Addie went on the attack and dispatched another drone that was approaching, one of ten or twelve still out there. They seemed to be walking towards us in a more relaxed manner, something I didn't like the look of.

'Damn,' I said, thumping the wheel, 'what a time to lose a track. Addie? Damage report!'

Addie ran around to the right of the vehicle while Wilson jumped off the half-track to more easily engage the closest drones. Addie had a look and then yelled:

'Reverse, but easy does it!'

I clunked the half-track into gear and reversed slowly. The vehicle seemed to move correctly at first but then lurched in the opposite direction, and Addie yelled at me to stop.

'Three swords jammed in the right-hand track,' she yelled.

'Let me see.'

I left the engine running and jumped out to have a look as Wilson and the Princess stood by defensively, ready for the slow-approaching drones. The swords were bent around the drive sprocket, jamming it completely. They weren't the only things jammed in the tracks – there were several Hollow Men, or at least their clothes. They hadn't really been fighting at all, just searching for a weakness, and they'd found it. The Achilles heel on a tracked vehicle is the same as its main advantage – the tracks.

I looked around. We had covered barely four hundred yards from our starting point and had not even reached the river. Tactically speaking, it was a good place to disable the half-track, and as I looked back to where we had left the jeep, six more drones popped up from the earth where they had been buried.

'They're cutting off the retreat,' said Wilson.

'Perkins,' I shouted, 'we're going to need something from you pretty soon.'

'Working on it,' he replied.

I grabbed a spare sword from the back of the half-track and faced the drones alongside the others.

'Hang on,' said the Princess, 'they're stopping.'

She was right. We were surrounded by at least thirty Hollow Men by now and they had halted about twenty yards out and simply stood at readiness, the gap between each drone and its neighbour precisely the same.

'They're waiting,' said Wilson.

'They're waiting because they have time in their favour,' said Addie. 'Look behind them.'

Behind the row of drones, other Hollow Men were popping into malevolent being all over the scrubby land and were walking towards us. Reinforcements. I looked again at the jammed track, swore to myself and switched off the half-track's engine.

'Okay, the half-track is dead. We need a new plan.'

Worryingly, there were no suggestions, and Perkins climbed out to join us.

'They're like a conjoined military mind,' he babbled excitedly. 'They don't need a chain of command because each individual is a general and a soldier combined. They will study their enemy, exploit its weakness and neutralise its strengths. The reason they've stopped is because they don't yet know how to neutralise our strength.'

'We have one?' asked Addie.

'It's me,' said Perkins. 'They know I'm reading them. And since they've stopped thirty or so feet away, we must assume they *do* have a weakness that we can exploit. Watch this.'

Perkins took three strides towards the line of drones, and they all withdrew. When he returned to us, they moved back in again.

'They're waiting until they have overwhelmingly superior numbers,' said Addie as more drones arrived behind the ones already present, 'and waiting is something we can't do.'

'They might be made of nothing but drip-dry terylene,' said Wilson, 'but if they charge at us, we won't stand a chance.'

He was right. The drones were now three deep, and more were arriving by the second. Just then, one of the Hollow Men who was wrapped around the track tried to grab me with an empty arm attached to a muddy empty glove. We had needed a break, and it seemed we had just got one.

'Bingo,' I said. 'Perkins?'

Perkins looked at where the drone's gloved hand was still feeling around, while the rest of it was jammed in the drive sprocket. The other drone costumes wedged in the track, I noted, were devoid of life, and just empty clothes.

'Ah,' said Perkins, 'wounded. Spellcode probably disrupted. Here goes.'

He held the gloved hand of the drone for a moment, then smiled.

'Now *that's* something I can use,' he said excitedly. 'Sickeningly simple, when you think of it. They were right to be nervous. Wait a moment.'

And he squatted down to prepare himself as the drones became five deep. There were, I reckoned, about a hundred and fifty of them fewer than ten paces away.

'Blast,' said Perkins.

'What?'

'I need twenty years of life spirit to make this spell work, and I wouldn't have made it past sixty-nine, so I've not got enough years to trade – I need a dozen more to figure out a countermeasure *and* to clear the swords out of the half-track.'

'Take it off me,' I said, 'I'll still be only twenty-six.'

'No,' said Wilson, 'use me. This way I get the Value Added Death I've always wanted. Dying, to protect you all. It is poetic. It is *heroic*. I insist.'

'I'm only twelve,' countered Addie, 'so I'm the most qualified to surrender any years. I'll be in my early twenties and I feel twice that old already. Perkins, do your thing.'

Addie's argument seemed the most sound, and already the drones, now six deep and in excess of three hundred, were beginning to tramp the ground in readiness for attack.

'Okay,' said Perkins holding out his hand to Addie. 'It'll be at the count of three but you have to repeat the count. One.'

'One.' She took his hand.

There was no time for any goodbyes or pithy final speeches. I didn't even have time to *think* before the Hollow Men drew their swords in unison – a sound, like the song of the Quarkbeast, that I hope never to hear again.

'Two,' said Perkins, eyes tightly closed, concentrating hard.

'Two,' said Addie.

The Hollow Men all advanced a pace. There were so many of them I could see nothing but black suits and white shirts in every direction.

'Three,' said Perkins.

But Addie didn't get to say three. Wilson jumped forward with surprising agility, and knocked Addie's and Perkins' hands apart – and replaced Addie's hand with his own.

'Three,' said Wilson, and Perkins summoned up every available second of his life and let fly. There was a high-pitched wail, a sudden bright flash and a pulse of blue light that moved rapidly outwards as Perkins and Wilson vaporised, the spell squeezing every last vestige of mortality from their souls. A moment later, Addie and I and the Princess were left standing there quite alone, the Hollow Men every bit as alive as before.

'This isn't good,' I said.

The Hollow Men charged, and the three of us, our tempers up, did the same and met the first wave head-on with an angry clatter of swords. I had expected a swift end but a second later and the first rank of Hollow Men seemed to falter and collapse inwards, quickly followed by the second row and the third. Within a second or two swords were falling to the ground and Hollow Men were collapsing like deflating parachutes, their clothes quite literally falling apart around them.

Perkins did not have the power to defeat drones, but he had the power to turn the complex co-polymer in nylon stitching to its component parts: gaseous nitrogen, carbon dioxide and quite a lot of hydrogen. If I'd had nylon stitching, my clothes would have fallen off too, but I didn't. I was sensibly dressed in cotton.

Addie and I looked around at the sections of clothing blowing in the wind. They were twitching as the three hundred or so drones attempted to make sense of their fate and develop a countermeasure of their own. But Hollow Men don't to do magic, they *are* magic, and short of their acquiring several hundred seamstresses in the next ten minutes, we'd won.

The last stand

Correction: we'd sort of won. Perkins and Wilson were no longer with us. On the ground where they had been standing were merely their dog tags, the change in their pockets and a few zips, gold fillings and Wilson's gallstones. I also noted the swords stuck in the drive sprocket of the track were now made of ice and were melting. Perkins had excelled himself. We were back in the game.

'I'm thinking we shouldn't be hanging about,' said Addie, pointing to where the Hollow Men in the most distant ranks of the surrounding army were not *quite* as dismantled as the rest – they were not dangerous, but already we could see more Hollow Men popping into life in the distance and heading our way. I jumped into the driver's seat and fired up the engine with Addie joining me in the passenger seat. We looked at one another. Someone was missing.

We found her crouched on the ground behind the half-track. She was cradling her arm and looked up at us with an apologetic smile.

'I took a hit the second before Perkins did his stuff,'

she said, showing us the wound. Her right hand was severed cleanly at the wrist, and bleeding badly. If we didn't do something pretty soon, we'd lose her to blood loss.

Luckily, Addie had dealt with this sort of thing before on the tourist trail, and pulled a bandage kit from one of her pouches.

'This will hurt,' she said.

'It already hurts,' said the Princess. 'Do it.'

Addie bound the stump tightly with several bandages, which seemed to help, although I could see that the Princess was in considerable pain. But there wasn't time to commiserate. We quite literally threw the Princess into the back of the half-track and I jumped back in the driver's seat.

'Hurry,' said Addie, 'they're redeploying.'

And so they were. All the Hollow Men that hadn't been affected by Perkins' spell – and those few that had, but were just about functional – were moving to cut off our escape by the river at the only place we could cross. I noted also that even though the swords jammed in the tracks were no longer a problem, the clothes also wedged into the tracks were impeding progress. I was flat out in second, and we were barely making the pace of a jogger. Even if we were to retreat back to the mountain, we'd still be overtaken by the drones, and to be honest, I wasn't big on retreating, and I didn't suppose Addie and the Princess were either.

Addie grabbed her sword and returned to her place on the bonnet. The battle was not yet over. The Princess climbed in next to me and stared forlornly at her stump.

'Laura Scrubb will be pissed as hell when she finds I've lost one of her hands.'

'I'm sure you can make it up to her.'

'Before I was useless but *with* a sword,' added the Princess. 'Now I'm double-useless without one.'

'Maybe not,' I said as I had an idea. I rummaged in my bag and passed her the Helping Hand™. It was a sound idea. A Helping Hand™ was memory preloaded with every dextrous act imaginable, from mending barometers to building box-girder bridges. With a pair of them you could even play Rachmaninov's Third Piano Concerto, which is *seriously* hard. More relevant to the here and now, a Helping Hand™ can wield a sword as expertly as it can conduct open heart surgery – which are not as remotely related as one would have supposed.

'There's some duct tape in the toolbox,' I said, pointing in the back. 'Get a couple of lengths and I'll tape it on.'

She did, and pretty soon the Princess had two hands again, even if her new one was too large, four decades older then her, hairy, and had 'No more pies' tattooed on the back. She didn't waste any time, either. The Helping Hand™ grabbed a sword and she and it joined Addie on the bonnet.

We covered the next four hundred yards in less than a minute, the engine labouring to overcome the drag of the clothes stuck in the tracks. We plunged down the slope into the shallow ravine and forded the river, barely glancing at the decaying bones of the massacred. We made it another hundred yards beyond this, and just as the engine temperature was nudging into the red, the Hollow Men closed ranks and presented an unbroken wall in front of us. There were fewer of them – Perkins had depleted their numbers by at least two-thirds – but even as we watched, more were streaming from Shandar's Guanolite facility, quite literally dropping their droppings to assist in this, the most important of tasks: protect the secret.

The half-track slowed to a walking pace, then stopped entirely with a clatter as it overheated.

We were less than three hundred yards from the Hollow Men, who were standing about an equal distance between us and safety. As their ranks swelled with their identical compatriots, they began walking slowly towards us, the outer edges of the long line curving around in readiness to attack on all sides.

I grabbed a sword and joined the others on the bonnet for what was now a last-stand defence. The Hollow Men would be upon us in thirty seconds, and unless we could each take down between sixty and seventy drones before succumbing ourselves, the end would not be long in coming.

'It's funny what runs though your mind when the end is near,' said Addie, 'and all I can think about is how annoyed I am that my sums didn't add up. With Perkins and Wilson dead we've lost five out of eight, and that's one more than the fifty per cent I'd calculated.'

'I was thinking of odd stuff too,' I replied with a half-smile, 'like who was going to look after the Quarkbeast – Tiger, I guess.'

'I was thinking about walking one more time in the Palace gardens,' mused the Princess. 'The fountains are very cooling in the summer.'

I looked behind us. Cadair Idris was almost three-quarters of a mile away. I could see the jeep, and the rock-hewn stairway. We'd be safe there, but only safe to die of starvation, or be attacked again on the next attempt.

'We'd never reach it in time,' said Addie, divining my thoughts, 'and I don't run. Not from anything.'

'Me neither,' said the Princess. 'Fleeing for one's life is so very . . . *unregal*.'

So we stood together on the bonnet of the half-track, swords at the ready, awaiting our fate. I wasn't thinking only about the Quarkbeast. I was thinking about the Eye of Zoltar, and where it might be. I was thinking that I had failed to find the Eye, and that the Dragons would die. And I was thinking about Perkins.

Then I had no more time to think, for the Hollow Men had charged.

The Princess was the most skilled with her new old hand, with Addie not far behind. They dispatched three each in quick order, keeping the drones from climbing upon the bonnet. We were, quite literally, defending the high ground. For my part, I simply swiped where I could with my sword in both hands. It was desperate but, given the numbers, we were not so much fighting as postponing the inevitable. I sliced through one that had jumped on the bonnet, then ducked to allow Addie to cut down another behind me. The situation was becoming increasingly difficult, and I could feel my muscles begin to tire. When they could no longer swing a sword, it would be over.

And that was when we heard a loud rushing noise. It was like a distant express train, but ahead of the noise was a call, like the sharp bark of a . . . *seal.* A sound that was familiar, but given that I was concentrating on the fight, a sound that I could not at first place.

The rushing noise increased to a thunderous roar and a moment later the Hollow Men in front of us scattered like playing cards, disrupted by a foe whose form was wobbly and indistinct. Almost instantly the drones we were battling disengaged to fight the new, larger enemy, and we were once more on our own. I had a cut on my thigh, had lost part of my boot and, I think, my little toe. I could also feel the salty taste of blood in my mouth from a cut lip, but we were still alive.

We heard the whooshing noise again, mixed with a faint 'Ook, ook!', and we saw the wobbly outline of the partially invisible Cloud Leviathan as it executed a steep hammerhead turn in the air and then dived down for the second attack, its large mouth open, a pattern of red marks upon its broad jaws where it had withstood the drones' swords on the first run. As the rushing sound increased again and the Leviathan dived down for the second attack we could see that it was not alone – it was being ridden. But this was not a pirate of some sort, this was Ralph. He was alive, well, and no longer a passenger: he was standing upright upon the Leviathan's back, riding the creature as a surfer, without fear.

The second pass was as devastating as the first. Those drones that were not gathered up in the Leviathan's massive mouth were blown apart by the high-pressure air venting out of its underbelly as it passed, leaving the Hollow Men in tatters. We jumped down after the second pass and moved forward to lend a hand, either by slicing to ribbons those Hollow Men that were momentarily disoriented, or attacking those that were awaiting the Leviathan's third run. It was an enemy in rout. Like all armies, they had weaknesses, and we had found two that evening: nylon stitching and a collapse of leadership when attacked on two fronts.

Ralph and his new friend conducted six passes in total until the Hollow Men either retreated or simply collapsed back into parcels of clothes. They were powerful, but even they knew when to call it a day. This time the battle was truly over, and we had won. We looked at one another, and were a picture of exhaustion, stress and relief. I wasn't the only one who had taken some damage. The Princess had two nasty cuts to her arm and chest, and Addie was wrapping her arm with a bandage.

The Leviathan parked itself nearby in a low hover and Ralph jumped down to join us, still carrying his large ladies' handbag in the crook of his arm. He was smiling in his odd Australopithecine way and he greeted us with a clasp of our hands and a soft chuckle. True, we had not been over-enamoured of Ralph when we first met, but when Perkins devolved him it was we who cared for him, and clearly, friendship and loyalty were something that went back a long way in mankind's history – even to a point before we were truly human. We'd looked after him, and he'd looked after us.

'Thank you, Ralph,' I said.

'No *Ralph,*' he said, his mouth making strange contortions, as though chewing the words together before he spoke. 'Name . . . *Pirate 'aptain Ralph.*'

'Ralph, Wolff? Why not. But a pirate?'

'Only for . . . good,' said Sky Captain Ralph with another semi-grin, before looking around. 'Others?'

'All gone, Captain.'

'Sorrow f' all,' said the Australopithecine, ''cept Curtis. Glad dead, 'natius too. Wilson, 'erkins – liked. Sorry.'

'We're sorry too,' I said. 'Who's your friend?'

I nodded towards the Leviathan, whose chameleonic skin made him look like the scrubby grassland he was hovering above, and Captain Ralph looked at the Leviathan, smiled one of his ancient smiles and touched all our hands again.

'Friend,' he said, and rummaged in his oversized ladies' handbag for a moment before handing me a small object carved out of Leviathan tooth and attached to a gold chain. It was a whistle. The captain pointed at the whistle, made a blowing gesture, then pointed at himself, the Leviathan and me.

'I understand,' I said, and he smiled again, snapped the clasp of his handbag shut, climbed back upon the body of the beast and they both moved off and up as one. By the time they were at a thousand feet in altitude, the Leviathan's underbelly was already looking like the clouds, and a second later we couldn't see it at all.

We stood there for some moments in silence.

'Well, Addie,' said the Princess at last, 'looks like your fifty per cent fatality rate was correct after all.'

Addie frowned as she counted up the numbers in her head. Eight had come out, and four had survived.

'Yes,' she said sadly, 'but I wish I'd been wrong.

Without Perkins and without Wilson, all would have been lost. Jenny, I'm truly sorry.'

And we all hugged. Spontaneously, and in silence, while the tattered remnants of the Hollow Men were blown by the breeze across the scrubby grassland.

We become sisters

The half-track had cooled down sufficiently to be started and move off once we'd cut the clothes from the tracks, and we didn't stop until we'd reached the cave in which we'd spent the night before. It was late when we arrived, and too tired to even bother about hiding the half-track or for one of us to stay awake as sentry, we all fell fast asleep.

I was awoken by a faint noise from outside the cave. I looked at my watch only to discover that a sword-cut the day before had removed the face and hands. I nudged the Princess, who mumbled something like: 'No,no, Nursey, a pedicure at ten, I said,' before turning over and going back to sleep. I looked for Addie but her bedroll was empty, and I found her crouching silently at the cave entrance, watching. It was painful when I moved, as all the cuts and nicks I'd received stung horribly.

'Who's outside?' I whispered.

'The Mountain Silurians,' Addie whispered back.

'Let's see what they want,' I said, getting up. 'They

know we're here, and after yesterday, I'm not sure much really scares me any more.'

We stepped out from behind the rhododendrons to find three warriors upon Buzonjis silently waiting for us.

'Greetings on this day,' I said, 'and all respects be upon you. But if you mean to kill us, then be quick about it. We have faced more death in the past twenty-four hours than we would care to see in a lifetime, so do it now or go about your business and leave us to ours.'

'We're not here to kill you,' said the middle warrior and the larger of the three, 'we are here to bring Geraint the Great's word of congratulations. He salutes the brave warriors who have faced the *Cavi homini* and returned, and thanks you also for the goat thing, which looks like sound financial advice. He deems you worthy of being called his sisters, and grants you free access upon our lands and the full protection of the Mountain Silurians, wherever you might be.'

'Oh,' I said, 'good.'

'Then you accept?' asked the warrior.

'Do we?' I asked Addie.

'Hell, *yes*,' said Addie enthusiastically. 'An honorary sister of Geraint the Great? You'll never have to queue in Tesco's again. And that's just for *starters*. Never mind all the other fringe benefits of being affiliated to the most terrifying warrior tribe in the whole of the Kingdoms.'

'I don't shop at Tesco's,' said the Princess, who had arrived behind us. 'In fact,' she added, 'I don't think I shop at all.'

'Laura Scrubb will have all the benefits when you return her body,' I said. 'Perhaps it might make up for the lost hand.'

'You're right,' said the Princess, 'I'm totally in.'

The warrior on the left slipped expertly from his Buzonji and asked us to sit down. An induction into the Mountain Silurians' affiliation was designated by a tattoo, in their case a small blue star on the right temple. It took about twenty minutes each, and after leaving us with an elegantly bound book of eligible bachelors within the tribe and three offers of marriage for 'The Fearless Tour Guide Addie Powell', the warriors remounted their Buzonjis and were gone.

'Mum will be furious I've had a tattoo,' said the Princess, looking at the livid red mark in the half-track's wing mirror. 'Yes, I *know* it's technically not on me. It's just that I've got so used to this body I'm not really sensing much of a difference. In a strange way, I'm actually *enjoying* being Laura Scrubb.'

We had a good wash in the waterfall before taking a half-hour to tension the half-track's tracks, as was insisted upon in the rental hire agreement. I even checked the oil and refilled the radiator with water.

We repacked, climbed in, checked Rubber Colin's straps were still secure, and headed off down the Llangurig road.

'Do you think Laura has had as interesting a time in my body as I have in hers?' said the Princess, who had been thoughtful for some time.

'I'm thinking almost certainly,' I replied.

'I'm going to free her,' she said, 'with a generous pension. In fact, I'm going to free all the orphans working in the palace. And when I become Queen I'm abolishing this whole bullshit orphan-based economy. The trade in orphans ends under me – the fast-food joints and hotel industry will just have to figure it out another way.'

I smiled. Things were looking good for the Kingdom of Snodd, and for orphans in general. Queen Mimosa had been right to send her daughter out with us, even if by every other measure the trip had been an abject failure.

'Maybe that's why we have the Troll Wars,' mused the Princess, who was turning out to be a lot less wooden-headed than I had first thought, 'to supply the orphan-based economy with orphans.'

'It's crossed my mind many times,' I said.

We came within sight of Llangurig at that point, and I was suddenly aware that the past few days, adventurous though they had been, had not helped us *one atom* in our fight against the Mighty Shandar.

In fact, since we'd lost Perkins and Colin was still rubber, we were actually worse off.

We found Llangurig a ghost town. The arrival of the railway had taken away its geographic relevance, and only a handful of residents remained, there because they loved it, and none of us had any issue with that.

We had lunch in the Bluebell and all of us ate two main courses, and sponge pudding to finish. Cadair Idris has that effect.

'So who did take the Eye of Zoltar?' asked Addie, calling for more custard.

'I don't know,' I replied, 'but whoever did has had six years to try to unlock its power, and I'm figuring they haven't – we'd certainly have heard about it.'

'Tell me if I'm pointing out the bleeding obvious,' said the Princess, 'but when did Able Quizzler die from that fall?'

'It was . . . six years ago,' I murmured.

'And how long since Pirate Wolff got changed to lead?'

'Six years.'

'Is that important?' asked Addie.

The Princess didn't need to answer. I knew *precisely* what she was getting at. I got up and placed the last of our money on the table.

'Where are we going?' asked Addie.

'We're going to find some shovels,' I said, 'because the Princess just picked up on something we all missed.'

'And then,' added the Princess, 'we're going to the cemetery.'

I had no difficulty finding Able Quizzler's grave again, and started to dig almost immediately, much to the outrage of the gravedigger, the same one we had met previously.

'You can't be doing tha'!' he said. 'We only 'cept deposits, not withdrawals!'

We ignored him and, after waving his arms at us for a while, he shambled off about as fast as he could go.

The ground was waterlogged and heavy, but we eventually unearthed a leaden foot, twisted and mildly flattened by the impact, about two feet beneath the surface.

'Kevin Zipp might well have been right after all,' I said as we continued to dig, 'and this is my theory: Able Quizzler found his way to Sky Pirate Wolff's lair, and as soon as the Eye was shown to him, he used the most easily accessible magic within the Eye to make his escape – in this case, a turning-to-lead gatekeeper. He prised the Eye from Pirate Wolff's hand, then killed every pirate in his way using the Eye's power before escaping on a Leviathan. But then the Eye's gatekeeper spell did what gatekeeper spells are meant to do – protect the jewel. Quizzler was himself turned to lead, and now dead, fell from the Leviathan.'

'And landed here, still – *hopefully* – clutching the Eye.'

'Fingers crossed.'

We uncovered his torso, also deformed with the impact, and a minute or two later uncovered his leaden features, still fixed in a triumphant grin etched there six years before and at a height of ten thousand feet or so. I knew then that my theory was sound. Quizzler was killed by the Eye's malevolence, just as he had achieved his lifelong quest.

'There!' said Addie as we brushed the dirt off Quizzler's body to reveal his hand clenched around a large, pink jewel. Despite the ground being wet and muddy, the jewel seemed to repel the dirt and shone with a brightness that almost invited avariciousness. It was actually, I think, even bigger than a goose's egg, and from somewhere deep inside the jewel there was a light – a pulsating glow, like that of a human pulse. It seemed that Zoltar's evil will, the guiding force of the gem's power, was still in residence. We'd found the Eye of Zoltar. But we were going to have to be very, very careful unless we wanted to end up like Quizzler – lead, and very dead.

We all stared at the jewel, hardly daring to breathe.

'I've got no magic in me,' said the Princess, 'but even I can feel it – a sort of dark wickedness.'

'I feel it too,' said Addie, 'and I'm also thinking that no one should touch it.'

I agreed with this and after a brief discussion I had

the Princess go into town to buy an iron cooking pot, several large balls of string and as many candles as she could carry. And then, without touching the massive jewel, we prised it from Quizzler's grasp and placed it in the pot surrounded by clay. Once this was done we bound the lid of the pot closed with string, then poured molten wax over the string to seal it tight. We then carried our treasure gently to the half-track, where it was lashed securely to the floor next to Rubber Colin. It was the most dangerous magical artefact that I had ever handled, and I wondered then about the wisdom of giving it to Shandar. But that was up to Moobin and the others to decide.

'Okay, then,' I said, 'just one more thing to do and we're heading home.'

'I really hope it doesn't involve going back into the Empty Quarter,' said the Princess.

'No, Cambrianopolis – to negotiate for Once Magnificent Boo's release.'

Negotiations in Cambrianopolis

Cambrianopolis was close to the border with Midlandia but a good hour's drive north of the frontier with the Kingdom of Snodd. It was a large, sprawling city built in the 'shabby war-torn chic' style so popular in the Empire. Most of the city seemed to be piles of rubble interspersed with roofless houses and half-dilapidated apartment blocks, leaning dangerously and blackened by smoke. It was all contrived, of course, like a large and uniquely complex Victorian folly, or a theme park celebrating mankind's ceaseless warmongery, or something equally daft. Most of the apparently empty buildings were fully occupied, and not unsafe at all. The overall effect was one of a nation in constant civil war, something that was not the case at all – the Tharv dynasty had ruled unopposed for over three centuries.

We found our way to Emperor Tharv's State-Owned Ransom Clearance House, which was a large building that, despite having bars on the windows, was run along the lines of a five-star hotel: there was an extensive menu, reliable room service and a health spa and pool. If you were going to be kidnapped anywhere, Cambrianopolis was the place. Some people even came on holiday deliberately to be kidnapped as the Clearance House was full of interesting people. One might, for instance, mix with long-term resident the Duke of Ipswich over breakfast, and be invited to buy tea for the deposed and penniless King Zsigsmund VIII in the afternoon.

Addie said she'd wait for us by the half-track, so I showed my credentials at the door, took a number and then sat on one of the benches and waited to be called. The Clearance House was designed to make negotiations as quick and easy as possible: agree a price, pay the money – release. Notwithstanding, negotiations *could* sometimes drag on for decades. The Duke of Ipswich had been here sixteen years as everyone tried to come to an agreement. The ransom was the easy bit; the argument was over who was going to pay for the duke's food and laundry expenses.

Our number was eventually called and we entered a small, cheerless room with dusty grey filing cabinets and a dead potted plant. Our negotiator was a young, tidily dressed woman with an intriguing scar running vertically down her cheek and across to her lower lip.

'Hello,' she said pleasantly, rising to greet us. 'Welcome to the Cambrian Empire's Ransom Clearing House. My name is Hilda and I will be negotiating on behalf of the Nation. Offers made in this room are legally binding and negotiations may be recorded for training purposes.'

I asked whether my handmaiden could sit in, which was okay, and then said who I was and who I wanted to release. Hilda's eyebrows rose as I spoke, but whether that was because of me or Boo, I wasn't sure. I'd like to think a bit of both.

Hilda the negotiator spoke into a phone to have Boo's file sent up and then made small talk about the weather and asked whether we had any news from the Kingdom of Snodd. I tried to fill her in about politics but she was really only interested in the Kingdom's most famous stunt performer, Jimmy 'Daredevil' Nuttjob.

'On fire last I heard,' I told her.

'Oh,' she said, 'news doesn't really cross the border. There could be a war going on and we'd be the last to hear about it. Ah, the file. Thank you, Brigitte.'

Hilda opened the file and scanned the contents.

'So,' she said after a while, 'Miss Boolean Champernowne Waseed Mitford Smith, aka "Once Magnificent Boo". Occupation: Sorcerer. Condition: Healthy but minus her spelling fingers so deemed "damaged goods". Charges: Unauthorised importation of a Tralfamosaur, illegal flight over the border and using magic to avoid detection. Charges dropped through the intervention of the Emperor, but after refusing to do any sorcery for him and threatening to "punch him painfully in the eye", she was transferred to the Clearing House for disposal. We've had two best offers for her, both of which are currently on hold. But since you are a recognised negotiator for Kazam Mystical Arts Management and have the prior claim, we will transfer her to you if we can agree terms. If you don't buy her release, we'll accept the highest best offer. Okay?'

'Not really,' I said.

'Splendid. Here we go: we're looking to get thirty back for her.'

Thirty grand was a lot of cash, but actually a little less than I thought they'd ask for. But Boo was, as they said, damaged goods, so her value was limited.

'Ridiculous,' I said, 'she doesn't even work for us. I'm here as a friend, and would be asking Boo to refund me once we get her home.'

'But she *is* a sorcerer,' said Hilda, 'and even though her power might be diminished, we understand she can still spell – just with limited accuracy and duration. Give us twenty-five and you can take her away now and I'll chuck in some B&Q vouchers and two tickets to the Nolan Sisters concert next month.'

'Twenty-five?' I echoed. 'Out of the question. Houses of Enchantment don't have that kind of cash and you well know it.'

The negotiations went on like this for about twenty minutes. We were both polite but firm, and I finally agreed at eighteen, which I thought quite reasonable.

It was always possible Boo might make a contribution of a few thousand, although somehow I doubted it.

'Excellent,' said Hilda, filling out a form. 'How will you be paying?'

I placed the twenty-thousand-moolah letter of credit that Moobin had given me on the table and slid it across. Hilda glanced at it.

'That'll do for her room service and bar bills. What about the rest?'

'Eighteen, you said,' I told her, 'this is good for twenty.'

'Oh,' she said, 'we seem to have been talking at cross-purposes. I meant eighteen *million*.'

'Eighteen *million*?' I said.

'Of course,' she replied. 'Boo was once one of the world's greatest sorcerers. The highest best offer was for eight million. Do you want to go away and raise the funds and then come back? I'll have to warn you that if we don't see any cash by Sunday, we withdraw our offer and take the best offer.'

'Hang on—' I began, but the Princess interrupted me.

'We'll pay now,' she said, rummaging in my shoulder bag. 'You do take all forms of currency, I take it?'

Hilda nodded and said that they took everything except goats 'as there was something of a glut at present' and the Princess presented her with the receipt I had received for the Bugatti Royale.

'There,' said the Princess, 'this should cover it.'

Hilda looked at the note, which stated that we were owed the value of the Royale, signed by Emperor Tharv himself.

'We don't take receipts,' said Hilda.

'It's not a receipt,' said the Princess. 'Technically speaking what you have there is a banknote. *Any* banknote is merely a promissory note issued by a government against its assets to enable the citizenry to more easily trade commodities. And by assets one might usually mean gold, although you could choose mice, turnips or tulip bulbs. Often you don't need any assets at all – if the citizenry believe their national bank will remain solvent come what may, a simple promise is enough, backed by nothing more tangible than . . . confidence.'

Hilda looked at the Princess blankly, then at me.

'Yes, I know,' I said, 'we've had to endure her for a while now but the funny thing is, she's usually right.'

Heartened by this, the Princess continued.

'. . . and since that receipt is signed by Emperor Tharv, who is the Cambrian head of state, that note is legal tender to the value of one Bugatti Royale.'

'But it's a car,' I said, 'it's not worth eighteen million.'

The Princess smiled.

'Not *quite* correct. There were only seven Bugatti Royales made, and the last one sold at auction for over twenty million. The Bugatti is not so much a car, more an exquisite work of art you can take to the shops. You've been driving around in a Van Gogh.'

'You like economics, don't you, handmaiden?' said Hilda, picking up the telephone.

'Is there anything else?'

'Hello?' said Hilda into the receiver. 'I need to speak to the Master of the Sums.'

We waited for a few minutes while Hilda explained the situation, and after a minute or two she put her hand over the receiver.

'The Bugatti Royale exchange rate stands at 19.2 million Cambrian plotniks,' she said. 'Would you like to take the deposed and penniless King Zsigsmund VIII in lieu of change?'

'No, I'll take a Volkswagen Beetle, please,' I said. 'One in particular. Pale blue, 1959 – the one Boo arrived in. The rest can be cash.'

Heading home

We stayed overnight in Cambrianopolis while Boo's paperwork was processed. We had a good meal, a very welcome bath and slept in clean sheets for the first time in what seemed like an age. Talk between the three of us had been muted, with each of us lost in our own thoughts. We'd all be returning to our usual lives over the next few days. The Princess would go back to being a princess, I would return to Kazam and Addie would be dealing with her usual bread-and-butter tour work – taking eager and very dopey tourists into areas of high jeopardy, then attempting to stop them being eaten.

We were waiting outside the Clearance House twenty minutes before it was due to open. I'd tried to raise Kazam on the conch again, but still nothing. The good news was that my Volkswagen had been found, repaired, filled with fuel and returned the previous evening. We had spent an amusing half-hour trying to squeeze Rubber Colin inside the car, only to give up and instead lash him on to the roof rack. Addie had returned the half-track to the hire company, and we were very glad we'd taken out the Additional

Collision Waiver as it was in a considerably worse state than when we hired it.

Boo did not seem particularly happy to see us, and stepped blinking into the daylight as soon as I had signed the paperwork.

'You shouldn't have paid the ransom,' she said as soon as she saw me. 'If no one paid, the kidnapping business would collapse in an afternoon. You're all fools.'

'It's good to see you again too, Boo,' I said. 'This is Addie Powell, our friend and guide, and this is Princess Shazine of Snodd.'

'A Sister Organza switcheroo?' asked Boo, staring at the Princess and prodding her with an inquisitive middle finger.

'My mother did it,' said the Princess.

'Once, I knew the Queen very well,' said Boo, raising an inquisitive eyebrow at the Princess. 'A good woman until she married that idiot your father. Ask her if she remembers the incident with the squid.'

'I will,' said the Princess, who seemed to have become immune to the insults her father's name attracted.

'Right,' I said as soon as we were in the car, Once Magnificent Boo deferentially allowing the Princess to sit up front, 'let's get out of Cambrianopolis before someone changes their mind.'

Luckily, no one did, and an hour later we were

heading back towards the border. Barring bad traffic or a breakdown, we'd be back at the palace by lunchtime, and the Princess and the handmaiden could be changed back.

'I used to think Laura Scrubb was the ugliest girl I'd ever seen,' said the Princess, staring in the courtesy mirror at the face she'd been using for the past few days, 'but I've got to quite like the snub nose, shortness of stature and lack of any agreeable bone structure.'

'You'll soon be yourself again,' I said, with mixed feelings. The Princess in Laura's body and I had got on really well, but I wasn't sure how that would translate once she was back to being beautiful and rich and influential once more.

As we drove towards the border I related everything that had happened over the past four days. I told Boo all that I could recall – leaving out the bit about Gabby – and expected her to make comment, ask questions, or say 'Ah-ha' or 'Really?' or 'Gosh' or something but she didn't say anything until I'd finished.

'At least it explains why there's a rubber Dragon strapped to the roof,' she said at last. 'I was wondering about that. Where's the Eye of Zoltar right now?'

I told her it was in the old saucepan in her footwell, and she drew her feet away.

'Has anyone touched it?'

'No.'

'Keep it that way. It'll be nothing but trouble. If I

were you I'd drop it down the first disused mine shaft you come across.'

I explained why we needed it, and that we'd hold a conclave to discuss everything when we got home. Boo merely shrugged at this and muttered darkly about 'meddling with powers you could not possibly hope to comprehend'.

We passed a road sign alerting us that the border to the Kingdom of Snodd was ahead.

'Thirty minutes,' said Addie, who would be picking up her next group from the tourist office, where we first met her.

'About time,' said the Princess, 'I'm really beginning to miss being me.'

I ran over my speech to Queen Mimosa as we drove along. About how I felt the Princess had progressed from being a spoilt brat of the highest order to someone who could, and would, think of others. On second thoughts, I probably wouldn't need to say anything at all – the Princess would simply open her mouth and speak, and the Queen in her wisdom would *know*.

We first spotted the smoke when we were still some way from the border. We thought at first that it was the result of a minor border skirmish or something. When I mentioned it to Boo she leaned forward in her seat.

'That's not the border,' she said, 'it's farther away.'

'Hereford?' I asked.

'Closer than that,' said Boo. 'Perhaps the palace.'

'The palace?' echoed the Princess, and urged me to drive faster. The palace was only ten miles from the border, and as we crested the last rise and the Kingdom was spread before us the Princess's home came into view. And what we saw was neither expected, nor welcome.

'No!' cried the Princess, and put her hand to her mouth.

I stopped the car at a lookout spot where several other people were already watching, and we climbed out. The royal palace was on fire, and a long pall of black smoke drifted across the land. There was a small explosion in the castle, then another.

'My lovely palace,' said the Princess. 'I do hope Mummy and Daddy got out okay.'

'The powder magazine must have blown up or something,' I said.

'Don't be a clot,' said Boo. 'The palace is under attack. See there, landships on the move.'

She was right. Far in the distance we could see the unmistakable rhomboid shape of King Snodd's defensive landships moving across the land, one of which exploded into fragments as we watched. Beyond the palace, another distant smudge of smoke was drifting into the sky. They – whoever they were – had attacked Hereford as well. I think I felt anger rather than fear, and concern over my friends and colleagues.

'Who would dare attack us?' said the Princess. 'A sneak attack by, what, Midlandia? But why? My cousin is the Crown Prince and the one I was most likely to marry. Our kingdoms would have been joined peacefully in the fullness of time.'

'It's not Midlandia,' said Boo in a dark tone. 'Look down there,' she went on, pointing towards the Cambrian–Snodd border. The Cambrian artillery, which had been pointing towards the sky as we entered the country, was now pointing across the River Wye towards the Kingdom of Snodd. Tharv had mobilised his troops to defend his nation, although quite how well they could do this wasn't clear. As we watched, we could see a single Snoddian landship heading towards the border.

'Boo,' I said, 'can you do a fingerscope?'

'Of a sort.'

She made two circles with her middle fingers and thumbs and then uttered a spell. In an instant there was a lens in each of her encircled fingers, and we crowded around her shoulder to see the Snoddian landship close up. It was badly battle-damaged, and from the forward hatch there fluttered a white flag of truce – whoever was in the landship was attempting to escape. This was a defeated army on the run. There was another explosion at the castle.

'Oh!' said the Princess, clutching her chest in pain. 'Oh, oh, oh!'

She dropped to her knees and tried desperately to regain her breath.

'She's frightened,' said the Princess, 'I can feel her.'

'Feel who?' asked Addie.

'Me – her – Laura, the Princess. She's running. Running for her life!'

I held her hand and squeezed it, and she looked up at me with the same expression of confused realisation I had seen on her face when her body was swapped.

'This is bad,' said Boo, 'and I think this war is all but lost.'

As if to punctuate her words a huge explosion tore through the palace, flinging masonry and rubble in all directions, and as we watched the remains collapsed in on themselves in a massive ball of dust and debris.

I looked at the Princess, who was silently sobbing on the ground, and then at Boo, who shook her head sadly.

'It's over,' she said, 'I can feel it in the air. A collective sadness, a negative emotion that is disrupting the background wizidrical energy. I'm sorry, ma'am, but your parents, the King and Queen, are both dead.'

'Oh no,' she said in a quiet voice, as tears welled up in her eyes, 'and my little brother Stevie?'

'Of this, I know nothing.'

'What about Laura Scrubb?' she asked. 'And my beautiful and elegant body?'

Boo shook her head sadly, and the Princess nodded, accepting what she knew to be the truth, that she could never truly be herself again. But with the King and Queen dead, her real body destroyed and the Princess's little brother's whereabouts unknown, this could mean only one thing.

'Your Gracious Majesty,' I said to the Princess, bowing my head, 'rightful ruler of the Kingdom of Snodd, you have my loyalty above everything. I wish only to serve, and serve well.'

'And I,' said Addie, giving a low bow, 'humbly request leave to be your personal bodyguard.'

'I, too, am at your disposal, Your Majesty,' said Once Magnificent Boo, 'in matters magical or wherever I can serve. Loyal, like us all, until death.'

'Loyal,' we affirmed in unison, 'until death.'

The new Queen stared up at us from where she was sitting, still on the ground. We'd not had confirmation that Laura Scrubb had gone, but something inside the Princess knew it was true. A small part of her that had stayed with the real Laura until her death, perhaps to guide her back in when the mind switcheroo was over.

'Okay, then,' she said, taking a deep breath, and wiping away her tears, 'I accept all the responsibilities of my birthright, and will not rest until the perpetrator of this foul deed is brought to justice. But I will not be calling myself Queen until I am once more in full command of my lands and people. Help me up, will you? I think I've got cramp.'

We helped her up and sat on a bench, all four of us, and watched the black smoke drifting across the distant countryside. The Princess broke the silence.

'Jennifer,' she said, 'I should like you to be Royal Counsel.'

'With respect, ma'am,' I said, 'I'm only sixteen. That's a job usually reserved for grey hair – someone with experience.'

'Nonsense,' said the Princess, 'you have plenty of experience, and what's more – I trust you completely and know you will always do the right thing. You accept?'

'I accept, ma'am.'

She thanked me, smiled, and looked at her hands. The left was still raw and calloused from the previous owner's years of toil, and the other was the hand of the ex-stoker, with 'No more pies' tattooed on the back, and held on with duct tape. It wasn't an ideal situation, and as far as we knew it, a first for royalty.

'This is my body now, isn't it?'

'Yes, I think it is.'

'Then I'd better start looking after it. Tell me, Jenny, am I horribly plain?'

I looked at her pale, sun-starved face, her brown hair, which was still lank with undernourishment, and her dark-rimmed eyes.

'It's not the outside that counts, ma'am.'

Aftermath

It was too dangerous to cross the border until we knew more about what was happening, so we stayed put. I tried over and over again to reach Kazam on the conch, but with no success.

The road to the border was soon packed full of refugees, vehicles and medical personnel tending to any wounded who had managed to escape across the border. Tharv, true to his cherished principles of unpredictability, had welcomed the refugees from the Kingdom of Snodd, and from the garbled reports of the inrush of displaced citizens, we managed to piece together broadly what had happened.

The Snoddian Royal Family were, as we had feared, killed when the Palace was destroyed. But it was worse than that: the victors had displayed their heads upon poles outside the shattered remnants of the palace, and fed their corpses to wolves, for fun. We also learned that the war had not been solely against the Kingdom of Snodd. Of the twenty-eight nations within the unUnited Kingdoms, all but nine were now overrun, or had surrendered. Information was scarce but it seemed that

Financia had been spared owing to the fact that it was a centre of banking, the Duchy of Portland Bill had been defended successfully thanks to their deep moat, and the seagoing nation of the Isle of Wight had been away conducting sea trials in the North Atlantic.

It was hard to describe the chaos in which we found ourselves as we walked up to the border. Homeless people had grabbed what they could before fleeing, and mothers desperately searched for husbands, their children clinging on tightly with a look of numb terror upon their faces. There were casualties, too – soldiers with appalling wounds being treated as best they could – and among all this, the Cambrian Gunners lay waiting, their weapons trained upon the invaders, poised to return fire if attacked.

For the invaders *were* there, sitting outside the Snoddian customs post on the other side of the River Wye, doing nothing, awaiting orders. The larger members of the group were six in total and each about twenty-five feet tall, dressed only in a loincloth and heavy battle bootees. The Trolls' skin was covered in elaborate tattoos, each had a dead goat decorating its copper war helmet, and their small, cruel eyes stared at us greedily.

'Trolls,' hissed the Princess when we saw them, 'I hate Trolls.'

'And not alone,' said Addie, 'look.'

The other members of the group she indicated

were fewer in number and stature, and looked like nothing more than businessmen in dark suits and sunglasses. The group had planted two flags in the ground denoting their allegiance and the extent of their new territories. The Troll flag was obvious, but the second standard gave me a shock. It had the sign of the flaming footprint: the Mighty Shandar.

'I can't see from this distance,' said Addie, 'but I'll bet good money there's nothing in those suits.'

'Hollow Men,' said the Princess, 'presumably there to relay orders from their master to the Troll warriors.'

'The Mighty Shandar,' said Boo, 'as treacherous as he is arrogant. Despite all that he has done, I never trusted him. Not one inch.'

'But Kevin Zipp was right,' I said, 'the next Troll War was going to be when least expected. It would be bloody, short, and the aggressors would be victorious. Sadly, the "victorious aggressors" weren't us – they were the Trolls.'

'It explains why Tiger and Moobin were so keen for us to find the Eye of Zoltar,' said the Princess. 'To defeat him we're going to need some serious magical power of our own.'

'It also explains why Moobin was telling you that the Princess needed to be protected at all costs,' said Addie. 'A defeated nation needs leadership.'

'I think they would have fought bravely,' said the Princess, 'my parents, the army, everyone at Kazam.'

'They'd have fought to the death,' I said, 'even the really strange ones.'

'They could be still alive,' said the Princess, 'we don't know anything yet.'

'I hope so,' I replied, 'but—'

'Jenny?'

I started. It was Tiger's voice. Very faint, but unmistakable.

'I can hear Tiger's voice now,' I said, 'it must be a last shout from the astral plane before he passed to the other side – or something.'

'I don't think so,' said Addie, 'because I can hear it too.'

It was the conch.

'Tiger?' I said after hurriedly removing the large shell from my bag, 'Where are you?'

'Thank goodness,' he said in a relieved tone, 'Shandar has finally stopped jamming the Conchways – probably because he thinks we're all dead. I'm in the basement of Zambini Towers along with the Quarkbeast, Mabel, the Mysterious X, and Monty Vanguard.'

I heard a Quark in the background.

'Okay,' I said, 'if it's safe to do so, stay put. I'll be there as soon as I can.'

'We don't really have a choice,' said Tiger, 'we're trapped. I think the building has collapsed above us.'

Tiger explained as much as he knew. Shandar had returned to the Kingdom of Snodd, and he had brought the Trolls with him. He was clearly not worried about the Dragon refund, because no one would be there to demand one. It seemed he had been biding his time all these years, remaining in stone for centuries until the moment was right to strike and strike hard. The previous four Troll Wars were not wars at all, but a series of warm-ups – preparing the Trolls for the ultimate invasion.

'Shandar targeted Kazam before the war began' said Tiger, 'Kevin Zipp was kidnapped so we couldn't see it coming, and Kazam was hit first the morning of the invasion. Feldspar came back from Princess duty to rescue us, but could only carry away one at a time. Moobin was first. I don't know if anyone else made it out.'

'Any idea why he had me look for the Eye of Zoltar?'

'To get you out the way, Lady Mawgon thought. You've bested him once before, and we think he's actually quite frightened of you.'

'I'm going to make sure of that,' I said, 'what about you guys?'

Tiger explained that there was ample food and water as they were in the basement kitchens. As far as they were concerned they were safe for the time being – they had heard the Trolls up above searching through the rubble, but they had moved on. I told him to sit tight, and not to use the conch in case Shandar decided to listen in, and I'd said I'd organise a rescue party as soon as I could.

'At least we know Moobin is safe,' said Once Magnificent Boo. 'We will need many people to retake the Kingdoms.'

'I hate to be a party-pooper at times like these,' I said, 'but with what are we going to retake the Kingdoms? We are a vanquished nation without an army, without weapons and, at present, without ideas.'

'We have hope,' said Addie, 'and a sense of moral outrage and natural justice. We will retake the Kingdoms, no matter what it costs.'

'I second that,' said Boo. 'Dark magic never triumphs. We will rally what sorcerers we can, and build up an army from scratch if we have to. We have my limited powers, your leadership, the Princess as a figurehead and Addie's unique survival skills. Moobin is still around somewhere and we also have the terrifying possibility of harnessing the awesome power of the Eye of Zoltar.'

We were silent for a moment. Things didn't seem so bleak after all.

'Holy smoke,' came a voice behind us, 'I feel like I've slept with a spare wheel in my mouth.'

It was Colin. He had reverted to normal, still strapped on the roof of the Volkswagen. That might have seemed unusual, but given the surrounding chaos, no one was paying us any attention at all.

'Oh, yes,' said Once Magnificent Boo, 'we also have two Dragons.'

Acknowledgements

I am hugely indebted for the editorial assistance of both Carolyn Mays and Katy Rouse of Hodder, and Jeanette Larson of Houghton-Mifflin-Harcourt. Once again, their attention to detail and unfailing support permitted me to complete this book vaguely on time. My thanks to you all.

My thanks also to Roger Mason, who undertook the task of completing the frontispiece at short notice and not only satisfied my brief, but added much more besides. Roger's talents extend to not just freelance illustrating but storyboard and graphic novels. Like me, he is also a big fan of illustrator Kevin O'Neill. Roger can be found at www.looksgoodonpaper.co.uk.

My thanks would not be complete without mention of Simon Pettifar for his invaluable companionship and words of wisdom, and to my family, for their continued support – especially the youngest two, whose continued drain on my resources will keep me motivated for many years to come.

Finally, to Ozzy, whose boundless enthusiasm for stick retrieval and walks keeps me well exercised.

Jasper Fforde, January 2014

About the author

Jasper Fforde is the critically acclaimed author of The Last Dragonslayer series: *The Last Dragonslayer* and *The Song of the Quarkbeast*, *Shades of Grey*, the Nursery Crime books: *The Big Over Easy* and *The Fourth Bear* and the Thursday Next novels: *The Eyre Affair*, *Lost in a Good Book*, *The Well of Lost Plots*, *Something Rotten*, *First Among Sequels*, *One of Our Thursdays is Missing* and *The Woman Who Died a Lot*.

After giving up a varied career in the film world, he now lives and writes in Wales, and has a passion for aviation.

To find out more, visit:
www.jasperfforde.com
www.facebook.com/jasperffordebooks.

Do you wish this wasn't the end?
Join us at www.hodder.co.uk, or follow us on Twitter @hodderbooks to be a part of our community of people who love the very best in books and reading.
Whether you want to discover more about a book or an author, watch trailers and interviews, have the chance to win early limited editions, or simply browse our expert readers' selection of the very best books, we think you'll find what you're looking for.
And if you don't, that's the place to tell us what's missing.
We love what we do, and we'd love you to be part of it.
www.hodder.co.uk
@hodderbooks
HodderBooks
You Tube
HodderBooks